About *The Wanting Life*

It's the summer of 2009, and the Novak family is in crisis. Paul, a dying priest, is haunted by a relationship forty years removed from his present life in Wisconsin, when he was a graduate student in Rome. Britta, his self-destructive sister and caretaker, is struggling to find meaning without her beloved husband. And Maura, Britta's daughter, is an artist who finds herself impossibly torn between a future with her young family and the man she believes is her one, true love. Told from all three perspectives, Mark Rader's debut novel examines each character's attempt to reconcile their deepest desires with the limits of their lives, and, in doing so, unearths a surprising emotional legacy.

....

"A cross-generational novel focused on happiness, fulfillment, and love... whose leads are unafraid to explore the complicated territory of human desire."
—*Foreword Reviews*

"Mark Rader's poignant debut novel explores the emotional costs of seeking and sacrificing romantic love... An insightful and compassionate family drama about desire, love, and the courage it takes to live a full life."
—*Kirkus Reviews*

The Wanting Life

a novel

Mark Rader

The Unnamed Press
Los Angeles, CA

AN UNNAMED PRESS BOOK

www.unnamedpress.com

Unnamed Press, and the colophon, are registered trademarks of Unnamed Media LLC.

ISBN: 978-1-944700-99-7
eISBN: 978-1-951213-03-9

Library of Congress Control Number: 2019951347

Cover Art by John A. Sargent III
Designed and Typeset by Jaya Nicely

Manufactured in the United States of America by Versa Press, Inc.

Distributed by Publishers Group West

First Edition

Wanting and dissatisfaction
are the main ingredients
of happiness.
To want is to believe
there is something worth getting.
Whereas getting only shows
how worthless the thing is.
And this is why destruction
is so useful.
It gets rid of what was wanted
and so makes room
for more to be wanted.

—Ruth Stone, "Wanting"

Say not, "Why were the former days better than these?"
For it is not from wisdom that you ask this.

—Ecclesiastes 7:10

For my family

Contents

The Wanting Life

I. Sister Bay

I t was only dinner with the McNamaras they were driving to tonight—the friendliest company imaginable—but Paul was already wishing he'd had the guts to stay home.

On his first night with his sister at the rental cottage two weeks ago, he'd accepted Georgia McNamara's invitation to their new summer place in the hopes that his darkness would have lifted by now. But it hadn't; in fact, he felt much worse. After waking from a nightmare on the couch earlier this afternoon, he'd pulled out his phone with every intention of canceling. They would be kind to him, but their kindness wouldn't help, as these two weeks with Britta had made clear. All he had to do was tell Georgia he wasn't feeling well and apologize for the late notice. But instead, phone in hand, his martyr complex—as Britta called it—had kicked in. He'd pictured Georgia whipping up a feast in the kitchen, humming Beach Boys songs. Then her phone buzzing, her *Hello?*, the disappointed drop in her eyes. He reminded himself that he'd declined their last three dinner invitations. He felt Gordon's disappointment too. And their adult children, whom Georgia had said would all be in town for the weekend, even Sophie who lived in New York...if he didn't show, none of them would likely ever see him alive again.

So, feeling obligated, he'd slipped his phone back in his pocket and sighed, and now here they were in his Camry, heading south along the bay side of the peninsula to Egg Harbor, Britta at the wheel. He hated being a passenger in his own car, but it was wise, with all the morphine he was on, he knew that. He was trying to see it as a perk: his mind could scatter and drift as it liked. Usually, when they were quiet like this, Britta turned on the public radio station out of Green Bay, but tonight his sister was letting their silence stand, the only sound the rush of air through their open windows, steady as white noise. Outside it was an unusually gorgeous early evening in July. A pink liquid sun hung over the bay on Paul's right, its oven heat steady on his face, neck, and shoulders, hot disks of light burning into the water's surface so brightly he had to squint, despite the shades clipped over his bifocals. Dark gray silhouettes of seagulls hung above the waves, suspended and swaying like kites, and along the sand, a boy so skinny you could count his ribs sprinted along the waterline, joy personified, a blue pail swinging from his hand.

Normally all this beauty would have made him close his eyes against the sun and melt into the glowing red sea behind his eyelids. Normally he would have inhaled and given praise. But he didn't have gratitude in him these days. For these weren't normal times. Nor this his normal self.

Three months ago—a few days after Easter, actually—he'd walked into Mercy Clinic a fit man of seventy with a nagging pain in his side. Strained muscle, he'd thought. Small hernia, maybe, from lifting too many books during St. Iggy's library remodel. Instead, Dr. Shah had blinked his big dark eyes and said, *I'm very sorry.* The *o* round and hollow, the *r*'s trilled.

In the X-ray of his liver, the two smallest tumors looked like fish eggs. The big, deadly one: a gray fist clenching a straw. The cancer was already stage three. The location of the big tumor made surgery impossible. There was very little that could be done. He'd get six months more if he did chemo. Four, maybe, without. So then, he'd decided a few days later, *without.* Quality over quantity being the idea. Which meant he'd be in the ground by September. October, if he was lucky.

As a pastor, he was no stranger to deterioration and death. In hospital rooms silent but for the wet rasp of a single throat, and bedrooms that reeked of fear and lemon disinfectant, and once in a sunny backyard, standing beside a very annoying Buddhist monk named Brother Larry—he'd led families in prayer, administered last rites, and given counsel the best he could. For thirty-some years now. He told the dying and their families that heaven was real, a realm beyond suffering. He gifted people *On Death and Dying* by Kübler-Ross, *A Grief Observed* by C. S. Lewis, Bibles with little Post-it tongues. Except for the few months after his mother had died, when everything made him cry, he never lost his composure. It was his job not to—and he was good at his job.

There was no predicting how people would handle it: that was something he'd learned. Usually people remained themselves, muffled a little by exhaustion and meds. But sometimes, at the last minute, they changed. Mean ones got sweet, sweet ones got mean, tough old guys sobbed like babies, terrified to let go. When it was his turn, Paul had always imagined he would be one of those who didn't change. He would accept his fate stoically, as he'd accepted so much in his life. Go honorably into that dark night. But about that, it turned out, he'd been wrong: never before had he been more troubled. Which was saying a lot.

All the hiding he'd done, the secrets he'd kept inside—he knew this had something to do with it. The official story of the life of Father Paul Novak was that he was a more or less happy man who'd lived an admirable life of service. He knew he wasn't as beloved as his best friend, Tim Cochran, pastor at St. Boniface in town, or Ed Warpinski over at St. Anne's: they were warmer and more charming, bear-huggers both. But in his own steady, generous, devoted way, he'd served his congregation well. Reserved by nature, he'd worked hard to become a man people could open up to, someone who listened. He showed up to appointments five minutes early, was meticulous and opinionated about matters large and small—yes, sometimes to a fault. But that was only because he cared so much, because he hated to disappoint.

In the twenty-eight years he'd been the pastor at St. Ignatius Parish in Northfield, and the five before that at St. Matthew's with Father Tim, before they were reassigned, he'd baptized hundreds of babies, married hundreds of couples, delivered thousands of sermons. As eloquently as he could, he'd shared his thoughts about the abiding love of God, the inevitability of suffering, the mystery of faith. And while the memberships of most parishes in the diocese were shrinking, St. Iggy's had grown bigger by nearly half since he'd started there—proof, he liked to think, that he was doing something right.

Still, even so, flowing under this story had always been another, fraught one, and in the month after he'd celebrated his last Mass and especially during these past two weeks in their rented cottage in Sister Bay, only this story had felt true. In this version of things, he was a coward who'd built a cage around himself but spent most of his life complaining how he wasn't free.

In the morphine-fueled daydreams that had arrived these past few weeks as he napped under Britta's umbrella at the beach, Paul had been visited by a number of handsome strangers: the men who could have been. They sat across from him at a dinner table, candlelight reflected in their eyes. They rolled over in bed to touch his face. Most of them had olive skin and dark eyes, like Luca, but they weren't him, not exactly. Though Luca *had* appeared to him once, directly, as himself. In that dream, Paul was climbing a staircase, carrying a white paper bag filled with cheeseburgers, Luca's favorite. When an open door appeared at the top, there was Luca sitting on the edge of an open window, his hair the same shiny, dark, curly mop it was in Rome, but his body was pale and skeletal. *Where were you?* he asked, and Paul realized that Luca had been waiting for the meal he'd brought for a long time. But now it was too late. *I can't eat,* he said, *I'm sorry.* Then he swung his legs over the ledge, pushed off, and fell, a slowly shrinking X....

Since Britta had flown in from St. Louis two weeks ago, three expensive suitcases in tow, she'd been trying to distract him from his nagging sadness. Every day, they ate out for lunch, her treat, and drifted through the tacky art galleries, half-heartedly scanning the walls and bins for hidden gems. Down at the beach, she insisted he get his feet wet at least, and even though he didn't feel like making the effort, he obeyed. Their first Sunday there, Father Tim drove up with his fishing gear, and they each caught exactly nothing with plastic night crawlers at the pier. When Tim asked him how he was doing, he said he'd been feeling depressed, to which Tim had nodded, understanding completely, he said. Though actually he did not.

Obediently, per Dr. Shah's instructions, Paul had been taking his morphine pills twice a day and double his usual dose of antidepressants. After breakfast, he sometimes called his secretary, Jean, to check in, and she made sure to pass on the well-wishes from the people who dropped by. But their concern didn't comfort him. It was like his heart was encased in glass.

Britta, bless her, had been trying to get him to open up more about his feelings, and mostly he'd been honest. When she'd asked him if he was scared, he said of course. When she asked him if he was worried about the afterlife—whether there was one—he said no: what scared him was the prospect of losing control of himself. The messy falling apart. When she asked him how he felt about having served his last Mass before they drove up to the cottage, he said he was glad he'd stepped down earlier than later, but that he felt a little lost.

Yet this matter of his thwarted heart—about that she had no clue. No one did.

It wasn't that he didn't want her to finally understand how, and how much, he'd struggled. A big part of him did. He knew well how cathartic unburdening your secrets could be, having heard so many in the St. Iggy's confessionals. It was the *actual doing it*—the kicking open of that long-boarded-up door—that was so daunting. If he told her how close he'd come to leaving, how often he'd wished he had and why, he'd have no choice: he'd have to tell her everything, starting with Rome and Luca Aurecchio. Which felt, at the moment, impossible.

At the first little crosswalk in Egg Harbor, Britta brought the car to a jerking stop as a family of five rushed across the street, fresh from the beach. The young parents were cartoonish beasts of burden: the father with a huge beach bag slung over one shoulder, a pink backpack slung over the other, a Dora the Explorer inner tube pressed to his chest. The mother half-heartedly wielded a beach umbrella like a sword, two huge plastic shopping bags drooping off her free shoulder. Their children—three blond girls—trailed behind, carrying nothing. The tallest had a beach towel wrapped around her head like a Bedouin. The middle girl wore hers like a cape. And the youngest, maybe six, was whipping hers above her head like a lasso, while also waving—at them, actually.

Britta waved back. Paul didn't. By the time he considered it and decided to also wave, the moment had passed. His brain was sludgy like this now—thus his banishment to the passenger seat.

"Oh my god. I feel tired just looking at them," Britta said, as she stepped on the gas.

"They'll sleep well tonight."

"The parents or the kids?"

"Both, probably."

The Australian lady in the GPS told them to turn right a block ahead, so Britta did, veering onto a road flanked on both sides by tall pines. The sun flashed and gushed through the gaps like Morse code. In a tiny park, an old pale-legged hippie in jean shorts conjured giant bubbles for two boys with a big yellow wand.

"Oh shit," she said. "We probably should have brought some wine." She scrunched her nose at him. "Should I stop somewhere?"

"I don't think it's that kind of party," he said. Had it occurred to her earlier, he thought, she could have plucked a bottle from the small arsenal she'd assembled in the garage of the cottage.

"No, I guess not."

The many hours Britta had spent lying out at the beach lately had given her normally pale skin a healthy-seeming pink glow, but it was an illusion: he'd never seen her in worse shape. She'd always been fat (that's the word she'd used herself since meeting Don, when the fact stopped mattering to her), she'd always liked her wine. But since Don had died three years ago, things had gotten out of hand. He'd seen it firsthand during her visit: every day she ate two helpings at every meal, every night she polished off a big bottle of Pinot Grigio all by herself. Then, in the mornings, a pot of coffee, as if that balanced things out. Even with the driver's seat pushed all the way back, it was a tight squeeze for her; the seat belt strained against her belly and thighs. Plus, just in the past few months, she'd taken up smoking again, after quitting ten years ago, though she claimed this was only temporary. A way to cope with what was going on with Maura, her daughter out east.

Maura. As the road scrolled under them, Paul thought of his niece. Not long after he'd called Britta with his bad news back in April, Maura had called Britta with her own: she'd been having what she called an emotional affair with a man she'd met at an art retreat. David something. Then in May, her husband, Harden, found out, and she wasn't sure what to do because, if she was being honest, she had fallen in love.

What her daughter had probably wanted from her, Britta told him later, was to simply listen. Absorb her news and pain. But she couldn't: she'd been livid. It felt personal: After everything she'd been through, now she was supposed to endure this too? She'd been blunt. Told Maura to break it off. Get counseling with Harden. Fix things while there was still a chance. And when Maura pushed back, saying she wasn't sure if she *wanted* to fix things, that was the whole problem, Britta told her she was being selfish. Selfish and stupid. She had two young kids, one of whom had special needs. How could she even think about leaving them, especially now?

At this, Maura had hung up, and for the past six weeks she'd been unreachable. In voice mails and emails, Britta had apologized for her tone, implored her to call or email back. A few days after they'd arrived, Paul overheard her leaving a voice mail message: *I'm with your uncle. I'm sure he'd love to hear from you.* Trying to guilt her into it. But that hadn't worked either. *It'll pass,* Britta said a few times, dismissively batting the air, *she can't ice me out forever.* But when she checked her phone and laptop every morning for messages, the disappointment in her eyes gave her away.

There was no room here for his own hurt, of course. This was his sister's cross to bear, not his. But that Maura hadn't reached out at all to him—it stung. Unlike her brother, Shade, lover of football and video games and possibly little else, Maura had always been a sensitive, creative creature. A kindred spirit. His favorite. As a girl, she called him Uncle Father Paul, so ever after in the birthday cards he sent—still sent—he signed off *Love, UFP.* Every time he'd visited them when she still lived at home, she had some elaborate art project going. A panoramic Smurf village drawn with Sharpie on a giant roll of brown paper, as detailed and busy as a Hieronymus Bosch. A string of origami cranes she was making for a pretend Japanese wedding. One year, moody charcoal drawings of dead birds, each title a song lyric from her favorite band, the Cure. When she was concentrating on her art, she furrowed her brow and bit down on her lips the same way he knew he did when he was at his kitchen table or in his office at the church, making notes for a sermon.

For the past twenty years or so, the period in which she'd been in Massachusetts, they'd seen each other only a handful of times—family weddings and funerals, two Christmases. To bridge the distance, he sent birthday cards to her and her family, a fresh ten-dollar bill taped inside. On Facebook he liked every post about her kids and every post about art she liked, though most of the stuff (the abstract stuff especially) wasn't his cup of tea. In return, only rarely did she like his posts back; the only card she sent was during Christmas. She was busy, what with her job as a graphic designer and her kids—her son, Evan, especially, who was a handful. Out of necessity, her focus was elsewhere. He didn't hold that against her. But to be silent at the news of his impending death, well, that was different. Even Shade had texted him twice. Whatever she was going through, it must be all-consuming. She simply wasn't herself.

"You're doing it again," Britta said now, flicking him a sharp look. He was staring at her without realizing it, another side effect of the drugs.

"Sorry." He cleared his throat and swung his gaze to the road. A mailbox that looked like a trout passed by on the right, then one with a Packers decal on it.

"You were giving me a *very* pitying look," she said.

"Actually, I was thinking about Maura."

"Is that right?"

"Yes, actually. It is."

When he looked back at her, Britta was staring ahead at the road, her jaw set, skeptical. Under normal circumstances, he would have said something to her by now about her drinking (and her eating and her smoking), but he didn't have the energy to deal with the repercussions. He didn't want them to argue. It was hard enough as it was. But she was right to imagine that he was secretly worrying about her. Judging her. With the tiny portion of his mind available for anything but beating himself up, he did.

"Just for the record, you give me pitying looks all the time," he said. It was true, he'd caught her at it exactly three times: once at the beach, twice in the kitchen. Raw little moments that burned with truth.

"It's not *pity*," she said. "I'm just worried about you. As I have a right to be."

She paused to let him respond, but he didn't know what to say.

"You're depressed and nothing I'm trying seems to help. If you were in my shoes, I think you'd feel exactly the same way."

He looked at the side of her big, round face. The dyed brown bob, dark with sweat at her temples. Her big, sun-kissed cheek.

"You're right," he said, his annoyance already fading. "And I appreciate you trying, I do." He just didn't believe it would do him much good.

The McNamaras' cottage was a huge two-story Cape Cod, navy-blue wood siding with bright white trim, set at the end of a pristine driveway flanked by little trees, each with a tidy collar of dark red mulch. Georgia had been angling for this for years, and after Gordon sold off his trucking business (surely in the millions), he finally said go for it. And Georgia had.

Before they got out of the car, Britta offered Paul a Tic Tac (the meds did a number on his breath too), and they walked up together, him in front. From the stoop, Paul rang the doorbell and listened to it echo joyfully inside the house. Quickly, Gordon opened the door, boomed his hello, and Georgia stood patiently just behind, waiting, a wince of a smile on her face. They handled him carefully, Gordon barely gripping his hand when they shook, Georgia barely pressing herself into his chest during their quick hug. They'd met Britta once many years ago but introduced themselves again, then, skipping right over any awkwardness, ferried him and Britta into the living room, where their children and grandchildren were waiting.

The kids, all in their twenties and thirties now, were pretty much as Paul remembered them, or maybe they were different— he actually wasn't sure. Bemused, affable George, the oldest and only son, thirty-something by now, his pretty wife, their two boys. Tall, slim Alice, her husband, their twin girls. Plain, wry Casey, divorced with a sullen, chubby daughter. But no Sophie yet. She and Darius, her new Greek boyfriend, were out playing mini-golf, Georgia reported, due back any minute.

Did he feel like a tour of the place? What could be said but yes? Each room was immaculate, filled with expensive, photo-shoot-ready things. Five bedrooms—one for Gordon and Georgia, and one for every child and their family. The walls featured the grandkids' drawings and paintings (crayon ninjas fighting dinosaurs, finger paint handprints radiating out like flowers) professionally matted and framed, set beside Cézanne-like landscapes of the area (or maybe it was Cape Cod) Georgia had probably bought at one of the galleries here. In the living room, a custom-built fireplace made from yellow quarry rock shipped up from Milwaukee; in the bathroom, a built-in marble hot tub the color of pumice stone. But the crowning jewel of the place was the dining room: a long, grand room with four giant windows facing the bay, and in the middle, an unusually large table with high-backed chairs, fit for a Viking feast. His friend Tim would be disgusted by this opulence, he who frumped around in his clerical shirts, baggy teal sweaters, and used chinos he bought at Goodwill. Even reasonable shows of wealth made him uneasy. The waste of it all! The good that could have been done with all the money! But Paul had always had an eye for quality. Beauty for beauty's sake. He was vain, he knew, about his checked dress shirts; he spent a good deal more than he needed to for nice Ital-ian leather dress shoes once a year; he splurged at least once a month on a thirty-dollar bottle of German Riesling. If God cared for only what was spartan and simple, he'd once asked Tim, why make the peacock? Or the human being for that matter?

Why not take a wrecking ball to St. Peter's? To which Tim, no fan of the pope, had shrugged and said, *I can imagine worse.*

"Tell Father Paul what we saw outside here yesterday," Gordon said, when they stopped in the kitchen. He was talking to the oldest grandson, maybe eight, who'd been shadowing them, taking long swaying, stomping steps, hands latched behind his back, like a drunk little Ichabod Crane.

"A pileated woodpecker," the boy said. He pointed. "It was in that tree."

"A *what* woodpecker?" Britta asked.

"*Pil-ee-ay-ted.* They're really big and more rare than regular ones."

Georgia rolled her eyes. "Gordon gets them all hot and bothered about this stuff," she said to Britta. "He acts like they saw a leprechaun."

"Hey," Gordon said. "You like expensive wallpaper, I like birds. To each his own."

To begin, at least, it appeared the family was content to carry on as though this were a normal visit—whether to put him or themselves at ease, it wasn't clear. But once they found themselves in the living room, and everyone had regathered on the floor and sofas, and Georgia had glided over with glasses of lemon water, Paul could see his moment of reckoning had arrived. Hunched forward, Gordon asked him how he was feeling. Like a lawyer, it felt, which made him the deposed witness. He spoke of the morphine and the vivid, crazy dreams it gave him; Britta's helpfulness; the strangeness of not saying Mass on Sundays—everything but the crucial thing: that he'd been regretting his life.

"Now, I know some people think it's nonsense," Georgia said, flashing a stink eye to Gordon, "but have you looked into any alternative pain medication for all this?"

"I didn't say it was *nonsense*," Gordon snapped. "I said I didn't think it would do much at this point."

"I haven't really, no," Paul said, looking at Georgia. "I'm pretty conservative when it comes to that stuff."

"See," Gordon said, pointing at him. "That's smart."

Georgia arched her back to reimpose her dignity. "How much longer are you two staying up here?"

Paul looked at Britta: this was actually something they needed to figure out soon. "I'm not sure," he said. "I can't seem to decide whether to stay another week or head back."

The Jaworskis, also parishioners of his, had offered up their cottage at a discount for two weeks, with the option of extending it if he and Britta so chose. The two weeks would be up on Monday, and they'd asked him to let them know by tomorrow what he wanted to do. But he'd been feeling utterly unable to decide. Where to spend his remaining time in this world felt immensely important and simultaneously beside the point. Back home at St. Iggy's he'd be in the company of people who loved him, which was good. But it would also mean the time had truly come to start falling apart, which was not.

"What's making it hard to decide?" Georgia asked.

"I don't know," Paul said. "I'm sure it doesn't help that I'm not firing on all cylinders lately."

"Well, I vote you stay two more weeks," Gordon said. "Not that my opinion really matters."

"Wait a second," Georgia said. "I'm going to write that down. 'On July 8, 2009, Gordon McNamara finally admitted his opinion doesn't matter.'"

Along with the kids, his sister laughed—a real one, straight from the heart; she and Don had bickered like this too: the everyday friction of love.

"I'm sure we'll figure something out," Britta said, turning to him. Like the mother she was, she patted his knee. "Maybe we can just flip a coin."

She smiled, a hint of coolness in her eyes. He knew he should smile back, so he did. A little. But her solution was no solution at all. Had he been the man he'd been even four months earlier, at this point in the conversation, Father Paul Novak, respected pastor, old man of some importance, would have turned to George or Casey or Alice and asked them about themselves. Or Gordon would have asked him how planning for the fall harvest fest was going or how his veggie garden was shaping up. But instead, sensing the awkwardness in the room, and his unusual shyness, Britta had taken the lead, wielding bright questions about the grandchildren, which Gordon and Georgia's children answered, before returning the favor.

"...Shade does computer programming stuff," Britta was saying now, wrapping things up. Paul realized he hadn't been listening for a while. "But I never remember his exact title. Do you remember, Paul? Shade's job title?"

"Head systems analyst."

"That's it." She looked at him. "Doped up on morphine and your memory's still better than mine."

"It's a blessing and a curse," Paul said, and everyone, relieved that he was still able to crack a joke, laughed too hard.

The arrival of Sophie and Darius was the sound of a car engine idling, then shutting off in the driveway, the door opening, and male and female voices murmuring. Sophie appeared first, hair pulled back into two little pom-poms, spry advertisements for her personality, a cautious look in her eyes. What demeanor was right for your last audience with a dying man? How natural or formal to be?

And then behind her walked in Darius, the boyfriend, the sight of whom startled Paul so much the glass of lemon water he was holding dropped from his hand.

"I'm sorry," he said, and Georgia scuttled quickly to the kitchen for some paper towels to sop up the stain on the carpet at his feet (the glass somehow hadn't broken). Gordon rose as if to help but then just stood there with his hands in his pockets, and Britta put her hand on Paul's forearm and asked him if he was okay (yes, he said, he was). But Paul paid little mind to the commotion around him: his eyes were fastened on the man who'd walked into the room, the ghost of Luca from forty years past. It wasn't the morphine either: Darius was the spitting image. The same head shape and dark eyebrows, widening as they headed toward the ears. The same long lashes, big-lobed ears, slightly too big forehead. The same stooped shoulders and wide-legged cowboy's stance. His dark hair was a bit shorter and he had a slightly different-shaped mouth. But even those differences only helped Paul better remember. Bigger teeth, the wolfish eyeteeth; that swollen dark pink bottom lip....

Sophie told him not to get up and held his hand with both of hers, a tender little clamshell. She smiled warmly, no pouty sympathy, thank God. Then Darius reached in to shake his hand too. "Nice to meet you, Father." A deferential nod. Paul forced a polite smile, not wanting the man to mistake his shock for a lack of warmth. But he couldn't speak. How were you supposed to talk to a ghost?

It had taken a couple decades of emotional scouring to diminish Luca's place in his heart. He'd prayed about Luca, told no one, conquered Luca, told no one, spoke sometimes to Luca, imagined how Luca would respond, told no one. During his fifties, a stretch in which he'd found himself strangely more energetic than his forties, his half-hearted sex drive had returned, and so had young Luca, often when he was in the shower, aroused. The Luca who graced the stall with him was Luca as he'd been during their weekend trip to Sperlonga, that night and that morning: thin-armed, soft-skinned, generous. Two faint stripes of sunburn running across his shoulders.

While there with Luca, he could sometimes feel the love that had been part of the act. But often he couldn't, or he didn't bother to try to, and then it was as though he were using Luca like a puppet, his unwilling servant. After those sessions, he'd feel awful and dimly ask God for forgiveness. But that phase too had run its course, and he'd settled into a period of relative satiation. In the last, more chaste fifteen, twenty years, Luca had existed as the idea of Luca more than the man himself. Faded into an idea. But here now, in the flesh: this Darius-Luca, resurrected.

By the time Georgia jangled an actual triangle dinner bell to call the family to the dining room, it was quarter past eight, and the sun was melting into the surface of the bay. Blood-orange sunshine obliged the space with an underwater light. It was, Paul thought, exactly the sort of scene Georgia must have imagined when she asked whomever they paid to build it, here on the west side of the house. The whole clan together. Not including, of course, the less cheery surprise addition of pale Father Death and his sister.

Everyone found a chair. The adults quieted one by one. At the head of the table, Gordon stood, licked his lips a little, eyes flitting around the table, nervously, patiently waiting for silence. *Oh no,* Paul thought, *he'll want a prayer from me.* They always did.

But Gordon said he wanted to do it himself tonight. "That all right?"

"Just this once," Paul said, trying to conceal his relief.

"Good," Gordon said. "Because I was going to do it anyway."

Presently all the flittering, disparate minds formed a single beam that pressed into Paul's chest; even as their eyes fell on the tablecloth, he felt it.

"It's so good to be here on this beautiful summer night to share this meal with Paul and his sister, Britta," Gordon began. "We're so thankful that they're able to join us, Lord. And we're thankful for all Paul's done for St. Iggy's all these years, and the many ways he's helped others and taught us about the love of God. We're also so grateful that he was able to marry off all three of our oldest children and say such beautiful things at the services. But most of all we're grateful for his presence in our lives, for his example of living like Christ. May you be with Paul in the coming weeks and months and give him comfort. As it says in Psalm Twenty-Three, 'Though I walk through the valley of the shadow of death, I will fear no evil: for thou art with me.' And so may this be true." Here he cleared his throat. "We ask this, in your name."

Everyone said amen.

Paul faintly smiled and nodded to Gordon. He was supposed to be moved by this, but he wasn't; terribly, he felt only relief that it was over. But as the hard dinner rolls were passed around in the slightly dumbstruck way people always passed around dinner rolls, that changed. He started to feel annoyed. *His example of living like Christ*—was that true? Was he any more Christ-like than any of them sitting here? He'd certainly given of his time and energy to the Church, despite the many ways in which he disagreed with the brass in Rome, but the impersonality of the compliment made him sad for how little they really knew him. They'd donated generously to the parish for nearly thirty years—more than anyone else. Gordon sometimes served Communion. Georgia had taught CCD. Every August, Paul would show up at their big pig roast and lead the group in a prayer. But all these years they'd kept their distance from each other when it came to talking about the awkward stuff of life. Instead, they'd had roles to play and played them well. How interesting it might have been if they hadn't, though, he thought, as he speared a leaf of romaine with his fork.

But too late for all that. Across the table, George's wife was asking Darius and Sophie about their upcoming trip to Europe. They were planning to do a sort of upside-down U-shaped thing, Sophie said. Fly into Athens, drive up to Thessaloniki to visit Darius's family first, then fly to Budapest and go west. Euro rail and rent a car from there. Stops in Slovakia, Prague, Munich, Brussels; two days with some friends of theirs whose parents lived in Alsace-Lorraine; and then Venice, Florence, and flying out of Rome.

"Paul studied in Rome," Gordon said. "Three years, wasn't it?"

"That's right," Paul said.

"And what is it that you studied?" Darius asked. He looked at Paul with interest, pinning him to his chair.

"Scripture," he replied. "And a bit of philosophy. I was there getting my licentiate degree, which is basically a master's."

"That must have been a fantastic experience," Darius said.

"It was," Paul said. "My first time out of the country too."

"Have you been back since?" Darius asked.

"No," Paul said. "I haven't, actually."

"I have to say," Gordon said, "I still don't understand that. You had a cat named Campari, for goodness' sake."

"He's explained this before," said Georgia sharply. "He prefers to see new places more than go back to old places." She looked at Paul. "Isn't that right?"

Paul managed a smile. "Yeah. That's right. More or less."

But Gordon was right to doubt his logic. There was more to it than that.

At first, he hadn't wanted to return because he was afraid he wouldn't be able to prevent himself from looking up Luca, and that Luca would dismiss him or make him feel like a fool, this American priest still carrying a torch after what had, after all, been less than two months together. Or worse: that Luca would be as happy to see him as he would be to see Luca. Then, after he'd learned that Luca had died, back in 1988, he didn't want to go back because he worried he'd destroy the magic the city still held for him if he dipped back into the old well, looking for something that had long ago disappeared, sunk to the bottom like a stone. And that's what he'd mostly told himself ever since.

"You know what?" Darius said. "I'm this way too. Always new, new, new. When it gets boring, *fft*"—he sliced at the air—"try something else."

Sophie looked at him, alarmed. "Oh yeah? Really? *That's* your philosophy? Always something new?"

Darius reared back. "What? Is that bad?"

"He's just saying he likes a little adventure," Alice chipped in. "That's all."

"Yes, of course," Darius said. "What did you think I meant?"

"Oh nothing," Sophie said, "I'm just giving you a hard time." She casually laid her hand on Darius's forearm, trying to sweep her fear under the rug. "It's a good thing to be like that. It makes you less boring."

"Well, good," Darius said. "I don't want to be boring."

He smiled his lady-killer smile at her, then looked around the table, as if for approval. But the mood wasn't light. The prospect of abandonment was out there now. It couldn't be taken back.

The panic attack that hit Paul a few minutes later caught him completely off guard. He hadn't had one for at least twenty years, at least not in public, but here one was, despite his daily Klonopin and the extra Wellbutrin he'd been taking to help him handle the anxiety that many people felt when they were close to death, or so he'd been reminded by Dr. Shah. Suddenly he felt as though he were separating from everyone, including, most frighteningly, himself. The room constricted and expanded like giant lungs. No one was noticing the change in him, but they would soon, and to prevent this, to recover properly, he knew he needed to be alone. For half a minute, his heart raced, and he couldn't move. But then Britta touched his knee under the table, and when he looked at the recognition in his sister's face, he excused himself to the bathroom, avoiding eye contact with anyone else.

Sitting on the closed toilet seat, Paul tried breathing deeply through his nose, to prevent hyperventilating. He imagined doing it into a helpful paper bag. What a stupid idea it had been to come. How narcissistic of him to assume they'd be crushed if he hadn't. They would have been just fine.

After a while, Britta knocked tentatively on the door. "I'm fine," Paul heard himself answering, falsely bright. "Just be a minute." Then he did actually lift the lid, sit, and piss—why not?—but managed only a trickle. His urine was the color of cloudy orange juice now, and from what he'd read it would get as brown as beer near the end, as his liver stopped working.

At the sink, Paul lightly rubbed his cheeks with cold water and looked directly at himself in the mirror. He took a big shuddering breath. *You look like a square version of Peter Fonda,* a curly-haired woman had told him at Luca's party that night— the one they'd left in order to take a walk. Everyone'd agreed and chuckled, because it was true. The big forehead, the square jaw, his big joker's smile with the small teeth and receding gums. People in the years since had said so too.

But that handsome face, the one Luca had enjoyed, was no longer a thing in the world. Only its saggier, softer cousin remained. Though his eyes were still nice. He'd always liked his pale blue eyes.

A half hour later, they left. After dessert and coffee, Paul had followed Gordon down a long flight of wooden stairs to the water, where Gordon showed off the dock he'd recently built. Paul tried but failed to follow the arc of the detailed story of its creation; for long stretches at a time his attention drifted. On the walk back up, he suddenly felt so faint, he grabbed on to the railing with two hands, and when they entered the house, Paul sweating profusely, Georgia snapped at Gordon for making Paul overdo it. Quickly, Britta found her purse, and they said their goodbyes. Georgia and Gordon hugged him gently. *We'll drop by to see you when you're back home,* she said, and Paul said, *Please do.* The rest of the McNamaras knew to just wave, not wanting to put him through the hassle of embracing everyone. And Paul waved back, forcing his eyes and mouth into a smile. It wasn't a goodbye worthy of the moment, but it would have to do.

They'd barely left the driveway when he nodded off. Fifteen minutes later he woke in the driveway of the rental. Britta was beside him, delicately rocking his shoulder back and forth, as if trying to slowly work it loose.

"We're here," she said.

He blinked at her, eyes gummy. "Okay."

"Let's get you inside to bed. You look totally wiped."

He inhaled deeply. "Probably a good idea."

As they walked to the front door, Britta linked her arm with his like they'd done with their mother during her last years at the home. Not that he needed this quite yet. But he knew what she was thinking: *Just in case.*

The next day, a Sunday, was the hardest yet. When Paul woke up, he didn't want to leave his bed, but after having breakfast, going to Mass at Stella Maris in Baileys Harbor, and eating brunch on the water, his mood lightened; he wasn't sure why. *Maybe,* a voice had whispered as he drank his sparkling water and squinted into the sun, *it's not as bad as you think.* Back at the cottage it began to rain, the first time in a week. He watched it fall from the sliding glass door, thousands of white stars flashing at once on the rocking skin of the bay. Then, as if trying to hoard the calm feeling inside himself, he took a nap.

But when he woke, all was lost again: sadness thronged him and wouldn't let go. The rain had stopped. The world was unspeakably quiet. The false hope that washed over him late in the morning had flown off, leaving him raw again, and as he stared up at the ceiling from his bed, the twist of regret tightening in his stomach, he couldn't help but think again about how close he'd come to changing his life, to *really doing it*. The summer of 1990 that had preceded his first breakdown, or whatever you wanted to call it, that fall.

He'd been fifty-one that year, almost ten years into his life at St. Iggy's; Rome was exactly twenty years past. In '84, he'd felt down enough that he got himself on antidepressants, which had helped him greatly ever after. Though he still felt hungry for what he'd had with Luca, and though he still sometimes spent whole Monday afternoons wondering if the sermons he carefully crafted and shared made a shred of difference, or whether he was just a functionary going through the motions, he felt—if not exactly happy—not so disappointed. Happy enough.

Whenever he felt his life wanting, he'd muscle out of it. He'd think of all the good people who looked to him to be strong and assured in his faith; he'd see himself as if through their eyes and straighten up. When he felt like staying in bed, he'd force himself to get out in his garden, go for a long walk, slip into a book, do ten reps of curls with his twenty-pound barbells, toss in a DVD of *Fawlty Towers* or Peter Sellers for a laugh, call Tim or Sister Mary over at the settlement, or wander over to the church building across the huge parking lot to chat with Jean. Once the darkness burned away, he became logical. Found the root of the troubling feeling and dissected it, until it was a harmless little pile of bones. To win the battles that were his cross to bear, he'd learned how to fight.

In the spring of that year, however, a few cracks appeared in the facade he worked so hard to maintain. On a whim, during a visit to Chicago for a conference, he'd called up an old friend from seminary, Gus Vreeland, now a pastor on the North Side of the city. He'd thought it might be nice to catch up and Gus agreed. But instead of suggesting a restaurant, he'd invited Paul over to his apartment in Edgewater and picked Paul up from his hotel downtown in his big white Cadillac Seville.

On the drive, they'd laughed about their oddball instructors at Sacred Heart, and Gus narrated the history passing their windows. Just like old times. But then, upon walking into Gus's apartment, Paul saw it wouldn't be just the two of them for dinner: standing at the stove, sautéing what looked like onions and leeks in butter, was a man Gus introduced as his good friend Sven, a librarian at Loyola University, a Norwegian immigrant with John Lennon glasses, a trimmed gray-blond beard, and thin, pale hands.

From the way they moved around each other, the way they looked at each other, it was obvious. All of the lightness Paul had been feeling suddenly disappeared. He felt wary and slightly offended—ambushed, even. It was as if Gus was trying to say, *Look what I've gotten away with.* But after two bottles of cabernet, Paul changed his mind and decided Gus had no agenda but to honestly show him his life, and Sven was a nice guy. Even now, almost twenty years later, he could clearly hear Gus's belly laugh, see the David Letterman gap between his front teeth. Still see sweaty Sven in his KISS ME, I'M NORWEGIAN apron, carrying out the bowl of rabbit stew with juniper berries, a family recipe. The two of them had achieved an impossible domesticity, at what seemed to him little cost. Not publicly, sure. But they didn't seem to be exactly hiding either.

On the short flight back to the airport in Green Bay after that Chicago trip, Paul knocked back two whiskey sours, as if trying to numb his envy. Well oiled and loose brained, he justified to himself why a Sven wasn't in the cards for him. Tiny little Northfield wasn't Chicago or New York or San Francisco. In a small country parish like his, everyone knew your business. Besides, what were the odds he'd find a Sven nearby? Not to mention there was Bishop Caldwell, who didn't like him, who *already* thought him too liberal, who might take action at the slightest rumor. Even if there were a way to manage some sort of covert relationship, his parish work would suffer. He knew this as fact. Unlike Gus, who seemed so at ease with his choice in life, he would have felt constantly afraid of being found out.

So no, this was impossible. In his particular situation, impossible. That was what he'd told himself, thirty thousand feet above the ground. And yet a few months later, in the summer, he'd found himself thinking about Dan Cotton.

They'd met two years prior in a watercolor class at the community college. The instructor had encouraged conversation because she felt it led to looser, more natural brushwork, and he and Dan, a man a few years younger than he was, had chosen to share a table near the back of the room. Dan was an architect (mostly of malls and big-box stores), an avid birdwatcher, a lover of Australian-rules football due to a brief stint living in Perth as a boy, and recently divorced. For only a few months now, he'd been living in a bachelor apartment in Howard, about ten miles from Northfield. The decision to break up had been mutual, he'd said: his wife still talked to him, they were still friends. But his oldest daughter—who was nineteen and now dating a Presbyterian divinity student—wasn't speaking to him. When Paul asked why, Dan said, *It's not because I cheated, not that you asked.* And that was as much as Dan chose to divulge.

Which was fine: there was plenty else to talk about. The geological history of northeastern Wisconsin, for instance. Spinoza. Kierkegaard. Gardening. Ginseng farming. Early Christianity. The governor. The migration habits of herons. Agatha Christie versus John le Carré. Dogs. Music. Dan was the far better painter—well, almost everyone in the class was better—but Dan always found something specific to compliment about Paul's clunky little attempts. A section that seemed "fresh." A combination of colors that "popped nicely." Paul's goals for the class had been humble: to produce a few paintings he could frame and give away as presents at Christmas, maybe turn into thank-you cards. He came prepared the first night with photographs—the farmhouse he'd grown up in, the black-eyed Susans in his garden, a few pictures he'd taken of chickadees in the snow—whereas Dan worked loose, sometimes going off of a picture he'd pulled from a magazine, sometimes simply playing around with shapes. In that class, from seven to nine thirty once a week, he wasn't Father Paul Novak, pastor at St. Ignatius in Northfield. He was a kid trying not to fall on his face.

At the end of their second-to-last class, Dan suggested they go out for a bite to eat afterward, and he accepted. In a booth at a diner Dan liked, they shared chicken tenders and drank coffee, and Dan told him the reason his marriage had broken up was that he was gay. Early in their marriage, he'd told his wife that he'd been with a man once in college, but that it was only a phase. He was bisexual, he said, and for years he—and they—believed it. But as the years passed, he understood that wasn't true, and when she discovered the sexts he'd been sharing with a man he'd met online, she wasn't exactly shocked. She didn't want to break up, for the kids' sake, and neither did he. But as soon as their youngest graduated high school—in fact, the June after the May ceremony—she filed for divorce. Which, as dramatic as that had been, was also a relief.

For the past six months, he'd been living in an apartment alone. He wasn't dating anyone, but he'd started hanging out at one of the two gay bars in town and had become friendly with a few guys online who lived not in town but nearby.

"It's scary as hell starting over at my age," he said. "But better late than never, as they say."

Paul could have said that he understood, the way he'd said it to Luca that night so many years ago. But instead he kept things pastoral. He said that on the matter of sexual orientation he and the Church didn't agree; he told Dan what he'd done was brave. But that's all he said because, though he wasn't physically attracted to Dan in the least, though Dan wasn't right *for him*, Dan was the sort of person who might help him make the leap. The perfect shepherd.

For a while they sent emails back and forth, but then Paul got busy during the fall and that waned. A Christmas card showed up at the rectory house and he'd sent one late in turn. And that was the last of it. Yet that summer after seeing Gus and Sven in Chicago, as he walked the country roads near his church in the evenings when it was cooler, yearning for someone to be with, a man with eyes to look into and a mouth to kiss and a body to hold close, he'd decided: *If I really do want this, I need to act. And if not now, it'll never happen.*

What he'd do for money if he left had always scared him, so he made calls to counseling centers and asked whether a man with his advanced degrees would be qualified to make the jump over to counseling. (The answer was: it depends.) He called rental agencies not far from where Britta lived in St. Louis. He rehearsed his speech to his mother, who would be devastated. Indulged, dangerously, in memories of his time with Luca. Made different plans for spending the six thousand dollars he'd saved.

The quality of his pastoring that summer had suffered. He was distracted and irritable. Already mentally walking away. Secretly, he felt proud of how brave he was being and wished someone else saw this bravery. But he couldn't tell Tim, or Britta, or anyone who might remember it later if it didn't happen. Which had put him in mind of Dan. Of *course* Dan.

One night, he looked in the phone book and there was the listing: "D. Cotton." He called the number, but it was disconnected, so he tried Theresa Cotton instead. The ex-wife.

Dan's daughter answered the phone. And when he asked if she happened to have the current number for her father, she paused and said, *Who is this?* He said he'd been in a painting class with her dad a few years ago. He was hoping to get back in touch.

Can you hold on a second? the girl asked, and then, a while later, another woman's voice. Theresa's.

Hi, she said, her voice alert and intense. *Amy told me you know Dan?*

I do, Paul said. *I mean, I did. I was calling to see if you knew how I could reach him.*

Well, she said, *I wish I did.*

He's not in town anymore?

Oh no. He moved away more than a year ago.

Oh, Paul said. *And he didn't tell you where he went?*

Well, she said. *The last I heard from him, he was in Vancouver, working at a bar there. And before that he was in San Jose, doing temp work, so he could have his evenings to paint.* She paused. *He writes us letters every three or four months but doesn't put his address on them. On purpose, I think.*

Oh.

He says he's trying to find himself, she said dismissively. *Which, you know, fine. Go ahead.*

Paul wanted to imagine Dan in a group of men, laughing, being welcomed as one of them. But for some reason he pictured him mostly alone.

Does he seem happy to you? he asked. It was the only thing he really wanted to know.

Happy? she said. *I guess I don't know. If he was unhappy, I don't think he'd tell us. Especially not the kids. He wouldn't want us to worry. If I could get him on the phone, I think I'd be able to tell. But he hasn't called since he left. And he won't give us his number. So your guess is as good as mine.*

To some people, he knew, Dan's story might have been inspirational: proof that huge changes late in life were possible, that you could really start over. But on hearing Dan's wife tell of his disappearance, so to speak, he'd felt deflated. How sad to turn into an absence. How selfish and reckless and unkind. What Dan had done seemed less about chasing freedom than the act of a man fleeing the scene of a crime.

Had he fixated less on Dan and latched on to some other, more inspiring coming-out story—of which he knew there were many—maybe things would have gone differently. He'd thought about that a lot since. But chance sometimes controlled your fate, and after hearing about Dan, the air had gone out of the whole thing. Made it seem silly. After that, he'd gotten so depressed he'd taken six weeks off from the pulpit. A bad case of mono was the public story. Tim and Ed and some others had covered for him. They'd upped his meds. And eventually, yes, he'd recovered. Gotten back to it. What else was there to do?

What he'd told himself so many times since to quiet his doubts was that instead of a Sven, he had Tim and Jean and his sister, and many other friends. All who loved him like a brother.

No romantic partner but love in other forms. Filial. Agape. Platonic. Which was still love. What he lacked in physical and emotional intimacy with a single person he'd made up for in breadth and depth. Instead of what Jean had with her husband and Britta had with Don and Gus had with Sven, a constellation of friendships. Meaningful work. Many other priests he knew called this enough, had chosen this on purpose, so he should be able to as well. They cherished their independence and didn't miss the other part of life, it seemed. Or didn't miss it as much as he did, at least. Which was to say, very much.

Curled up in bed at the cottage, Paul tried falling back to sleep to escape his thoughts but couldn't. Instead, he forced himself to check his email. He paged lamely through *On Death and Dying*, revisiting the sections he always highlighted for others. He stood at the window overlooking the bay and watched the sailboats in the near distance skidding effortlessly across the surface.

Around six, Britta, who'd been politely not bothering him, knocked on his door and announced that she'd made tarragon chicken and rainbow chard salad, if he was up for eating something. He wasn't really, but he walked over to the table as if in a dark waking dream. When she asked him if he was all right, noticing something, he surprised himself by starting to sob.

"Oh, honey." She set down her fork and hustled over. She put a tentative hand on his shoulder. "What is it?"

"I don't know," he said eventually. The convulsing of his chest and stomach shot more pain into his side—a barrage of little punches.

"Do you want to talk about it?"

He did, in a way, but he said no. She looked at him tenderly, then squeezed his shoulder gently. All he knew for sure was that he wanted to be close to her, to defer to her suggestions and blindly follow. So after dinner, as she washed dishes, he stood there and dried them, mute. Then he sat beside her on the porch to watch the sun set, as she ate a bowl of popcorn and drank two big glasses of wine. When she left him to take a cooling shower, he felt the urge to stand outside the door and talk to her, like a boy afraid to be away from his mother. But instead he lay on the sofa, favoring his good left side, and closed his eyes. When Britta finally appeared in the kitchen in her pajamas, hair damp, sighing with relief, he went over to hug her. His crying jag ended quickly this time. It was like throwing up.

"I wish you'd just tell me what's going on," she said. "If you don't talk to me, I just feel...helpless."

"Just you being here is helping," he said. "Really."

She put her hand on his back and rubbed it. Her expression didn't change. "Maybe you should just take some Unisom and go to bed. Tomorrow's another day."

The pills worked: within ten minutes, he was asleep. But when he woke up, it was dark, still not morning.

He stared at the darkness until it brightened a bit, his eyes adjusting. It felt like the hour before sunrise, and at the thought of it being a new day, he remembered he'd blown his deadline with the Jaworskis, who had been so nice about all this. He'd have to call them later, but he still didn't know what he'd say.

Cool air from the rotating fan grazed his skin like a paint-brush, moving all in one direction, then the other. Paul could see it dimly—big off-white plastic design like a spoked eye—and then, elsewhere in the room, the bad beach scene painting with the chipped white frame, the pineapple-patterned wall-paper, the light fixture in the ceiling like a gold-nippled breast.

The bed exerted a pull on him he didn't like, so he carefully stood up and shuffled to the window, as if not under his own power, like a moth drawn dumbly to light. Under the bright full moon, a few windows, lit a pale orange, stared back across the bay, muted squares on dark square faces. Just outside the window, the tops of a few trees performed a slow sashay.

Out of habit, he tried putting his hands into his pockets, but his boxer shorts didn't have any, so he clasped them loosely outside his fly. *Find a third way:* the phrase arrived unbidden, and it made him unclasp his hands, as if he might need them for something. He'd said these words at marriage retreats, the phrase stolen from a pastoral counseling seminar he'd taken once. Fighting couples got stuck in *you're right, I'm wrong, you're dumb, I'm smart, you're weak, I'm strong.* So the challenge, he told them, was to think in terms of both/and. A third way. Not just a compromise—a reduction of possibilities—but a new creation, with contributions from both. Getting past an impasse involved humility, faith, and, possibly most important, a kind of deep imagination. The creativity to dream up a different way forward that incorporated your challenges instead of pushing them away.

In other words, why were his only choices to stay here or go home? Wasn't life more full of possibilities than that?

And that was when the idea flew into his head. *Rome.*

As if physically weighed down by the mere possibility, he walked stooped to the edge of his bed and sat facing the wall. The city this time of year would be scorching hot—though, of course, accommodations could be made. They'd drink lots of water, stay in a place with great A/C, hire taxis to limit their walking. If he felt like wandering the streets, they could head out after sunset, when the air was cooler. Britta, a night owl, wouldn't mind.

He cornered the idea, slapped it around for being ridiculous, only to find that it was still standing, unharmed, blinking and eager, like an idiot pet. They could find a direct flight out of Milwaukee or Chicago, the soonest one possible. Maybe stay in the Campo de' Fiori—his favorite. They could leave as soon as tomorrow night if tickets were available. Pack up their stuff. Drop it off at St. Iggy's before driving down to Chicago. None of this was impossible. If he wanted to make it happen, it could.

For how long he sat there, waiting for the idea to turn into a decision, he couldn't say. He saw Piazza Navona on the far wall, a flapping gush of pigeons. The sun would already be shining, seven hours ahead, so he cast light along a dusty dark stone facade, like a sideways stain. He saw the view from St. Sebastian's. The hofbräuhaus, Antonio's little corner place, without a real name. His little room at Il Castello. Luca's little room in Trastevere. Luca sitting across a table from him, tucking his hair over his ear.

He could feel it growing in him now, the thrill of being impractical, of surprising himself. It was odd to want this right now. But it had been just as odd to never go back.

At some point he clicked on his nightstand lamp so he wouldn't stumble as he walked across the room and into the hallway. The TV in the living room was still on, the sound low. A rerun of *Magnum, P.I.* was playing, Tom Selleck leaning across a table, a bad guy with a toothpick between his lips scowling back. Britta hadn't made it to her bedroom again; she was snoring loudly on the couch, head awkwardly on a pillow, one thick arm reaching up, another thick arm bent, hand pressed demurely to the drooping belly peeking under her shirt. Another empty bottle on the coffee table, her pack of Mistys on the magazine beside the glass.

He stood over her for a while, watching her breathe. It seemed wrong to disturb her. She seemed as though she was somewhere good.

But he really didn't have a choice. He needed her help to see this through. So as carefully as he could, Paul lowered himself to the floor, one leg at a time, and gently shook her shoulder until she opened her eyes.

II. The Pilgrimage

He was too nervous and excited to read the books in his carry-on, so during the first few hours of the Alitalia flight Paul watched programs on the little console embedded in the seat in front of him, and gazed out his little window at the pink-edged clouds, and looked, trying not to stare, at his fellow passengers. A motley group of people of all ages, all quietly facing the same direction, all there for the same purpose; they reminded him of his congregation, whom he had not seen for almost a month and whom he missed. Across the aisle, a freckled boy kept showing his mom his video game player. In the seat in front of the boy, a hunched old man in a green sweater and matching cap stared blankly and sadly at his gnarled hands. Three rows up he could see the tops of the heads of two young Carmelite nuns in their black habits—making a pilgrimage, no doubt. As was he, in his way.

The second half of the flight, he mostly slept, like the sick person he was. When he was awake, Britta read or drank wine beside him. The plane surged over the ocean. Dinner was bland. At one point, he awoke to see Angelina Jolie in a leather jumpsuit, holding a gun in each hand, shouting silently at some bad guys not long for this world.

And then, finally, the descent.

Outside the airport, as the cabbie stuffed their shared suitcase in the trunk of the taxi, Paul asked him in Italian to drive carefully—that he was feeling ill—and to his surprise, the man obeyed. Cars and Vespas flowed around them, beeping, accelerating, impatient, and he remembered the wild taxi ride he'd taken into the city more than forty years before, the day he'd arrived as a graduate student, so jarring after the long, calm hours he'd spent reading John Ruskin on the flight in from New York. As their driver swung wildly from lane to lane, honking his horn, barely watching the road, Fred Womack, the second-year assigned to accompany him from the airport to the residence, had sat with short legs crossed, calm as a monk. He smoked four cigarettes, one after another, and only when almost an inch's worth of ash accumulated would he tap his cigarette out the window. Every time, Paul worried that it would fall into his lap, but it never did. Fred was from Wisconsin too, a suburb of Milwaukee, but seemed to him that day as exotic as Rome itself. A vision of a possible, more civilized future self.

Back then, in 1967, Rome was poor, an epic city in decline. The shacks with their corrugated tin roofs along the autostrada had shocked him. Though it was also true that seeing them first had, by contrast, only enhanced the grandeur of the Arch of Constantine and the Colosseum as they glided past his window, impossibly real. Since then, he'd seen a fair share of the world. The Holy Land. India, to visit the sister church St. Iggy's had there. Maybe ten countries in Europe. But there was nothing like your first time abroad, feeling strange in another world.

At a stoplight, Paul asked the driver the temperature.

"Trentatré," said the driver, "trentaquattro."

"Ai, molto caldo," Paul replied. *Very hot.*

The cabbie shrugged. "Eh. Juli."

The hostess from the internet, Amalia, was pleased to see them but not mawkishly so, like an American hostess would be, and Paul appreciated that, because it confirmed he was really here. As promised, the apartment was two stories above the Campo de' Fiori, the rooms pleasantly cool. Everything was just as it had appeared in the photos online: the white library in the main room, the oval mahogany dining room table, the gnarly-treed Constable reproductions on the walls. Amalia showed them the two bedrooms, the coolest rooms of all, and the narrow bathroom with a stylish shower. Some iced coffee and half a rum cake was in the fridge, she told them, and handed over the keys.

Britta wanted a quick shower, and as she did, Paul sat on the bed in his room, then laid down. For a while the air was healing, but then he began to feel *too* cold, so walked back into the living room and stood by the big bay window to warm up.

Down below, the morning market was in full swing: an encampment of plain beige tents with bright things beneath them: slick silver fish, yellow tomatoes, maroon hunks of prosciutto hung with twine. Locals and tourists flowed in the aisles; vendors stewed in the golden shade of the café table umbrellas. A horse and buggy for tourists clomped past the tents, the age-old *pock* of hooves on stone, a faint whiff of manure on a gust of wind. And lording over it all, on the far side, was the black brooding statue of hooded Giordano Bruno the heretic, eyes cast down, as if deep in thought.

Convincing Britta to make this trip had taken most of a morning and afternoon. She'd been alarmed when he'd woken her on the couch, thinking something was wrong, then confused, then annoyed, before she told him they could talk about it in the morning, which did seem like the sensible thing to do. *Why now?* she asked, and he said, *Because I've put it off too long. I want to see it again.*

Over eggs, she'd raised practical concerns, as he would have had their roles been reversed. What if they found themselves stuck there because of some complication with his health, unable to risk a flight back? She shared a story about a friend's sister who'd insisted on camping up in Manitoba two weeks before her baby was due and died during childbirth on the two-hour drive to the nearest clinic.

Keep in mind I'm not pregnant, he'd said.

You know what I mean.

Back at the cottage that morning, he'd felt a surge of purpose. He left a voice mail with Dr. Shah, who returned the call within the hour to confirm that there was no medical reason he couldn't go. Then, as if it were the easiest thing in the world, the other dominoes fell: he told the Jaworskis he'd be leaving Tuesday, as planned, then Tim and Jean at the church, to make the news official—something she could share with the parish. Before he knew it, he was sitting beside Britta as they scrolled through travel sites, making a plan. A flight. This apartment, four days, three nights. Full breakfast every morning, a great view of the square. Day one he'd show her his old haunts: the university, the residence where he'd lived, the German bar they'd go to for a beer. Do a little sightseeing along the way. Day two they'd go wherever Britta wanted to go; this being her first (and possibly last) time in Rome, that seemed only fair. And then, on day three, at last, he would visit the places that reminded him most of Luca. Borghese Park. Trastevere... maybe he could even find the old apartment. If they were up for it, a train ride out to Sperlonga, where they could sit on the beach, staring out at the same slice of ocean, feeling the same sand between their toes. Britta, oblivious to the mission she was accompanying him on, but hopefully enjoying herself all the same.

After Britta dried her hair and changed into a fresh shirt, they descended the stairs slowly to the square. If they needed to take pit stops where it was cool every fifteen minutes, so be it. With her weight and his condition, whatever was needed, they'd do. They'd already agreed to be sensible.

Down at the market Britta bought a little bag of nectarines to eat on the way, and at a fountain along one of the alleys, they filled their water bottles, as Amalia had suggested they do, and walked east along the narrower streets, partially in shade. Forty years ago, he'd walked this city to death; in three years he'd had his brown shoes resoled five times. The walks were both exercise and his best way to empty his mind after jamming it full or to jog it back to life. As he walked carefully beside Britta, both of them veering toward the shady patches, Paul felt, faintly, in the knife-bright parts of the street, the anxiety he'd lived with back then. It was mostly self-imposed: he'd been so tightly wound. Not that people would exactly call him mellow *now*; he still worried over little things, took seriously all the tasks asked of him, big and small, had his moody side. To put it mildly, considering the past month. But in the years since then, he'd come to understand that his mission in life was bigger than perfecting his mind. His heart had expanded, making room for all forms of human weakness, especially his own.

The Pantheon was only a few blocks out of the way, so they killed two birds with one stone. Ogled the dome, passed the farmacia where he used to buy his cigarettes, passed Santa Maria sopra Minerva. One of the three great doors that led into the front of Gregorian University was open, and as they walked into the cooler atrium, Paul heard two men's muffled voices. Summer classes were in session, but only a few. Forty years ago, it was like a beehive when classes let out, but now the only other person here was a plain teenaged girl sitting against the wall in very short red shorts, legs flared open like wings, reading a book, absently but provocatively mouthing an orange Popsicle. His first thought was that she came here because it was cool and quiet. But it was possible too, wasn't it, that she came here to tempt the young priests. Here where she held more power than she did in the world outside, this plain girl who would seem prettier for being so available.

The graduate student residence he'd called home for three years—a place they'd nicknamed Il Castello—was just down the street. But when Paul rang the doorbell, no one answered, so they continued to Trevi Fountain. The crowd around the fountain was only three or four people deep, not nearly as thick as it would have been in May or September. The glaring noon sun cast harsh shadows on heroic Neptune and his tritons. In the open area beyond the ring, sometimes venturing their way into it, African men in bright silk shirts hawked spinning whirligigs, hats with propellers on them—junk Paul couldn't imagine anyone would want. Those at the front sloshed their hands in the water or tossed coins over their shoulders, smiling for their Facebook photo op. They pressed forward through the docile crowd, Britta smoking a cigarette like a local. Sunlight blinked and flashed off the water.

And then they were beside it. A blazing pool of aquamarine, the impossible blue of a hot springs, but cool. Paul cupped some water, splashed it on his neck and face, like aftershave, and sighed at the pleasure of it. Britta dug through her purse and found two quarters.

"Want one?"

Paul shook his head. "That's okay. You go ahead."

Throw a coin over your shoulder, they said, and you'd return to Rome. *Yeah, well,* he thought, *unlikely.* He watched his sister face the fountain with the coins clasped in her hand, hypnotized by the water. She didn't move. *So much to wish for,* Paul thought: peace for him, a merciful death. Some resolution or clarity for Maura. Maybe something for herself too. Though what would that be? Strength to deal with it all? Something completely unrelated? He didn't really know what she wanted in life anymore, beyond avoiding more heartbreak. But maybe that was wish enough.

Finally, Britta bent forward, as if lowering a biscuit to a dog, and tossed the two quarters as reverently as possible.

"What'd you wish for?" he asked when she was back beside him.

She flashed him a wry smile. "Wouldn't you like to know?"

"Yes," he said, "that's why I asked."

"It's a secret," she said, and looked at him with sad, bright eyes. "How you feeling, by the way? You want to keep going or go back?"

He was tired, he realized. He could use a nap. "I think go back."

In his room, Paul took off his shoes, socks, and shorts and drifted off under the cool bedsheet. When he woke, it was too hot. He took a cold shower, pulled down a book of old maps from Amalia's family library, watched TV with Britta, gathered the gist of the nightly newscast. Around seven, they went out for dinner two streets away. The heat today reminded Britta of her trip with Don and the kids to the Grand Canyon forever ago. How hot it had been at the bottom, her recurring fantasy of the canyon filling with water like a gigantic swimming hole to cool them off. When a breeze snuffed the candle set out for ambiance, a young busser arrived quickly to relight it, his nervous, earnest manner familiar, exactly like something else. An altar boy, he thought. Exactly that.

"Is there a patron saint for people who're stuck?" Britta asked, as she dropped her credit card onto the little black tray beside her second glass of wine. Paul thought she was referring to him, but before he could answer, she added: "I'm trying to think who Mom would pray to about Maura. Not that I would have told her about it."

"Saint Dymphna is for anxiety," Paul said unhelpfully.

"I need one for when you're having an emotional affair with a painter from Maine and thinking about ending your marriage."

"I wouldn't be surprised if there was one for that too."

Paul recalled Maura's most recent Facebook profile photo: shoulder-length hair, a soft smile, face lit by a morning sun, the top of Ella's head resting under her chin. Happy seeming. But obviously not so happy. There was something she'd been hiding from the world too—and now, against his will, he imagined his niece pressed against a wall, passionately kissing a man in a black shirt speckled with dust, one hand on the man's ass. The soft, placid face in sunlight overcome with desire, like a still from a melodramatic B movie. If the specifics he was imagining were wrong, at least the longing was real. And beneath the longing, he imagined, love. Maura was an artistic soul, but practical too. Committed as she was to her kids, as sensitive as she was to the opinions of others (though perhaps not his opinions anymore), she wouldn't have entertained the thought of divorce unless her desire was grounded in love.

Now Britta found her phone in her purse and swiped at it intently with her thumb.

"Still haven't heard from her, huh?" Paul asked.

"You'd be the first to know."

"Shade texted me to wish me a good trip," he said. "Not sure if I told you that." The message was short—vintage Shade—but sweet: *Hey Uncle Paul—hope you have fun in Rome. Eat some pizza for me. Shade.*

"Raised one of them right, at least," Britta said.

But the joke was neither funny nor true. They both knew that Maura was normally the more thoughtful one. And yet this radio silence. She was preoccupied with her own drama, of course—maybe it was as simple as that. Or maybe it was fear. Or discomfort. Some people, even good, thoughtful ones, simply couldn't stomach death. Avoided it at all costs, blind to their fear.

"Here we go," Britta said now, looking at her phone. "Saint Margaret of Cortona, patron of the sexually tempted. Good ol' Maggie C."

"That was going to be my next guess."

"They should really test you guys on this stuff. Keep you on your toes."

"If they did, I'd be in trouble."

Their waiter appeared and whisked away her card. Britta crossed her arms loosely over her belly.

"So, is everything how you remember it?" she asked him.

"Well," he said, "yes and no." The buildings and the streets were the same, of course—Rome, eternal as ever. But he hadn't come to merely see familiar buildings, familiar streets. He was after something more. The old feeling, silly as that seemed. As if by simply being physically present in the place where it had happened, the young man he'd been and everything he'd felt so intensely would be resurrected. Here, he'd hoped, in the hectic days they'd spent preparing for the trip, his well-worn memories might be buffed to a shine. Or even better: a few that had slipped through the cracks might be recovered.

Britta was giving him a bemused, concerned look. "Where did you just go?" she asked.

"What do you mean?"

"You drifted off for a second."

"Oh," he said. "Maybe I did."

His sister leaned forward a little, eyes squinted slightly. She was trying to figure him out. Failing, but he appreciated the effort.

That night, they went to bed early. Tomorrow would be a full day and they needed their rest. But when Paul woke, ten hours after falling asleep, he was exhausted down to his bones. It was jet lag, of course, but this was worse than any jet lag he'd had before: jet lag on top of dying, it almost wasn't fair. Lying in bed, he considered begging off sightseeing altogether, but when he shuffled into the kitchen to find Britta already showered and happily eating the breakfast Amalia had brought up for them—salmon and butter sandwiches, chocolate biscotti, espresso, sparkling water, two huge bottles of blood orange juice—he thought better of it. To fly eight hours to Rome and not see it was criminal. And just look at her—as bright-eyed and eager as he'd seen her since she'd flown in.

He drank his espresso, though he wasn't supposed to have caffeine. In the shower, he made the water cold and bracing, and as he stood under the spray, droplets streaming off the edges of his face, he prayed for the first time since before Sister Bay: *Please give me the strength to get through the day.*

A few minutes into their cab ride to the Bone Church—the first stop on Britta's itinerary—an old Italian love song came on the radio. Flamenco-style guitar, flute, a wistful male voice. He closed his eyes, trying to remember its name. It had played from transistor radios set out on balconies and the radio the nuns in the kitchen listened to for company; he saw railings bound with silver tinsel and placed it: a pretty, melancholy song among the usual cheery Christmas carols, the winter of either '68 or '69. And then the name appeared: "Lo straniero." A memory that only being here could have unearthed.

Remembering the song buoyed him and made him greedy for more. Though of course you couldn't force it: memories either arrived or they didn't. When the song ended, another one much like it began: guitar, oboe, another earnest baritone pining for lost love. He didn't know this one but listened to it intently, sinking slowly into its dream world, his lungs growing heavy and calm...until Britta was shaking his shoulder, saying his name. He'd fallen asleep. The cab's engine was idling. Beyond the half-open window loomed the church: three stories of white trim and pink brick.

"We're here," she said.

"Oh," he said. "Okay."

He unbuckled his seat belt, and that tiniest of exertions told him something. He was beyond exhausted. His arms and legs felt hollow, his face thick and heavy, as if caked with clay. Just to enter the church, he'd have to climb a big flight of stairs, then all the claustrophobic wandering underground. He imagined trying to do this and realized he couldn't. He felt angry. Duped.

Britta stood hunched beside the car, holding the door. "Aren't you coming out?"

"I don't think I can," he said. "I suddenly feel wiped out."

Britta's eyes were sympathetic, but her pursed mouth was disappointed. "Do you want to go back to the apartment?"

"I probably should. You should stay here, though. All I'll be doing is sleeping."

"No," she said, a faint note of exasperation in her voice. "I'll come with you. I can always leave after you're settled in."

"Okay," he said. "Thank you."

Already the indignation of being fooled was giving way to a fear of his own helplessness. Compared to the will of his body, his mind didn't stand a chance.

"I'm sorry about this," he said. "I should have just stayed home."

"No apologies allowed, Paul," she said. "This isn't your fault."

He slept the entire ride back, head rocking gently on the headrest. On the walk up the stairs to their apartment, he grabbed the railing and Britta gripped his right arm to steady him, mirrored his steps. At the kitchen sink, one hand gripping the counter, he drank half a glass of water, collected his breath, then filled the glass to the top and drank it all down. The moment he felt the cool fabric of the pillow against his hot cheek, he fell asleep.

When he woke, his watch said it was noon: two hours had passed. But he didn't feel much better. His whole body felt heavy as stone, but for the tumor on his right side, which was also on fire. In the bathroom, he swallowed a morphine pill with a palmful of water, then returned to bed. Soon, the drug set in. His heart and fingertips hummed, his jaw unclenched, the sharp teeth gnawing at his side retracted into their gums. For a while, the beginnings of thoughts darted over his head like small, quick birds, but they were impossible to grasp, which made him anxious.

To ground himself, he tried focusing on the delicate pinholes and sunbursts in the lace curtains framing the window, the fine white hairs on the knuckles of his folded hands, the ebb and flow of his breath. *I'm in a hotel bed in Rome,* he thought. *I've finally come back. I have jet lag but soon I will feel better.*

He closed his eyes and slowed his breathing, but sleep didn't come. When he opened them again, the air in front of him was vibrating. The effect reminded him of the honeybees that sometimes thronged one of their maple trees back on the farm: at a glance, the mass of them seemed still, but if you looked closer, you noticed the way they boiled with energy. Once, as a boy, he'd been stung all over his legs by some of these bees while walking past the tree, and suddenly here he was, lying on his family's living room couch, his mother beside him, plucking the stingers out with dirt-rimmed fingernails. Then the sofa became his childhood bed; he was sick with fever, and his mother draped a cold, damp cloth on his forehead. And then it wasn't his mother beside him but Luca, looking at him with soft eyes. *Can I lie next to you?* he asked. *Of course,* Paul replied, and Luca moved from his chair to the bed and curled up beside him in his white T-shirt and ill-fitting jeans, one of his thin arms cradling Paul's head.

The second time Paul woke, his watch said it was two fifteen: he'd been in bed more than four hours. He pushed himself carefully to a sitting position, then slowly rose and shuffled into the living room. In the ornate mirror on the far wall, he caught a glimpse of himself: rumpled khaki shorts, saggy blue T-shirt, hair sticking up in three directions, sleepy, tired eyes— like some doddering fool at a nursing home. Britta was lying on the couch like a fat Cleopatra, head propped up by a tasseled red pillow, watching TV with the sound off.

"He lives!" she said, turning to look at him.

"Just barely."

"How're you feeling?"

"Rested," he said. "Better, actually." It was true.

"Good," she said. "I napped a little too. The jet lag started hitting me after lunch."

"When did you get back?" Paul asked.

"Oh, I don't know. About an hour ago?"

"Did you have fun?"

"Well," she said, "I don't know. I had a weird experience at the Bone Church place. Nothing to do with the church itself, just...there were these two assholes on the tour."

"Oh," Paul said. "What happened?"

Britta clicked off the TV. "I'll tell you, but how about we grab something to eat first. You must be starving."

The market had been officially closed for more than an hour—most of the tents were already broken down and whisked away—but as they walked to the trattoria Britta had in mind, a few vendors remained, sweaty and stark as they packed up in the midafternoon sunlight. A middle-aged woman set an armful of red flowers onto a bed of burlap in the back of her truck. An old man lugged a crate of artichokes. A sleepy girl sat in her father's car, sideways on the passenger seat, legs dangling, listening to music with earbuds. Within the hour they would be gone, along with all the little piles of trash. A fleet of garbage trucks would arrive and eat them all up and the place would look pristine again by evening for the tourists. Like magic.

It was even hotter today than yesterday, but when Britta asked him if he wanted to eat inside, Paul said no: he wanted to sit on the square under the faint shade of umbrellas, where he could watch the world go by. And after lying in air-conditioning most of the day, his bones felt cold; he wanted to warm up.

When their waiter arrived, Britta ordered fresh mozzarella to share and deep-fried artichoke hearts and a Campari and soda for herself; Paul chose a small plate of pumpkin gnocchi and sparkling water to calm his stomach. The tour this morning had started off fine, she began, handing over her menu. The guide was this nerdy young guy with thick glasses she'd found immediately endearing and who knew his stuff inside and out. The shrines—built from the pelvises and spines and skulls of dead monks—were just as beautiful and creepy up close as she'd hoped. She'd been having a lovely time, all things considered. But then, near the end of the tour, two young Scottish guys had appeared behind her. How they'd found a way to come down unaccompanied, she wasn't sure. But within a minute, she wanted to strangle them. They weren't paying attention to the guide at all; instead they snickered and snorted at their own private running commentary, probably stoned. *Fookin' this, fookin' that.* A couple of knuckleheads. Like the couple ahead of her, who'd frowned at them to no avail, she tried to ignore them. For a few minutes, she'd succeeded. But after one of them made a joke about nun abortions, she couldn't help herself. Not that she was even Catholic anymore, but still.

"I turned around and I said, 'Hey, guys. We're in a church. Show some respect.' And for maybe a minute after they didn't say a word. And I thought I'd shut them up. But then, as we were headed to the next spot, I heard one of them make a sound that sounded like 'Move. Moooove.' So I turned around again and said, 'Excuse me? What did you just say?' And then the tall one just said, 'We didn't say anything. Must have been a skeleton.' And of course his buddy snorts, ha-ha. But when I turned forward again, they said it again, and I realized they were saying 'Moo.' To me. As in, *Look at the fat cow. Moooo.*"

Paul felt his stomach drop. "Are you serious?"

"Yes."

"How dare they?"

"I know. I couldn't believe it either. I wanted to kick them in the nuts, I'm not even kidding. But what could I do? I didn't want to make a big fuss and ruin the tour for everybody else. And I didn't want to *leave*, because they'd feel like they won. So

I just kept going and bit my tongue." She took a big stuttering breath. "I was so angry though, Paul. My heart was going a hundred miles a minute. And so finally, when the tour was over, I went up to them and I told them, 'You know what? You guys are real assholes to say that to me. You should be ashamed of yourselves.' But they just stared at me with these little shit-eating smirks on their faces, like me being angry was somehow funny to them. And then they walked away."

"This story is pissing me off," Paul said. His whole body felt tight, as though tensed to spring into action. Though what exactly was there to do?

"Thank you," Britta said, "me too." But she wasn't done. "I told myself as I left the church that I wasn't going to cry. I didn't want to give them the pleasure. But as soon as I got in the cab, I couldn't help it. I kept thinking, *Did that really just happen?* And then I thought, *If Don was with me that would have never happened.* And then, well"—and here her voice broke—"I started really missing Don."

She cleared her throat, momentarily overcome. Behind her big Jackie O. sunglasses her eyes were surely tearing up. She was right: with Don there, all six-foot-four, three-hundred-plus intimidating pounds of him, the idiots wouldn't have dared. And if they had, instead of getting right up in their faces, the way they would want it, Don would have put himself between them and Britta, turned the spotlight on them, and cut them down to size. Carved them up with the sharp blade that was his lawyer's mind, calm in tone but brutal in content. What an intimidating but gentle man he'd been, what a good man he'd been. Paul imagined him for a moment among them, wedged into one of these small chairs, tree-trunk legs in the wide stance that helped keep his big body stable, a Coke or whiskey set on his belly as he awaited his food. Mischief and an expectation of pleasure glowing in his eyes.

"I'm sorry that happened to you," he said. "And here of all places."

Britta sniffed. "I know. Anyway. By the time the taxi dropped me off, I'd decided I wasn't going to let those pricks ruin my day. So I walked over to Piazza—what's it called, Navona?— and I bought myself a very pretty, very expensive necklace. And then I stopped for a slice of very tasty pizza and had a couple very delicious limoncellos. And then I bought some postcards and took a nap."

"You made limoncello out of lemons," Paul said.

She smiled, happy to hear him joke. "Well," she said, "I sure did try."

The food arrived, and they dug in with unusual determination—both of them eager to do something other than talk. Every now and then, Britta looked up at him smiling. "So good," she said. "Yes," he agreed. And it was. Small pleasures, the gnocchi reminded him, could still be had. He wasn't past that yet.

As they waited for the check, Paul lifted his head to the buildings flanking the square. All but a few of the windows were shuttered. In one, an old woman looked down, her fingers scratching the back of a gray cat. In another, a drooping ficus plant. And two windows over from that, a tall man with a shaved head standing beside a shorter man with uncombed Mediterranean curls, arm slung over his shoulder. Partners, clearly. A couple in love.

Paul decided to watch them; from this distance he could look and look. Shaved Head was talking passionately about something, his free hand whipping the air beside him. Curls nodded, but his gaze was unfocused and distant: he was somewhere else, as if hypnotized. For a while, Paul stared at the man's vacant face; he decided there was an imbalance at work here. Curls had fallen out of love with Shaved Head but didn't have the heart to tell him. But then, just as he'd convinced himself his theory was true, Curls snapped out of it and smiled. Shaved Head was saying something and laughing, and now Curls chuckled to himself, lips still closed. Encouraged, Shaved Head continued, free hand chopping the air like a cleaver, his face more expressive, until, finally, he got what he'd been after: Curls laughing, exposing a set of perfect teeth. Satisfied with this outcome, Shaved Head turned and kissed his partner's ear, right smack in the middle. Then, as if to seal his victory, he thumped his partner's chest twice with the hand hovering near his heart, and they turned away as if one unit and slipped out of sight.

For a while, Paul stared at the empty window. Then, as if hoping they might pop up elsewhere, he scanned the rest of the building, until he realized how silly that was. When he dropped his head, Britta was across the table watching him: one of her squinting, pitying looks. It lasted only a moment: caught, she guiltily glanced down at the table. But he'd seen what he'd seen. And she'd seen what she'd seen. The pity this time wasn't for his recent suffering, all wrapped up in death. It was for what she would imagine must be going through the mind of her gay older brother—a stranger, she'd assume wrongly, to such intimacy—caught looking at two men in love.

According to their plan, it was still Britta's day to call the shots, but when Paul asked if she wanted to see anything else this afternoon, she said, adamantly, that from now on they should only do Paul things. This trip was for him, not her, and who knew how he'd feel tomorrow. He didn't protest. And he knew immediately where he wanted to go.

In the cab, Britta unfolded her map of Rome and laid it on her lap. Borghese Park was near the middle, in the shape of a green cartoon heart, if half of its left curve had dissolved away. But he didn't study it like she did: he remembered it well enough, each area in his mind leading to the next like the verses of a song.

At Paul's request, the driver dropped them off at Porta Pinciana, and they passed through the arched Roman gate, heading northeast down the hardpan paths, keeping to the edges for shade. In clearings, the sunlight was laser-bright, so he slipped his clip-on shades over his bifocals. When they arrived at the Galleria Borghese, Britta asked if he wanted to go inside, but he realized he didn't—not here or anywhere. All he wanted to do was walk.

Everywhere he looked, he saw both what was here and what was missing, a kind of double vision. Near the zoo, a peacock strutted past them, its tail feathers lightly brushing the ground behind it like a regal broom, the descendant, no doubt, of the peacocks that had strutted around these paths forty years ago. At the edge of the duck pond beside the Temple of Asclepius, an Asian father and mother rowed their daughter to the middle of the pond, at which the girl, afraid of being so far from shore, began to cry—and he remembered how, once, he'd watched two teenaged boys rock their rented boat until it capsized and come walking out, white T-shirts soaked to transparency, laughing. Happy swamp monsters.

Over there, he told Britta, pointing to the lawn in front of the Villa Giulia, was where the hippies liked to hang out, smoking pot, napping on blankets, playing guitar, trying and failing to do headstands. Here by this fountain, a young man with a fifties pompadour, hopelessly out of style, always played the trumpet, curled in on himself like Miles Davis. And in this spot there once was a gelato stand; he could still remember the woman who did the scooping, a shy creature in her forties who was very pretty but for the tufts of dark hair on her chin.

And then, finally, they came to the spot he'd been guiding them toward all along: a span of close-cut grass beside the Fontana Rotunda, where he'd met Luca. He could see it all so vividly: the old men in vests and caps, hands clasped behind their backs; Luca crouched in his feline way, eyeing up his shot, red ball heavy in one hand like an alien egg, the other hand rubbing his jeans to wipe the sweat off. The wedge of tan skin this exposed between his jeans and the bottom of his T-shirt. How all this made his stomach contract, his heart quicken.

Tears rushed to his eyes but he blinked them away. "I used to play bocce with some local guys over there," he said at last. But immediately he wished he hadn't: it was such a meager thing to say. *One of them became a close friend,* he thought, trying out the words. *His name was Luca.* It was as if he were standing before a door, behind which was a pile of heavy boxes, pressing against it, his right hand on the doorknob. All he had to do was open it, a quick turn of the wrist. *This whole trip is really about him.*

"I remember you mentioning that once," Britta said. She looked where he looked but saw nothing. "Neat."

By the time they reached the puppet theater near the park's other entrance, it was almost six. As if to ceremonially acknowledge the end of their walk, Britta treated them to pistachio gelatos and they dispatched them on a bench, wiping their lips and fingers with thin brown napkins.

"So," she said, once they were finished. She set a comradely hand on his knee. "Anything else you want to see here?"

"Nope," he said. He smiled to reassure her. "I think I got my fill."

It was true: there was nothing more he wanted to see. And yet, as they returned to the apartment in another cab, and as he stood beside Britta while she bought two bottles of limoncello at a corner store, and as they sat for a while in silence in their apartment's living room, both of them on their laptops, checking email, and then sat watching TV, Paul didn't feel like a man who'd gotten his fill in the least. Anything but.

At quarter till eight, Britta announced that she was hungry again and suggested they grab dinner in Trastevere tonight instead of tomorrow: strike while the iron was hot. And though Paul didn't feel exactly ready, or hungry, he agreed.

Twenty minutes later, they were sitting at a table outside a trattoria overlooking the Tiber River. The sun was setting, a pink sky softly glowing in the spaces between the peach and orange buildings before them, their windows on fire with reflected light. The air had cooled and was silky against his skin. From inside the restaurant came trickles of laughter and the sweet sound of a guitar, and along the river walk, little packs of tourists moved as unhurried as the water beside them. At dusk, it was as though the anxious creature that was Rome had decided to yawn, curl up in sunlight like a cat on a windowsill, and, finally, rest.

A reasonable person, Paul knew, would feel content right now: this morning's collapse aside, everything had gone according to plan. He'd wanted to return one last time to Rome—and look, here he was. He'd wanted to visit his old student haunts and the places that reminded him of Luca and to remember things that only being here would dredge up. And that had happened too. After dinner tonight, he could direct their next driver to meander through the maze that was Trastevere until he found Luca's apartment building, to stop at the Basilica di Santa Maria, where they'd gone for that walk. Tomorrow, body willing, he could ride out with Britta to Sperlonga, do his secret pilgrimage there.

Yes, he thought, sipping his sparkling water, *I should feel grateful to be here.* Leave it at that. And yet, what he felt blooming at the bottom of his throat was a pang of desperation so familiar he couldn't help feeling a perverse fondness for it, despite the pain it caused. The question wasn't whether he'd gotten what he'd come for. It was whether it really mattered either way in the end.

Deep in his life's routine, it had been easier to not question the path he was on. There was no time to; his duties led him forward like a horse. But sometimes, of course, the routine fell away and he became vulnerable. A feeling of fruitlessness would take hold. Sitting on his sofa on a Saturday afternoon, all his errands complete, no plans for the evening. Sick with the flu or a cold, his schedule and all its urgent demands suddenly beside the point. Sitting at a table on a beautiful night in Rome, thousands of miles from home, the usual rhythms of his life gone perfectly silent...

He knew he wasn't alone in sometimes feeling that nothing he did really mattered in the end. Many people lost the thread at some point in their lives, usually after a loss. And it was during those times, so often, that they had turned to him, their pastor, for help. In his office at the church, he would listen to their heartbreak or their dilemma, asking questions when necessary. When it came time to respond, he would speak plainly, look them in the eyes. In whatever way seemed most appropriate to the person, he'd offered counsel, doing his best to remind them that, in a world that seemed void of meaning, void even of God, there was still, always, the call to love. Their job, above all else, was to love. And if they weren't up to giving it, to accept what was given to them. No more, no less.

If someone asked directly for his intercession, he would push the chair from behind his desk to a spot beside them and pray on their behalf. Always he closed his eyes; sometimes he held their hand. Before they left, he would remind them to lean on friends and family and their community here at St. Iggy's. Remind them that God wasn't out there somewhere but here, all around them. Then he'd escort them to the front doors of the church, and if they asked for a hug, or just seemed to need one, that's how he'd leave them.

There were many times, of course, that he'd felt insufficient to the task. That in retrospect he wished he'd done things differently. In some cases, even his best hadn't mattered. The two suicides. Three, if you counted Tom McAllister's overdose. But more often than not, his counsel, imperfect as it was, had seemed to offer people solace.

So why was he so bad at consoling himself?

By the time they finished dinner, night had fallen. The pink sky was now a rich dark blue, and the buildings now appeared vaguely medieval—a dramatic study in lantern light and shadows.

As they stood from their chairs, the bill paid, Britta asked if he might have any interest in walking back, at least partway. He took stock of how he felt and decided he did; though it was past his normal bedtime, after this morning's long rest, he felt okay.

When they arrived at the apartment twenty minutes later, neither of them was ready for bed. Britta said she might read for a bit and picked up her true crime book, and Paul decided he might try reading too: Amalia had left them yesterday's *New York Times*. But as he held the paper in his hands, he realized, as far as world news was concerned, he couldn't care less.

As they'd walked, arms linked, along the river and over the bridge and then slipped into the narrow streets that would lead them west, he'd glanced over at his sister a few times and felt a surge of affection for her that nearly made him cry. Drunk on wine, as she often was at this hour, she wasn't the steadiest walking partner. But he forgave her that.

Careful not to stare, he glanced at her now, sitting in a high-backed chair, her glasses halfway down the bridge of her nose, his recent caretaker. Growing up, it had been the opposite, of course: six years older, he'd been the one to look after her. When they'd go fishing at the lake, he'd grab the crook of her arm to keep her upright as they carefully descended the hill that led to their spot. The Saturday nights their parents went dancing, it was up to him to put her to bed, hum her to sleep. That dynamic had held into their early adulthood: after Ray, her first husband, left her, the kids still too young for school, she'd been bitter and desperate, and he'd supported her from five hundred miles away. Called her often, sent what little money he could spare. Prayed for her too, though she wouldn't have cared much about that.

After Don came into the picture and saved her from her misery—he still thought of it that way, and maybe she did too—things had evened out. She was safe now, finally at home, and when they talked over the phone or visited, she assumed he was too. And sometimes that was true. As they settled deeper into their lives, they needed each other less—or at least this was what he'd come to believe. They checked in every month or so on the phone, caught each other up on news. They weren't each other's confidants, like some siblings were, usually a brother to a brother, a sister to a sister; it wasn't quite like that. But she knew more about him, say, than their mother had. Not everything, but a lot.

Though she claimed she'd known he was gay as far back as the seventies, they'd talked about it only once, about fifteen years ago. It was the year *Philadelphia* had come out, a winter night; they were talking on the phone. Had he seen it yet? she asked. He had, he'd replied. And what had he thought? *Loved it,* he said. She told him she'd cried at the ending, that she kept playing the theme song by Bruce Springsteen on repeat. *Yes,* he said. *I like it too.* And then, out of the blue, she asked him.

Well, he answered after a moment, *what do you think?*

I've always assumed you were, she said, *but you never actually said it.*

I didn't think I needed to, he replied.

Then silence.

Has that been hard for you? she continued.

What do you mean? he asked.

Always around guys, you know, in school?

I don't think it was any harder or easier than it would have been anywhere else, he said.

She asked him if he'd ever had a crush on anyone, rather abruptly.

Of course, he said.

Yeah? she said. *More than one?*

Well, yeah. A few.

Like who? she asked.

He said she wouldn't know who any of them were, so why bother naming names?

Oh, come on...tell me anyway, she said.

But here he'd balked. Her tone was all wrong for the moment: too proprietary, too slight. She didn't think him capable of more than schoolboy crushes, and he wasn't going to be fooled into convincing her otherwise.

I'm not sure how much I want to get into this, to be honest, he said.

Okay! she said, slightly taken aback. *We don't have to if you don't want to.*

Yeah, he said, trying to be polite now. *I guess I don't.*

In the years since, she must have considered returning to the subject but, out of respect for his wishes, decided against it. Really, she would have thought, what was there to know? So he'd had crushes. And the crushes had names. So what? In matters of the heart she assumed he knew nothing of what he'd seen today in the square. That he was a virgin who'd put his desires in a jar on a shelf. Poor Paul, who'd done so much good, but who'd missed out on so much.

Of course she'd think this: he hadn't told her anything about any of it on purpose. He didn't want her pity. He wanted to prove to her, with his devotion, that he'd been right to serve the Church she'd long ago left. So he'd shown her the person he wanted her to see, the one who had chosen wisely and wouldn't trouble her, instead of the person he really was. And if he wanted to, he could continue being that person for her, right up until the end. Take his secrets, as they say, to the grave.

When he said her name, she didn't look up from her book.

"Hmm?"

"Can I talk to you for a minute?"

"Of course. What is it?" She closed her book on her finger, slowly looked his way.

"I want to tell you something."

She set her book facedown on the armrest to give him her full attention. "Okay," she said. "Shoot."

And here it was. He hadn't planned how to say it, so he would just say the first things that came to his mind. Just tell the truth.

"I wanted to tell you why I've been so down lately. It's more than you think."

"Okay," she said cautiously.

"I've been feeling a lot of regret. For things I didn't do."

"What do you mean?" she asked.

"Like"—he took a breath—"not leaving the priesthood. And never having a partner."

Blunt. Direct. But there it was.

She scooted an inch forward and frowned, still gauging him for sincerity. "Seriously?"

"Yes," he said.

Her frown softened. Not pity, only concern. And then something on his face made her say, "Oh, Paul."

He wasn't crying yet, but he knew it was only a matter of time; he could feel his chest swelling, his sinuses thickening. Britta pulled her chair closer beside him, sat, and clasped her hand lightly on his forearm, a loving shackle.

"I always thought you liked your life at St. Iggy's."

"I did," he said. "Some of the time, at least. But I always wondered if I might have been happier if I'd—" Here his voice broke.

Britta nodded and searched his face, a wince disguised as a soft smile. "How long have you felt this way?" she asked.

"Oh, you know. Thirty-five, forty years."

She inhaled slightly, then nodded. "So why didn't you do it, you think? If you wanted it so badly?"

His chest quivered when he exhaled. "I was afraid," he said, "of what people would say, at first, at least. Back when it was more of a scandal. And I guess the older I got, the more I was afraid of where I'd end up if it didn't work out."

"It can be hard to meet someone," she said. "For anybody. The most wonderful people in the world struggle to find love."

She was trying to show him he hadn't been foolish to be wary. But it was odd how quickly she'd jumped to this particular thought.

"You can't even imagine it, can you?" he said.

"What do you mean?"

"Me in a relationship. You think I'd have no clue."

"It's not that!" Her face curdled, protesting too much. "Of course I can imagine it."

"I'm not as innocent as you think," he said. "I'm not even a virgin."

She blinked. "Really?"

"Yes," he said. "It happened when I was here, actually. The end of my last year. I was in love with him. He's partly the reason we're here."

"You're being serious."

"Yes," he said, "I am."

For a long moment, she looked at him, as if for the first time. "Does anyone else know about this?"

"No, you're the first."

"Not even Tim?"

"Not even Tim."

She didn't seem to know what to say, so he kept talking.

"You know the bocce court I pointed out today? That's where we met, actually. I would sit and watch Luca play with the old men there, until he finally came over and talked to me."

"Luca," she said.

"Yes," he said. "Luca Aurecchio."

For a while, Britta said nothing, slowly absorbing the news. Above the big Persian rug in front of them, invisible dust was still settling from the crash of this meteor. The lamps seemed stunned, unable to do anything but obediently shed their light.

"I honestly don't know what to say," she said. "Here I was reading my Mormon murder book, and suddenly you're telling me you had a boyfriend."

"Sorry to kill the mood."

"It's okay. I just need a second to get used to it, that's all."

"I understand."

"Have there been other guys since then? Or just him?"

"No," he said. "Just him."

It was true, but hearing himself say the words out loud, it didn't feel true. There *had* been other men besides Luca—they just hadn't known it. Crushes that lasted a few months and stopped, like Charlie Evans, the shy mechanic son of his deacon Bill, who sometimes served Communion, the faint outline of grease forever on his fingernails. Crushes that lasted years, like John Barnes, a boyish man well into his forties with a woman's long lashes, husband of Gail, who always shook his hand firmly on the way out of church and had lent his pickup to the land-scaping project they'd done on the church grounds years ago. And in a different category altogether—a place built purely for lust—the mysterious young man he'd summoned to his hotel room in Chicago, during a conference the year after he'd discovered Luca had died. Bobby. Though who knew if that was his real name. Dark hair, dark eyes, according to the woman on the phone. But he'd never seen the man's face. When Bobby had knocked three times on his door, his courage had failed him. A condom in his pocket. Hands shaking. He'd slipped ten twenty-dollar bills under the door and told him to leave, and for years after had rewritten the ending a dozen different ways.

"I know the Catholic Church wouldn't approve of me saying this," Britta said, "but I'm happy that happened to you. And I'm glad it was with someone you loved."

Paul nodded. "Me too."

"Having said that," she added, "you realize you'll have to pay me to keep this a secret now."

"Don't even joke about that," he said.

"Okay, fine." She was faintly smiling. "I won't. On one condition."

"What's that?"

"You need to tell me the story."

He looked at her: her eyes were bright and curious. "That's a pretty big condition," he said.

"I mean, you've gotten this far."

He nodded. He had. And what an odd destination it was. Here in this apartment in Rome. Late at night and strangely not tired.

"I'm ready whenever you are," she said.

"Okay," he said. He smiled and took a deep, shuddering breath. "In that case I guess I'll tell you everything."

III. Everything

T he first of the strange events that transpired early that spring in Rome was the arrival of Norb Sensenbrenner's shocking news, airmailed from Cincinnati.

It arrived a week into February, three months before Paul would finish his exams and return to the States. Inside the envelope were two folded sheets of impossibly thin paper. Blue ink. His friend's unmistakable microscopic lettering. The usual niceties to begin, but then a revelation that had made him literally break out into a cold sweat and sit on his bed. Norb was putting in his papers; it was already in the works. All for some nun named Sister Marie.

I'm sure your mouth is open wide enough to stuff a golf ball inside right now, the letter began. *It surprised me too. I'm sorry if this disappoints you. I know from our conversations how you thought it best for certain people to leave if their hearts weren't in it, but I'm sure you never counted me among them. To be honest, neither did I. But she's a great person, Paul, and I'm in love with her. I want you to know that. She's prettier than I deserve and the kindest woman I've ever met. You'd like her, I think. She sees the absurdity in things like most women don't and that's probably one of the things that struck me about her. I hope you can be happy for me.*

Holding the letter in his hands, Paul had considered the possibility that it was a hoax. Stupidly, he looked for another sheet, behind this sheet, with *GOTCHA!* written big. The priests they both knew who had already left—a dozen at least—had seemed either ambivalent from the start or the hale and hearty sorts who had realized, a little late, that they couldn't waste their manly charms. But Norb? *Norb Sensenbrenner?* It hadn't seemed possible. And now here was Norb, wanting his support.

In the three-page reply he'd typed up that very night on his portable Smith Corona, Paul tried, admirably he thought, to keep his emotions largely out of it, choosing instead to eloquently log his concerns, as was his obligation as a friend. How long had Norb actually known her? Was it possible, considering he had so little experience with women, that he was mistaking friendship or a crush for something more? Could this desire for an escape be a knee-jerk reaction to the boredom of having his first real job? What about his plan to open the eyes of the masses to the surprising complexities of Scripture? Had he talked to anyone about this?

This wasn't a decision to be made lightly.

This was disowning a whole life.

The tone of his response, he'd thought, was just right—deeply concerned without scolding—and Paul had expected a long reply, a bulletpoint defense. But Norb had returned only a short paragraph. He understood Paul's concerns, the note said, but it was as simple as this: he was following his heart. *I don't think the wedding will be until next spring,* Norb concluded, *so unless you plan on staying on as assistant doorman at the dorms, I presume you'll be back. I really do hope you'll be able to make it.* Then, under his typed initials (*NFS*), as if to squelch any further debate, he'd typed out an excerpt from the Song of Songs.

My beloved speaks and says to me:
"Arise, my love, my fair one,
and come away;
for now the winter is past,
the rain is over and gone.
The flowers appear on the earth;
the time of singing has come,
and the voice of the turtledove
is heard in our land...."

To satisfy his inner scold, Paul imagined the flak Norb would surely get back home from his relatives, the scoffing of some of their fellow classmates in Rome. But he knew that all that would be temporary. In a few years, once Norb and this Marie person had escaped the shadow of their past, they would seem just like anyone else. A normal man and woman doing what normal men and women did. They'd probably even have kids. No one would know. And if they did, they wouldn't much care.

Whereas if *he* were to leave for love, if such a thing was even possible, he'd never be forgiven. His parents, his mother especially, would be destroyed. His hometown, family, and friends scandalized. All the reason not to even consider it. Except that he did. Hopeless and reckless as it was, he considered it all the time.

By that first spring of the new decade, he'd been in Rome nearly three years, there to get his master's in Scripture. He'd chosen to go to graduate school mostly to avoid teaching the boys at Sacred Heart, the minor seminary he'd gone to himself ten years before—the job he'd had since his ordination. He'd thought he'd like it, teaching biblical history and American history, but he hadn't. He hated having to entertain and discipline the boys; resented the conveyor belt of mediocre student papers, the feeling that he'd stopped improving his own mind. The excellent teachers, like Father Ketchum, who'd taught Latin, and Father O'Hara, who'd taught Greek and Roman history, took an obvious contagious pleasure in sharing what they knew. They were natural performers and they cared. He wasn't and didn't, not as much as he should. He'd been at the very top of his class, loved to learn, loved the subject matter for its own sake. It was having to explain it to others that was annoying. When he admitted to himself that he wasn't happy with what he was doing, he'd appealed to the bishop to let him return to school. Three years of graduate studies in the Eternal City, the idea being that maybe he'd then go on for his Ph.D., teach older, smarter students at a college somewhere where he would feel more fulfilled. All that beauty, all that history, and only the expansion of his mind to worry about. His bishop—a kind, bug-eyed old guy with a penchant for cigars and an arch sense of humor—had agreed. *Go forth, young man, and bring back the treasures you find* had been his exact words.

Young Paul hadn't done a ton of traveling, but he wasn't some country bumpkin either. Twice he'd been to Chicago, once to Minneapolis and St. Louis. Even so, Rome might as well have been Mars. Its narrow, mazelike streets, all its layers of history there but not there, worked on him like a pulsing lingering subconscious. Turn a corner and there was the Pantheon. Turn another, Piazza Navona. The endless foul-smelling Gypsies and beggars. The business girls made up like Brigitte Bardot. Grime and splendor, splendor and grime.

He'd immediately fallen in love with the energy of the place, though often those first few weeks, walking through it, he'd felt afraid. Not of being pickpocketed so much, though he'd been warned about that. It was the ordinary Romans who scared him. The boisterous men and women who were every-where, shouting, laughing, arguing, thrusting their arms and stirring the air with their hands as they talked. Staring at you like a cat when you walked by. Was he supposed to be this way too? Would he *need* to be? But soon, as the boundaries of his life got settled, he'd seen it was silly to worry. His world and theirs wouldn't intersect much. If he did find himself walking past a group of young machos eating their bagged lunches against a wall on one of the days his clerical collar was required, he wasn't expected to be anything but who he was. Just like the people with whom he went to school and the members of his parents' church back home, the Romans wanted to hold their priests slightly above, or at least apart. When he passed, they nodded with a neutral look in their eyes.

Buon giorno, he'd say. And they'd nod back. And that was that.

The place where he and the other American graduate students lived was a building its residents lovingly called Il Castello. The castle. Set into the city a block from the college and a ten-minute stroll from Trevi Fountain, the building had served as a convent in the sixteenth and seventeenth centuries, and sometimes, when the place was quietest, Paul was able to imagine dozens of Sally Fields in their white flying-seagull headdresses moving serenely down the halls, polite ghosts. Now the ancient lease served to house seventy to eighty American priests. Open the gigantic castle door, and you entered a tall three-story atrium. At the middle stood a gray stone fountain, radiating silence. Faded peach impasto walls wept soot black and seaweed green. Up above, walkways wound around walls, leaving a trail of closed wooden doors. A sanctuary. But they weren't monks. You heard conversation, laughter. The place was old but alive.

Most of the residents were on the bishop track, here to study canon law. A few others had come for degrees in liturgy, choral music, and history. But only he and Norb were here for Scripture, Norb a year ahead. From the get-go, Monsignor LaRouche had paired them up; they couldn't have avoided the other if they'd wanted to. And in this way, they'd come to be friendly and, after a few tentative months, friends.

Norb was strange looking but had developed the ability to joke about it. This was his long-established defense against teasing. Short, thin, stooped; sporting a protruding Adam's apple, a weak chin, close-set eyes, thick horn-rims set on a big nose, pockmarked skin from adolescent acne; bowlegged as a cowboy—it was hard *not* to imagine Norb getting bullied as a kid, and, as it turned out, exactly that had happened, his personal schoolyard hell having played out behind his grade school in suburban Cincinnati. Like Paul, he'd been an academic ace all the way through. Loved philosophy and Barth, baseball more than football, and had gone through a martyr phase as a boy, every abuse merely setting the stage for his eventual sainthood. Unlike Paul, he'd grown up with money, the son of a successful accountant and a devout mother, so was a connoisseur of things Paul couldn't have afforded to appreciate even if it had occurred to him to: as a boy, catalog-bought seashells and stamps; more recently, Spanish sherries and jazz. A little full of himself, Paul's mother would have said, had she heard him criticize Mass wine as being too sweet or seen him snort at the cheap Michelangelo's *David* replicas for sale in the little shops near the school. But Paul had developed a far higher tolerance for snobbery than his mother. He wanted himself, and all things within his domain, to be better than just good enough. Had he not been ambitious, he would never have made it off the farm. His high standards were a gift.

Neither of them was part of the social scene. Some of the guys were friendly enough, good for a game of chess or a quick salted pretzel and beer at the hofbräuhaus nearby, but the dominant force was a loose fraternity of loud, boastful, and moneyed guys from the bigger cities who seemed to spend a lot of time zipping around on the Vespas or in the Fiats their parents had bought them; playing pranks; having loud, self-serving arguments about Johnson, then Nixon; going out of town for four-day weekends; doing the *New York Times* crossword; and playing hearts or pinochle. Everything, it seemed, but study. Norb had no problem asking them to keep quiet when they were hooting too loudly at someone's Bob Newhart record, but Paul feared their scorn too much to be so bold. When he did occasionally enter their orbit, during the beer hall dinners monsignor set up twice a quarter, or happened upon a little group in the cafeteria, he tried to be pleasant. He had always been very intentional about being pleasant; by taking careful note of those mannerisms people associated with homosexuals and ironing the few that came to him naturally out of his repertoire, he'd managed to avoid getting teased—and had managed to arouse little suspicion from most everyone. In the company of the other residents, he laughed at the good jokes, told stories about odd professors, colorful characters from back home, like Otis the junk man. He was liked well enough, nodded to, abided...but they understood he didn't want to be part of their world. And vice versa. It was fine. They did their thing; he did his.

Mostly, his thing was studying, reading for pleasure, playing chess with Norb, and, when he could spare the time, taking walks around the city. Lectures ran from eight to noon every day, then it was studying all afternoon, a break for dinner, and more studying late into the night. He was used to this rhythm by now, but the first year had nearly killed him. The language classes were murder. He already knew Latin and some Greek and a little German and French from seminary. But now he was required to learn Hebrew and Italian too. And to add to the degree of difficulty, the Hebrew section was taught in Latin by a Spaniard with a strong accent, who sometimes switched from Latin to Italian for his more off-the-cuff remarks. *It's like the Tower of Babel around here,* Paul wrote his parents that year. *But no miracle in sight.* Years later it made for a funny anecdote—Who's on First, priest edition—but at the time it had been hell. He was used to digesting things quickly, sinking deeply into books, but here learning seemed to be done on the fly. Words flitted off professors' lips, and he had to grab them before they flew out the window. Worse, all the final exams were in Latin and few were written, as he was used to. Instead you were to stand in front of your professors and answer questions while being looked at, waited on. He had survived in the end, of course. Worked his tail off and had prayed every morning at Mass for the strength to keep his focus, and thought, more charitably than he ever had when he was in front of them, of the future seminarians back home who were counting on him to get through the program, so he might bring back the secrets they did not know.

And secrets were what they felt like, when that second year began. What he hadn't known—what his education even as an undergraduate studying theology hadn't taught him—was staggering. The catechism he knew inside out. The rules, yes. And Bible verses he could quote at length. But how had it come to be? How had it been put together? What had been left out? All this had been willfully, it seemed now, kept in shadow.

His professors here were odd, formidable, and razor-sharp. Scripture wasn't a given, as he'd been taught to think as a child, but a puzzle, a pastiche, carefully constructed for certain audiences and contexts. An onion of many layers to be unpeeled. The detective novel buff in him liked the feeling of tracking something down, of homing in on original intentions, of determining where errors were made, where a translator went wrong. It was, as he'd hoped, more stimulating than teaching, and he would often take a moment to feel thankful, at Mass and at night, as he had since he was a boy, and also while walking around Rome after dinner, hands clasped behind his back or smoking a Nazionale, as he absorbed the roiling energy of the place, the molten light of evening bleeding over the ancient buildings. It was a solitary existence made less anxious because whenever he wanted a little companionship he could simply go knock on Norb's door and vice versa. Theirs was a friendship of the mind, of convenience. In his life there had been other friendships, two where he was attracted to the friend, errant but welcome daydreams of something more. Handsome boys. But Norb was just Norb. Goofy, harmless, and straight.

They played Scrabble and crazy eights. Every so often a check from Norb's parents arrived, and Norb bought a bottle of good sherry and then they were sophisticated and tipsy as they played Scrabble and crazy eights. Walking around the city, Norb glanced blatantly at the breasts of young Roman women, once dreadfully using the term "milk wagon" to describe the rack on a girl of maybe eighteen, and referenced certain pretty girls back home, Roman versions of which seemed to be everywhere. But his ardor for the opposite sex had seemed harmless, in the way of a twelve-year- old boy, or wistful, in the way of an old man long out of the game.

When Norb completed his degree and returned home to Cincinnati at the end of Paul's second year, Paul knew he would be lonely. He'd always been the type to latch on to a single person a little too much, to put all his eggs in one basket. There were three new Scripture students that fall—Tom and Dale from Michigan, Dom from Indiana—and it fell to him to show them around, play the role of knowing old vet. But they had their own thing going, those three, all of them oppressively witty. So that third fall he read Le Carré and Agatha Christie paperbacks bought for cheap from the American bookstore's bargain bin. Listened to the Ornette Coleman records Norb had bequeathed him, trying to not resent them for being chaotic. Became friendly, after a forced study group, with two ruddy-faced Benedictines from Alsace-Lorraine, with whom he'd gone skiing in the Alps over the Christmas holiday, practiced his conversational German, and drunk too many hot buttered rums. But it was small consolation. They weren't just down the hall; they didn't play chess. He had arranged his life so as to have privacy, and that's what the others had given him. Sometimes he wondered if anyone would even have noticed if he didn't leave his room for a week, just stayed inside smoking and playing solitaire.

They had promised to write, he and Norb, but managed only one exchange that year after Norb left in July. Paul's long letter, sent in August, hadn't been answered until early October, a few weeks later than he would have liked. Norb's first letter had mentioned nothing of Sister Marie specifically, only that he and Father Gary, the other young priest who taught in his department (*a bit of a priss but likes Ping-Pong*), had been going to Sunday dinner with a few nuns who worked in the campus ministry office (*pretty good gals*). Lots of half-interested students, lots of numbing paperwork, was the verdict, though the dean was a good guy. A fellow lover of dessert wines. Paul had replied right away, complaining uncharacteristically of the slog that third year was turning out to be, mentioning only in passing the three newbies, and in return there had been nothing but a Christmas card: embossed angel, star, manger, and two lines of generic holiday greeting inside, a promise to write more later. But then in February, the bombshell.

Rome was eternal, sure, but it also existed in 1970. As unbelievably strange and still stranger things had happened over the past three years back home, Paul had followed along, of course, as did all the Americans. Three copies of the *Times* and two copies of the *Tribune* were bought and set out in the common area every day, courtesy of the recreation budget, and they pored over everything, the way Paul's father always did on Sundays, his one day for catching up on the world. Martin Luther King Jr.'s assassination had led to a prayer meeting; the same had gone for Bobby Kennedy. Vietnam was proving hopeless. Sea changes were happening everywhere—you saw that even in Rome, where crowds gathered to oppose the war, where grizzled, languid hippies, who looked exactly like the hippies back home, were yelled at by old men with their undershirts showing: *Lazy beggars! Get a fuckin' job!* Britta had become one of them—that was the subject of most of his mother's monthly letters. She wasn't going to church anymore, just because it was run only by men. As if *that* was a reason. And yet—and on paper he could hear his mother's tone of utter disgust—

she seemed quite unopposed to sleeping with as many men as she pleased. She was getting swept up in the tidal wave of the times, and his mother prayed every day for her soul. *Could you talk to her?* she had asked. *I hate to bother you when you're so busy, but she might listen to you more than me.* So he'd called home, to hear it straight, and called Britta three times at the number his mother had given him, but when she finally called back, the conversation had led nowhere. Her stubbornness, actually, was what Norb's response would immediately remind him of. She knew what he believed: she'd gone to the same schools, had the same nuns, had the same parents, been confirmed and done First Communion and all the rest just like him. And she got that it was his job to keep his sheep in line, being a shepherd of souls and all. But what it came down to was that he didn't understand the first thing about what it was to be alive and young right now, and she was sorry, but she wanted to find out.

I understand the appeal of doing things a new way, he'd told her. *That part I get. But what you're talking about doesn't sound like love,* meaning her sleeping around. *You're too smart to get caught up in all that.*

Funny you say that, she'd said. *Because I think I'm too smart not to.*

That had been in the summer after his second year. Since then they hadn't talked or written at all, except for the birthday card she sent him. *I'm fine, don't worry,* it read. *Hope you are too. With love, your pagan sister.*

For the past nearly three years, whenever he felt the need for a walk, Paul took one of three little routes he had devised, all of which took around an hour, making a jagged loop in the city center that brought him back on schedule. But in the wake of Norb's letter, an hour hadn't seemed long enough, so he'd gotten more adventurous. The walks went farther out, lasted sometimes two hours, sometimes three. Sometimes he just jumped on a bus and walked around in a neighborhood he hadn't seen before, on the edge of the suburbs. Noon to four, the dead siesta hours in the city, was supposed to be study time, but Paul found it hard to sit still and concentrate in the middle of the day.

One day he took a bus north and wandered up into the Borghese Gardens. During the dead hours of the city, it was still more or less alive and cooler for being up higher. Mothers pushed their strollers; the usual hippies lounged on blankets, playing their guitars. Sometimes handstands. Sometimes dancing or competitive paper airplane flying.

In one spot near the Fontana Rotunda, a group of older men were playing bocce. Paul knew the game. He'd played it a few times with the monsignor in the first week he'd spent in Rome and a few times with Ernie Betterman, who used some of his parents' allowance to buy himself an actual set. Paul was quite good at it, which he attributed to having played horseshoes on the farm and at the seminary. And there was the stone-throwing game he and Britta would sometimes play on the farm: who could get closest to a certain dandelion, a certain fence post. At six-two, two-ten, he'd been recruited for the seminary basketball team, but he was disastrous at team sports. If the game required reacting to many things at once, responding on the fly, he was doomed. But games that asked you to master one movement, one thing, and do it well, over and over—with those he could hold his own. He didn't dare ask to play with the old Romans: they were in their world; he was in his. Instead, he decided to sit awhile and watch. Dip into his Le Carré mystery if need be. But that hadn't been necessary. It was entertaining, listening to the old men curse at each other, and tease, and quibble about the measuring done with a piece of string. The two youngest of the group—men maybe in their late fifties—were very good.

He returned twice, sat, kept his distance, pretended to read, watched. But on his third visit, someone new was playing with them: a small, skinny young guy, early twenties, a hippie type. Mess of black hair, pinned-back greyhound's ears, a few days' stubble, and he wore a white T-shirt that was a little baggy at the neck. Quite beautiful, in a gangly way, and his method of bowling the ball was telling. Deliberate, cautious. His crouch low to the ground, the release all long, fine fingers. Knowledge swooned through Paul's stomach. Though the bigger, broader mystery, of course, was why these old-timers put up with such a delicate young man at all.

Though Paul's book was open, he hadn't read a word. Instead, he watched and strained to hear a name, but this wasn't a place where names were needed. The young man held his own, though twice he faltered at the crucial moment. When he listened to one of the men's stories, he looked innocent, like a boy. When it wasn't his turn, he set the ball in between his feet and stood with his arms hugging himself. The signs weren't glaring, probably, to the old men but glaring enough to Paul. Such a rarity, especially here. In his mind's eye, Paul imagined putting down his book and boldly walking over, asking if he could join in the next game. The old men would give him his due respect once he said he was un padre; it was the young man he had to fear. His judgment, his serious dark eyes. But he wasn't actually going to do that. He watched as the young man and his partner lost. The partner, it seemed, had a chance to win, or at least extend the game, but missed. The young man had shaken his head no, smirked sympathetically, and too firmly gripped hands all around. Compensating, clearly. Then Paul watched the young man leave, pedaling away on an old orange bike, mop of hair flouncing around his ears. The young man glanced at him as he passed. The sensation took a long moment to fade, like a sunspot when you close your eyes.

Paul told himself the next time he came to the park—he'd come the next day at the very same time—that he hoped the young man wouldn't be there. Easier to try his luck without competition. But when he was there again, Paul felt no irritation at all. Quite the contrary.

At one point, the old Italians took a break, uncorked some of the homemade red wine they'd brought to drink. The young guy walked off, heavy on his heels, and bought a Fanta from the old woman sitting on a bench with a tin washing bucket, bottles of sodas floating in what had once been ice. On the way back, he looked Paul's way and stopped.

"Are you a cop or something?" he asked in Italian.

"I'm sorry?" Paul replied in Italian.

"Weren't you here yesterday?"

"Yes. This is the time I take my walk," Paul said. "I'm not a cop."

"You're an American," said the young man.

"Is it that obvious?"

"Ah—yes," the young man replied in English.

Paul nodded. His neck flushed. "I played something like this back home," he said, nodding in the direction of the old men. "Well, sort of."

"You played this in America?"

"Something like it. Horseshoes. But it's different."

"Do you want to play?"

"I wouldn't be very good."

"Yes, but do you want to?"

"I wouldn't want to intrude."

"I'll say I know you," the young man said. "No problem." He drank the soda down and had a beautiful neck.

They exchanged names. Luca reached out his hand.

This was their beginning.

The old men were annoyed that Luca had added to the ranks of those who were not old men, but they shrugged and let Paul play, this Americano, about whom none of them asked anything.

Luca explained the rules, and though Paul knew them already, he listened as if he didn't. He took three practice rolls, to get a lay of the course, throwing too hard, still too hard, and then pretty well. When he'd played before with the monsignor it had been on the grass; the difference was considerable. It was more like playing pool than bowling, really—the way you had to calculate your banks off the side, hit other balls glancingly to move them around. The subtle grooves in the hardpan lane that pushed the ball right or left were his greatest disadvantages: everyone else knew them by heart.

"How long have you played with these guys?" Paul asked Luca in Italian, after the first game ended.

"Since I was a kid. I used to come along with my grandfather. Three of them were old war buddies of his. Now there's just Gustavo."

He imagined little Luca: mop of hair, dark eyes, gangly boy arms. "The First World War?"

Luca nodded. "Grandpa was their commander. He hung out with Mussolini, actually. Y'know, before he was Mussolini."

"Is that right?"

"He always beat him at cards. Or so the story goes."

There was a twinkle, as they say, in his eye: he had loved his grandfather, obviously.

"Are you on holiday?" he asked.

"No, I live here. I'm a graduate student," Paul said.

"What for?"

"I'm studying the Bible. Scripture."

"Oh," said Luca. He frowned. "Are you a priest?"

After he was first ordained, he was so proud to be able to say, *Yes, yes, I am.* Father Paul at last! But now he felt like saying, *Yes, but...*But what? *I'm not what you think? I'm more than just a priest?*

"I am, actually. And you?"

"I'm not a priest, no."

Paul laughed. "No. I mean what do you do?"

Luca shrugged. "Try to survive, mostly."

"Are you a student?"

"I was. In photography. But I quit. Now I just work in a restaurant, waiting tables."

"Why?"

"Why did I quit?"

"Yes."

"It was a horrible school. All they cared about is the figure, the figure."

"As opposed to what?"

"Everything else! They didn't care about anything new. Anything not traditional, you know. Overexposures, double exposures, the pictures that look like a mistake...that's what I liked doing. But they thought I was crazy. Besides, I couldn't afford the film anymore. And the darkroom made me throw up. And my mother stopped giving me money."

"She didn't like you doing art?"

"No," he said. "Not that." Luca stared at him and weighed a thought in his mind.

"So do you like waiting tables?" Paul asked.

Luca frowned. "No, of course not. I hate it. I'm horrible at it. I'll probably get fired today, actually. Last night I spilled Alfredo sauce on a very important person."

Paul laughed.

"Why are you laughing?"

"I'm sorry," Paul said. "The way you said it sounded funny."

"Yeah, but...without my job I can't pay rent."

Chastened, Paul asked where he lived in the city. It was occurring to him that he hadn't really met a new person in quite some time.

"Guess."

"Trastevere," Paul said.

"Correct," Luca said.

Trastevere: hippie central, the Haight-Ashbury of Rome. He looked like its poster boy, actually.

"I'm not a lazy bum, if that's what you're thinking," he said. "I make my own money. It's not like I'm a freeloader."

"I didn't think you were. Plus, I already know you're a successful waiter."

Luca studied Paul for a second with a smirk on his face, eyeing him up and down. It was as if being brushed by a very soft wing.

"They don't make you wear the priest suit, huh?" Luca said.

"No," Paul responded. "Only for formal things. When you're a student, it's different." He paused. "Do you ever do this with your friends? Play bocce, I mean?"

"No. They only want to smoke grass and play pinball. I don't know how much I even like them anymore. They say I'm a fussy old lady."

This moved him, this admission of vulnerability. They had something in common: they lived with many others but felt alone.

"Maybe we can team up again tomorrow," Paul said.

"Okay," said Luca. "I'll try to come at two."

"I'll be here," Paul said.

They looked at each other, waiting for the other to say something.

"Well," Paul said, "I'd best be off."

"Nice to meet you, Padre."

"No 'padre.' Call me Paul."

That night, Paul sat at his desk trying to absorb the notes he'd taken on Father Bennini's lecture about the recently discovered Ras Shamra tablets (an example of Ugaritic or Hebrew poetry? it was unclear). But what kept rising up from his legal pad, unbidden, was Luca. His face. How he'd rolled the ball, gently, vulnerable on his heels. How natural it had felt to tease him, when he wasn't at all a teaser. What this was, at the very least, was an opportunity for camaraderie. As it had been with Norb, except Norb was Norb, and Luca quickened his heart the way Troy O'Neal had in seminary, when he was fourteen.

As early as eight or nine years old, he'd figured out that he didn't feel about girls the way his classmates did, and he had suspected something was truly wrong with him in sixth grade, because of how red his ears would get when he watched Rudy Helmsbach, their sometimes hired hand—a handsome, wiry kid of sixteen—pound nails, shirtless, into the roof of their tool shed. He'd dreamed of Rudy stripping off his clothes to jump into a lake, unaware he was watching. But he'd not realized there was a name for what he was until first year of seminary, the year he turned thirteen, when he heard a group of class-mates talking about someone being a faggot. As if that were the most horrible thing one could be.

Troy had liked girls, very clearly so, which was why Paul chose him to pine after, naturally. The impossibility made the longing safe. Oh, the things he thought about Troy! The vivid scenarios he begged forgiveness for! That was around the time he came to learn some interesting things about ancient Greece, poring over the chapter on homosexuality, his head growing lighter, the most stirring passages already underlined by some-one else, probably a gay predecessor. (And wasn't Troy's name, as in the Greek city of Troy, some sort of sign? Yes, he decided, it was.)

Historical facts soothed him. Achilles and Patroclus had been in love with each other. There was Alexander the Great and Hephaestion, his boyhood friend. These, the bravest of soldiers, had had their young lovers. And wasn't that beloved culture the foundation of everything to come? Whenever needed, these arguments found their way into his thinking. But the fact was that he was now thirty-one, a man who knew nothing about it.

He wasn't supposed to know anything about it, of course; he'd taken a vow to not find out. He understood the love of God, which he did feel powerfully, genuinely, sometimes in silence, or under the thrall of beauty, and in the general loving presence of his family. You were supposed to love one another like brothers and sisters, in the way of the earliest Christians, and he had done that too, felt that love in return—when saying Mass, when with his extended family, sometimes when hanging out with his classmates. But never had he been chosen and accepted or chosen and been accepted. God he now imagined more as Emerson's transparent eyeball than a limitlessly expansive bearded man frowning down on him, arms crossed, from on high, as he had as a boy. A force something like a fire, a pilot light that never went off. Though a knowing fire, a force that kept tabs—that saw what others didn't. So he knew to be careful when it came to Luca. He promised himself he would. It was true, on the other hand, that God had watched Norb do what he'd done too,. and Norb wasn't yet a pillar of salt. But Norb was straight. The critical difference.

The next day, on his way to meet Luca, the bus Paul was riding hit a Fiat trying to beat a red light. The car's driver was a young Ethiopian guy, who emerged from the wreckage improbably unscathed, only to be assaulted by their bus driver, a bald middle-aged man, who cursed him—for endangering his passengers, for being a stupid immigrant—before kicking the man in the knee and ribs. A minute passed this way, the driver kicking, the Ethiopian holding up his arms and pleading for him to stop, until a cop on a motorcycle finally arrived and dragged their driver away by the arm. As Paul and the other passengers emerged from the bus, the cop told them to stay put. And yet, if he did, he'd be late to meet Luca, even later than he already was. So Paul slipped away, trotting down an alley even as he overheard some of his fellow passengers calling after him.

He was slick and itchy with sweat when he arrived, more than forty-five minutes late, and resigned to Luca having already left. Walking quickly despite his certainty that every step was beside the point, he felt angry at the Ethiopian man for his carelessness, then angry at himself for not bringing extra money in case of an emergency so he could have hailed a cab, then vaguely guilty that he hadn't stopped the bus driver before the cop showed up. But as soon as he caught sight of Luca, sitting on the bench they'd agreed to meet at, arms slung over the back, all of his dark thoughts evaporated and he felt only relief.

Up close, Luca's blue T-shirt was dark with sweat at the armpits, and there were thatchy green stains on the knees of his white jeans.

"I'm so sorry I'm late," Paul said.

"I was just about to leave," Luca said. "I figured you'd stood me up."

"I would never stand you up." He explained what happened: the accident, the assault, his long walk over.

"So that's why you're so sweaty," Luca said with a smirk, glancing down at his chest.

"Yes, that's right."

"I take it you weren't hurt in the crash."

"No, I'm fine. Sweaty but fine." Paul took a big breath and smiled; how nice that so quickly they'd turned disaster into a joke. "I was worried you wouldn't be here."

"I was going to leave in five minutes," Luca said. "Good thing you walked so fast." He smiled back. "So, since we seem to be without a bocce set, want to grab a drink instead?"

Paul said he did, he just didn't have any money.

"That's fine," Luca said, waving his excuse away. "My treat."

The place Luca led them to was nearly empty: two German couples, an old man with an enormous wart on his nose, reading the newspaper, and them. Luca ordered a Campari and soda, Paul ordered a glass of the house wine, and for a while they talked about their families. Luca was the baby, the youngest by eight years. "An *oopsie* baby," he said in English. He had two sisters, one who had left the country right after high school and worked as a stewardess; the other was married with four kids in Sicily. His father had fought in World War II and had left their mother when Luca was four for the mistress with whom he had a daughter, his half sister, on the other side of the city. His mother had never agreed to a divorce—holding out was the last bit of power she had. And she still lived in the apartment he'd grown up in, in the southeast suburbs; managed a dress shop; and, other than going to and from work, rarely left the house. No other men since then. He'd lived there, he said, until he was nineteen.

"You must be close with her then, being the only child for all those years."

"We were, yes," he said. "But now we don't speak."

"What? Why?"

He cleared his throat and shifted back in his seat. "She turned me away. She thinks I'm a bad person."

"How is that possible?" Paul said.

"It's complicated," Luca said, picking at the cuticle of his thumb with his pointer finger—a nervous tic. "Family stuff." He squinted one eye. "How about you? What's your family like?" Sidestepping the subject, just like that.

Paul described the farm he'd grown up on, his mother, his father, Britta. He'd planned to talk about seminary life a little, but Luca wanted to know more about back home. Was it a big farm? A small farm? What kind of animals?

"It must have been nice," Luca said. "All that space to yourself."

"I guess it was," Paul said. "But it wasn't an easy life. If things didn't go right, there was nobody to fix it but you. And the work never stopped. My parents have taken a vacation maybe three times in thirty-five years."

"That's very American, no?" Luca said. "Nose to the headstone," he said in English, "right?"

Paul laughed. "Nose to the *grindstone*. You're close."

"And your sister?"

"She's a little like you and your friends. A free spirit. I'm a little concerned about her, to be honest."

"And me? You're concerned about me then too?"

"No," Paul said. "I didn't mean it that way."

"Why are you concerned about her?"

"I just don't want her to get hurt. She sometimes thinks she's tougher than she is."

Luca downed the last of his drink. This answer seemed to satisfy him. "So you never wanted to fall in love and get married then, I guess?"

Here Paul looked at him closely. Luca seemed tentative, curious, unaware of where they both stood. It was disappointing: he would have preferred if they could have understood each other completely already.

"I don't feel it was what I was put here to do," he said. "I feel I have a different calling." *See, Norb,* he thought. *See how that works?*

"So you've never kissed a girl?" Luca asked.

Paul was used to this by now: cousins' kids were full of the same questions, which of course were apologized away by their parents. Though the parents tended not to leave until they'd heard his answer either.

"Just one. Sally McPherson, my third cousin. It was at a family reunion. But it was against my will."

Luca laughed, fulfilling the point of the deflection.

"I'm sure you've had many girlfriends," Paul then found himself saying, thinking, *A face like yours.*

Luca sized him up for a moment. "No. No girlfriends."

"Really?" Paul said. "The way you look?"

Luca looked at him and blushed. Paul felt his own neck get hot as if in response.

"No," he said. "None."

For a while, the noises around them seemed a little louder, as if someone had turned a radio dial to the right. The warty old man coughed up phlegm. A German woman shook her head no but said, "Ja, ja, ja." Luca avoided Paul's eyes.

"So what do you do for fun?" Luca finally asked. "Other than play bocce and pretend to read books."

"That's about it. Movies sometimes. Actual reading sometimes too."

"My roommates are having a party tomorrow night," Luca said. "You should come."

"Oh, I don't know about that."

"Why not? Are parties not allowed?"

"No," Paul said. "It's not that."

"Then why not? We're friends now, aren't we? Yes?"

"Sure." It was alarming, Luca's saying it this way. But it was also a relief. A new friend. He was right: Why not just call it what it was? Fast-forward to that being clear?

"Think of it as research for understanding your sister."

Paul thought of what it would be like being at a party with Britta. She would be protective of him. She whom he'd protected as a girl, now the worldlier of the two of them by far.

"Are these the friends who think you're an old woman?"

Luca smirked. "Only two have said that."

"Won't they think it's strange?" Paul asked. "You bringing along a priest? I'd be really out of place."

"I think they would find you interesting. They'd ask you all kinds of questions."

"I'd be a curiosity, you mean," Paul said.

"If they're rude to you, I'll kick them out."

At the idea of this—slight, gentle Luca wreaking havoc—Paul had to laugh. "But they live there."

"Well," Luca said, "I'll do something. I'll insult them in very creative ways."

"It's nice of you to offer. I'll think about it."

"Or you could just say you're coming right now," Luca said. "I already know you have nothing else to do."

Paul looked at him, absorbing the challenge. "What time will it start?"

"Nine, nine thirty."

Paul pictured himself in his room, rereading *The Spy Who Came in from the Cold*. Maybe wandering down to the social table to challenge someone to a game of chess. Lying on his narrow bed, listening to the sounds echoing up from the street. Alone.

"All right. You win."

"So yes?"

"Yes."

"If it's too strange for you, I'll leave with you," Luca said. "I don't really care."

"Wouldn't that seem rude to your friends?"

Luca shrugged and bunched his lips. "I've only known them a few months."

They stayed awhile longer, neither of them ordering another drink, the conversation somehow breezier in the knowledge that they'd be seeing each other soon. When it was time to settle up, Luca took out a battered old leather coin purse that opened like a clamshell.

"And you wonder why they call you an old lady," Paul said.

Luca bugged out his eyes, mock angry. "Maybe I won't pay for your drink after all."

"I'm sorry," Paul said, smiling. "I take it all back."

"Hmm." Luca squinted a single eye at him, pretending to be upset in a way that made Paul's heart swell, and as he tugged at the tightly rolled lire inside, a few coins fell to the ground and careened in a circle until they fell. Two German marks, a U.S. quarter and penny. Paul bent down to pick them up and set them on the other side of the table.

"Why do you have American money?" Paul asked.

"I find it sometimes," Luca said, not meeting his eyes, pretending to look around for other coins. "The tourists drop them everywhere."

He was hiding something: Paul could already tell.

The question of what to wear, which reared its head late the next afternoon, was made easier by the fact that all of Paul's clothes looked alike. Four button-down short-sleeved shirts in blue, light blue, dark green, black. Two light blue dress shirts with sleeves. Two dark sweaters with leather patches at the elbows. Two clerical shirts, collars tucked inside, for the formal events where that was required. All variety of dark or light beige cotton trousers. Two black belts. It didn't matter which arrangement he went with: he'd stick out like a sore thumb. But what was the alternative? Go out and buy a fringed buckskin jacket? Go back in time and grow out his sideburns?

Sideburns: they had nearly caused him an identity crisis. Some of the guys at Il Castello and a few of the priests back home had grown theirs an inch below their ears; some still had the same hair they'd had as teenagers in the fifties. After much consideration, he had ended up somewhere in the middle. Just an inch down from where they'd been three, four years before, but still above the bottom of the ears. Enough to acknowledge his awareness of the progressive movement in the world, but not so much as to make people think he was part of the irresponsible crowd. Of course, to the people he'd meet tonight, the extra inch would mean less than nothing; they'd see a square, or whatever the word was now. Though, he told himself, this insecurity was silly. He was a grown man, more accomplished than any of them. In front of his little notebook-sized mirror, as he combed his not-short, not-long hair, defining the part a few inches above his right ear, he regrouped his confidence: *I am what I am.* Popeye's motto, it occurred to him. But, tonight, his too.

He couldn't imagine curfew would be an issue, but of course he didn't know *what* to expect, which was why his heart beat like a jackhammer as he walked down the steps to the courtyard, hair still damp from his shower, and toward the giant doors, nodding at Tom and Dom, who were loitering at the entrance, smoking, surely off to see a movie, and waiting for Dale, who was always late. (Oh, the useless things he knew about people!) A nod hello and he walked south.

In his pocket were the gate key, his room key, his wallet, directions he'd figured out from consulting his disintegrating city map, and the bar napkin with the address in Trastevere written down in Luca's left-leaning hand. He'd memorized it, but thought it wise to bring it anyway, just in case.

As he crossed the moon-lit river, Paul thought of something the monsignor had told them when he'd arrived in the city nearly three years before: *Gentlemen, Trastevere late at night can be an unsavory place. By day? Fine, sure, go enjoy the history, check out the flea market, chat up the hippies, buy a pin of Che Guevara for your commie friends back home.* (Har-hars from the crowd.) *But at night, you'd be advised to be careful. It can get a little wild.* Until now, Paul had obeyed. He knew Trastevere from his walks, but when he did head out in the evening, it was always east of the Tiber, in the city center. He knew no one in Trastevere: it was simple as that. But now he did, and suddenly here he was striding alongside the river, then veering south, a vague vertiginous feeling, nervous about the party, but not scared of the neighborhood at all. Why would he be? It was fine: middle-aged guys in work pants; a young local girl riding a bike, hands at her sides; cars, trees, lights; rumpled young people and, naturally, a whiff here and there of marijuana. A group of white men with Afros hogging most of the sidewalk, playing "House of the Rising Sun" badly on guitars. No one cared that he was here. Whatever judgment he felt came only from himself.

The streets narrowed and darkened the farther he got from the main roads. Less traffic, more trees, less shops, more silence, but for the whoops of laughter and music escaping from open windows. An ancient man with dark eye sockets passed him on a bicycle. A young man swayed and zipped on a Vespa. Out of sight but close by, two cats fought, crying out in waves, like sirens. And then he was close, on a street narrow as an alley, the buildings flanking it three, four stories up. A street like a tunnel. Up ahead, on the other side, a drunk swayed a little, dipping in and out of the light of a streetlamp, furtively digging into his pants pocket. Above, an old prostitute stood smoking in her window, waiting for him to find what he was looking for. Finally the drunk freed his hand, held up two coins. "I only have one thousand lire!"

"For that, just one," she said.

"One? Not one! Both!" he said.

"One or nothing," she said, and began to close the shade.

"All right, one! One!" the man said, understanding he was powerless.

Paul was too far down the street now to turn around and find another way past, and besides, he'd written down only this one way and didn't want to risk getting lost. The drunk tossed up one coin and then the other, surprisingly focused, and the whore snapped them up—one, two—hands like two Venus flytraps. Then, without fanfare, she pulled down the right half of her dress, and out flopped a huge, veiny breast, dark areola pointing to the ground. It was as big as her head, a cow's one-nippled udder. For a few seconds, the drunk just stood there transfixed, feet nailed to the ground but the rest of him swaying as he took it all in. Worshipful. As he passed, Paul couldn't help but stare either, and the woman caught his eye. A look of bored hatred.

"Hey!" the drunk man yelled, now behind him, now in the past. "Not yet! Not yet!"

"Basta," said the woman, "Go home to your wife."

Soon after, he was at Luca's building—one of the many in Rome that seemed cut from one long, gigantic block of rust-colored stone. Paul buzzed and waited. A minute passed, then another. He buzzed again. Finally, a tall, pale guy with long, thin brown hair and a necklace strung with giant wooden olives appeared, his bulbous features rearranging into annoyance the moment his eyes landed on Paul. Not who he'd hoped for. He asked Paul who he was and seemed dubious somehow of his answer. But then he nodded Paul in, and Paul was following him up the stairs.

When the white door at the top opened, Paul saw two rooms: a living room and what would have been a dining room if not for the mattress taking up half the floor. The space was lit only with old lamps, Christmas tinsel hanging like strands of limp silver seaweed from the dead fixtures, and a poster of Mussolini with two huge tits spray-painted on it was tacked to one of the walls. The incense inside was thick as fog, and huddled here and there were about twenty people. His stairwell guide walked over to a still-burning cigarette perched on a speckled ashtray and yelled, "Luca, someone's here for you!" and a few faces swiveled toward him. As he'd decided whether to come and as he'd walked over, Paul had thought mostly of Luca—of talking to him, looking at him, making him laugh; the other people would be backdrop, curiosities. But of course there was the obligation to account for oneself. The eyes on him now reminded him of this, and for a moment he was paralyzed with fear. He was a stranger in a strange land, a babe in the woods. But then Luca appeared in the hallway: tan stains in the armpits of his white T-shirt, dark blue jeans, a coffee mug in hand, sweat glossy at his temples. He smiled a good, pure smile—his face was happy—and when he reached out his hand, Paul shook it. In this room, Luca was the person from the park—and someone else.

"I didn't think you'd actually come."

"I said I would, didn't I?"

"Well, I worried you might not anyway."

Paul cast his eyes around the room. "So this is where you live?"

"For better or worse."

Luca pointed out his roommates, of which there were five. Renaldo and Elise shared a bedroom; Luca and the other three guys split the other two. Elise was the one who'd convinced Renaldo to let him move in; Luca knew her from art school. The others were okay—his roommate Berto was barely around. But one person he really didn't like: Sandro, who shared a room with Guillermo. To identify his nemesis, Luca jutted his chin at a man standing near a lamp across the room. Curly light brown hair pulled into a tiny ponytail, white pants, green cowboy boots, tight black shirt. His extremely bored expression poleaxing the face of the person talking to him.

"Why don't you like him?" Paul asked.

"Because he's an asshole."

"Do the others think that too?"

"Elise doesn't like him, but the others don't mind him so much. I hate him the most."

Paul could imagine well enough: Sandro would guess what kind of man Luca was and hate him for it.

"Anyway," said Luca, "can I get you something to drink?"

Paul looked at the mug Luca held, four fingers wedged into the negative space within the handle. "What are you drinking? Coffee?"

"Chianti."

"In a mug?"

"I like the heaviness of it," he said. "It feels more special that way."

Paul smiled: the idea had a strange logic to it. "I'll do that too, then. Chianti in a mug. As they say, *when in Rome*."

Luca shook his head slowly. "Please. Never say that again."

Paul could count on one hand the number of mixed parties like this he'd been to in the past decade. The last had been the bush party his cousin Fred brought him to the second summer after he'd gotten his B.A., when he was home visiting his parents. A mild night, a clearing in the woods, a bonfire, and thirty, forty young people like him drinking lukewarm Blatz as a car radio played songs about California girls. Most were Fred's year, but a few were his elementary school classmates, names attached to vaguely familiar faces he hadn't seen since he'd left for seminary the fall he was thirteen. The bonfire warmed one half of him, then the other, as he followed Fred around his circle of friends, feeling both the distance of his difference and the dim light of their respect. Few chose his path in life—only two others from their parish in the past few years—but, being Catholic, they respected the sacrifice, the commitment. Like soldiers, priests were held slightly above: noble men, slightly mysterious, admired. Some girl, visiting from out of town, probably a little drunk, had clucked at hearing he was a priest, said, *Well, that's a crying shame*, and he was flattered, as he always was when women implied he was good-looking.

That night, he had very quickly stopped feeling the anxiety he'd arrived with, but tonight was going to be different. Luca was no easygoing Fred—in fact, he seemed nervous himself as they eased their way into the fringes of a group containing Elise and Renaldo and a few others. A chubby faun of a man with red-tinted glasses was holding forth about the acid trip he'd had in Venice over Christmas, and as he talked he looked only at Naldo and the man beside him. Wasn't it odd how feeling invisible in moments like this could threaten to drown you in some awful realization about your unworthiness, about the real feelings of the world toward you? When it was nothing at all? Paying attention to the story the best he could, Paul gulped down his wine quickly and then, when it was gone, faked sipping to have something to do. Only when the story ended were they acknowledged. Luca introduced him as his American student friend from the park, but it was clear Elise and Naldo had been told nothing else. They asked him what he studied and where, and he answered.

"You're being serious?" Elise asked. She glanced at Luca for confirmation and he nodded yes.

Renaldo, who was clearly very drunk already, took a closer look, one eye open, one eye squinted, like a sea captain looking into an invisible telescope. "I mean, he *looks* like he could be. Don't you think?"

Elise ignored this rudeness. "You're so funny, Luca," she said instead. "Always so mysterious."

Luca shrugged. If this was so, Paul thought, wonderful. It was true, of course, that since the day his family drove him to the campus of Sacred Heart he had enjoyed being seen as more special than most. Who didn't like to feel special and have evidence to back it up? But recently—especially since Norb's happy, guiltless shedding of their status—he hadn't been able to work up the old assurance his standing in the world once gave him. The reliable ego boost. What he had actually been craving lately was a way to feel less special, more down-to-earth. In fact, it occurred to him, as he stood there with his empty mug of wine, this desire was what had prompted his longer walks, his lingering over that which he usually walked right past. It was the reason he found himself here.

To Elise, that he was an American was perhaps more interesting than his being a priest. Wisconsin she hadn't heard of, but Chicago, yes. Al Capone and gangsters and, most recently, the riots there before the Democratic National Convention. The brave young protesters. He provided a sketch of where he studied, where he lived. Then Naldo asked him if he could ask a personal question, and Paul knew exactly which question was coming. Even ready for it, his ears burned hot. No, he responded, he hadn't ever had sex.

"See?" Naldo said. "That's the killer right there. No way in hell could I do that."

Elise snorted. "No shit."

"How do you even deal with that, man?" Naldo said. "Knowing you'll never do it? Doesn't that make you, like, totally frustrated?"

Naldo wasn't right for Elise, Paul saw that immediately. But women made stupid decisions when it came to men. Britta was doing that too, according to their mother.

"You don't have to answer that," Luca said.

"It's fine," Paul said. "I guess since I don't know what I'm missing, it's easier."

"So what then," Naldo said, "do you guys, you know, take care of yourselves? Or do you just pretend it's not there?"

"Jesus Christ, Naldo!" Elise said. "Show some respect."

"What? I'm curious."

"Don't even listen to him," Luca said. "He gets even more stupid when he's drunk."

"Okay," Elise said. "Sorry. Change of subject. How about this instead: What's the worst confession you ever heard? Can you talk about that?"

Here, he actually had a story that might satisfy her. "Well," he said, "the worst one was actually a prank a friend of mine played on me. Another priest. He got into the confessional and pretended to be one of the students where I taught and told me he'd fallen in love with one of the cows on his family's farm. Buttercup, if I remember correctly."

At this, Elise burst into beautiful silent laughter.

"Would you do that for me?" Naldo now said.

"Do what?" Paul said.

"Hear a confession."

"Oh, stop it," Elise said.

"No, seriously. I think it's about time I get some things off my chest." Naldo looked at Paul. "Couldn't I just whisper it in your ear or something?"

Elise looked at Paul with bugged eyes and shook her head. "Naldo, you're being a shit."

"I'm serious," he said.

"But we're not in a church," Paul said.

"Does it have to be?"

"Yes," he said, but he realized he wasn't completely sure. "That's the standard, at least," he added.

"But would you? If I asked you to? As a personal favor?"

"I feel like you're putting me on."

"No, I'm serious," Naldo said. "There's something I'd like to get off my chest."

Paul tried to read his face to see if he was serious, but Naldo's swimming eyes made it impossible to tell. "If you're serious then, fine. As long as you haven't killed anyone."

"Don't be so sure," someone said behind them.

Given the green light, Renaldo came slowly toward him, laid a hand on his shoulder, and moved them both away from the circle. Swaying a little, he leaned in, put his mouth close enough to Paul's ear that Paul could feel his heat and smell his bad breath. "Okay, here it is," he whispered. "I jerk off too much, I killed my brother's ferret on purpose, and I've cheated on Elise three times." He paused for a moment, wondering probably if there was more to say, decided against it, stepped back. The expression on his face, the dare in his eyes, told Paul everything was true.

He should have known not to glance at Elise, but he did.

She frowned. "Wait, what did he say?"

Paul looked down at the hardwood floor.

"What did you tell him, Renaldo? Did you say something about me?"

"It's a confession, Elise," Naldo said. "The whole point is that it's confidential."

Her nostrils flared. "Naldo! That's not fair!" She looked at Paul. "Was it bad? Can you at least tell me that?"

Paul blinked very quickly. "I really can't say." *Though,* he thought, *maybe I'll tell you on the way out. Slip you a note.* Though that would be even worse than never agreeing in the first place.

"Fuck," said a sleepy-looking somebody on the fringes. "Must've been pretty heavy."

"You have to tell me what you said," Elise told her boyfriend. "Right now. I'm not kidding."

Here Naldo decided to change his tack. Paul could sense the lightbulb going off and then watched his face soften, a little curl appear in his lip.

"Elise, relax," he said. "I made it all up."

"You're lying."

"No, I'm not. I wanted to get a rise out of him, that's all."

"Okay. Then tell me. If it's made up, what's it matter?"

"Exactly. If it's all made up, what's it matter? Exactly."

The sleepy guy looked at Paul. "If he was lying you can say it, right? I mean, that changes the whole thing."

He felt ashamed: he'd turned a sacrament into a party trick, and it had blown up in his face. But he wouldn't hurt this woman. There was a whole evening to get through. "It's really up to him," Paul said.

Elise looked at Naldo, waiting, and when Naldo looked back at her, shaking his head, throwing up his hands in the exasperated Italian way, she hated him once more and walked across the living room and into their room, slamming the door shut.

"So fucking sensitive," Naldo said.

Now Luca looked at him. *I'm sorry you got caught in the middle of this,* his eyes said.

It's my own fault, replied Paul's.

In the awkward minutes that followed, Paul had the urge to flee. Luca had said that if he wanted to leave, he would go with him, to where he'd never said. But Paul didn't want to look back on tonight and remember himself as a coward. Was he so weak that he couldn't handle some mockery? Was he so delicate? *No,* he thought, *I'll push on.* Fall, if need be, into the role of anthropologist, as Luca had suggested he do. To understand Britta better. To get a flavor for her life. When Luca apologized for Naldo and asked if he was okay (he apparently looked a little pale), he said yeah, he was, it was fine. And they resumed their wandering.

Talk in one huddle was of a band simply called Love and then of a Super 8 film two of the huddlers had been extras in, some hippie take on "Jack and the Beanstalk," with the giant played by an actor dressed up as the prime minister. Then people slid into a discussion about a magical human named Tony Piazzi, deemed "wacko" and "hilarious" by all who knew him. Paul had little to share—besides jazz, his tastes in music tended toward classical, a little bit of early Dylan, and Peter, Paul and Mary, and he couldn't feign the drowsy awestruck demeanor the others had if he tried—so he simply sipped his now-refilled wine. But when one of the guests asked him who he was exactly and discovered he was American, and when one of the interlopers from the Naldo farce piped in that he was not only that but an American *priest*, he found himself again the center of attention.

"You don't *support* the war, do you?" one of them said, and he'd had the pleasure of saying no, he didn't. The Church did, still believing it met the criteria for a morally just war, but there he and the Church disagreed (this perked people up). Not wanting to disappoint, he shared the story of how an old classmate of his had grown his hair to his shoulders, driven around in a VW Bug with daisies wound around the antenna, and been disrobed for holding secret Masses at his brother's place, where collections went toward the printing of antiwar pamphlets and where he'd given Communion to all in his red silk pajamas. Having hooked them, he then laid out all the sensational details he could recall about the disobedient shenanigans of Fathers Philip and Daniel Berrigan: how the Baltimore Four had poured chicken blood on draft records there, how the Catonsville Nine had burst into a draft board and burned draft records with homemade napalm. Maybe he'd too greedily lapped up the attention and let them assume, by his eagerness in spreading the details, he was as headstrong and political as the characters he trotted out before them. But of course, when they did directly ask him if he felt the same way, he had to admit he did not. The whole Berrigan thing stunk too much of righteousness, a hunger for attention. There were better, less combative ways to protest. One of the huddlers, whose name he never did find out, came forward then, a swollen look on his face. "You call *that* combative? When innocent fucking women and children are being slaughtered at My Lai? The *war* is fucking combative. The problem with those guys is they didn't go far enough." By this, the man meant, quite literally, that someone needed to kidnap Pat Nixon and the Nixon daughters and hold them for ransom. For ten minutes they sparred. The man was intelligent and frightening, and little flecks of spit flew from his lips the more passionate he became. But Paul liked the chance to argue for moderation. It felt like he was defending his perspective on life.

When the discussion hit a lull, Paul excused himself to the bathroom. He was a little drunk now, and after he'd peed two mugs' worth of processed Chianti into the dank mouth of the toilet, he communed with the mirror. His eyes were the ones swimming now, his face damp. Wasn't he doing fine out there, holding his own? His intelligence was his life preserver, even here. Also interesting was that, during the entire argument in the kitchen, Luca had stood beside him, sipping his wine, nodding at him whenever he looked over, hoping for confirmation. Loyal already, though they'd been through nothing together. If he wasn't mistaken, he'd seen pride in his friend's eyes at knowing someone who knew so much, who was so good with words, even in his second language. This man liked him, this Luca whom he had tried so hard not to think about these past few days. But what did he *want*? What did he see in him, someone so unlike himself? Was Paul more trustworthy than these people? Less likely to hurt him? Had he seemed a kindred lonely spirit? Or was it as simple as he could tell they were the same in that other, important way?

Blood thumped in his ears, like a second heartbeat. Lust whistled up and down the inside of his stomach. *Be careful,* he told his reflection. *Remember who you are.*

A low Arabic saxophone solo from some jazz record played him back into the living room. A man and a woman were ravenously making out on the sofa, their grasping faces tinted pink by the lamp wrapped like a head injury with a gauzy red scarf. As if inspired, but feeling more experimental, three cross-legged people had begun a drowsy back-massage train on the bare floor mattress, two men bookending a woman, all eyes closed, the masseuses' hands probing blindly, the man in front with his palms on his knees like a yogi. From the kitchen, though, there was still the serious energy of conversation, to Paul's relief. And when he entered, Luca was where he'd been, leaning against the sink, half listening to an argument about the Italian soccer team. On seeing him, his friend brightened and walked over.

"Hey," Luca said. "You want to see my room?"

"Your room?" Paul said. His mind wasn't right. He sensed his own fear.

Luca's head tilted like a dog's. "Yeah. My room."

An innocent request, Paul realized. But tell that to his steaming red ears. "Okay," he said. "Sure."

The twist of a doorknob, Luca pulling the chain to the lightbulb, and they were inside. The room was a bit bigger than his own at Il Castello, though considering Luca shared it with a roommate, smaller, really. Far less privacy. Paul's room had no windows, as it was on the inner ring, facing the Castello's courtyard, but this had a little square one. Flush against the far wall was a wooden twin bed and a flaking metal bunk bed that gave the room a boyish, military flavor. A shabby lamp sat on the floor beside the bed. A big grubby rug lay over the floor, two corners bent slightly up, suggesting a grounded magic carpet. A stereo flanked by two tan speakers sat under the window. Paul was going to ask which bunk was Luca's, but then he noticed, hanging by a strap from the top farthest bedpost, a small but serious-looking silver camera and, taped randomly to the ceiling above and the wall beside the top bunk, an irregular assortment of white-rimmed photographs. Another difference between them, then. Never would he have taped pictures directly to the wall, without frames, much less done it in such an erratic way. And yet they formed a pleasing, irregular whole, the way a flock of birds could, or stars.

"I like it," he said of the space, not sure if he really did.

"It's tiny," Luca said. "But I don't mind little spaces. My mother always said I was happiest playing under the kitchen table."

"It smells different in here too," Paul said, just noticing.

"No incense. It's bad enough out there, with Elise." Instead, here, a faint breeze of lemon, the origin of which was the homemade fruit fly catcher on the floor under the window: tapered funnel of paper taped to the mouth of a dirty vase; within, a limp browning lemon wedge crawling with fruit fly captives. Sister Angelique, one of the cooks at the residence, used them too.

"I presume those are yours up there?" Paul asked, pointing to the ceiling above the top bunk.

"Yeah. You want to see them?"

"Of course."

They walked over and Paul pressed his chest against the bed frame, tilting his neck to look up.

"Pretend you like them even if you don't," Luca said.

What this was, Paul felt immediately, was the Sistine Chapel experience in miniature: the eager looking up and literal pain in your neck, gravity's hard push on your forehead. Except no figures here, no discernible story. Double exposures, all of them, instead, just as Luca had described. Some were a kind of visual joke: in one, a man's face (*whose?* Paul wondered), eyes and mouth closed, overlaid with the open mouth of one of the fountain gargoyles found around the city, a stream of water pouring out. In another, a tiny hunched-over woman stood in the palm of a cupped hand. The rest, though, were harder to pin down, absurd or haunting or both: A long-nosed woman's profile superimposed on a sunrise, the sun where her brain would be. A ghostly mother and son, hovering over a cemetery. An overly bright brown river, the Tiber, surely, and hovering above, the dark genderless shadow of an angel, a friend wearing a winged costume of some sort, arms outstretched. If the images had a theme, it was that there is a real world and a dream world, and a place where they intersect. The world of the naked eye wasn't enough; enhancement was needed. As he looked at them, Paul realized that underneath his attraction to Luca had been an arrogant assumption that the young man was somehow beneath him, not his intellectual equal. But how flat and stale that logic seemed now. Luca was lovely and formidable. Paul could never have dreamed these up; his mind just didn't work that way.

Paul dropped his head and looked straight at Luca. "I really like them."

"Thank you," Luca said. "Have you seen the film *Persona*?"

"Last year, at the Venetio, in fact. They had a Bergman night."

"That's when I saw it too." Luca paused. "Remember the way he put one half of the one woman's face next to the other half of the other woman's face, to make a new face?"

"Of course."

"That was the inspiration."

Actually, Paul remembered the movie very well. Norb had spent most of the walk back home trying to shed light on the mysteries of the movie using what he knew of Jungian psychology—but he, Paul, hadn't been in the mood to parse it out. He'd felt gonged in the heart, rapt with the movie's dramatization of the perfect confessor, more perfect than even God, in that a human confessor had eyes to look back at you with, to forgive or accept you with. The disturbing, alluring idea of losing yourself in another person. Merging. The bit about the tryst on the beach, the nurse's long-repressed ecstasy. Thinking of it again, now, he actually felt its addictive darkness, distilled into the pungent smell of lemon constant in the room.

Luca was waiting for a response, looking at him.

"I think they're fantastic," Paul said. "Your professors should have their degrees revoked."

"Thank you," Luca said. "Maybe you could write a letter and tell them that."

"If it would help, I would."

The job of looking done, Paul smiled quickly at Luca but felt terrified. Luca was looking at him differently now: waiting himself, it seemed. What else was there to show a person in one's room?

"Anything good in there?" Paul said, nodding to the two crates of records stacked beside the turntable.

But before Luca could answer, the door opened and the head and torso of Sandro appeared. He jerked up his head once. "Hey. Father."

"Yes?"

Sandro nodded at Luca, a cool Mafia sneer on his face. "Be careful with this one."

"Leave us alone, Sandro," Luca said.

"What do you mean?" Paul asked Sandro. He instantly wished he hadn't.

"I don't know if you've noticed, but he's...you know"—Sandro put out a limp hand and wobbled it—"a little funny. Just saying, you might want to watch your back. Never know what he might try to pull."

Paul flushed and went mute. What he was supposed to say and what he might say if he could express his anger pulled him in two directions. So he just stood there, hands in his pockets, vibrating and paralyzed and looking at Sandro so as to avoid Luca's eyes.

"You're such an asshole," Luca said, more mournful than angry.

"See? He doesn't deny it. He gets angry but he doesn't deny it."

"Get out of here. Now!"

"As you wish, sweetheart," Sandro replied. Then he tipped back his bottle of beer, two big swallows, and nodded at Paul before closing the door.

When Paul turned to look, Luca was blinking his eyes at the magic carpet rug, shoulders hunched, hair grazing his eyebrows, breathing deeply. Hot eared and full of a sour energy. So strong was Paul's urge to go over and embrace him, maybe kiss him passionately on one hot ear, that he made a fist, pressing his nails into his palm to stop himself. Maybe ten seconds passed, until he said, "Listen. It's okay. I had a feeling."

"I like women," Luca said. "Just not, you know..."

And here Paul did something completely out of character. Was it bravery? Giving in? He wasn't quite sure. "I'm a bit like you too, you know. In that regard. Exactly like you, in fact."

Luca looked up quickly at this. Alert to it, but not shocked. It was the look of a person who had wondered but not given it much of a chance of being true.

"Really?"

"You're surprised?"

Luca smirked. "I thought it might be possible."

"That's only for you to know, of course," Paul added.

"Of course," Luca replied with a nod.

For a while they just looked at each other, then Paul looked down at the floor. When he looked back up, Luca had broken into a bemused little smile.

"So," he said, "should we head back into the fray?"

Paul replied, "How about we take a walk?"

The piazza nearby might be a place to go, Luca said, and Paul agreed that was fine, though he didn't care either way. In the new light of what had been said, as they took the stairs down, Luca seemed more familiar to him, maybe a pal he'd gone to school with. Though, no—that scenario didn't work. Luca's difference was part of it too—his not being American. A person he'd needed to cross the ocean to find. Just out the door, Luca pulled a joint from his jean pocket, then a matchbook, and offered Paul a hit, as if the streets of Trastevere were the private spot and the apartment crawling with cops. Paul waved it off—now was not the time to find out how marijuana affected him—and felt worried, despite his happiness. Was he not fun enough by himself? But he shook it off. Maybe Luca simply wanted to relax. Because he was feeling something too.

Luca said it was a little chillier now, Paul agreed, and they walked side by side, footsteps barely audible on the concrete. His parents had walked together in the beginning too: that's what he thought of. How bold, young Anna Dombrowski pursued quiet Virgil Novak, dropping by with the sour hard candies he liked whenever she saw him plowing the fields. How she'd walked beside his slowly moving horse, getting him to talk, to laugh, tart little lumps in their cheeks as they said the words that made them fall in love.

"Can I ask you a question?" Paul said, seeing that someone needed to start.

"Of course."

"Why do you live with these people if they're not really your friends?"

Luca squinted one eye. "Elise is sort of a friend. More than the others. I needed a place to live and they let me pay less since I do all the dishes and clean things up. That's our agreement. I can't afford much more."

"Your mother doesn't help even a little?"

"I told you. I haven't seen her in two years."

"Can I ask why?"

Inhale, exhale. "I'm no longer her son anymore. Her son is dead to her."

"She found out," Paul said. It didn't even need saying.

He didn't nod but said, "I was so stupid."

(They were on a wider street now. A radio high up somewhere was booming opera. An old woman yelled, "Just bring me the damn ice tray, Gio!")

"She found some pictures under my bed," Luca said, hands in his pockets. "Dirty pictures, you know. Or maybe you don't. Anyway, I usually kept them in the back of this art book I had. But I forgot to put them away one night. They were just lying under the bed, plain as day, and she saw them when she was cleaning—even though I asked her not to. That day, I was in class all day, and when I came back home, she was sitting in the kitchen, smoking, looking out the window with this strange look on her face. Ravel was playing on the record player, which she usually only plays when she has a big meal to cook and is tired and needs something to get her going. But nothing was on the stove. When I asked her if something was wrong, she didn't answer me. Then I asked her again. And she wouldn't even look at me. Then, finally, she said, 'I packed your things.' Very calmly. Still looking at the floor. And I asked her, 'What do you mean you packed my things? Why would you do that?' Because, you know, this was my mother. 'Go to your room,' she said. 'Look on your bed.' And even then—even when she said 'bed'—I had no idea. But when I saw the pictures laid out on the pillow, my heart just sank. The thought that she'd seen that. And she wasn't kidding: everything else was in garbage bags and boxes. It must have taken her half the day."

"That's awful."

"I couldn't believe it. I mean, I knew how she felt about, you know, men like me. But I always hoped if something happened she'd understand. When I went over to her, just to touch her shoulder, she pushed my arm away. 'How could you?' she said. 'First Papa and now this?' As if I'd done it on purpose to break her heart. And the more I tried to touch her, the more she shoved me away. And then she stood up and slapped me, hard—*bam!*—on the face."

They were approaching the piazza now; Paul could hear faintly the hollow hooting of a pan flute, lazy guitar chords.

"That first night, I didn't know what to do. I was panicking. I couldn't eat, but I threw up anyway—I didn't have a place to go. I couldn't bear to even put the sheets back on my bed before I slept. The next morning, she was gone by the time I woke up, and I thought maybe we could talk about it, maybe she just needed to get it out of her system, and I decided to wait for her. But in the afternoon, I heard somebody messing with our front door, and it was a locksmith. He told me he'd been told to come change the locks on the apartment—that my mother said there'd been a robbery. And that's when I knew I couldn't stay."

Paul's head felt hollow, his guts pinched and aching. His mother would have been crushed too, but would have gone straight to crying, to praying for his soul. That was how it would have gone: she would have been determined to save him.

"But she's your *mother*. How could she do that?"

"When my father left us, she changed," Luca said. "Her heart got tough. She was already not very nice sometimes, but when he left, that sort of killed her."

They passed an open bench and Paul suggested they sit. Halos encircled the streetlights. Some hippies were drawing chalk outlines of each other on a section of the square, like whimsical forensics experts.

"It was very sad," Luca continued, as he lowered himself to the bench. "I had nowhere to go, nowhere to live. I didn't have any friends at school, and nobody would give me a job, probably because I seemed a little crazy. For a while, I slept in the park, but one night I was beat up—one of them was a cop, I know because I saw him later on his horse. I was just washing my face and feet in the pond, and they came over shouting at me, shoving me. And when I kicked the smaller one in the nuts, they beat me up. You should have seen me. I was in the hospital for three days."

"You kicked a cop in the nuts?" Paul said.

Luca raised his eyebrows. "Yes. Bad idea."

Paul smirked, then sobered. Back to the plot. "I can't believe this."

"It wasn't even a year ago."

"So when did you move in with Elise and everyone?"

"Eight months ago? Something like that."

"And in between? You were still in the park?"

"Well," he said, "I..." And he hesitated. "There was a man who I stayed with for a few months. But I didn't like him. He was disgusting."

Paul could guess at the implications. The arrangement, the deal. He thought of the tarted-up old queens he'd seen and been made sickly dizzy by in *La Dolce Vita*: wrinkled, prancing, dressed in silk kimonos. He thought of the American money Luca had dropped at the café.

Paul looked up from the ground he'd been staring at, glanced at the square, the lounging, squatting, drawing hippies. So. Sleeping with a man for a place to stay. The whore's droopy breast he'd seen earlier in the night flashed into his mind, and he was thankful not to be facing Luca now. He felt disappointed, knowing that this knowledge would make it harder for him to love Luca purely. But then as his mind fell on the mother, and the man who'd taken advantage, the judgment fell quickly, surprisingly away.

Instead he felt angry. And he wished he were the right man for the job of comforting Luca now. The truth was he wasn't the comforting type. Britta, of course, had run to him for comfort, crying when she fell and skinned her knee, horsing around in the barn, and there was the time she'd jumped off the silo ladder and twisted her knee, and he'd run in to get help and told her it would be okay when he got back. But his guidance had always come paired with a scolding. A lesson. She was wild and impetuous—always getting into trouble—whereas he was smart and together. His job, as brother, was setting her right. He thought of her as a wayward pest, and he sighed when he had to help. The quicker he could flee, the better. At seminary too this had happened, when his roommate Ted Willabrand found out his father had drowned during a fishing trip on Lake Michigan. *Thank you for being there for him,* Ted's mother said, when she came to pick him up three days later, but he *hadn't* really been there. In the days after, he'd made himself scarce, always heading off to study elsewhere. He'd felt not up to the job. *Tell me if you need anything,* he said, that first morning after, hoping to God Ted didn't ask for anything, and mercifully Ted hadn't.

"You can go if you want," Luca said. "You don't have to stay."

Intensely, Paul could feel the safety of his room, the companions that were his desk and bed. But he didn't want that now. "Please," he said. "I'm not going to leave."

He put his hand on his friend's shoulder. Luca flinched a bit, blinked quickly, and searched his eyes for something good, not relenting until he was sure it was there. Then he looked down. They sat there awhile like that. A peal of female laughter erupted on the other side of the square—a hunched-over American girl with long blond hair shielding her face like a weeping willow, pointing at something her friend had drawn on one of the chalk outlines.

He could give advice: *Well, Luca, if you ask for forgiveness, God will forgive you.*

Let he without sin cast the first stone. But words felt mealy in his mouth.

His hand was still where he'd put it and by now seemed to belong there. The silence they sat in had become something solid but light, like a cloud. After a while of searching for something to say, he gave up trying.

"You got more than you bargained for tonight, didn't you?" Luca said finally.

Paul snorted happily at this, relieved to be back in the world of language. "Well," he said, "beats pretending to read all night."

At the door of Luca's apartment, they first shook hands, army private to army private, but after the shake, Luca's eyes went liquid and he stepped forward with his arms out, and they embraced, his thin chest pressing against Paul's, the warm imprint of his hand on Paul's back.

"I'll see you soon," Paul said, not having any idea what that meant. Back to playing bocce together? Continue to meet for drinks? But neither path seemed right. Why regress, why plateau, when obviously this was a beginning?

"Yes," said Luca. "I hope so."

The worst had been aired, their cards were on the table, but now what? Where did this thing go? The question stalked Paul in the days to come. Beautiful Luca. His face, his lean body, his dangerous, pitiable past, his clever, slippery mind. The quickening in his heart at the thought was more intense than it had been with his other crushes. For a simple reason too: with Luca, there was finally a chance of being wanted back.

Of course, to even think *in love* was utterly ridiculous. For someone in his position, for Father Paul Novak, the master's candidate in Scripture, the committed celibate, to be thinking in such gooey terms was laughable. Something Britta would think after two dates. And yet, there it was. More than simple attraction, more than simple camaraderie. More, he felt, than friendship. An overflow. A new combination. *Okay,* he thought one night, when he should have been making flash cards for Liturgical Practices: *Love. Let me do some clearheaded thinking on love. Come at it like a space alien, the way Father Benton always said we should approach the familiar.* So he flipped through Buber's *I and Thou*, jotting down its ideas about the other as "thou," not "it." He unfolded Norb's letter, reread the psalm in all its bold and flowery language, a poem about love of God, but still. For the three millionth time, he thought of good old Achilles and Patroclus, good old Alexander the Great and Hephaestion— brief, comforting touchstones always quickly rebutted by a voice saying that they were pagans, untouched by the truth of Christ. Not worth much.

He thought of himself and Luca like Romeo and Juliet, star-crossed lovers, victims of circumstance and fate: the limits marked by societies. He thought about the civil rights movement back home, the recent rise of the blacks, small good steps, and he dreamed forward of a time when maybe the same acceptance would apply to himself and Luca. He imagined his mother citing the quotes in the Bible that were always quoted to argue its wrongness, the passages in the catechism.

The words that had sent the fear of God into him, made him so cautious. But if he'd learned anything in his studies thus far, it was the importance of understanding the context of things. Understanding that the Bible was a document of its time. Overseen by Providence, his mother would say—but about that now he wasn't so sure. The more you investigated, the less magical it became.

Day after day, he sat in his classes and wallowed at his desk. He showered, and Luca bloomed up before him, thin, naked, light in his dark eyes. He did not sleep well, but decided he was on the right path—working past his troubling desire.

Then, midweek, the monsignor yelled his name, just after suppertime. "Novak! Phone call!" His mother, he'd thought at first. Something's happened to Britta. Or Dad: a heart attack, dead. But the voice on the line was Luca's.

"I hope I'm not bothering you," he said. "I wasn't sure when to call."

"Oh, hi."

"How are you?"

"I'm good. And you?"

"Oh, fine," Luca said. "But listen. I'll get right to it."

He explained that his roommates were going to be away for the weekend, camping out at some concert, and that he figured why not have some company and have Paul over for dinner.

Paul blushed, before asking, "What are you making?"

"Something delicious, I hope. Why? Are there things you don't eat?"

"No, I'll eat anything."

"Good. That helps. Right now I'm thinking some scampi in garlic and spaghetti carbonara. That sound okay? You like those things?"

"Sure," Paul said. It appeared he wouldn't even have a moment to mull it over. Luca required immediate action. "When did you say this was?"

"This Saturday. Say eight? That fit into your busy schedule?"

"Yes," he said. "I'll come." He was being carried along by a force not under his control, but had no desire to fight it.

A minute after he pushed the broken buzzer that night, Luca appeared, first feet, then legs, then torso, then smiling face, hair dark and springy as moss, at the bottom of the stairs. He was smiling, his neck shiny. On seeing him, Paul stuck out his hand, and Luca said, "Yes, shaking's better. I'm sweating like a pig." Then Paul handed over the gifts he'd brought along: a cheap bottle of Chianti, a little bag of figs, a container of melting vanilla gelato. The treats had cost him a week's worth of pocket money, but it'd be worth it, he'd thought, to see Luca hold and be pleased by the things he'd given him. And it was. Luca loved figs.

As he followed his friend up the stairs, Paul couldn't help but glance above at Luca's ass as it shifted in his white jeans, and then he could hear the music coming from the apartment. Berlioz's *Symphonie fantastique,* second movement; Norb had the record too. It was dim inside, the same two lamps lit, but without the crowd of partygoers the place seemed enormous. The air smelled faintly of bacon and garlic and incense.

Luca said to follow him into the kitchen and set Paul's gifts on the little counter beside a sheath of pasta, a carton of eggs, a wedge of pecorino, and a handkerchief. He motioned to the chair he'd already placed to the side. There was no table, just the chair. Obediently, Paul sat.

"I love this piece," he said. "The Berlioz."

"It's beautiful, isn't it?" replied Luca, as he clicked on the burner under a chipped white pot of water. "I like the Italians too, but for me it's the French. Ravel, Berlioz, Debussy. My mother could never understand it. For her it was Verdi or death."

The horrible woman conjured by their talk in the piazza flickered briefly to life. But now, under the glare of a single lightbulb,

Luca was dumping out the figs, quartering them, and squeezing them so the pieces flared open like a fleshy flower. They wouldn't return to all that. Tonight, their only job was to be happy.

Paul asked, "Did you know Berlioz almost murdered his fiancée?"

"Really?" Luca walked over and handed him a fig.

"She decided to leave him for some other man and he couldn't stand it. So he planned to dress up as a woman and sneak into her house. He bought a dress and a wig and a gun. But on his way there—it must have been pretty far—he forgot the costume in one of the horse carriages. And by the time he realized he'd forgotten it, he wised up."

"That's what would happen to me. I'd have a big plan to shoot somebody and forget my gun."

"Are you forgetful?"

"I'm getting better. But when I was a kid, my uncle used to say I'd lose my head if it weren't screwed onto my neck. Now I write things on my hand to remember. See? Like this."

He extended a clenched fist, and Paul leaned forward to see.

Buy chianti, it said in Italian, the letters compressed at first, then unraveling.

"And did you?" Paul asked.

Luca backed up to a cupboard and pulled out the same cheap bottle Paul had brought.

Paul laughed. "Perfect! One for each of us!"

A bottle each had been a joke, of course, but Luca quite liked the idea and insisted they do it. To show he was serious, he began drinking straight from Paul's bottle like a wino on the street. Bizarre and sort of crude, but if Luca was going to do it, if this silliness was a test, Paul would do it too. Tonight, he would get drunker than he had at the party: he immediately knew it. He would walk quickly home in that proud, drunk stomping way, a target for thieves. Unless, of course, he was to stay over. For safety's sake. And then leave early enough to make morning Mass. He could explain to the monsignor if necessary—and would anyone even notice? By the time Luca was stirring the egg and cheese mixture into the spaghetti, Paul saw this all might happen; his friend, eyes glassy, cheeks touched with pink, slightly softened, looked as warm and expectant as he felt.

After two figs each, they had bread and butter and wine and, finally, the spaghetti, which they carried into the dining room, where there was a proper folding table to eat at. Mostly they spoke in Italian as they usually did, but when Luca was comfortable he tried out his English, which was better than Paul expected. As if to balance out the darkness of their conversation in the piazza, they stuck to what was light: meals their mothers made, their oddest teachers, the crazy relatives who had cameos in their childhood—swinging from vine to vine across the abyss.

When he was eight, Luca said, he snuck a big glass of his grandpa's homemade wine during a cousin's birthday party and fell asleep, snoring loudly, in the middle of the floor, to the amusement of his sisters. Paul told the story about his father's first hired man, a troubled World War II vet named Harlon, who'd been so drunk one morning he nodded off while milking a cow, one hand still tugging down on a teat. The stories were particular, but the *what* of it all entered him less than the story of themselves developing at the table: potential being made good. He tried hard to entertain Luca, to perform his best, freest self—and was rewarded with Luca's raspy laugh. In his dorm room on the other side of the river, waiting for him, were his notes for the approaching exams, two stacks of books on the early Christians, his Smith Corona typewriter, the letter from his mother he hadn't responded to yet. Monkish silence. It was the place where he had learned things, where the Bible had been opened up to him, where the moving parts of the old gold watch had been removed and oiled and laid out on velvet. A studious and somewhat lonely place—but a good place, because he'd learned so much there. Wiser Paul: that was what he'd hoped for three years ago. That and a vague desire to be made worldlier, maybe, to discover something about himself he hadn't yet—and it was that desire that he was reminded of most now, sitting across from Luca.

Slightly drunk, feeling younger than usual, on the verge of leaving Rome, ringing with pleasure in his head and heart: this was him too. He had desire in him that wasn't willing to be shut up; the pleasure and attraction were becoming an adult thing, as the minutes ticked away—something less shirking and guilty and, instead, natural and strong. Always, he admitted to himself, just after Luca disappeared into his room to change the record, it had been thin, dark-featured guys for him: Bobby Darin, Montgomery Clift, lately Alain Delon. Thick brows, but fine features, not hairy—no more than a dusting of hair on their arms and knuckles. Half his life now he'd sought out and savored these physical charms, the whole shameful enterprise below the level of words, felt more than thought—and now they had gathered in the form of the man sitting across from him, accompanied, of course, by unprepared-for touches: the mop of hair, the pinned-back ears, the tiny smudge of a mole on his chin. A real person, who thought he, Paul Novak, was good company and a confidant. At the very least.

The levels on their bottles sank. Time breathed. There came a point when Luca got up to find the ice cream, which he had neglected to put in the icebox. Unnecessarily, Paul followed him into the kitchen with a vague notion of offering to help and watched as he poured it out, soft lumps and liquid, into two bowls. Ice-cream soup. Luca poured a little Chianti in the ice cream, just to see—then Paul did too. Boys' silliness, but even as a boy he'd been so serious, hadn't he? So serious and eager to please—anything to preemptively win the favor of those who might scorn him if they knew what he was. But here he was happy. Good music, a full belly, a light head, laughter. The white windows framed the darkness outside. The occasional car and motorbike Dopplered past. It was a warm spring evening in Rome. He was here and nowhere else.

As the third movement of the piece began—expectant, then building, then retreating—the cursing of two angry men drifted up from the alley. What they were arguing over wasn't clear. One yelled, "What's your proof?" and the other yelled, "Who else knew about it? Huh? Who else did I tell?" Luca cocked his head toward the west wall, a conspiring smirk on his face.

"You want to see what's going on?" he asked, nodding to his bedroom.

"We probably should," said Paul.

Both men were old and wore a white T-shirt and brown pants. The short bald man seemed to have just passed by the tall man with an Elvis pompadour, out for a walk. In the Italian way, they jabbed at the air with their hands as they talked, as if brusquely conducting music.

"I don't *know* who else you told! Ask your big mouth!"

"Big mouth? Me? You! *You* have the mouth! Now even the grocer knows! I heard them laughing at me! You fucking sneak!"

"Maybe it was your wife! You ever think that? The biggest mouth there is?"

"Ah—fuck you. Keep her out of it!"

Luca smiled and raised his eyebrows, amused.

"What do you think he told him?" Paul asked.

"That he's too old to screw," said Luca.

That guess did seem exactly right. "And do you think he's guilty?" he added.

"No," Luca said. "I think it was the wife."

Paul agreed. For a while, they watched in silence, as the men continued to purge their anger and indignation. Finally, the accused man began walking away, talking over his shoulder, jerking his arm up in the air. "I know you how many years? Sixty? And you don't believe me? Then fuck you. *Fuck* you *and* your wife." And then the accuser shook his head and kept walking the other way, shaking his head, until he was out of view, offstage.

"Well, that was entertaining."

"We lucked out," Paul said. "Dinner *and* a show."

The Ravel was still playing. Ambiguous hours lay ahead. Paul looked at Luca and then, seeing something in his eyes he feared, he glanced around the room. The bunk bed, the photographs, and, just beside them, on top of a little bookshelf, another little pile of coins. Not Italian—the biggest one a Kennedy silver dollar.

"Are those new?" Paul said.

"Sort of," Luca said.

Paul walked over and took the silver dollar in his hand. Just the presence of American money twisted him up inside, reminded him of who he was supposed to be.

"Do you want to know where I really get them from?"

"I thought you just found them."

"I take them from the Trevi Fountain."

"You're serious?"

"I don't do it much. Only when I really need it. If you go there late at night, there's no one there to stop you."

"I still can't tell if you're kidding." It was true: right now Luca's face was unreadable.

"I'm being honest. Other people do this too."

A thief then too. And yet, Paul instantly forgave him. "But they're not yours to take."

"Then whose are they? The fountain can't spend it. And the wishes stop when they hit the water."

Paul frowned. "That's a proven fact? The water ends the wish?"

"That's my own theory, I admit."

"Doesn't the city take them? Give them to a charity or something?"

"Yeah," Luca said. "The charity of the police chief. I mean, I only take what I need. *I'm* kind of a charity myself."

Paul looked at the coins again and thought of the wishes that might have been attached to them. Mouths and their private whispering.

"You think I'm bad now, don't you?" Luca said. "I can see you thinking it."

Paul blushed and felt angry. He wanted to feel only good things about Luca, but Luca was making that difficult.

"No, I don't."

"I do things I shouldn't, but I don't hurt anybody."

"I'm sure you don't."

"Never on purpose at least," he said.

He was thinking, Paul thought, about his mother.

"Anyway," Luca said, snapping out of it, "I don't even cash all of them. Most I just keep."

Now he walked over to his bed, plunged his arm under his mattress, and pulled out a little purple velvet cognac bag. Stolen, Paul guessed, from the man he'd lived with. Beside Paul, he shook out a palm's worth. Silver from Bolivia. Gold from Ghana. A well-worn Buffalo nickel.

They returned to the sofas, and when the Ravel stopped playing Luca disappeared into his room again. For a while Paul was alone. The future rushed into the vacuum. In less than five weeks' time, he'd be back in America. His exams in early May, a Pan Am flight back—back to life as he'd known it, except now with a new, impressive degree. Rome behind him, tonight would be a cherished memory—but of no real consequence whatsoever. His responsibilities at home would swallow him up, and if anything, he'd write Luca now and again. Maybe that was enough.

From the other room, a saxophone began playing "My Favorite Things." Luca emerged with a red leather book in two hands. A giant illustrated Bible? No. A photo album.

He handed Paul the album and dropped down beside him, arm flat on the top of the sofa. The photos at the front were in black and white, then around Luca's teenaged years, suddenly color. Luca at his First Communion in a white collared shirt. Luca holding hands with his mother as they walked out of a building. The pictures all revealed the same tentativeness and shynes, with the exception of a Polaroid of Luca, at eight or nine, holding up a drawing of a cross-eyed clown, his own eyes crossed to match. His mother wasn't as attractive as Paul presumed she'd be—a little chubby, a knobby nose—though she was thin when Luca was very young. The interiors of the house, the one he had been cast out of, were studies in gaudy reds and purples and loud patterned furniture. As Paul flipped the pages, Luca added commentary ("that guy ended up drowned in the Tiber," "my cousin is a corporal now, just like my dad was") and Paul nodded, showing interest. Halfway through, Luca moved his hand so it gently gripped Paul's shoulder—and Paul flinched and then let it burn there, a hot, heavy starfish. It was an audacious, awkward move: romantic, not comforting, as his gesture had been at the piazza. Gathering what was happening, Paul's ears burned, and he opened his mouth to protest—but what was the harm in this? If he tried something more, *then* he would speak up. But not until then.

The unmoving hand seemed to push things along, and after a while Paul barely felt it there at all. Many of the color pictures near the end showed Luca and his siblings and mother at the beach. He explained that, every summer, his family would go to the coast for two weeks. The beach at Sperlonga. He hadn't been, of course, since everything happened. Of his sisters, only Ilana had come to see him after diligently tracking him down through the art school. "But anyway," he said, "enough of all that."

"I've only gone to the beaches here twice, if you can believe that," Paul said.

"We should go then," Luca said. "Before you leave."

He imagined it: Luca wearing very little, in the one place where this was acceptable. "Maybe we should."

Luca turned to him slightly. "You know, I really don't like that you're leaving."

Paul looked into Luca's big dark eyes, improbably locked on his. "What is it you like about me?" Paul said. "I don't think I know. I mean, we're not really alike, are we?"

Luca frowned. "What do you mean?"

"I mean..." said Paul, but what *did* he mean? Beyond the obvious differences that didn't need explaining.

"You're good to talk to," Luca said. "You're smart. You're funny. I know I could count on you if I needed to." He paused. "But mostly I like your eyes."

The saxophone played on. Paul's heart lurched and ached, and he tensed his shoulders so hard they got warm. People would be disgusted. His mother, everybody. He felt disgusted too, for a moment, before receiving what Luca actually had said.

"Is that right."

"Yes," Luca said, his eyes dancing over Paul's face now. "Ever since I'm a boy. Blond hair, blue eyes." So honest. So unrepentant.

Paul inhaled deeply, the hand on his shoulder rising like a leaf on a swell of water. "Do you know what time it is?" he said.

"Hmm," Luca said. "Eleven thirty, maybe twelve?"

"I should walk back."

"Maybe I said too much," Luca said. "I'm sorry."

"No," Paul said. "It's okay."

"You could stay here, you know," Luca said. "You drank that whole bottle."

"Where would I sleep?" Paul asked. "On the couch?"

"I suppose, yes," Luca replied. "If that's what you prefer."

"Okay," Paul said. "I think I may do that." His words were clipped and robotic, his heart singing and sad.

That night, Paul washed his face and pissed, and then Luca did the same. They parted ways at the edge of the living room and said good night. For a while, Paul's heart thumped dumbly as he stared at the dark ceiling, the night silent but for the occasional chain saw buzz of distant motorbikes, shouts from the street. Before dawn, after waking from a shameful dream, he got up to pee again and stopped beside Luca's slightly open door. There he was, asleep on his top bunk, nose whistling. A slab of flat tan stomach between his ghost-white T-shirt and underwear. Legs tangled in sheets. The hand at the end of his dangling arm branched with thick veins. All of which might have been his—had he only been less virtuous.

In the morning, after a shallow sleep, Paul woke to a blur that was Luca, wearing jeans and no shirt, standing a few feet from him, watchful, sipping coffee, holding another cup in his hand. He patted the floor for his glasses, curled them on, remembered where he was.

"I made you coffee," Luca said, skipping past pleasantries.

The kitchen was softened with cool light like a Vermeer painting. Church bells faintly gonged. They ate small, hard clementines and buttered bread. Luca told him he'd dreamed of being in school again and everyone was supposed to make a papier-mâché version of themselves and fill it with things to fall out, like a piñata. But the kids near him kept taking all the candy he'd chosen and started beating the piñata in advance. Maybe, he said, this was because they had been talking about teachers the night before.

"Did that happen to you as a kid?" Paul asked. "Getting teased?"

Luca raised his eyebrows. "What do *you* think?"

Around seven thirty, still early, they took the stairs down and stood together at the door, not embracing or shaking hands. Luca squinted and said, "So, the beach? What do you say?"

Paul agreed. He couldn't bear for this to be the end. Simple as that. Not next weekend, because Luca had a shift at the restaurant, but the weekend after. He could look into the cost, the place. Maybe they could stay the weekend. Paul said might as well. "You never gave me your number," he added.

Luca smiled. "We don't have a phone here. I'll just call you from the pay phone in the restaurant."

"You sure?"

Luca smiled and playfully reached out to shake Paul's shoulder. "Don't worry. I'm not going to stand you up."

In the days that followed, Paul swung between trying to forget himself inside his books and notes and feeling desperately social. He sought out the Franciscan brothers he'd gone skiing with in Switzerland for lunch, twice. He tagged along to a beer hall dinner he would have usually waved off, got quite drunk on Dunkel Bräu. Obediently, he replied to the letter from his mother (maple syrup season decent but not great, Britta had taken up with some guy named Ray, any news on what flight he'd be taking back? any requests on a homecoming cake?), mentioning, in only a sentence, and not by name, a local guy he played bocce with occasionally—an acquaintance. He was looking forward, he added, to being finished, to having his degree, and was curious (he'd lingered before choosing this word) about what the future would hold. Curious, concerned, terrified: take your pick. The food and the beauty of the city he'd miss, but it would be nice to be able to turn on the radio and listen to Braves games again, though apparently they were now called the Brewers. The usual stuff, in other words: trumped-up platitudes, a spirit of gratitude, and only mildly cheeky, gentle humor. His mother, an optimist, would not have done well with knowledge of his continued uncertainty—an uncertainty he had referred to only in the most oblique of ways. He was her pride and joy, and in the letter he let her think he was happy.

Usually he attended Mass on Wednesday and Sunday mornings, but he found himself going more often. In the quiet moments of the service, on his knees, he asked God to guide him. Wrapped in prayer, he felt safe, but a bit like an automaton. When he took Communion and felt the wafer slowly dissolve on his tongue, Paul tried with all his might to imagine the act as the taking in of the spirit of Jesus—the greatest possible human wisdom and goodness. Always it was a trick of the imagination, a test of faith—to imagine this wan little circle as sustenance for the soul, a flat white pill to eat away the darkness inside you.

One night, after listening to a Bach cantata, whittled down to his most vulnerable self, he remembered the talks he'd had in the fellowship hall of St. Mary's with Father Allan after school, Father Allan who had recruited him, given him the recruiting literature, talked about the clerical life. Father Allan, probably gay like him, now that he looked back on it. Tommy Ott had been there too, though he'd shortly thereafter bowed out, not certain he really had the call. Folding chairs, the smell of cleaning product, Father Allan bent forward, elbows on his knees, one hand gripping a fist, as if ready to both fight and pray. *There are sacrifices to this life, Paul, as you know,* he'd said. *But they pale in comparison to the bounty of the rewards.*

The bounty of the rewards: the phrase had been noble enough to stick in his mind ever since. Spiritual rewards, Father Allan meant. An elevation of the spirit. The earthly transcendence one might get in serving Christ full-time—and the richness of heaven. A special place beyond the regular, vulgar, judging world, he'd thought at thirteen. The position he'd always wanted, in other words. A place above, a place to hide.

They met at Termini Station in time to take the nine A.M. train to Formia. Luca was wearing black shorts and a white T-shirt and carrying a tan canvas beach bag. Paul was in his khaki shorts, a yellow shirt, and stuffed in his school bag was a change of clothes, his three-year-old guidebook, his toothbrush. On the way out of Il Castello, he'd hoped not to run into anyone, but Jim Conklin, an eager first-year from Nebraska, seeing that he seemed bent on leaving, stopped him to ask where he was off to.

Naples, Paul said, still walking, as if in a hurry. *I'm going to see if their pizza is as good as advertised.*

You know, Jim said, *that sounds like a great idea.*

For a woozy moment it seemed like Jim might invite himself along, but Paul kept moving and soon was gone.

Then Paul and Luca were sitting together, a few inches apart, two friends going on a trip, amid other young people, families, a sweaty old couple slugging water from wine bottles. Paul had missed him; only a few seconds in Luca's presence again confirmed it. He had busied himself so he wouldn't feel himself missing Luca, wouldn't be overwhelmed with missing Luca, but he had missed him still. Luca smelled faintly of incense, his temples were slick with sweat, and he had stories to tell of his roommates' time at the concert. As Paul listened, the city giving way to the scruffy countryside, he felt his chest contract with pleasure. It was hot, his armpits were dripping onto his sides, but the cooler air streaming in the windows was the promise of cold water, relief. Two days they'd have together. One night.

At the train station in Formia, they hopped on a bus, which led them into town. Most of the buildings were whitewashed, as the guidebook had said they would be. Check-in at the hotel wasn't until the early afternoon, so Luca suggested they go straight to the beach. On the walk there, they stopped at two stores for a little bottle of sun lotion, two Cokes, water for

Paul's Thermos, salami, and a loaf of day-old bread, so they wouldn't have to leave the beach to eat. A narrow road widened to a view of the water, sapphire blue. Along the beach, grand hotels faced the water, each with umbrellas for rent. But the free spots were what they wanted—what spending money they had they agreed not to waste on an umbrella. Their own hats would do: a straw fedora for Luca and an old Milwaukee Braves cap for Paul, a present from his uncle so he wouldn't forget Wisconsin while he was gone.

The towels they'd brought were not beach towels but bathroom towels, and side by side they rolled them out, one green, one white. Luca immediately peeled off his shirt, shoes, and socks, then dropped his shorts to reveal a smaller swimsuit. He was eager to be here, the grown-up boy who spent all those summers on the water. Paul felt self-conscious. Underneath his shirt, he was as pasty white as his legs and arms were, with a little winter gut. Not that Luca didn't already know this, not that he or anyone else would care. But even so, he was aware of how he was on display here. Part of the big skin show. In fact, what was he doing but already gawking at the men wearing what was really just skimpy, shiny underwear?

Luca sat, back hunched, knees bent, and glugged water. He asked Paul if he could help put sun lotion on his back, a logistical necessity. But this time the job seemed illicitly slippery. Already, Luca's back was a little warm.

"Aren't you going to go in the water?"

"I will," Paul said.

"What? With your shirt on?"

"I'll take it off," he protested. "I don't see what the rush is."

When, ten minutes later, he did, Luca looked at him.

"You're so pale." He picked the sun lotion back up. "Turn around. I'll get you too."

"I'm half Polish," Paul said. "We don't tan, we burn."

"I'll make sure to give you extra then."

Well covered, Paul lay down, head propped up on his bag. The clip-on shades over his glasses reduced his squint. There wasn't the slightest breeze. In the stillness, he sank into a silence within himself that was like the space he made for prayer, which shouldn't have been surprising. Beaches were places of worship too. Pagan churches. God, the sun—a powerful force that could scald you if you weren't careful, but also a giver of light, of life. *Hmm,* he thought, his mind drifting, *I should really jot that down.*

As the sun rose higher in the sky, the beach came alive and Luca said he was going in. He jogged to the shore, small hipped and loose legged among the flashing brightness of other bathers. He wasn't an Adonis; he was slender in a boyish, nonmuscular way, a creature who had endured a shocking and lasting hurt and who wanted happiness. He ran until the water reached his crotch, then walked a bit and dove forward. Gone for a moment, then a wet shaking head. In less than three weeks, Paul thought, he would be flying back, to return to his early life. But now, here he was.

"How is it?" Paul asked when Luca walked back.

Luca's poufy hair was a slick waterfall spilling in all directions. Droplets fell from his elbows, his ears. He slid a little wet curtain of hair clear of his right eye. "Cold but nice. You should go in."

When Paul did, the water was so cold he gasped. But he knew he'd get used to it—his body would adjust. Soon they were eating their bread and ham. They napped, swam again, and napped again, hats covering their faces. Paul suggested they drop off their things at the hotel and said he'd like to go visit the ruins of Tiberius's grotto, a bit farther east along the beach. It was one of the former emperor's many summer villas, built around A.D. 14 inside a cave that looked out to the sea. His *Fodor's* had called it a must-see.

Luca shrugged. "Okay. If you really want to."

"You don't want to come?"

"It's just that I've been there many times," Luca said. "I used to come here as a kid, remember?"

"So I should go by myself?"

"Well," Luca said, "maybe I'll see how I feel after we go to the hotel."

The room was even smaller than Luca's. Two beds, one chair, a view of a white alley. A dusty ceiling fan that wobbled side to side when Paul turned it on. Luca said he was going to take a quick shower, wash the sand off. There was a shared bathroom at the end of the hall. Paul waited, imagined the shower, waited. He heard the sound of an ice-cream truck coming down the street. Clouds shifted, giving way to a sheet of sunlight that made the whitewashed wall blinding for a moment. He pulled the clip-on shades from his shirt pocket and clamped it back over his glasses and looked out. No view of the water here, only a wall, the tips of trees.

When Luca emerged he was shirtless, drying off his hair, his armpit hair straight and patchy. The top button of his shorts was undone, something forgotten in haste.

"Okay," he said. "I'm going to come with you."

The relief Paul felt was almost embarrassing. "I think you made the right decision."

Luca smiled. "I didn't want us to fight."

There was only one person standing at the railing that looked out onto the grotto when they arrived—a balding redheaded man sitting on a portable stool, sketching the scene expertly in his notebook with a brown crayon. The rock face above and around the cave's dark mouth was craggy and a dirty tan color, spotted here and there with dense bushes that looked like broccoli. Behind the shallow amphitheater the entrance of the cave made were two deep hollows like empty eye sockets, and jutting out was a pool of cloudy green water lively with dark fish cordoned off by a huge square wall. Standing before it, Paul felt what he felt when looking at most of the ruins he'd seen in Italy: a sadness at how forlorn the thing seemed—so far removed from its original function—muted by an appreciation for its resilience. Except the sadness wasn't as potent here, maybe because of the cave, which had existed for millions of years before Tiberius and his ambition...and would exist for millions of years after.

Paul's *Fodor's* said that statues depicting scenes from *The Iliad* had once been on display in the grotto; replicas of them were in the museum nearby. He'd always loved reading aloud, and now he read verbatim from the entry to Luca, three paragraphs long. But when he finished and looked at Luca for a reaction, Luca had his camera to his face and was sizing up a shot.

"Were you even listening?" Paul asked. He tried not to sound annoyed, but he was.

"It's hard to listen when I'm trying to look."

Annoyed, Paul closed the fat book on his finger and let the moment pass. Norb, he thought, indignant, would have patiently listened to every word, then followed up with a comment or question of his own; that was the reaction he'd wanted. But Luca was different from Norb, wasn't he? Different from anyone else he knew. More vulnerable, less serious, not one to read books. This difference bothered him in theory, because it meant the things that made him happy weren't necessarily going to be the things that made Luca happy, and to sniff those out felt like work. But he knew it wasn't necessarily bad, the differences between them. Opposites attract and all that. Maybe that was the kind of couple they were.

Neither of them was hungry yet; it was only six. So after leaving the grotto they walked around the town as Luca looked for things he wanted to photograph. As he walked beside his friend, Paul couldn't help but size up the scenery too, cropping things into white rectangles, remembering from his grade school art class the rule of thirds. The shadow of Luca's straw hat, he noticed, looked like a nest. The white walls all around reminded him of a landscape after a huge winter storm. Home. A few times, he and Luca lingered on the same things at the same time. Two little boys crouching, playing marbles, the slanting sunlight hard against their faces. A chicken peeking out of a balcony frontispiece. An old man fanning himself with a folded newspaper in an alley. But more often than not, the opposite was true. Paul wondered if, by watching Luca long enough, he might come to understand the man better—recognize what he liked, what he ignored. Think and see like Luca did.

A half hour into the walk, they fell silent for a while. It worried him. He didn't want to yammer on like he had at the grotto, but with every passing second of silence, he felt judgment was being cast on their compatibility, the foolishness of his hopes—this friendship, or whatever it was. On seeing an old man on a bike, he told a story about his great-uncle Anton, who owned one of those turn-of-the-century bikes with a gigantic front wheel and tiny back wheel—and Luca said things in response, never not looking around, then fell back into silence. Every little shift now in mood seemed critical, either a warning flare of conflict or an opportunity to get closer that shouldn't be missed. He had the urge to touch Luca, a hand on his shoulder, a big daring embrace from behind. When they exited the side streets and were back walking along the main road, a kelly-green Alfa Romeo convertible slid by, an old man driving, a beautiful young thing with wild blond hair beside him. Young enough to be his granddaughter.

"Which do you think cost him more, the car or the girl?" Luca asked.

"In the long run, the girl," Paul said, and they laughed.

Relief.

They window-shopped the restaurants near the town center, went into the cheapest one. Dinner was a bottle of the house red, spaghetti with sauce, and a cup of cuttlefish soup, the local specialty, to share. They ordered, ate the free bread, drank. Luca told Paul he had some color on his face now, and Paul said Luca did too: a flush of pink strongest under his eyes, at the top of his cheeks.

"So," Luca said, "what are the two most interesting things you learned in your program?"

"Why two?"

"I don't know. Because two is better than one?"

They hadn't talked at all of his studies, his priestly life—in fact, they'd steered clear of it almost completely. "You're sure you'd find this interesting?"

"Yes," Luca said. "That's why I'm asking."

Paul thought for a while before he answered; he wanted his answer to be true. The first most interesting thing he'd learned, he said, was that there weren't really just four Gospels. There had been about a dozen, but only four had made the cut.

"Really?" Luca said.

"Yes. Not many people know that. Some of them are quite beautiful, actually."

"Why don't they tell people that? It seems kind of important."

"It's more than most people want to know, I think," Paul said. "There's probably a fear that it could challenge people's faith."

Luca nodded. "Yes. That makes sense. And what's the second thing?"

"Well," Paul said, leaning back in his chair, "I think it was that...Jesus was really a human being. I mean, I knew that in theory, but never really thought of him that way. He was the angelic blond guy with blue eyes in the pictures my mom had around the house. This supernatural person. But the more you dig into the history, the more you understand he was a man too, a Jewish man from a certain place and time. Who most definitely didn't have blond hair and blue eyes."

"No," Luca said. "Probably not." He smiled, his mouth half full. "Too bad for him."

Paul smiled back and his neck flushed with heat.

"Did you like finding out these new things?" Luca asked.

"Well," Paul said, and then stopped. The truth was the sleuth in him had enjoyed getting to the bottom of it all—but the process had left him a little disoriented. More curious and more skeptical both. "I guess I think more about the source material now. Why they were written and to whom, and what they tell us. How's that for an answer?"

"I think that answer is very good," said Luca. "It would be bad if you lost your faith, being a priest and everything."

"Yes, it would."

"You know what's funny," Luca said, "when I was a boy, after my father left us, I would sometimes think what it would be like if Jesus was my new dad. How he'd say nice things to my mother, make her less sad. How he'd come to school and I'd say, 'Hi, Papa Jesus!' and he'd tell the kids to stop picking on me. Very silly, I know. But that's what I'd think of in church. Jesus telling Oscar Berlucci to leave me alone."

Paul laughed and liked imagining this. Never would he have dared imagine, as a boy, Jesus as his father, actually walking beside him like an uncle or friend. He'd been taught that Jesus was *with us*, yes, but that presence had more to do with his example, the constant light of love he gave off, the warmth of which you would feel only if you got near enough. Jesus's presence required his absence. But Luca's boyhood daydream was a nice new convergence. Beautiful Luca speaking of matters of the soul. Worlds blending together. He wanted to lean forward and give the man a kiss.

"You had quite an imagination," he said instead.

"It's my very best quality," said Luca, smiling.

When they walked out to the street, it was dark and they were a little drunk: they'd gotten another half carafe instead of coffee after the waiter whisked away their plates. Now they walked past another restaurant, where a band was playing jazz. A well-dressed mess of people watched the music develop, fanning themselves with programs. Some sort of private ceremony. A wedding reception.

"What should we do now?" Luca asked.

"I don't know. What do you feel like?"

"Are you tired?"

"A little." He was simply telling the truth. The sun had sapped him. The idea of a rest was appealing.

"Then maybe we should go back to the hotel."

Thinking only of a little nap, he said okay.

They'd left the fan running so the room would be aired out when they returned, and there it was, the one moving thing.

"It's almost a little too cool now," Luca said. "Mind if I?" motioning to the fan.

"No, go ahead," said Paul.

Luca clicked on the lamp on the little table and reached up to turn off the ceiling fan, which also turned off the overhead light. Smoothly, he spread himself out on his bed, put his hands behind his head. He exhaled like a man who'd worked hard all day.

Paul sat on the other bed, kicked off his sandals, breathed, lay back as well. The change in temperature was already noticeable. Humidity opening like a flower. "Do you think the people here call themselves Sperlongians or Sperlongites?" he asked.

"Hmm?" said Luca. Paul's attempt at this idea in Italian had been poor.

"What do you think the people who live here are called?" he tried again.

"I think they're called rich."

Paul laughed and turned his head to look at his friend. "I think I'm a little sunburned on my shoulders," he said. It was strange—this saying exactly what was running through his head, no filter.

"Oh, really?" Luca said. He sat up.

Paul didn't move. "It's not that bad. Just pink."

"Let me see."

Paul unbuttoned the top button of his shirt and tugged at the collar to reveal a shoulder.

Luca's mouth cringed a bit. "Well. You should maybe put something on that. If we had some aloe here we could do that. Cold water, at least."

It was a good thought. "Actually," Paul said, "maybe I'll take a cold shower. Brush my teeth and get ready for bed while I'm at it."

"Okay," Luca said. "We'll get a good night's sleep."

Paul took his towel, grabbed his little Dopp kit, and walked down the hall to the bathroom. There was a sink with a toilet's oval mouth and a big speckled circular mirror. A shower with a mildewed white curtain and a rusting wide spout. The air was thick and smelled sharply of soap—someone else must have just left. He locked the door with the little eyehook, stripped, and showered. Afterward, he was brushing his teeth, towel tied around his waist, when there was a knock at the door.

"Someone in here," he said in his clearest, manliest voice.

"No, it's me," Luca said. "Can I come in?"

Paul opened the door. Luca, shirtless, was holding his own toothbrush and toothpaste. He quickly locked the door behind him.

"May I?" he said, motioning to the sink.

Paul was still brushing, and not knowing what else to do, he kept at it. Luca wetted his brush, started in, and as they brushed they caught eyes in the mirror. Paul spat in the sink. Luca too.

"You really did get some sun," Luca said. "You might want to cover up tomorrow."

"You're probably right."

They were talking to each other's reflections.

"I wish I could help," Luca said.

"Help?" Paul said.

"Help make you feel better."

"It's not so bad," Paul said. But as he said this, Luca traced a hand down his back, sidled up behind him. Wrapped his arms around him, fingertips brushing the top of his towel. Chin level with his shoulder. Embarrassingly, without underwear and pants to hold it back, Paul got excited. He was glad the mirror was high up enough they didn't have to look at it.

"I've wanted to touch you all day," said Luca.

Paul's lungs and mouth suddenly didn't work. Proof that this was happening was right there, in the mirror, and yet it didn't feel real. Was he trembling or shivering from the cold water?

Luca pressed one hand tight, rubbed the other softly over his stomach.

"I—"

"Can I?"

Paul kept his eyes on Luca's in the mirror, so as to not see anything else. The hand he could not see drifted lower, touched the elevated towel. Then loosened it—and it dropped to the floor.

"Luca," Paul said, as a warning.

But Luca touched him, reaching forward a bit. Soft fingertips. For a little while, he let it happen, heart lurching, looking at the growing pink in Luca's cheeks and neck. Until he glanced down at himself—at what was happening—and said, "Wait. Stop." Then whispered, "Stop. Stop!"

"What?"

"I can't." He couldn't look below or in front, so he cast his eyes to the corner of the sink.

Luca had stopped moving his hand but hadn't removed it. Paul snatched his wrist and flung his arm aside.

"I can't."

"Why not?"

"You didn't even ask me," Paul said.

Luca looked at him, glassy-eyed.

"I did ask. You didn't answer. I thought that meant it was okay."

"I'm answering now." He felt angry, but it was a murky anger. "I want my towel back on. Give it back."

"Okay," Luca said. "Calm down." Face unchanged, half erect in his swim trunks, he crouched and handed it over. "Here."

Then he undid the lock and left.

As if threatened, even though he was in a locked room, Paul quickly put on his underwear, pants, and shirt. He leaned against the sink and suddenly his stomach churned. On the toilet, he felt dizzy, and when he was done voiding himself, he walked down the hall and into the room. Everything was as it had been, except for Luca, who wasn't there.

Sitting on the bed, Paul felt his blank mind racing and, under that vague commotion, an urge to pray. A need to center himself. But the world he was in now was screaming its own truths too loudly to go there. *I wanted to touch you all day.* This was Luca telling the truth. Luca taking a risk and paying for it. Only because Paul didn't know how to accept it, though he'd wanted it very much.

Yes, Luca had offered without being asked. Because that was what Luca had had to do to make it happen.

Though really Paul shouldn't have let him.

Except...

Except, except...

For a while, he stood at the window. The blazing white-washed wall was now a dim butter color in the lamplight. Where would he go if he were Luca? One of the bars, for a drink, maybe, except he didn't have enough money for that. They'd talked about the need to skimp so they'd have enough to eat tomorrow. So no, not there. The beach.

He imagined Luca walking toward the water, as he had during the afternoon, but now in darkness. As he walked farther and farther out, Paul thought of the Luca he'd only heard about—the vulnerable kid beaten in the park by the cops, the outcast son, the reluctant lover. Remembering, he feared he'd hurt him more than he realized. He worried that in a moment of weakness Luca might do something stupid.

Crazy, silly thoughts.

But once they latched themselves on to him, he couldn't shake them. He stood. And then, as if not in control of himself anymore at all, he slipped on his sandals, found the key, and went out, without a clue of what he'd say when he found him. In the nearby bars and restaurants, no sign. He kept walking. And then, away from the lights, he was at the entrance to the beach. To the left, a couple huddled under a blanket. Nearer the hotel, folded umbrellas piled like cordwood. And sitting on the shore to the right, his friend looking up at the sky.

At about fifty yards, Luca noticed him but quickly turned back to the water. When he was close, Paul said, "I had a feeling you'd be here."

Luca said nothing.

"I'm sorry about before," Paul said.

"Don't be," said Luca. "I mean, it's not like I should have been surprised."

It wasn't right, him standing while Luca sat, as if they were teacher and student, parent and child. So Paul lowered himself to the sand and sat, legs out, shoulders bunched at his ears. The water was both in the distance and slightly shifting close by.

"I'm just not used to that," Paul said, his words sounding stupid. "I don't have your experience."

"Yes, I know," Luca said brusquely. "I'm a whore. I get it."

"That's not what I meant."

Luca looked at the sand. "What *do* you mean exactly?"

"I mean what I said. I have no experience. Not any."

Luca squinted, let the sentence stand. "Well, obviously not."

"It's not like you didn't know that. You know my situation."

"Yeah, well, don't pretend like you're so innocent. You knew this could happen just as well as I did."

Paul had no answer. This was true. Luca sized him up until something in him softened, then, snipping off their fight, tipped back his head. Paul looked up there too. The stars were in their full glory.

"Clear sky tonight," said Luca.

"It is."

"You see the two little stars under the handle of the Big Dipper? Those two little specks?"

"I think so."

"When my nonna died, my mother told me that Nonna was that little star, the first one on the left. She said that when you died and you went to heaven, God put another star in the sky for the people left behind to know you're there."

"Did she come up with that herself?"

"I don't know. Probably so."

"It's a nice idea," Paul said. "Romantic."

"I know. I always liked it. I'd look for the star, like it was a game. Try to find Nonna quick as I could. And of course when Nonno died a few years later, my mother pointed out the little one nearest it and said that that was Nonno next to Nonna now. If two people loved each other very much and their love was true, they would get to be together like that forever. That was what she told me."

"This doesn't sound like the woman you told me about."

"She was different back then."

We choose the truths that serve us best. This was the thought Paul nursed as he sat beside Luca in the wake of his story. You chose what to believe in and chose what not to believe in too. Even if you were religious, even if you were the most pious person in the world. And so Paul decided that he would be

153

with Luca, just this once. The stars wouldn't care, the world would keep on spinning, and he would at least know what it was like to love and be loved that way. As soon as it was over, he would start asking for forgiveness. For who knew how long. But if he was truly sorry, God would forgive him. He truly did believe that. And he was glad for that belief, thrilled suddenly that he believed in a God who forgave even the worst of sins, as long as the sinner's repentance was pure. Lying, cheating, adultery, rape, murder. And what he was about to do...though how could that be a sin, when nobody would suffer? Yes, quite the contrary. Looking out over the water now, the long calm plain of it, his future penance pleased him: it would give purpose to the months and years ahead.

Finally, Luca said, "Well, shall we get back then?"

"Yes," Paul said. "We should."

As they both stood up and slapped away the sand from the seats of their shorts, his past grew infinitely quiet. Walking back, his heart beat heavily in his chest. The present was dense but delicate, and in the middle of it was a single note, a barely perceptible high G, growing slightly louder as they walked down the dark roads, entered the front of the hotel, climbed the stairs.

Luca unlocked the door. The light was still on. When the door was shut behind them, Paul grabbed Luca by the crook of his arm and held on.

"What are you doing?" Luca said.

"I changed my mind. I want to."

Luca frowned at him, then danced his eyes around Paul's, first dubiously, then seriously, and for a moment Paul feared he'd missed the moment, that he was going to be mocked.

"You're sure?" Luca asked.

"Yes."

"You're not going to blame me later?"

"No."

"Because I don't want to be the bad guy."

"No. I promise."

Almost forty years later, Paul would sit in a rented apartment overlooking the piazza, his riveted sister across the room from him, the memory still impossibly vivid. The two of them suddenly against the wall. Mouths. The faint taste of toothpaste. Veering onto Luca's bed. Quickly undressing, Luca struggling with the zipper in his haste. No thinking, no doubting, a surge forward as if they might run out of time. Luca's hand stroking him; his returning, clumsily then confidently, the favor. Luca lowering his head to him, putting him in his mouth. After his embarrassing, but not embarrassing, yelp and shudder, the reassuring kiss Luca had given his thigh. Luca then going to the sun lotion in his beach bag, covering himself with it, asking if this was okay, both of them knowing what he meant. The worry it wouldn't fit, that he would fail; the gasp when Luca was inside him. The way his jaw had fallen open, the way he'd felt vulnerable and entirely safe simultaneously, the way Luca had shuddered against him. Stayed in place even when it was over.

Afterward, the room was a vortex of silence, with them at the center, on their backs on the bed. He was taller than Luca by five, six inches, but Luca had scooted up so as to curl his arm around Paul's head, as though he were the tall one. Not touching anything, just curling around. His sweat smelled like soy sauce. They hadn't even bothered turning off the lights.

"Are you okay?" Luca asked.

"I think so," Paul said.

"Good. Me too."

The next morning, Paul awoke to light through the slats of the blinds and, on the other side of the room, a blur that was Luca, straddling the room's single chair, pointing his camera at him. Awake first again.

"Hey," Luca said. "Look alive." The shutter clicked.

"I want that photo so I can destroy it," Paul said. A joke. Destroying it was the last thing he'd do. Hide it but not destroy it.

"Why?" said Luca. "You look nice."

Last night's dream, it seemed, had not quite ended. This time, when Luca came over and rubbed Paul's shoulder, Paul initiated, and they did the opposite of what they'd done before, as if to confirm that it too was possible. He'd dreamed in the night of doing this again, and here he was, doing it, almost immediately. And so the first time became a second time: the same but completely different.

After showering separately, they left the hotel. Church bells rang out as they stood in line for coffee and a roll, and so strong was the joy of the morning, Paul felt protected from shame. In line he wished he could stop time completely so he could more deliberately savor the feeling, but then the man behind the counter was asking, "Yes? Yes? What do you want?"

They swam and baked on the beach. Ate lunch at two, then swam and baked some more, their suitcases beside their towels. For most of the day, the looming dread—he knew it was there— was ironed flat by the heat, kept cool by the water. But it wasn't gone. As they walked to the bus stop, to catch a ride to Formia, where the train station was, he felt it, corkscrewing his stomach. The return to ordinary life.

Halfway to Rome, Luca fell asleep and rested his head on Paul's shoulder. Paul was touched but worried; he looked around to see if anyone had taken notice. But others were in their own world. A little girl stomped up and down on the thighs of her father, like Godzilla, feeling her power. A young woman and her friend loudly ate potato crisps from a crinkly bag in the seat in front of them. Others slept or looked out the windows.

So he let Luca be. Moving only his head, so as not to disturb Luca's sleep, he watched fields the color of sand and high-branched pines scroll past, his reflection sometimes surprising him in the watery glass. Father Paul Novak stared back. Son of Anna and Virgil Novak, from Edgar, Wisconsin, with a moppy-haired man's head making peaceful sounds on his shoulder. Never would he be a virgin again. What had happened was as permanent as the summer landscape shooting past was fleeting. The reality of Italy outside made him fantasize for a while: the two of them in a small Italian town, quieter than Sperlonga; he a teacher of religion at some local school, Luca a photographer for the small local paper. Roommates to the world, of course, but inside their home, whatever they wanted. A private universe. In the back, a garden, a miniature of his mother's; Rome just a train ride away whenever they had the need for culture. Summers free, time to read. The town—and this was the unlikely, impossible part—a quiet place in which their neighbors wouldn't suspect a thing. Drifting, he thought of Norb and his Marie: now they had this in common. Though of course it was something he could never share.

Only as the train pulled with a hiss into the station did Luca wake up, lift his head, inhale deeply, arch his back. When he looked at Paul it was with a sleepy smile and eyes that could only be described as sexual, and Paul smiled back, proud of having been privy to the feeling the look implied. They waited their turn, then filed out into the walkway beside the train, until Luca stopped in his tracks and grabbed the back of Paul's sleeve. Ack, his sunglasses. They must have slid out of his pocket and onto the seat. Paul stopped with his own bag to wait, turned back to watch Luca jog nimbly toward the doors, and it was then that he saw a familiar face. Three faces, actually. Atwood, Fenno, and Durst. Second-years in canon law. Always together, those three, names strung quickly together by other people like they were a law firm.

Had Paul not so fearfully reacted to Atwood's glance at him, had they not been coming right for him, they might have avoided each other. But here they all were.

"Novak," said Atwood.

"Oh, hi," Paul said with fake cheer. His ears were preemptively red with embarrassment. "That's funny. That you're here."

"Yes, indeed," said Durst coldly.

"Were you...on this train too? I guess so."

"We were a few rows behind you, actually. Somebody in our car got sick and so we relocated. We were in Naples for the day."

They'd seen Luca, then; his and Paul's sweet little tableau. Paul felt dizzy. The best thing to do here was to keep a calm, straight face. But he couldn't contort his expression into something even close to calm. Surely he looked guilty.

"You're traveling with a friend, it looks like."

"Yes," Paul said. "My friend Luca. We met playing bocce."

"A close friend, it seems," Fenno said.

"Well," Paul said, blushing even more, "we get along, yes."

Only Atwood nodded. "How nice."

Five seconds of silence. "We'll see you back in town, I guess," said Durst.

"Right," said Paul. "Yes, I'll see you there."

He stood frozen, eyes unfocused, as they left him. Other people flowed around him like water around a stone. Then Luca was back, sunglasses perched on his head. His relieved smile faded when he looked at Paul.

"What? What is it?" he said.

"Some of my classmates were sitting right behind us," Paul said.

Luca blinked. "So?"

"Your head was on my shoulder. They saw that."

"You're paranoid. You didn't want to wake me up, that's all. What's the big deal?"

"I acted guilty. It wasn't good."

"My head on your shoulder doesn't mean anything, Paul."

"Of course it does," he snapped. He felt disappointed that Luca was so naïve to not see that. "People gossip, especially them."

"And if they do and someone asks you..." Luca said. "You just say we're friends. And that I fell asleep and you didn't want to wake me up. Okay? It's not that hard."

Paul felt like smacking him. In a few minutes, Luca would return to his wayward, meandering life with no consequences to face, this weekend just another blip in the ongoing drama of his life. One day Paul would be but one of Luca's many flings—a colorful story to tell his future lovers. A priest? How scandalous! Whereas he would be expected now to fall back into line. Pretend as if he weren't altered forever. No, Luca had no clue about the stakes for him because he was a silly, unserious person. Paul had a strange urge to shove him to the ground, show him how flimsy a thing he really was.

"You look angry right now," Luca said.

"I just want to go home."

"Fine then," Luca said, frowning. "We'll go." Then under his breath: *"Gesù Cristo."*

They walked in silence toward the bus line together and boarded. In the same way something bright and daring had bloomed in him on the walk from the beach to the door of their room the night before, something equally dark was growing in him as they moved through the city. He said nothing, and Luca didn't speak until a few blocks before his stop.

"So," he said, "when will I see you again?"

Maybe we shouldn't, Paul thought. But at the idea of an actual end, he panicked. "I don't know," he said.

"When do you leave again? What day?"

"May the eleventh."

"Then we should see each other before then," Luca said. "Shouldn't we?"

"I don't know if that's a good idea," Paul said, still sick to his stomach. The dream had ended the moment Atwood had said, *I see.* He felt naked, unable to think.

"Paul," Luca said, "you can't be serious."

"Why not?"

"You're angry at me, and I don't know why."

Paul said nothing. His stop was coming: strained relief. Luca looked out the window.

"Don't let them ruin this," Luca said, voice lowered. "You can't let them do that."

The bus creaked and stopped with a jerk.

"I'll call you soon," Luca said.

"Don't call there now."

"Then call me at the restaurant," said Luca. "Okay? Please."

"Okay," Paul said. "I will."

That night, and the nights that followed, Paul was constantly found out in his dreams. The judges varied. First it was Father Krzyechek, the priest of his boyhood, then his mother, then the monsignor. He always woke in a panic when the disappointment reached its peak, piercing him like the high whistle of a kettle—but one morning, sheets damp with sweat, he wondered what might've happened if he waited out the disgrace in the dream, remained present for his reckoning.

Monday, Tuesday, Wednesday, he went to class. Kept his eyes peeled for the Law Firm, whom he did not see. Read the faces of everyone at Il Castello, looking for but not finding evidence that they knew. He barely ate. He dry-heaved twice. In class, he remembered with amazement the encounters at Sperlonga: the power he'd had over Luca in certain moments, the power Luca had had over him. The pleasure of pleasing and being pleased. Many times a day he felt equally guilty and then wondered if, truly, it had been a sin. The Bible said that it was wrong; the Church he had given his life to did as well. And yet, when else had he felt so fully himself? Every night, he went to Mass and knelt. Closed his eyes, squeezed his hands together, and tried to summon through the murk the flickering sunbeam of God's love, the same love he'd been summoning since he was a boy kneeling beside his sister at St. John the Baptist or on the cold, warped hardwood floor of his bedroom. It took time to sense it, to shut up his mind completely enough, but he was relieved that it still came through: a heavy, warm presence above and inside himself, though not just there—beyond. Beyond his imagining, beyond himself, beyond them, beyond the Law Firm, beyond his confusion. A feeling he sometimes imposed on the smiling face of Christ.

It was still there, despite it all. His eyes filled with gratitude.

Wednesday, after dinner, someone knocked on his door. When Paul opened it, there was Monsignor LaRouche. As always, the hair on the back of his head was sticking up, and his glasses were smudged. These hygienic blind spots were some of the traits they all loved about him.

"Evening, Paul," he said. "Sorry to bother you. But do you have a few minutes to speak with me in my office?"

Paul's face fell. "Sure thing," he said. He slowly followed the monsignor along the external hallway and down the stairs. When Paul glanced up he saw Fenno and Atwood loitering by Durst's door, eyes following him. His heart sank. In the office, Monsignor LaRouche motioned for him to sit in the red leather chair across from his desk, worn and cracked in spots like an old baseball glove.

"So you'll be leaving us very shortly," he began.

"Yes," Paul said. "Two weeks. I can't believe it's already here."

"Amazing how time flies, isn't it?" Monsignor LaRouche said.

"Yes, but I've enjoyed it immensely," Paul said. "Some of the best years of my life. Without a doubt." It was a pathetic attempt to charm the man, but he didn't know what else to do.

"Good, good. I'm always glad to hear that. That's part of the reason I'm here."

Paul smiled.

"So then," he added with a sigh. "I'm upset that I even had to call you in here. But"—he began rummaging in his shirt pocket—"last night, someone slipped this under my door."

He took out a white rectangle the size of a postcard and unfolded it once: a piece of typing paper cut in half.

"Maybe I'll just let you look at it," he said, and pushed it across the table.

You might want to keep an eye on Father Novak.
"Do not lie with a man as one lies with a woman;
that is detestable." Leviticus 18:22.

Though he was sitting, Paul felt like he was free-falling down an elevator shaft. Had he been a good liar, he might have quickly assembled his features into a look of indignation. But he wasn't a performer. His lies, when he lied, were lies of omission. All he could manage was a deep frown he held as long as he could, until the blush on his neck passed and he could figure out what to do or say.

"I..." he said. "I'm...surprised."

"Now," said the monsignor, "I don't know *who* might have wrote this, or *why*—and I don't want to know, frankly. It's a cowardly thing to do, and I'd think the men here were above such a thing. But I felt the need to make you aware. Not that you're here much longer anyway. But even so."

"It's—it's quite a charge to make," Paul said, which he realized also wasn't a denial.

"Indeed, it is," Monsignor LaRouche said, his face serious. "Do you have any idea who might have found reason to do such a thing?"

He felt paralyzed, until his mind landed on Luca's advice at the train station: *Play it down. Explain the situation.*

"The only thing I can think of," he said, "is that this weekend, I went to the beach with a friend I've made in town. A guy

I play bocce with. A few of the second-years saw us together on the train and may have gotten the wrong idea."

"In what way?"

"Well, if I was to guess, at one point my friend fell asleep and his head slipped off his seat and onto my shoulder, you know, accidentally. And I didn't want to wake him up. Maybe they read something into that."

"Well," scoffed Monsignor LaRouche, "that's a rather big leap to make."

"Yes, exactly," said Paul. He was still flushed but now saw the monsignor wanted this to go away as much as he did; he would—at the end of this—be safe. "It is."

"Well," Monsignor LaRouche said, "I'm not going to ask you who it might be, as much as I'd like to give them a piece of my mind. But I understand if you'd feel the need to talk to them yourself. To clear things up."

"Okay," Paul said. "I'll consider that."

Monsignor LaRouche cocked his head to the left, nodded. "Okay then. Good." He exhaled, relieved. "It's nice that you've made friends outside of our little compound here. Gives you a different sense of the place, I bet."

"Yes, it does," Paul said.

"A local fellow, you said?"

"Yes. He's a photographer. Well, a waiter. We met playing bocce in the park. Nice guy. He's helped me with my Italian too."

"Very nice," Monsignor LaRouche said. "I never got the hang of bocce. Though I suppose that's because I've only played it twice."

"There's a learning curve for sure."

Now the monsignor reached for his pipe, opened a drawer, and began packing the bulb with tobacco. This signaled that the worst was over, and Paul relaxed, so much so that he felt a little faint.

"Anyway," Monsignor LaRouche said, "I'm sorry we had to have this conversation."

He struck a match, lit his pipe, and set fire to the edge of the note. The corner flared orange, and the fire slowly ate its way to the middle, at which point it died out. The monsignor swiveled back to where a small metal fan sat on the floor and turned it on, to diffuse the smell, then plucked the half-destroyed evidence and tossed it in the trash can under his desk.

"Thank you for understanding," Paul said.

Monsignor LaRouche took a puff, and a faint smoke genie wriggled its way to the ceiling. "Of course. Good luck on your exams."

That night, after his first decent meal since the weekend, Paul felt himself getting seriously ill. By the next morning, his body ached, his eyes and muscles most of all. He had a sore throat, fever and chills, diarrhea. Only twice had he gotten sick in Rome: a winter cold that lasted four days, and a twenty-four-hour calamari-inspired case of food poisoning. But this was going to be something worse, he knew it.

Not wanting to fall behind, he forced himself to dress and go to class, returned immediately to Il Castello, took aspirin, sweated up the sheets, slept. All he ate were the saltines he kept in his room for a snack; all he drank was water from the bathroom tap. The second day was worse. Feeling that he should, he put on pants and a shirt and walked down to the monsignor's office to tell him he wasn't feeling well, and within the hour, Sister Angelique had left a tray of chicken broth and bread outside his door. The salt in the soup tasted good, but he threw it all up, and the third day was more of the same. Looking up at the ceiling in bed, Paul imagined he was in his childhood bedroom, his mother downstairs making chicken soup the way he liked it, with dark thigh meat, the globs of fat strained out. Then a vision of Luca entered the room, sat at the edge of the bed, placed a cold washcloth on his forehead. *How nice this would be right now,* he thought—Luca's attention, Luca's touch. But of course, that was impossible, now that suspicion was in the air. Even before, it would have seemed suspicious. But if they were still in Sperlonga, it would be quite fine. That room, away from the world, two friends on vacation...though, for that entire Sunday, something like a couple. A pair. But now? There was nowhere else for the thing to go. Already they were on the verge of goodbye. His family and his diocese were waiting. His life as a priest. To think that a whole life filled with days like those he'd had with Luca was possible was utter foolishness. Very soon, he would have to begin his penance.

He was supposed to call Luca, but he didn't. What was the use, when he couldn't see him anyway? Best to focus on merely getting through the days, getting his rest. So Thursday turned to Friday, Friday to Saturday, Saturday to Sunday. His sheets did finally get changed, and a few of the guys he was friendly with stopped in to wish him well. Three times a day Sister Angelique brought up broth and fruit and a bland cheese sandwich, encouraging him to eat. On Sunday, the fever finally broke, but he still felt too exhausted to sit and kneel his way through a service, so the monsignor brought up Communion to his room. He tried to study, as he had the past two days, but didn't have the strength to concentrate. He didn't want to even think about the test: worrying about that wouldn't help him get better.

Early Sunday night—time had become strange, it felt like morning—there was a knock on his door. It was the portiere. "Call for you in the office," he said. "Your friend Luca. Should I tell him you're coming?"

"Yes," said Paul. He absently combed down the back of his hair, even though he was only going to use the phone.

"I thought you were going to call me," Luca said, first thing.

"I have the flu. I've been in bed for pretty much the last week."

"Really?"

"Yes, really."

"You poor thing," Luca said. "Are the people there helping you at least?"

"Yes. The sisters here bring me food." *But I'm feeling lonely*, he thought.

"Me coming to see you there isn't possible, is it?"

"No," Paul said. "That wouldn't be wise."

He told him of what had happened with the monsignor.

"Those assholes," Luca said. "I guess you were right."

"I will be very nice," Paul said, "and not tell you I told you so."

"But it all worked out in the end, right? So in a way I was right after all."

"I guess I should listen to you more often," Paul replied.

"Anyway," Luca said, "I don't want to keep you. I was going to suggest we meet for coffee, like you said. But now that you're sick..."

Paul felt offended that Luca might even consider not seeing him. Unfair, of course, as that was exactly what he'd considered on the bus. "No," he said. "I want to see you. Of course I do. I still have a week. I want to say goodbye."

"You'll give me the flu to remember you by..."

"You don't like that idea?" Paul said.

"We'll be careful. No touching whatsoever. Not even a handshake."

Warmth rippled through him.

The tenth, it was decided. Coffee at the place just across the river. The Thursday before he flew out.

By the next morning, the ache and fatigue had lifted, and Paul was in the clear. He had a week before the exam, and in that time, he crammed like his first-year self again: the growing tree of all he'd learned pushed its branches all the way out, sprouted leaves, and he climbed up and bounded from limb to limb, until he knew every knot, every flutter.

On the appointed day, his questioners were tough, but there were no big surprises. When he got a question he was less confident in answering, he stalled by giving context and setting the foundation, before winding his way forward to an answer. In answering the questions, he was reminded of the breadth of what he'd discovered, how far he'd come. At the end of his defense, each member of his committee shook his sweaty hand, and he passed, as he expected to do. A seven plus, which was very good, though not great.

Then two yawning days remained. Freed of the burden to know things, his head felt light. Also, his stomach hurt and he felt impossibly distracted. He packed up his suitcases, took a few long, meandering walks, made one last visit to St. Peter's because he felt he should—who knew how long it would be until he returned to Rome? There was a farewell dinner— all the graduates, good Pinot Bianco, and he got unusually drunk.

The next morning, he woke up with a pounding headache. Rain had fallen all night, and when he left to meet Luca, there were puddles in the shallowest spots on the streets to avoid, glaring with a harsh gray light.

Walking along those damp streets, he felt detached from his body, as if it were a puppet he was only partially operating. He was going to see Luca to say goodbye, probably forever, yet this was an absurd thing to do. In the days since they'd spoken on the phone he'd vaguely justified this one last meeting: he'd be busy studying; he didn't want to overdo it, sour the lingering good feeling. But now he cursed himself for being so stingy. They should have spent as much time together as they possibly could. He should have found the time.

He arrived at the café first, ordered a macchiato, and sipped it nervously, keeping watch out the window. About ten minutes past the hour, Luca finally rolled up on his bike, stopped, looked around inside, waved. He had a new, unfortunate haircut: that was the first thing Paul noticed. Too much off the back, not enough in the front, like a curly black mushroom.

"Don't say a word," Luca said, first thing. "I need someone to fix it. I tried doing it myself."

"I didn't say a thing," Paul said.

Since it was awkward to sidle around the little table he was sitting at, Paul didn't stand up to embrace him, so Luca just sat down. At first, they talked only of the previous few days. There was some horrible news: Luca's camera had been stolen, and he suspected Sandro, though Sandro denied it. And Luca had no proof. People did get robbed, and Elise's glass-blown ashtray was also missing, though of course Sandro could have stolen that to keep up the appearance. Paul was pleased for this drama to listen to, the chance to tell Luca he was sorry. To feel something other than his own sense of loss. Luca asked Paul how the last little while had been, since he'd been sick. Paul summed up his test and his wanderings, exaggerated how busy he'd been.

"I can't believe I'm actually going back," he said. "It hasn't sunk in yet."

"You were here three years, right?" Luca said, though he knew.

"Yeah, three years."

"I wish we'd met sooner," Luca said.

"Me too."

"I'm going to miss you," Luca said. "I feel we have a very special friendship."

Paul teared up: very special, yes. But please, this was more than friendship. He had the useless urge to take Luca by the hand and walk him into Il Castello and up into his room, where they could lie again, naked, curled into each other one last time. "I will too," he said. "But you already knew that."

"Yes," Luca said. "I did."

They veered toward inevitable talk of the future, and he steadied himself. Luca thought maybe he'd show his portfolio to some art magazines, see about moving into a new apartment— put up a ROOMMATES WANTED sign at the pinball hall. Paul talked of the worry he still had that, even after all this, he wouldn't like teaching, when it was the thing he was supposed to do.

"What about being a priest at a church? In a parish?" Luca said.

"No," Paul said. "I don't think so. I'm not that good with people."

"*I'm* a person," Luca said. "And you're good with me."

"You're not like most people though," Paul said. "You're not like the people I'd be asked to serve."

"See, I think you don't know yourself that well," Luca said. "You think you're so cold and smart, like a robot, but you're not. You'd be better than most of the deadbeats they've got doing the job. I mean that."

Paul didn't know what to make of this: Was this truth, or the biased perspective of a man who loved him—or who seemed, at least, to love him? He'd always looked down on the yeoman's work of being a pastor. He was too smart to waste his mind on something so pedestrian. But maybe that was another way in which he was ignorant. Maybe he'd dismissed that life because he was secretly intimidated by it. Maybe being in the trenches trying to help people make sense of life was an even greater challenge than educating the future priests of America in Scripture. Of course it was. Of course.

Outside, a dog barked, and they both looked its way. An old lady reached into her purse as a schnauzer jumped up on its hind legs with an embarrassing level of excitement.

"So you leave tomorrow then?" Luca said. "The afternoon?"

"That's right," said Paul.

"I don't know what else to say," Luca said. "I wish you could stay."

Paul bit down on his lip to keep from crying. "There's nothing to do about it now," he finally said.

"I guess not," Luca said.

For a while, they just sat there. People biked past the window, rushing off to who knew where.

"I have something to give you," Luca said. He sat up, reached into his pants pocket. And what he laid beside Paul's coffee cup was a print of him in the hotel, in bed by the window. The photo paper was slightly curled. He looked younger without his glasses. *Look alive*—that's what Luca had said the moment before he snapped it.

"I think it turned out nice," Luca said.

"I look a little out of it."

"You look dreamy," Luca said. "There's a difference."

Holding the picture lightly with his fingertips, Paul suddenly wished himself to be Italian, and single, someone who might live around the corner. One of the young men all around them, with no reason to ever leave.

"Luckily, I took out the film before Sandro stole it," Luca said. "If not, I think I would have killed him."

With this, finally the tears came, and Paul put his hand over his eyes as his back shook.

"Hey," Luca said, and when Paul looked at him, his chin was shaking too. "Let's get out of here."

Paul nodded, opened his mouth, bottom teeth out, breathed. Luca set a few coins on the table, then Paul followed him outside. Luca unlocked his bike, then turned to Paul, grabbed his forearm, and pulled him into a hug. In view of the café, Paul held on a little too long, and Luca lowered his head to Paul's shoulder. Then, too quickly, Luca pulled away and moved to his bike. He swung a leg over the frame and straddled it.

"Maybe I'll see you again someday," he said.

Paul nodded. "I hope so."

"Travel safe."

Paul nodded. "You too." Which didn't make sense, exactly, he realized. Though maybe it did, in the bigger picture.

Luca set his foot on one of the pedals, then stood up to push down on it, and the wheels turned. Paul watched him roll away— the moppy back of his head, the little wedge of skin exposed between the bottom of his shirt and the top of his jeans—until he turned onto a street and out of sight. Then he lowered himself to the ground and wept.

There were tears in Britta's eyes when he finally grew silent.

The furniture that held them seemed precarious, as if instead of a hardwood floor below them, it was the membrane of a giant balloon.

"Is he still alive, or you don't know?" she asked.

"He died years ago," Paul said. "Almost twenty years ago, I think it was the fall of 1990, I tried to track him down. This was before the internet, of course, but I ordered a Rome phone book and had it shipped to me and found his mom's number. When we talked, she told me he'd died two years before. From the way she described it, I'm pretty sure it was AIDS."

Britta nodded. "So that was the last time you saw him?"

"Yeah," he said. "That was it." He cleared his throat. "We did write letters for a little while after. But then he stopped writing back." Five letters total on his end, three total from Luca. What he'd told himself, when the replies stopped coming, was that Luca had lost the return address or moved out of town. But in his heart he knew it was just that Luca, being so young and free, had decided that he couldn't live in the past; he needed to keep his heart open for the next one who would come along.

"The summer you got back was the summer I was pregnant with Maura, wasn't it?" Britta said now.

"Yes, it was."

"I remember when I came home to see you, you seemed sadder than usual. Quiet."

"I was."

"I thought you just missed living it up in Rome."

"That was certainly part of it."

"But most of it was missing Luca."

"Yes, that's right."

She nodded, appreciating how it all made sense.

"Mom could see something was wrong and kept asking me what it was. But then, lucky for me, once you told everyone you were pregnant, she stopped worrying about me and started worrying about you."

"You're welcome," Britta replied, a smile in her eyes.

"Yes," he said. "Thank you for that."

He wondered if she ever thought about the conversation they had one morning that June, a month and a half before she'd told their parents her news. Right after breakfast, they'd gone for a walk in the woods—her idea—the way they had as kids, on the hunt for the wild morels their dad liked to eat fried up with butter. As they walked, dew dampening their shoes, she asked him what he'd been up to since being home, what he missed the most about Rome, whether Mom was driving him crazy yet. Then he asked her to tell him about Ray, whom he'd heard about only from the letters their mother sent. She said that he was very good-looking, like a more handsome Mick Jagger, but that she wasn't sure if she loved him. That sometimes she hated his guts. And then, in a clearing, a few moments later, she stopped and told him she was pregnant. Almost three months along.

She looked surprised more than scared when she said the words, as if she still couldn't believe it was true. *I presume this wasn't planned,* he said, and she said, *No, it wasn't.* She always imagined having kids someday, she told him, just not so soon. Not only did she and Ray barely make enough money to afford their shitty little apartment, but she didn't even know if she wanted to stay with him long term.

To be honest, she said, hesitating, *I'm not even sure I want to have the baby.*

You're talking about adoption, I hope, he said.

No, she said. *I'm not.*

His heart had sunk at the thought. If their parents knew that their daughter was even contemplating an abortion, they would have been heartbroken—though, at this point, probably not shocked. Which was why, of course, she hadn't told them.

You know how I would feel about that, he said.

Yes, I think I do.

I obviously can't tell you what to do, he continued. *You're going to do what you want. But I worry, Britta, knowing you, that if you don't have the child, you might regret it the rest of your life.*

She nodded. *I worry about that too.*

If you gave it up for adoption, you'd make some other family very happy, he said, *as hard as I know it would be to do that.*

She looked down at the ground, avoiding his eyes.

But if you ask me, he continued, *I think if you did have the child and decided to keep it, you would make a wonderful mother, whether you had your life figured out or not.*

At this, she lifted her head. And he saw what he'd not understood: that she secretly wanted it and hoped he was right.

Ray doesn't want you to have it, does he? he said.

No, she said.

But you're not sure if you agree.

She sniffed and nodded. *Yes.*

Looking at her then, in the morning light of the forest, he'd imagined her as a mother for the first time: long Venus de Milo hair, big white caftan, warm laugh—cradling an infant in her big freckled arms. The most natural thing in the world. There was a little life growing in her, he realized. Three of them were present. And as they stood there in silence, the strangest thing had happened: he'd imagined he heard its cry—clear as day. Her cry. The creature that would become Maura.

After they'd embraced and brushed their teeth, Paul went to bed feeling lighter—for having finally told the story, maybe, or for having relived that spring so long ago. That night, he had a wordless dream in which he and Britta had paid a visit, here in Rome, to an older man with a big mop of white hair, whom he understood to be Luca, if he were still alive—room upon room of his apartment filled with giant photographs of faces overlaid with birds, sky, buildings. The next morning, around six, he woke to the patter of light rain, a sound he usually loved. But as he lay in bed listening to it, an old man alone in a bed in a rented room in Rome, any remnant of relief the previous evening had given him curdled into sadness. Little by little at first, and then, without warning, a free fall.

Tomorrow morning, he thought, they would fly back, and this desperate little grace period would end. And then no more distractions. Nothing left to do but suffer and die. As he lay there, looking up at the ceiling, he sensed the poison in his cells gathering like storm clouds. His side throbbed, his head hurt, his tongue was dry. Feeling suddenly, achingly, claustrophobic, he got up as quickly as he could, walked to the bathroom, filled the water glass he kept there, and drank it quickly down. In the mirror was his face, fear glinting in his eyes.

When he went into the living room, last night's sofa and the chair Britta had pulled up beside it reminded him of his confession. But instead of lingering in the relief he'd felt in its immediate aftermath, the adrenaline that had coursed through him as he'd lay down to sleep, his mind, no longer under the spell of last night, delivered a stark and bitter truth: just as he'd survived the sharing of his secret fully intact, he would have survived leaving the Church. He'd always wondered what it would feel like on the other side, and now, too late, he knew.

By the time Britta emerged from her room in running shorts and a T-shirt, his defenses had deserted him. It was nine in the morning, he was sitting stunned in Britta's chair, and he felt despondent.

"Paul?" she said. "What's wrong? Are you all right?"

"I'm such a coward," he said. Bile climbed his throat. He felt faint.

"Are you talking about not leaving the Church?"

"Yes," he said. "What else?"

"What happened this morning?" she asked. "I thought we had a good night."

"I don't know," he said.

"Listen," she said. "I know you've been stuck on feeling regret lately. And it's your right to feel whatever you want. But I have to say, when I look at your life all I see is how much good you've added to the world. I mean, Paul, seriously. Just think how many people you've helped."

He said nothing.

"The things you did at Iggy's had a real effect on people. A *profound* effect. I mean, how many people can really say that?"

"A lot, actually," he said.

"Oh, stop."

"I know I've done good things. Everybody has. But I could have done good things and had a partner too. If I'd left."

At this, Britta didn't know how to respond. *Good,* he thought. *Now you're getting it.*

"I mean, look at you and Don," he continued. "Think of how happy you were together. Do you really think you would have been as happy on your own?"

"But we were lucky," she said. "Not everybody's so lucky."

"Yeah, well, maybe I could have been lucky too."

She lowered her head. "What would you have done for money? If you left?"

"I don't know. Teaching. Counseling. Something like that."

"Would you have stayed in Northfield?"

"No," he said. "Maybe Madison or Milwaukee. Maybe Chicago. For a little while, I thought I might move to St. Louis, to be near you."

"Oh, Paul," she said.

"Nothing to do about it now."

He wanted this to be the end of the discussion. He wanted to wallow in awful certainty. But Britta said, "I feel the need to remind you that you're *depressed*, by the way. You can't trust everything you're feeling now. This isn't the real you."

"It *is* though. That's what I'm trying to tell you."

"It's part of you. But it's not all of you."

"Fine. But it's an important part of me."

"Okay," she said. "I understand that. I do."

He didn't care if he saw more of Rome or not at this point. What he felt like doing was curling into a ball and sleeping away the day. But Britta said if he was going to be unhappy all day, he might as well be unhappy amid beauty and unhappy with her, and he felt too weak to resist.

First they went to the Basilica di San Clemente, with its great gold ceiling, its soft peachy frescoes in front. Then to Santa Maria, with the gorgeous ceiling, the ancient mosaics with the crudely depicted shepherds, the children with long adult faces.

The air in the churches was cool. Blocky footsteps hollowly sounded. Sitting in a pew, Britta beside him, Paul closed his eyes and let the bowl of air above him push into his shoulders, trying and failing to feel the presence of God. At the Spanish Steps, they drank iced tea and watched the people trickle up and down. Then back for a nap, an early dinner in Trastevere again, but then, instead of heading back for the night, Britta told him she wanted one last thing: to watch the sunset from the top of Gianicolo Hill.

The taxi wound up the long corridor of trees before dropping them off at the end of the road. Two African priests were having their photo taken by the Garibaldi statue, and maybe thirty, forty others stood at the edges of the plaza, looking out. During the ride, Paul slid his clip-on shades over his glasses to protect himself from the low light flaring from the gaps in trees and buildings, but up here he took them off.

This was his last night in Rome. The light was general and muted. He wanted to see everything exactly as it was.

There were no chairs or benches up here, so they stood at the southernmost tip, hands at their sides. Paul squinted west at the setting sun, bulging now as it met the horizon, then settled his eyes east, where it cast light over the city. A blocky carpet of tan and gray houses and offices and government buildings—tinted pink now—curled around the hill. Church domes bobbed above here and there, unmoving buoys in an unmoving sea. Here was St. Peter's, tallest of all. Here the low gray turtle shell of the Pantheon, the harmonica mouth of Victor Emmanuel. The radio in an idling taxi played some peppy Italian pop tune, which was distracting—but at the moment that was a blessing. Better to skim along the surface of his senses. Better to not think.

"There were trees like that in Door County," Britta said after a while, looking ahead at a stand of tall pines, peach-gray trunks and branches bare but for a high, wide canopy of leaves. "Weren't there? Along the main road?"

"I don't know. You might be right. I believe they're called umbrella pines."

"Ah," she said. "That'd make sense."

They looked back out at the city. The pale pink light was steady and general. Everything was beautiful and meant nothing.

"Good call on coming here for this," he said.

"It's nice, isn't it?"

177

"It is."

A long silence passed between them. The other tourists nearby had quieted too.

Then, without warning, Britta put her hand on the inside of Paul's arm, dropped it down to his wrist, and lightly pulled his hand from his pocket. She took it in hers and rubbed her thumb over his knuckles, back and forth, back and forth. When he turned to her, her eyes were shiny.

He knew what she felt. He felt the fear and fullness too.

Three times she squeezed his hand, as if to say, *Still here, still here, still here.*

IV. Maura in Love

For the past ten minutes, as her son and daughter steadily dug trenches on the beach in front of her and hustled buckets to and from the water and clawed the sand like puppies, Maura Novak Williams had been sitting motionless in her beach chair, staring at the same blazingly bright page of her novel as if into a portal, trying to imagine herself saying the words that would destroy her family.

Back in Newton, before they left for the Cape, she promised herself she'd tell Harden her intentions the last night of the trip, once the kids were in bed. Then, in the morning, she'd tell them too. For a few weeks, the time to do this had always been a little bit in the future. Mercifully, always later. But now that day was today, that night was tonight, that morning was tomorrow, sometime before the checkout deadline at noon.

Six weeks ago, she'd confessed to Harden about David and he'd demanded she end it immediately. When she said she wasn't sure she wanted to, he barked, *What?* And then: *What do you mean? You're leaving me?*

I don't know what I mean, she said. Which was true: she really didn't. And when he said, in that case, they would need to go to counseling to figure this out, she'd said she wasn't sure she wanted that either.

With every day that passed since Harden knew, she felt more inclined to do the unthinkable: ask him for a divorce so she could be with David. She had a plan for making it work, one that David had suggested. She'd ask for joint custody and move into a cheap apartment as close to Harden and the kids as possible. David would split his time between the apartment and his house in Portland, Maine and on the weekends she didn't have the kids, she'd drive up to Portland to be with him there. With the help of email and Skype, the distance wouldn't be so bad: every day she'd be in touch with the kids, virtually, and every other day or so she'd be with them in person, too. They'd all have to get creative to make it work, but she was nothing if not creative. *I need more time to think it through*—that's where she left things with Harden. And though he was insulted by her request, he was giving her the long leash she'd asked for. Because, unlike her, he wanted them to stay together.

Since finding out about David, Harden had burned with a justified righteous anger, his resting face red and swollen. But over the past few days, up here at the cottage, he seemed to realize his best chance of changing her mind was to reverse course, to remind her, with an attentiveness and kindness she hadn't seen from him in years, why she was making a mistake. He was a good father and not even that horrible a husband, objectively speaking—it wasn't about that. She simply wanted David instead. In fact, just a few days before they packed the car for vacation, she told David of her decision while sitting on a bench at the park she liked to walk through at night. To which he said, *This is the very best news.*

The kids would be blindsided. Crushed. Sitting here fake-reading, wading out into the water, watching them play, she'd been overcome again and again by a flood of tears and waves of vertigo exactly like those she'd felt when looking down a hundred stories from the clear glass platform off the edge of the John Hancock tower they'd visited in Chicago last year. As two thin boys on inner tubes blasted each other with water guns, she thought, *I'm a terrorist. Except instead of blowing up strangers, my victims will be my family. Instead of forty-seven comely virgins, David.* Though it was about so much more than sex. He wanted to be stepdad to the kids, everything. And he'd be great at it, she was sure. All this could be hers, theirs, later. All she had to do was rip off the Band-Aid now. Just that one tiny, impossible thing.

She hadn't willingly confessed: Harden had found texts from David on her phone and forced the issue. After, he'd coldly told her she was a bitch, stormed out of the house, and peeled out of the driveway in his Wagoneer. A minute later, Evan wandered into the room, hesitant but curious, and found her ugly-crying on the bed. He'd heard the front door slam. *Don't worry,* she'd said. *Dad's just mad about some money stuff. Okay,* he'd said, eager to believe.

Already stocked in the cottage kitchen, bought yesterday, was the pancake mix, the big carton of strawberries, and the whipping cream she would whisk until it was perfect for the dollops the kids liked on top of their pancakes, plus two bottles of cranberry juice (Ocean Spray, every other brand Evan wouldn't drink), a thing of turkey bacon, a bag of red (never green) grapes. With love, tomorrow, she'd make a nice breakfast for everyone, as she had a thousand times before. And as Harden sat there, heartbroken, still stunned by what she'd tell him tonight, they'd eat and talk. He'd stay for the kids, be their safety net. That was the right thing to do and Harden almost always did the right thing. She'd always respected him for that.

At some point, the world would shrink to the few cubic feet of air between their faces and she'd just need to open her mouth and say the words. Probably she'd cry in advance. Of course she would: she was already doing it now. Evan's eyes would get big and anxious, sensing trouble. *Guys,* she would say, *I have something very difficult to tell you.* Evan would ask her, already upset, if she was sick, because he had started worrying about people dying on him lately. It started three years ago when Grandpa Don died suddenly of a heart attack and intensified again this spring when she'd told him about her uncle, Paul, the priest, who had cancer and whom Grandma was with for the summer. That's where his mind would go. That, or he'd ask her if Paul had died, to which she would answer no, fortunately, not yet.

Thinking about her kids' brown eyes locked on to hers—
shocked, sad, vulnerable, not registering anything but *I'm leaving*
and *divorce*—Maura sucked in air, her chest stuttered. Imagining
details was torture but necessary: projecting the scene in all its
awful detail would make her less scared to actually do it.

"Hey, Mom?" Evan said now.

Maura looked up. He was kneeling in the sand, one eye closed,
Popeye style, against the sun.

"Hey, bud!" she said, overcompensating. "What is it?"

"Do we have any duct tape in the car?"

"I don't think so. Why?"

"Can you go check?"

"Actually, I know for sure it's not there, I would've seen it
when we packed. Do you need it for what you're building?"

"I want to make trapdoors. Like make a hole and put tape
over it? And then maybe sprinkle sand on it to camouflage it."

"Hmm," she said. "I bet there's something else here you could
use instead."

"Like what?"

"I don't know—like some bark or a piece of cardboard or
something?"

He tilted his head to the side, like a dog hearing a distant
whistle. "Do you have anything in your purse I could use?"

She looked: in fact, she did. Two brochures from the cottage.
"Would these work?"

Evan scrambled to his feet, took them, then scrambled back
to his spot. What they were making was unclear to her, but she
liked the pattern: from above, it would look like a target. Fully
engrossed like this, locked into a state of pure play, he could be
such a sweetheart. Look at his gulping boy belly, his faintly exposed
ribs. The Valley Girl way he blew hair out of his eyes. Stretches of
easy time like this made you forget about how hard he often was
to deal with. (She'd have to make so much up to him, after this.
The one who would be wounded most deeply was him.)

"Is this some sort of castle or something?" she asked.

"We're just making moats," Ella replied.

"A castle's a little-kid thing to make," Evan said.

"Though if a little kid walked by and wanted to *pretend* there's a castle there, that would be okay," Ella added.

"As long as it's invisible," Evan chimed in.

Quietly, for maybe a minute, they kept digging, saying nothing to each other, and the world was good.

"I really like how you two are playing together today," Maura said. The literature said positive reinforcement was key. For any kid, but Evan especially.

Ella shrugged. "It's easy when he's not being mean."

"I'm not being mean!" Evan said.

"She said you *weren't* being mean," Maura said.

"Oh."

"By the way, just so you guys know," she said, seizing the moment, "we should start back home in about ten minutes."

"Noooo!" Evan said. "Fifteen!"

"Fine," Maura said. She'd do ten and say it was fifteen: he wouldn't know the difference. "But that's it. I need to get dinner started soon."

"Okay," Evan said. "Deal."

He sniffed twice, his allergies acting up, then wiped his nose with his forearms; his hands were so caked with sand they looked like brown sequined gloves. A seagull landed behind them, a breeze blew, the pages of her neglected novel riffled in one direction, over the stopper of her thumb. The eye of the seagull was reptilian and yellow. A villain in a feathery package. How could it be she was going to move out? Not see them every day? Not scoop them up for hugs every morning? Was she insane? But it was true she'd been without them for long stretches before. At the Blue Woods retreat where she'd met David, for example. For two weeks at her mom's place after Don died too, and they'd all survived. It was so rarely nice like this anyway; usually she was yelling at Evan, or he and Ella were fighting. And if it was love on the table, what about the love she got from David, a love that had resurrected her as a person? It felt equally impossible that she break things off with him too.

What she'd need to learn how to do, she thought, as both children stiffly shuffled with buckets and great purpose toward the foam of the tide, was to need them a little bit less. Love them as much as ever, but *need* less. When kids were teenagers a little gulf often opened between them and their parents—the first steps toward leaving the nest; her moving out would merely speed up the process. It would be the hardest thing she'd have to do. But if she didn't do it now, while she had this clarity, she'd never forgive herself. Or that's what she told herself.

Ask her a year ago whether it was possible she could leave her husband, and she would have snorted and said, *Please. Never in a billion years.* It wasn't that she didn't daydream about being with someone else or living in a sleepy bungalow alone. She'd been more unhappy than happy for many years. Frustrated with her relationship with Harden, who was so distant and difficult to talk to; worn down by all the heavy lifting it took to keep Evan on the rails; and by her job. But she knew she wouldn't ever do anything about it. Who got everything they wanted? Real adults knew to be stoic and accept their fate.

But then, last year, the year she turned thirty-eight, that particular line of thinking had stopped working for her. Specifically, it stopped working in the patio room of the Emporium Bar and Grill, during her twentieth high school reunion back in St. Louis. She and her girlfriends—Sarah, Kris, Amity—had dove quickly into drinking, laughed too hard at the semi-embarrassing stories they decided to share, before a shrugging cynicism about kids and husbands took hold. If it was a little superficial, at least they were trying to be honest, unlike certain other people (she knew who) probably humblebragging at other tables. They weren't here to pour their hearts out, only to do a little bonding with whatever glue did the job. So be it.

But when Alison Ranier arrived, the night utterly changed. The high school version of Alison (never Ally, she refused to answer to Ally) had been, like Maura, one of the five smartest girls in their class. She was sweet and awkward and plain: her thick glasses and baggy sweatshirts put you in mind of a sloppy mole. Because she was a threat academically but not socially, Maura liked her; it was nice to have someone who pushed her to study harder whom she also felt superior to. But as social media proved many years later, Alison was a classic late bloomer. Turns out there was a hot body under those sweatshirts and a strikingly pretty face behind those glasses. In her late twenties she wrote a series of successful YA books about an awkward teenaged girl with superpowers, one of which was optioned but never made into a movie; and along the way she married a guy who looked like a cuddly Josh Brolin who had directed a pair of well-received indie movies and was personal friends with the movie star Ewan McGregor. Alison's public photo stream dried up suddenly, however, after a freak diving accident paralyzed her from the waist down, leaving Maura to wonder, and to aimlessly google, and to patch together a picture of Alison's life as some dim existence, filled with quiet suffering. There had been little activity on her blog. No new books in the works. No new movies for her husband. Life as they knew it had obviously been stopped cold.

Around nine, though—very late, considering the dinner had started at 5:30—Alison arrived. She was swarmed instantly by the three other formerly shy nerds she'd called her friends, leaning down to hug her in her wheelchair, rocking back and forth. Soon, this improbable incarnation of Alison held court in a beautifully stylish and expensive-looking dress, sharing—if the gaping mouths and hooting reaction of her audience was any indication—truly funny and slightly shocking things. Confident, beloved, unbroken Alison. Drinking a vodka cranberry.

It was possible that the handsome filmmaker, aware he was being watched and judged, was simply playing the part of the sweet husband and had a nonparalyzed mistress on the side. With all that access to beauty, time away on movie sets, you could imagine it. But Maura didn't think so. Along with her small audience, he smiled and laughed—real laughter—his dark eyes molten, it seemed, with a warm, admiring love. Not once, she thought, had Harden ever looked at her this way, not even when they were dating.

Sitting in a white plastic folding chair, her third vodka tonic held loosely in her warm hand, Rick Astley's "Never Gonna Give You Up" the latest in a maniacally on-theme playlist of pop songs exclusively released in their graduation year of 1988 thumping from a rented sound system, Maura felt pinned to the wall by a truth she knew but never let herself feel: that she'd never given the kind of love she'd wanted a fighting chance. A few too many painful breakups in college with art boys and music boys, and she'd sworn the whole romantic equals/partners in art idea off, already cynical by the age of twenty-one.

Before that, however, she'd been devoted to the idea of a soul mate; though she always mocked the word, she utterly believed in the idea of it. In Mrs. Alpert's painting class she wrote a paper on Georgia O'Keeffe's cow skull paintings, which yielded an A- but, more importantly, introduced her to the true story of the long, passionate, complex, ahead-of-its-time relationship of Georgia and Alfred Stieglitz, the famous photographer. Her mom and Don were a rare real-life love story, her first model; but Georgia and Albert had attracted her much more because they were (let's face it) more attractive. And they were both artists—what she desperately wanted to be.

For thirty years, first as lovers, then as a married couple, Georgia and Albert had written constantly to each other, sometimes twice a day. Early on, they made love in Albert's studio. Then, after sex, while she was still naked, he'd taken photos of her, but not pervy ones—artful, honoring ones. There had been something about young Georgia that young Maura found thrilling: her flinty confidence in her muscled yet feminine body; the breasts she often held in her strong, veined hands in the portraits, as if to say, *Yeah, I like 'em too*; her unplucked, mannish eyebrows. Albert, with his brushy white train conductor's mustache and rimless glasses, didn't do anything for her (back then it was Rob Lowe in *St. Elmo's Fire*), but the heady brew of serious, disciplined, ruthlessly critical artist plus big-hearted lover plus wry, playful, funny man of the world evidenced in his letters was something she'd decided she would be requiring in a man. In the four, five years after finding this example—from her junior year of high school to the spring of her junior year of college—she'd been on fire with the goal of finding her own Albert, her equal in making art, the one whom she'd never want to stop hanging out with, talking with, figuring out life with, passionately fucking and going to art shows with. And if Maura had patience and a steelier heart, she might have kept searching, as some did, as Alison seemed to have done, into their thirties. But she'd not been patient. She'd given up. Too soon, too soon.

At their table at the restaurant, Maura suddenly felt her heart beating so quickly she excused herself to the bathroom. For a few minutes she sat on a closed toilet taking deep breaths, trying not to hyperventilate. *Everything okay?* Kris asked, after she returned. *Oh, I'm fine*, she said. *The veggie lasagna did a number on my stomach, that's all.* But she wasn't fine: she wanted to leave, immediately, before she started to cry, here in full view of the Class of 1988. So she'd taken a fake call from Harden, pretended Ella was sick and needed her mom, and called a cab to take her home.

A month after the reunion, she applied to the Blue Woods Center, an arts retreat in Connecticut. Since having the kids, she'd not done much painting, though who was she kidding? She hadn't done much in the eight, nine years after college and before the kids either. Even so, ideas for paintings flew into her head sometimes, including—most promisingly and recently—a series of Edward Hopper–esque domestic scenes in which the mother was a mythological creature. A Minotaur-woman, say, sitting on a bus glancing at her iPhone. A gryphon-woman waiting in line at a Walgreens. Medusa in a dirty bathrobe watching David Letterman with a glass of Pinot Grigio. The key to making these scenes work would be to make them poignantly, authentically sad, otherwise the painting would be nothing but an arty *Far Side* cartoon. It had seemed gravely important that she do this—that she do *something* to put her back in touch with her hopeful, less jaded self. So she had.

For three weeks, late at night in the basement, she worked on a painting of the Minotaur-woman on the bus, and it turned out better than she'd hoped. For the application, she wrote a statement of purpose that used the phrase "the tragi-comedy of domestic life"; she sent photos of the new painting as well as her favorite four from college, which she still had as slides. And unbelievably, they'd accepted her—she who'd barely touched brush to canvas in fifteen years. There was a fee of $200, but beyond that, all she had to do was show up and work in the little Danish modern studio that was all hers, with a loft up top to sleep in. Every day a big, communal dinner was cooked up by the resident chef and served at the main house, at which point she could get out of her head and meet some fellow artists, if she so chose. At first, Harden had groused at the prospect of rolling solo with the kids for two weeks. But when she reminded him that he'd gone on a fishing trip with his dad for ten days a few years back, he backed down and agreed.

The first night at what the staff called the "big table" everyone introduced themselves, and as it turned out, most of the people there were as she'd imagined they'd be—full-time artists or artist-teachers. When it was her turn, she said she was a graphic designer who worked in advertising, but she was trying to get back to doing her own art. Elena, a white-haired poet wearing bright pink overalls, jumped in quickly to announce she'd brought a case of great Shiraz along, and they'd started to eat, thankfully.

Across the table was David, smiling. He wasn't as traditionally good-looking as Harden—his spiky hair was thinning on top, his chin was weaker, and faint acne scars ran along his cheeks—but she was immediately attracted to him: something about his kind, dark eyes and his small compact body and the way he leaned forward to listen to her when she talked. He was on the fine arts faculty at the University of Southern Maine–Portland, a sculptor, separated from his female partner of fifteen years for a year now but apparently, finally, okay with this. Though he had to be in his late forties, he seemed young in a way that reminded her of the supposedly senior citizens you saw throwing footballs in Viagra ads, the only geriatric thing about them being their suspiciously white hair.

The second night after dinner Ryan, the cabin manager, started a fire for them in the common room. Big stone hearth, comfy couches and chairs, arty ski lodge vibe, glasses of Scotch. For maybe an hour the storytelling and laughter ebbed and waned until, one by one, people excused themselves to go back to work, or sleep, or watch porn and jerk off (or so Josh, an irreverent young composer, had informed everyone he was about to do). She and David, on the other hand, who had begun talking halfway through dinner, had stayed.

What it felt like was college, first few weeks of freshman year, opening up to her lovely roommate, Wendy—if she'd also wanted to sleep with Wendy. For three hours, their conversation meandered in the best way: whatever one brought up to talk about, the other was happy to run with. David had grown up dirt poor outside of

Cleveland, the youngest of six, and he'd briefly studied art at Cleveland State on scholarship, but dropped out and gotten his M.F.A. and a teaching job only a decade ago, in his late thirties, after years of eclectic jobs. He'd lived on a houseboat in Amsterdam for three years where he paid his rent by playing Hank Williams songs at a cowboy-themed bar; served as an apprentice at a glass-blowing studio in Tucson for a year after that; spent a summer as a nurse's aide at an old folks' home—and every odd experience had left a few wry, funny stories in its wake. Unlike Harden, who'd stopped being curious about the world sometime around 1995 and so rarely tried to make her laugh, David seemed hungry to entertain her. And so eager to listen.

She asked to see his sculptures and he showed her pictures of them on his phone. The latest were a series of surrealist beds and stairs. One had a whirlpool spiral carved in the middle. Another was made of plastic and half submerged in a polyurethane block, like ocean trash. Another was a real, antique four-poster bed but with legs he'd added that were twenty feet tall, and beside it he'd placed a small child's trampoline, spray-painted a bright red. *The Impossible Sleep*, it was called, and though he said it was about insomnia, she read into it something about the elusiveness of peace in life, period, that struck a chord. *Is he pretentious?* she asked herself. *Because I can't do pretentious.* But he wasn't, she decided. Just deep.

Like her, David was drawn to nakedly symbolic things and not embarrassed by that (Harden would find such a preoccupation weird and unmanly). As for her, he kept cutting off his own stories to ask her more: about life as a graphic designer, her childhood, her kids, her favorite artists. Their talk had wrapped up around two fifteen, and by the end of it, she'd already fallen in love with his wonderful sideways grin, the deep dimple faintly visible in his scruff.

See you tomorrow then, he'd said.

Yes, she said, beaming. *See you then.*

That night, lying in bed, her heart thumped in her neck with adolescent joy. If he was to come to her studio, say, because he'd gotten caught in the rain and slipped and fallen into the mud, and the drain in his shower was clogged, which would require he use hers, and if after this shower, he walked to her from the bathroom wearing only the white towel that hung in there, his chest hair (which was thick, she guessed, white with a smattering of black, a bit younger than his head hair) exposed, his stomach yoga-flat, well—would she do anything if that towel somehow came undone and fell to the floor? She didn't know. But not knowing was infinitely more interesting than *no*.

In the days that followed, she threw herself into her work. She got up at quarter to six, drank a huge mug of coffee on the couch while listening to Erik Satie for maximum poignant feelings, then set to it. She was painting, she knew, as well as she could, and for him as much as for herself. She wanted him to see that she wasn't some fluky suburban dilettante but deeper than even she knew, deserving of his affection and respect, this David of the interesting lonely life and the warm, clicking mind.

They respected the other's space, and neither visited the other's studio during the day. But after dinner, they made up for it by walking along the path cut through the forest beside the center with flashlights to guide the way: two friends, yes. Just two new platonic friends. Not even in college had she ever felt both so new and so comfortable, so impatient with her usual doubts and hesitations. Swiftly, she followed her instincts at the easel in laying down a base, then, for hours at a time, homed in like a surgeon, often unconsciously holding her breath, moving faster than usual, as though the Blue Woods review committee might appear at any minute and tell her it was all over. *Sorry! Time's up!* The sense of urgency was giving her paintings a vitality that felt unfamiliar but that she liked very much.

On their walks they were extremely chaste; they walked not touching, with arms crossed or hands in their pockets. They were, she thought, like characters in an Austen novel—the space between their faces (exactly the distance they'd need to bridge if they kissed) alive with the light of their eyes or the expectation of the next look. Until high school, she'd gone to Catholic school—at Don's insistence—and considered herself Catholic. But freshman year of high school she'd arrived at her mother's position—that the Church was a sexist crock, unnecessary to her development as a female human. She started telling people she was agnostic, though secretly she was an atheist. Except that sometimes she thought, *Maybe I'm not.* God the judge up in heaven didn't do it for her, but there was one conception of God she'd always liked, something her uncle Paul had shared during an Easter vigil service they'd been in Northfield for, the one at which candles had been passed out to everyone in the pews, the wicks of which you lit with the candle flame of the person beside you, before passing on your flame to the person on the other side of you—the operation like a reverent assembly line. *Do you notice how the flame flares for a moment, when you touch it to the wick of another candle?* he'd asked the congregation. *I like to imagine God like this, flaring higher for a moment whenever we deeply connect with another person or God's creation. Yes,* she'd often thought, *that was a God she might believe in.*

In college, she'd taken an elective in which she read poets who searched for and documented what her professor called the "secular divine": Gerard Manley Hopkins, Wordsworth, Rumi, W. S. Merwin, Sharon Olds, Mary Oliver. In the little wooded groves of language they made on the page, what was worshipped were the delicate things of the world and love in all its forms. What endeared her to these poets was that they didn't find the emotional life to be secondary to the practical world: to them, it was something worth devoting their whole lives to...and in her walks with David, she knew she was in the presence of a person who felt this way too, a man who maybe didn't *write* about the bittersweet sadness of life, but who thought about it and enjoyed talking about it. He was someone who liked discovering new things as much as he felt it necessary to eulogize lost things. Within a week, Maura saw she had fallen in love.

With four days to go, she started to dread leaving the retreat so much that her stomach hurt; her sessions at the easel were interrupted by bouts of loud, stuttering, acidic shits. Every other night, she'd called and talked to the kids—and especially around their bedtime, she missed them: their lean-strong limbs and soft cheeks, the chicken bouillon smell of the tops of their heads when she kissed them there. But more than that she missed David, already. On the last night, after a feast of paella and chocolate baklava that Debbie, the center's cook, whipped up for them, there was a small reading, and then the poets and essayists and the lone fiction writer wandered over to the artists' studios for an open house. The smiles that instantly crept onto people's faces on grasping the theme of her project receded into something more pensive upon further looking. This made her happy. If it had been only grins she'd have been hurt. That night, she and David felt the need to talk to other people more than they had been, and after it was all over, she went to her room, and he went to his, with a little wave. But an hour later he sent her a text, his first to her—which meant he'd put her number, from the roster they'd all been given on their first day there, into his phone.

Okay if I drop by?

Hollow with fear, she texted back: *Yes.*

Sex, if she wanted it, was imminent, and she let slip the thought: *Just this once.* Upon closing the door behind him, he walked to her, put his hands on both sides of her face, and finally kissed her, his breath smelling of the pot he must have smoked for courage. At the point when they were on her bed, and her bra was off, Maura's phone buzzed from the floor where it had fallen from the pocket of her puddled jeans—and Harden, the kids, her other life, came roaring back. *David, I'm sorry,* she said. *I have to stop. Don't say that,* he said, but she'd crossed a line she couldn't uncross. He sighed and said he understood, kissed her on the forehead and left, and she kicked the side of the sofa three times, hating herself for her stupid morals. As compensation the morning after, in bed, she completed the fantasy, and naked, spectral David made her come twice.

After breakfast that last morning, standing beside his old Dodge pickup, which he used to ferry materials to and from his studio at home, and was now going to drive back to Portland, he held her in a firm embrace.

I feel like I want to stay another month here, just with you, he said.

She nodded, unable to speak.

Can I call you—or write you after this?

Yes, she said.

I actually feel like asking if I could come see you, he said, *but that's probably asking too much.*

It might be, she said. *But we'll see.*

Two days passed before he emailed her—and they picked up right where they left off. For two years before all this, a few times a week, she'd been in the habit of going on a nighttime run, two or three miles, to clear her head and—to be honest—to avoid Harden, who preferred to spend his evenings in front of the TV in the living room scanning channels, drinking his Newcastles (always Newcastle), decompressing from his day. So it was during these runs that turned into walks that she would talk to David. They had unlimited calling on their cell phone plan, same bill every month; there would be no reason for Harden to ever check or suspect. The route she took around the neighborhood, always the same, became a ritual, the scenery that slid past as familiar and welcome as the sound of his voice.

She talked about Harden: how he didn't seem to think about her when she wasn't right in front of him, how he was a good dad but how he bored her to tears, how she just wasn't interested in talking to him anymore, and how it seemed the feeling was mutual. David talked about his ex, Sarah: how narcissistic she was, this part-time actress/grant writer/only daughter of two shrinks; how she'd cheated on him with an old college friend; how she'd emotionally checked out on him when his dad was dying a year ago and he'd had to go to Cleveland to care for him. *You, though,* he said, one October night after a rain, pale orange leaves plastered to the black shiny sidewalks, *I knew before I even talked to you that you were a good person.*

I don't think I'm that good, she replied. *I'm probably not even in the top fiftieth percentile.*

David chuckled. *Spoken like a former grade grubber.*

I'm serious though, she said. *I mean, just think about what we're doing right now.*

Maura, he said solemnly, *I think you're definitely in the top twenty-five.*

She laughed. *So I'm basically a C-minus human being.*

I can't even make a joke about that, he said. *To me, you're off the charts.*

A month of this turned to two, early fall turned to winter—and in between their Tuesday and Thursday night talks, David began sending her things. Jack Gilbert was one of his favorite poets, so he texted her his poems, in real time, without prelude, as if he were writing them just for her (she loved the suspense of waiting for the next line—and the autocorrect mistakes that popped up now and then). He sent her iPhone videos of himself in his studio or out on his boat, narrating what was on his mind, showing her his dog, Ralphie. The blood trapped under a thumbnail after he'd dropped a pipe on it. A giant moth wrapped in a spiderweb like a mummy. She didn't send videos back; she was worried she'd not be able to bring herself to delete them and would be found out, so she'd simply made do by mining her days for pictures or articles that would make him laugh his David laugh—or make him say, in all earnestness, *Isn't that something.* The two distinct selves she'd been before—Work Maura and Home Maura—had sprouted a sister: Maura in Love. The belief that life was obligation, that only the lucky few experienced true love in their life, that there was a ceiling on how fulfilled she would ever feel—all that was burning away like fog to reveal an almost sacred truth: Connection is everything. Stagnancy, death.

She did what was needed of her at work, no more, no less. With the kids she felt more full of love to give, but she also felt guilty over what she was doing to their dad and (who was she kidding) greedy to do things that would demonstrate to David what a loving, tough, wonderful mother she was. The only person who suffered from her new brightness was Harden. Because it was impossible to not punish him with even more than the usual distance. He who was committing the unforgivable sin of not being *him.*

I wish we'd gone through with it that night, David said one night when she was a block away from home.

I know, she said. *I'm sorry.*

A fluffy white Maine coon was stretched out on the windowsill of the house she'd been passing by, face in shadow, furry back lit by the ambient lamplight of its owner's living room. The air was damp and thick, like cold jelly.

There is *something we could do instead,* she'd said, and immediately her neck had flushed.

What do you mean? he asked.

Over the phone, she said. *We could pretend.*

For a few long seconds, David hadn't responded, and she wondered if she'd proved herself unworthy of him with this smutty talk. Then he'd said, *Where could you even do it?*

She'd already ruled out going down to the basement once everyone was asleep; doing anything while they were in the house seemed wrong. However, the garage could be seen as a separate building from the house: if she just got into the Wagoneer and sat there with the lights off, her ears half aware of the door to the inside....

When she called him back, she asked him where he was, and he said, *In bed, where do you think?* and that made her laugh out loud. And when he asked her where she was and she told him, that was enough to get them going—the ridiculous wrongness of it. David wasn't good at dirty talk. Twice he said, *I'm bad at this,* until he saw how his reticence wasn't helping. So he opened himself up to the awkwardness of it because, for her, he'd be willing to feel ashamed and to fail—another thing Harden would never do. His words were the only things available to get her off, so he found the words she needed and meant them, and she found the words he needed back. At one point, she inclined the seat back to create more room. And when they were both finished, David let loose a beautiful little moan.

You're sitting in an SUV with your pants down right now, aren't you? he said.

And together they'd laughed at the absurdities people submitted themselves to for love.

All three months of winter—a period that saw her walks in the snow at night evolve into talks in her heated car in the parking lot during lunch—they spoke futilely about a way to meet up, if only for half a day somewhere, a ruse.

Maura began thinking about the mechanics of being with David for real—not just in secret, but openly. She was building her case (for herself and maybe, subliminally, she realized later, for her mom): millions of marriages break up every year, and many people, knowing themselves better now than they had when they were young, were much happier the second time around—this wasn't just true for her mom, it was true of half her parents' friends. People of her generation were supposed to be savvier about marriage than their parents, having been children themselves of divorce; most were careful not to jump in too early. Instead, they'd bided their time, dated around a bunch, figured out what they really, truly needed in a person, married in their late twenties, early thirties, had kids a few years later, if that's what they wanted. So many of her friends, but not her and Harden. The divide between the sexes had collapsed; couples were friends, equals, as much as lovers.

You saw this dynamic presented so well in commercials, on TV, in indie movies. Honest communication and authentic friendship were the great new magic available to the modern couple. Men at least understood the importance of it, even if they sucked at it. Women demanded it, in a way their mothers— even the hippie moms—hadn't. This, so the theory went, was why her generation's marriages were more likely to last.

Except that she and Harden had never been good at talking to each other—that had always been their relationship's great weakness. He'd been there for her from the beginning: reliable, handsome, funny in a dry, half-assed, slightly superior way that made her feel safe. He was salt of the earth; with him around, she'd known she wouldn't need to change a single thing about herself, which was one kind of freedom. He legitimately admired her talents, even if he didn't understand them. But he didn't care about his own inner life or hers; he wasn't curious or forth-coming or funny in the ways she wished he was; after college, he'd fallen far too eagerly into the mold of his brothers, his dad. The Williams men were like World War II veterans who hadn't been through anything particularly traumatic, just looking for a comfortable life, a place to call home. Wry, TV-loving providers. Good with their kids, but not passionate or ambitious. And no way would that ever change. That was the fucking killer.

In May, eight months after she and David met—after she'd shared her worries about her mom's drinking and the news about her uncle's cancer diagnosis; after she'd been there for him, virtually, checking in every hour, when Ralphie had to be rushed to the vet after eating some guacamole he'd left out after a party; after sending Ralphie get-well biscuits she found and shipped online with the old Bank One credit card she never used anymore; after probably a dozen more trysts over the phone, in the car, in the tub when she was alone and working from home in the afternoon; after sharing three topless pictures (stored in the Taxes 2003 folder on her work computer); and after many more long, deep, conversations, more brazen now, stolen as she drove home from work and sat idling in the driveway or at work in a spare conference room—they finally set it up, a rendezvous.

She had a meeting in Boston with a client in the morning that was done at eleven A.M. Instead of going to the lunch, she'd taken the rest of the day off. He was already in the hotel room on the seventh floor; she knocked, and the door opened, and there he was, fully clothed and smiling. They hugged a long time, squeezing and squeezing, her cheek roughed by the bristly scruff he kept trimmed to a week's growth, and then she kissed him, a warning shot. And then they were finally doing with bodies what they'd done only with words. What she expected and what actually was happening flickered back and forth. In the heat of it, she said the same things she said when they were pretending, as did he, and the syncing up of the imagined and the real was its own pleasure. Afterward, they showered together and ordered room service from under the covers. Lying beside him, his heavy arm across her chest, she realized she would never again be a fully faithful wife; in a matter of minutes she'd been relocated to a different corner of humanity: the land of cheaters.

They ate their tiramisu; David took two forkfuls and let her have the rest. Then, for an hour or so, they slept. On waking to the alarm David set on his phone, as if it were morning instead of three in the afternoon, he put his jeans back on, pushed the room's huge, ugly, heavy, shiny teal curtain aside and looked at the harbor. Lying there alone, she felt lonely, even with him and his strong back a few yards away, so she got up and stood beside him, slipped a hand in his back pocket, like some tween girl at the mall with her boyfriend. Below them was a cove of still water, a scattered assortment of sailboats stuck to it like toothpicked hors d'oeuvres left over after a waiter's first pass through a crowd. One yacht looked asleep under the hazy late spring sun.

There really is a place for you up in Maine, you know, he said, as they embraced before she left.

I know, she said.

In fact, he said, hesitating, pausing, gathering strength, *I could even live here half the time. So you could be closer to your kids.*

She stepped back to look at him, eyes big; this was news. *Really?*

Yeah, he said. *Someone I know in the classics department has an arrangement like that. You'd just have to get an apartment.*

You're serious, she said.

We could try it out, at least, he said. *If*—he paused—*that's something you're willing to do.*

David, she said, *that's so nice. It's amazing you'd do that.*

Well, David said, *what can I say? I'm in it to win it. But you knew that already.* And he smiled a little lovesick smile.

On the elevator ride down—she went by herself, just in case she saw someone she knew—the woman reflected in the tall, narrow mirror looking alarmed but happy. She had feared, she was realizing now, that she was part of some ego trip for him, some fling. But if anything, he might want her more. How about that?

Two weeks later Harden went through her purse while she was asleep and found the many, many text conversations (but not the photos and videos from David—those she offloaded on to her computer immediately). And thus the era of her double life ended and a new torturous era of exposure had begun.

Around four, Maura helped the kids gather up their beach stuff, and by ten after, they were walking into the driveway of the cottage. Ella and Evan poured into the front door recharged by the sun, but she was exhausted.

Harden was on his laptop at the kitchen island, drinking coffee. Blue golf shirt, cargo shorts, flip-flops that revealed his thick yellowing toenails. (David had beautiful olive toes, beautiful olive fingers.) Ella grabbed a plastic cup and filled it at the sink; Evan went to the freezer to grab a frozen Snickers bar.

"See any sharks down there?" Harden asked, just as he'd asked the last three days.

"We made a bunch of moats," Evan said. "I called it Moat-apalooza."

"We didn't fight once either," Ella added.

"It's true, actually," Maura said. "You guys did really well."

Evan was already gnawing on the Snickers with his back molars. Ella jerked her head back to down the last of her water.

"You feel like doing takeout?" Harden asked her.

"I wouldn't mind that, no."

"Anything in particular?"

"I don't really care."

"Okay."

"I'm actually feeling pretty wiped," she said. "I might go lie down for a little while if that's all right."

"Sure," Harden said. This was fair. She'd had them for hours now. It was his turn anyway. She smiled her eyes at him, the tiniest possible amount in thanks, then shut that down and looked away: the kinder she was toward him the harder it would be to do what was necessary later. Soon.

For two hours she slept, dreamless. On waking, she was sweaty and hot, so she took a cold shower. The kids and Harden were gone when she walked into the kitchen; a note on the table said, *Out shopping,* in Harden's blocky handwriting. When the Wagoneer pulled up in the driveway, Maura was standing at the kitchen sink with a glass of water, watching a red squirrel undulate along the power line in the backyard. Instead of two white pizza boxes or two white plastic sacks of Chinese, Evan walked in the front door proudly holding a paper grocery bag on its side, awkwardly against his belly, one hand pinching shut the top, as Ella skipped alongside him. Their faces were alive with suppressed glee. Something was up. Evan set the bag on the dinner table and said, "Want to see what we got for dinner?"

"I'm almost afraid to look," she said. "You guys are acting *very* strange."

Unable to wait a second longer, Evan quickly opened the top, then slid out, on a piece of white butcher paper, two big whole fish, each at least a foot and a half long. Green-brown skin, rosy spots, dull here, shiny there. Mouths open as if in shock. Their smell hit her faintly at first, then expanded like a sponge.

"We got them at Shaw's," Ella said.

"They're sea bass," said Evan. "We can each share one. You and me, and Ella and Dad."

Harden had come in past the doorframe with one more grocery bag in his arm, his keys in his free hand.

"What happened to getting takeout?" Maura asked.

"It was Evan's idea," Harden said. "I stopped for some booze and he asked if we could eat these instead. He said he saw something on TV where they caught and cooked a whole fish over a campfire and wanted to try it."

"Bear Grylls," Evan said. "He did it when they went to Tahiti."

"Oh. Okay. Did you get a say in this too?" she said, looking at Ella. Sometimes Harden and Evan railroaded her, she who was so eager to please.

She nodded. "Yeah. I picked one out. That one. Rosie."

"You named them?" Maura said.

"The one with the poking-out eyes is named Bug-Eye," said Evan.

Oh, these kids. She couldn't not go along now. But the project annoyed her a little. Now they'd have to figure out how to cook them, when all she wanted was to be fully awake to this last night of their innocence, stress-free.

"So what's your plan?" she asked Harden. "Just throw them in the oven?"

"Yeah. Should be super simple. Some lemon, oil, salt, and pepper. Maybe some of that rosemary we still have from the chicken you made."

"By 'we' you mean who exactly?"

"Me. And the kids. They wanted to help. You can just sit there and man the wine."

"Mom can't 'man the wine.' She's a lady," Ella said.

"Woman the wine," said Evan.

"It's just an expression," Harden said.

"So you'll do it?" Maura asked.

"Yeah. Sure."

"Okay," she said. "Thanks." Civility would be necessary once they parted ways. Couldn't hurt to practice that too.

"We're still all good with this plan?" Harden said. "Evan? All systems go?"

Evan made a dramatically confused face. "Why would I change my mind after it was totally my idea?" he said. "That doesn't even make *sense*."

Harden grew up fishing with his dad but didn't know the bone structure of sea bass, so he watched a quick instructional YouTube video on his laptop, his nose scrunched as he took mental notes. First, he sawed swiftly down their dirty-white bellies.

Then he scraped away the bloody black, white, and beige guts with the side of his knife onto the cutting board and into the trash. Almost tenderly, he lifted each gutted body up, thumb hooked under the head, and rinsed the body cavity clean. Then he placed the fish—each still very much a recently alive creature—on a clean towel, patted them dry, before setting them, heads and tails intact, on a sheet of tinfoil. He knew the kids wanted to be involved in some way, so he sliced some lemons and told Ella to stuff them into the body cavities, along with a sprig of rosemary. He poured olive oil on top of the carcasses and asked Evan to wash his hands before he rubbed the oil around the skin with his fingers. He gave Ella the salt-shaker and told her three shakes on each. Then Evan with the pepper. So it would be even. This man who knew them so well. Their one and only father.

Watching him from where she sat at the kitchen island, drinking the not-great Pinot Grigio he'd bought at the store, Maura felt a flare-up of the old affection. He wasn't the right partner for her, but he was a good man. About that there had never been a doubt. Someday—probably it would take years, once his heart had healed from their divorce—he'd find a more easily satisfied woman who would appreciate him for that goodness more than she could. His future, better partner was out there for him, Maura thought, feeling generous. He just didn't know it yet. As David had been out there for her.

They ate at the picnic table set in the weedy backyard as they had the past three nights. The trees swayed ever so slightly in the wind the ocean sent up the coast. The mosquitoes showed mercy. Eating the sea bass was difficult, what with the endless bones they had to pluck out of their forks and their mouths, but even Evan found this to be novel and interesting rather than a pain in the ass. His weird, spontaneous idea had been honored and made real, and that blessed the entire thing. Maura was quiet and watchful: her family's happiness and the golden light warming their faces were making it all too hard. How much easier tonight would be if they were at one another's throats! If Harden hadn't been making such a point, the past few days, to be so goddamn nice.

After Harden went in and returned with a tub of ice cream and four bowls, Evan said, "I want to do go-carts next time we come."

"Who said there'd be a next time?" Harden said.

She looked at him, wondering if this was meant for her, but it wasn't. He was looking at Evan.

Evan raised his eyebrows. "Why? Is it too expensive?"

Now Harden shot Maura a look: he was aware of her lie to them about money troubles.

"No," Harden said. "We just might want to go somewhere else next year."

"Aw, man!" Evan said.

"Hey," Maura said. "Be thankful we could even do this."

"That's right," Harden said. "Listen to your mother."

After dinner, Harden offered to do the dishes, but when Maura offered to dry (maybe showing she was decent was a better approach, she'd thought), he said he had it covered. Which meant he either was trying to impress her with his goodness or merely didn't want to be forced to talk to her. Even though he'd been softer in his demeanor toward her here, they'd still found ways of avoiding each other. They sat at their laptops in different rooms; he went to bed first, she followed later. For a while, she and the kids watched Animal Planet together, and then Evan suggested they keep the games going and play some croquet. They'd played at her sister-in-law's place last summer and he'd kicked everyone's ass, so this would be, Maura knew, a chance to end what had been a good day for him—a great day, really—on a high note.

"I think it's a bit late for that," Harden said. Which was technically true. It was eight fifteen, and their summer bedtime was eight thirty.

"Come on. Just one game," Evan said. "It's our last night here."

"We'll let you go first," Ella offered.

"We could probably do just one, couldn't we?" Maura said, wanting to be on their side this one last time.

"Okay, fine," Harden said. "Just one."

Evan set up the course. White wickets in each hand, he moved around the lawn like a little robot, pacing out distances, crouching to eye up whether this wicket was even with that wicket over there. Every time he stuck one in, Maura enjoyed the satisfyingly soft puncture it made in the ground—*boop!*—like sticking candles in a birthday cake. His intense need to have things *just so*, his *disability*, would serve him well, if properly channeled: that was what she liked to believe. Some kids with what he had became engineers and computer programmers. Thomas Edison—some people on Asperger's blogs thought even *he* had it. You had to stay hopeful. There was no other choice.

Ella asked them what colors they wanted to be, then handed out mallets and balls, trying to be useful too. Youngest to oldest. To the other side and back would be a game. In a single turn, Evan moved all the way to the other side, so it was playing catch-up from there. But on the return trip, he faltered. The terrain along the far left was bumpy and unpredictable. His ball seemed on line at first but veered past the outer edge of a wicket at the last second. When it happened again, the same way, on his next turn, he pounded his mallet into the ground, hard, four times.

"This ground fucking *sucks*!"

"Hey!" Maura said. "Language!"

"It's all bumpy!" Evan said. "It's messing up my shots!"

"You're the one who set up the course," Harden said, his mallet wedged between his crossed arms.

"I didn't set up the *ground*!" Evan said.

So, here it is, Maura thought, as she watched the tendons in Evan's neck grow taut. A return to reality. The bubble had burst. It was actually a relief.

"Just calm down," Harden said. "We're all going to have the same problems with it."

"*You* calm down!" he said.

"I am being calm, actually," Harden said calmly.

"*No, you're not!*" screamed Evan.

For a moment, the two males sized each other up, one wild, one not. Since the night he'd come to her as she sobbed in the aftermath of her confession to Harden, Evan had been testier with Harden because he believed his dad was to blame for their money-related disagreement more than she was; as a rule, he tended to take her side. She'd tried her best to disabuse him of this. But because she stayed so vague, he presumed she was protecting Harden and believed what he wanted to believe.

"Seriously," Harden said. "If the ground sucks for you, it sucks for all of us."

"Except maybe you won't hit it the same place I do!" Evan said.

Harden sighed, then bugged his eyes out at her, beseechingly. This was a look they'd shared so many times, in the grip of an Evan meltdown, for many years. A way to touch base.

"Evan," she said, "we have a choice here. Either we can play like this, or you can stop playing and we'll play without you. But none of us wants you to stop playing."

"If nobody else has problems, then the game doesn't count," Evan said.

"Let's just play and worry about that later," said Harden.

All of them endured an awkward limbo state for a second, waiting for him to go with the flow. She thought of her painting series—the Edward Hopper sadness in a moment of what was supposed to be fun. Maybe next would be Wonder Woman playing croquet, wielding a striped and starred mallet like a sword, her children flipping out around her.

"Mom," Ella said, "I think you're up next."

Whatever charm the idea of family croquet had once held by now had evaporated; at this point it was whimsical punishment.

Games like this were fun only with a lively running commentary—the kind of teasing and encouragement her uncle, Father Paul, always brought to the occasion when he played croquet with her and Shade on visits. *Give it a nice little whack,* he'd say. *That a girl! You better watch it, kiddo, I'm hot on your tail!* Her sweet, supportive uncle, whom she hadn't seen in years, who was dying. Whom she still hadn't even bothered to call.

She'd resolved to call ten times but hadn't followed through. She was afraid to: it was that simple. He wouldn't be unkind to her, but he might tell her things she didn't want to hear. Ask her questions she didn't have good answers for. She wasn't prepared enough yet for a reckoning, even if the reckoning was mild. Though maybe, she thought now, watching Ella line up her shot, once she'd made her announcement, that would change. The whirling in her head and stomach would stop, and she'd know exactly what to say.

Now, though, there was this game to endure. After every one of Evan's frustrating shots, Maura bit her tongue, because no matter what she said, he'd lash out. Her *ooh, not quite*s after Ella's shots were so feeble they'd have been better left unsaid. And then Harden knocked her ball with his.

"Well, well," he said. "Look at what we have here."

The rule about hitting someone else's ball, of course, was that you could, as a reward, whack their ball off course or take two extra strokes. Hitter's choice. When Paul would knock their balls away, he'd just tap them, a harmless little *bonk.* But Harden wasn't in the mood to be merciful. He scanned the yard until his eyes fell on the woods. Then he crowded the ball in that direction. Whether it was Evan's anger or the beers catching up with him, she didn't know, but his face was swollen with anger again.

"Do you really have to?" she said lamely. "It'll just make the game take longer."

"Sorry," he said. "That's not how it works." Right foot securing his own ball, he went into a full golfer's wind-up. And with a bold, fast *pock!* her ball barreled eagerly over the grass and into the woods, where a bush swallowed it whole.

I deserve this, she thought. *For David, for being a bad daughter and niece, for what I'll do tomorrow.* At the bush, she moved to her knees, reached in, face turned away so as not to get jammed in the eye. Blindly, she found the ball with her fingers and dropped it back in play. With her first swing, she only topped the ball: it went a foot. Frustrated, she swung again, this time chunking the ground six inches in front of the ball, sending it nowhere.

"Hey!" Evan yelled. "That's cheating! You can only swing once per turn."

This was true, but she couldn't help herself, she needed the satisfaction of a decent strike. Which her next one was—a great hit, actually. Even so, it stopped ten feet away from the nearest wicket: that's how far away she'd been.

"Mo-om!" Evan's voice sounded mournful. "You can't do that!"

"Fine, Evan," she said, hating herself. "Then I guess I'll just lose."

But he wasn't having that. Like a demented gym teacher, he stomped over, grabbed her ball, walked with purpose toward the woods, and dropped it where it belonged.

"There," he said. "Now do it right this time."

Back inside, after Evan had won to the relief of everyone involved, Maura got the kids ready for bed. As Harden watched ESPN from the couch, she gave Evan melatonin to help him wind down, then read them *Bartholomew and the Oobleck*, a recent favorite, and *Frog and Toad*. She stood watch as they brushed teeth, turned on the white noise machine as they slipped under the covers of the beds pressed side by side in the room they'd been sharing all week, and then squatted beside their beds and kissed her fingers and pressed them to their foreheads, her nightly blessing. Before she left, Harden showed up to say a quick good night, and then she said good night too and closed their door until it was almost shut. Evan liked at least a two-inch gap to remind him he wasn't alone.

Finally, it was adult time—just she and Harden left to their own devices. She might need to invite him out to the deck for the conversation, she realized; he might stay on the couch watching TV until he felt tired enough to tuck in. Wanting the courage, she found her empty wineglass on the kitchen counter and refilled it, almost to the top.

Beside the sofa, she watched the baseball highlights Harden was watching, the usual parade of macho wit. Harden looked over at her, acknowledging her, then turned back to the screen, so much smaller here than their giant TV at home.

"Wanna come join me on the porch?" she said.

He turned back to her, skeptical. "I don't know. Do I?" No one could accuse him of being dumb.

"I think it might be good for us to talk," she said.

The owners of this house had strung two strands of Christmas lights along the perimeter of the enclosed porch, and for the past few nights they'd plugged them in. The lights gave the space an intimate Mexican cantina vibe, but tonight Maura realized such cheeriness would seem discordant, so she left them off. She sat in one of the big, supremely comfortable chairs and waited. When Harden finally did appear, he was backlit at the entrance and then engulfed by the dimness as he sat on the other side of the big square coffee table between them.

"So," he said, looking at her coldly, "what is it you have to tell me?"

He already sensed it. The refrigerator droned in the next room. A half-moon, not visible from this angle, was casting its silver dust over the bumpy, impossible lawn. The children hopefully were asleep.

"I think I want a divorce," she said.

The word was profane, after the day they'd had. For a moment he was quiet. Then he cleared his throat. "You *think* you want a divorce," he said. "Okay. Well, you've said that before. Are you saying you want it or not?"

She took a big, shaky breath. "I guess what I'm saying is that, yes, I want one. I want a divorce."

Harden nodded and stiffly took a pull from his beer, and for a moment she was afraid he'd stand up and throw it against the mesh wall.

"So," he said, "you don't even want to try to make this work. You're just done, and that's it."

She couldn't look at him. "I just think, at this point, with the way I feel, I'd just be wasting our time."

"Yeah," he said. "A waste of time. Seventeen years. Big fucking waste."

He leaned forward, like he was experiencing stomach pain, then turned his head toward her and looked at her, like a predator.

"You realize this will screw up the kids," he said. "You know that, right?"

"I know it'll be hard. Divorces are always hard."

"But I guess you're okay with that. Because you're not going to be around for it."

"That's not true. I will be around for it. Just the same as you." She paused. "I'd get an apartment somewhere, maybe in Brighton. This is something that people do."

"How progressive of you."

"Harden," she said.

"We have a son who freaks out about normal things every day. And now you're going to add this to his plate? It's selfish. It's beyond selfish."

"I know it is," she said. "Of course it is. But I'm sick of being unhappy."

"Yeah, well, welcome to the club."

He shook his head at her ever so slightly.

"So," he said after a while, "what am I supposed to do now? Get a lawyer? Is that the next step?"

"I don't know."

"You planning on telling the kids about this?"

"I thought I'd do it tomorrow morning."

"*No,*" he snapped. "*Fuck* that. Let them enjoy their last morning here, at least. Tell them back home or something. But not here. No fucking way."

"Okay," she said. "I'll wait until we get back then."

"I want to be there when you tell them," he said—and here he choked up. She saw his lips retract, his eyes close. "I want them to know I'll be there."

"Both of us will be there," she said. But it took everything in her not to cry.

What a horrible person I am, she thought. But they were just words; she didn't really believe it, not right now. For a while, they just sat there together, looking out at the lawn. The bass line to "Brown Eyed Girl" thumped faintly in the distance. A woman whooped with joy. Someone a few houses down, probably outside having a campfire. What it made her remember in the dark here, faint sounds around them, just the two of them, was camping. The trip they took about five miles north of here, the year after they'd graduated from Boston College, their second year together. The plastic tarp of the tent had smelled like canned mushrooms. A sweet evangelical couple staying at the lot over came by offering them peanut butter cookies, and with their innocence in mind, every night but the first, when they'd been too tired, they'd fucked as quietly as possible, so as not to make it weird for them. Which had only made it more exciting, every tiny peep the equivalent of a moan. How was it possible that that young couple had been them?

Harden cleared his throat, twice. His gaze moved from outside to the floor beyond his feet. "Do you remember that conference I went to a few years ago? In New Orleans?"

"Sure."

"There was a woman I met there who basically asked me to her room one night."

"Really?"

"Yeah. She was hot too. Dirty-blond hair, big boobs. Tall Amazon type. We got pretty drunk. She'd just dumped her husband and was hot to trot. Sandra. That was her name."

"Okay," Maura said, not sure what else to say. If he was trying to dredge up some jealousy in her...he'd succeeded. She shouldn't have felt anything, but she did. It was something physiological, it seemed. Beyond her control. "Did you do it?" She hoped he'd say yes. Then he'd have sinned too.

"I thought about it, I'll be honest," he said. "I mean, nobody would have ever known. But then I reminded myself that I was married and went back to my room. And rubbed one out instead."

This was funny, but it wouldn't be right to laugh. He wasn't smiling.

"You're a really good person," she said. "I mean that."

"Yeah, well," he said. "A lot of good it's done me."

Again, they fell silent. Maura felt the impulse to crack a joke, to maybe tell him about the camping trip she'd just thought of. But that was a cop-out. That was just her trying to slip out of the grip of Harden's pain, fool herself into thinking, because he wasn't crying or screaming, he was going to be fine.

This would be her penance too. To force herself to sit with those she wounded. To watch the bleeding.

"If it doesn't work out with him," he said, "I'm not going to take you back. You think I would. But I wouldn't. I just want you to know that."

"I wouldn't expect you to," she lied. She'd imagined he would.

"Guy like that," he continued, "never married, no kids, might get sick of always having to share you. He might decide it's not worth the hassle, dealing with a kid like Evan. And then what? What's to stop him from finding another person to moon over at his next little retreat. Stuff like this happens. Every single day."

This Harden was more familiar to her: the one who considered all the angles, like everything was a business deal. But about David he was wrong.

"It's not like that," she said. "I wouldn't do this if it was."

"Well," he said, "I hope you're right."

A few moments later, Harden pushed himself up to standing.

"Anyway," he said bitterly. "Good talk."

She looked at him.

"I'm going to go inside now."

"Okay," she said. "I might stay out here awhile longer."

"I figured."

I love you, Maura almost said. Because it was true. In a dusty, nostalgic way that didn't matter anymore, she did. But that would be rubbing salt in the wound.

"Good night," she said instead, and Harden nodded and left her sitting with her empty wineglass in the dark.

Now the difficult thing was done. Well, one of them. The least difficult of the two. She didn't feel relief or joy, but, instead, a cool richness to the passing of the seconds that reminded her, very oddly, of the first time she'd held Evan in her arms, the doctors finally gone, Harden hunched forward in a chair beside her hospital bed. Fifteen stories up in their hospital downtown. *He's finally here,* she'd thought—*my baby's here!* Yet you didn't start cheering or high-fiving, even though you'd waited nine months for this moment to come; immediately, *immediately,* you sensed the immensity of the task ahead, not as a burden but as a welcome call to grow up. This wasn't a joyful moment, of course. But it was important. No doubt about that. A step had been taken she wasn't sure she could take.

Maura wanted to go inside and refill her glass, but from the kitchen came the sound of the refrigerator opening and closing, so she waited. Let Harden get his beer and retreat to their room. Give him space out of respect.

When it sounded as though he was gone, she went inside and filled her glass to the top and took a sip. The kitchen here was old but cute—part *Design*Sponge*, part old maid. White cabinets with midcentury black handles, white-veined blue Formica countertops made to look like marble. One of those Elvis clocks where his hips rock back and forth, measuring time. How odd that this giant moment in her life would happen here of all places. The owners would never know.

One thing she could do was go back to her chair, turn on the Christmas lights, and text David to tell him she'd done it. But that seemed crass to her, something a teenaged girl would do, not a woman dumping a Pandora's box of hurt onto her family. Tomorrow, after they got home, she could go out for a walk and debrief him. Though it wouldn't be real, she knew, until she told the kids.

The porch held nothing for her anymore. It was spoiled.

Nor did she want to sit in the living room or go to bed.

But if she wanted, it occurred to her, her mind listing now slowly to David—the reason for all this drama, lover of boats, his lake—she could slip on sandals and walk down to the beach. Take her wine with her.

Within a few minutes she was out of the house, walking under the night sky. As she passed the second house on the way to the steep stairs, the sounds of the nearby party flared louder; behind a house she glimpsed a smear of fire and laughing people in demonic chiaroscuro. She walked on the gravel along the edges of the road, the grit shifting with every step, just the tiniest give. Already she was regretting bringing a wineglass—it was a thing she had to worry about now, to hold and keep track of, so to remove its power over her she downed it all and then carried it, lazily, by the bulb. The head rush was nice. It matched the velvety air.

The view of the beach was obstructed by trees until there was a clearing. Then: an orange wedge of moon, a dim halo effect around its curved side. She couldn't see the tide from here, only the dark plain stretching to a horizon, but she could hear its hypnotic sound. The sky was clear, and as she descended the stairs, using the light on her phone to navigate, she snuck glimpses of the stars embedded in it. There was a Jack Gilbert poem David once texted her that she'd loved, that she'd come to hold close as a guiding light in the conversation she constantly had about leaving. Not since she was a girl in Mrs. Morneau's English class had she memorized a poem. Her favorite part was the beginning:

> We find out the heart only by dismantling what
> the heart knows. By redefining the morning,
> we find a morning that comes just after darkness.
> We can break through marriage into marriage.
> By insisting on love we spoil it, get beyond
> affection and wade mouth-deep into love.
> We must unlearn the constellations to see the stars.

"Break through marriage into marriage," of course, had made her wonder if Jack was talking about finding joy within commitment, rather than setting it aside for something riskier and more honest. Maybe so. But in her case, it served as a reminder of what a social worker friend had once said of the benefits of therapy—that sometimes you had to dismantle a thing completely in order to see it clearly and to be able to build something new. Before you can rise like a phoenix, you need to be ashes first.

In the past months, whenever she needed to feel her struggle was noble, not just some craven midlife crisis, she'd think of her college friend Natasha Barron, a pediatrician in Olympia, Washington, with a flair for theatrics and bold pantsuits. Married with three girls. On National Coming Out Day a few years back Natasha had come out, at the age of thirty-six, as bisexual... and maybe a year later announced that she and Trent were separating, splitting custody, and that with the help of her new girlfriend and Trent and both their extended families, she was confident the girls were going to grow up in an environment of love and support. The comments section had wished her well in her new brave, authentic life. Knowing it wasn't the same, but wishing it were, Maura hoped the world would support her the same way. If she left for her own truth. But her awakening wasn't so appealing a story, was it? The unoriginal tale of a straight woman realizing, when it was very inconvenient to realize it, that she needed a certain kind of love to feel whole. Only certain types of awakenings were in vogue now, she'd thought, disgusted at how right wing and intolerant that sounded in her head. How petulant and self-serving. But there it was.

Now though—as her flip-flops hit sand and she moved closer to the shoreline—she thought, *I'm past that. I've jumped out of the plane. I'm falling, yes, but falling, at least, is moving.* Once she landed safely—and the landing might be dangerous, she knew—there would be a morning when she'd wake early in David's bed in Portland, and walk out with him to his pontoon boat, painted baby blue, and in the middle of his lake sit on the lawn chairs he had with their coffee and watch the morning bleed over the water. They wouldn't have to hoard time anymore; they'd be present to enjoy the small moments, to talk about their ideas as they occurred to them. If he needed time to work in his studio when she was there, she'd read in the house and go visit him, or no (!), she'd have her own spot in his house to paint. Maybe a spot in her apartment, too. Would she be with him the rest of her life...the way the kids would be? It was dizzying to think of David old, herself old. But this unknown was a better kind of scary than the future she'd dreaded for so long.

Every talk they'd had all these many months was her testing him like an apple for rot, pressing him to find the bruises, the worms. What more could she have done than that?

The only other people within a hundred yards of her here were a young couple to her left, teenagers, gauging by their languid slouches, sitting in the little valley between two sandbanks. To her right, scattered along the long jawbone of coast arching north, were three beach campfires, even though it was a warm night—and at the tip, dim, like a controlled fire, the lights of Provincetown.

Sometimes a clear night sky pulled you up toward it, as if extending an impossible challenge. But tonight, it pushed down, the stars and the darkness a firm weight on her chest. Maura closed her eyes and burrowed deep inside the silence, lowering herself as if by rope into a deep cavern. She didn't pray anymore, but sometimes at night, most often when she was drunk and alone, she would extend her antennae out into the silence like this, listening not for the voice of God, but for reassurance that there was more to life than what there appeared to be. Wanting that, remembering to want that, whether you got the reassurance, was maybe the point. Nights snug in her bed as a little Catholic girl, she'd sometimes imagine shadowy gangster figures cornering her in the clothes closet she could see from her pillow, asking her if she believed Jesus was really the son of God. If a gun barrel were pressed to her little head, would she say yes and die a martyr, or would she lie and hope God understood her predicament? (She'd lie. Her parents would be very angry with her if she were dead.) A few times a year, their teachers marched them to the church basement beside the school and they'd done their confessions. Those little phone booths with the light fastened above the door—white for open, blue for occupied. Everyone giggling in their chairs, counting who'd been in longest, who was the biggest sinner. Father John, who ended up leaving the priesthood when she was in high school (and no wonder, Father John was a *hottie*), had listened to her talk about being mean to Shade, about telling Emma Johnston that her hair looked like someone pooped in it. This poor guy—how seriously could he have taken this exercise? These silly non-sins. Yet you didn't feel it had been official unless there was a penance. Father John got creative, playful with his power. Two Hail Marys and give your brother two hugs this week. Smile at Emma the next time you see her. But what penance, she wondered, would Father John give her if she confessed her sins now? Her stomach puckered: Or Paul?

She didn't really want to hear the answer, so she opened her eyes. A bubbly scroll of water unfurled along the shore, then receded, as if it had abruptly changed its mind.

She could wade in wearing these clothes; the water would be bracing, but she could take a warm shower when she walked back. She glanced over to where she hoped the teenaged kids had disappeared from, but they were still there, watching her.

To them both (she could feel it so sharply here in the dark) she was nothing but some middle-aged lush with a wineglass at the beach, tank top, hair down to the middle of her back, pinned up but loose in places. To the boy, not even a MILF, so what good was she? None. Maybe they were so naive to have thought this beach was private enough to fuck on. Or no. They just wanted a place to make out that felt big but their own. It warmed her to think that even for this particular weasel, who surely knew his way around internet porn, there was still this ageless romantic notion of lying under the stars. Their animal dislike of her reminded her of Evan, how he yelled at her sometimes when she popped by his room to see what he was doing: her mere existence an imposition. She was off the hook for tomorrow morning, thank God. She felt grateful to Harden for insisting it happen later. But that still meant she'd have to tell them soon. And what she didn't imagine earlier today, beyond their shock and sadness, was how they'd maybe come to hate her. For a while. Hopefully only for a while. Though it was possible that Evan might, in his black-and-white way, decide that she was the enemy, full stop.

The dim peace she'd lulled herself into was already receding. Nothing would be clean about this, nothing.

She felt like lowering herself to the sand, lying on her back, and drifting to sleep. That was how exhausted she suddenly was. But though it wasn't exactly dangerous out here, it wasn't exactly safe either. She needed to go back home.

The steps from the beach up to the road looked impossibly steep, but she reminded herself she'd walked up them many times this week, carrying far more than an empty wineglass. As she ascended, she wondered: *Am I a bad person? It can't possibly be true, can it?* Feeling unsteady, she gripped the railing with her right hand. Narrowed her focus to her feet, like a horse wearing blinders. The farther she went, the more her ass and calves burned.

She didn't want to stop until she'd reached the top, but halfway there she felt light-headed and stood still. She felt vaguely uncertain, then woozy. For a moment she thought she'd throw up, but the moment passed.

Usually her answer to the question of her goodness was to say, *Of course I'm good. Good and bad, trying my best and flawed, like everybody else.* The internet memes about personal strength and self-forgiveness some of her girlfriends posted on Facebook and some of the things her therapist had told her helped her believe that too.

But at the moment, as she looked up at the top of the stairs— a few more minutes' work—and the starry sky above, such thinking offered no comfort. Of course she wanted to believe everything she wanted and everything she did was, in the big picture, okay—a big, beautiful mess. And of course the people who were in the business of making other people feel okay about themselves would reassure her that this was true.

The truth, Maura suspected, would be far less forgiving. The truth would cause her and her family pain, delivered in ways she couldn't yet imagine. But, she thought, if that was the cost of finally being true to herself, so be it, and with her tiny light making a path in front of her, she carried on up the stairs.

V. Homecoming

Their plane landed at O'Hare around five in the afternoon, and for the entire four hours it took Britta to drive them from Chicago up to Northfield, Paul slept, hands folded in his lap, head wobbling against the headrest, as if even in sleep he was protesting the situation.

There was plenty of time for her to worry about what lay ahead during the flight, but she'd intentionally avoided it. At thirty thousand feet, she was technically still on vacation, and so—even though it was still only early afternoon—she'd indulged in a few glasses of chardonnay, watched the in-flight movie, read a few chapters of the other murder mystery she'd brought along, then had two cups of black coffee to straighten out. Even after they'd disembarked and were waiting for their luggage to come around on the carousel, Paul standing beside her, grim and withdrawn, she'd distracted herself by scrolling through Facebook on her phone and chatting with the young couple standing beside them. Not yet. Not yet.

But in the silence of Paul's car, heading north to his home, there was no choice but to face things. Since his little breakdown the morning after his confession—an unburdening that had surprised her by making him feel worse—she'd been trying to be strong for him. Depressed as he was, he needed someone to challenge his misery—and clearly that person was her. But as she stole glances at him now beside her, vulnerable as a child, she wondered if his story *was* a little tragic. Could that actually be true? History, as she told her students, wasn't necessarily truth, but a story wrapped around facts by those who held power to control the story, and as new people gained access to power, the story changed. So what was the truth about her brother? What would a cold-eyed journalist decide? How would she weigh the testimony of Paul's friends and parishioners against Paul's feelings now? The truth would land somewhere in the middle, probably—somewhere between tragedy and triumph. Like most people's lives. But the thought didn't reassure her. If only he'd told her about his struggles years ago. She would have done anything to help him. But he hadn't said a word, he'd held it all inside, and the time for big changes was long over. All she could do now was help him accept that. And show him all the ways his version of the truth was wrong.

That night, within a few minutes of walking inside his house, his rolling suitcase rattling behind him, Paul said good night and excused himself to his bedroom. After reading the note his secretary, Jean, had left on the table (*Welcome back! Lots of frozen food in the fridge! I have mail for Paul at the office!*) and taking a long, lukewarm shower, Britta laid on the pullout bed in a fresh T-shirt and shorts but could not sleep. For a while, she thought about Maura, imagined her unable to sleep in her bed at this hour too. Or the couch—maybe Harden had banished her there. She imagined Shade sitting in the dark, playing one of his video games, sunk into his fake leather sofa, legs splayed out the same way Don always sat, colored light from the screen flashing on his face. She imagined her empty house in St. Louis and missed it: her huge king-sized ComforPedic bed; all the space in which there was to roam; the kitchen island where she sat with her black coffee in the morning, listening to NPR and looking out at their side yard, in which her hydrangea bushes would just be starting to bloom. And then, to complete the circuit, she hugged the two big pillows she'd taken from the linen closet, closed her eyes, and imagined she was hugging Don.

In their thirty years together, she'd never stopped feeling lucky to find him, and now that he was gone, she'd never get over it, never. When they'd met, she'd been a broke, single thirty-one-year-old mom. Ray had left them to move to Alaska the year Maura was four. Reason one was that she'd gotten so fat; reason two was because he'd realized he just wasn't *wired to be a family man*, as if it were a matter of genetics, not character. When he'd left, she'd been relieved—their fights were exhausting and near the end he'd started shoving her around—but she'd not at all been prepared for life as a single parent, working two soul-sucking crap jobs just to barely get by.

So then to meet Donald Allan Williams, on only the second date she'd been on with anyone since the divorce, two years later—this funny southern gentleman who couldn't have, but very badly wanted, kids himself; this big, cheerful guy who'd told her she was beautiful two hours into their first date, who was even fatter than she was and therefore in no danger of turning on her the way Ray had; a man who so quickly warmed to Maura and Shade—well, it had felt like returning home after a brutal war. A gift she sometimes wondered if she deserved.

Some of her girlfriends, postmenopause, had confessed to losing their appetite for sex. Just didn't want it anymore. But not her, not them. Up until the very end, both of them past sixty, their sex life had remained a reliable pleasure. During their life together, she'd come to see their weight as a mutual dismissal of what the world considered weak, even disgusting. They were united in their bounty. They overflowed and didn't care. As they'd gotten older, Don had gone from 250 pounds to 300 to 325. The last few years of his life, his formidable gut covered all but the tip of his penis when naked, and they'd had to get more creative in bed with positions. But even those accommodations had felt like something uniquely theirs.

Once a week, or twice if the first time was especially good, she'd come up to him and either touch the top of his head, as if in blessing, if he was sitting in his giant Barcalounger, or kiss him firmly on the lips, if he was standing. She'd say she was going into the bedroom to "tidy up"—would he care to join her?—and heart beating fast, she undressed, got completely naked under the sheets, and waited. A bit later, he entered, dark eyes sparkling, and at the foot of the bed, took off all his clothes except for his plaid boxers, which he liked her to remove herself. His chest blushed, the pinkish shape always a diffuse thick diamond. His big teardrop earlobes swelled hot with lust. Atop their king-sized bed, they discovered each other again and again, exchanged reliable and original favors. In the heat of the moment, he sometimes grabbed handfuls of her, gently shoved her flesh around, reveling in it. *Oh, Brit, yeah, Britty, you're so fucking good...*in that molasses voice of his, which she missed almost as much as his touch.

After he'd died, some of her friends had suggested, unprompted, that she sell the house. Take the profits, buy a condo, start fresh. Get away, they didn't have to say, from the room in which Don had lay dead as she'd screamed at him to breathe and the ambulance raced uselessly over. To which she'd thought, Why? Was his death supposed to scare her? Did they think her beautiful home had somehow been *spoiled*? What she could have told them, putting on her history teacher hat, was that for centuries your dead went right smack up on your kitchen table at home, coins laid on their closed eyes. Your children, your parents, everyone. So no, she wouldn't sell the house, thank you very fucking much.

And she hadn't—she'd weathered the temptation and stayed on and had no plans to move. But as fond as she was of it, it wasn't the same place. Nor would it ever be again.

For three days straight, Paul didn't leave his room except to use the bathroom and have a little toast and soup. In Sister Bay and Rome, she'd been able to drag him out into the world, even when he didn't feel like it; like a child, he'd let himself be led. But when she tried that now, more desperation in her voice despite her attempts to conceal it, he simply said he wanted to be alone, and the dark, drowning look in his eyes told her she shouldn't push it.

He wasn't the type of person to kill himself—that was out of the question—and yet Britta didn't like the idea of him being alone in the house. Even if he didn't want visitors (and he'd told her that directly—not even Tim or Jean) and was mostly sleeping, or trying to sleep, it seemed important that she was there. He was refusing her help, but she resolved to be useful nonetheless: that was why she'd come.

Their first day back, she called Dr. Shah and asked him to up Paul's dose of antidepressants and then arranged with the pharmacy to let Jean pick them up. That afternoon—which was, despite the gloom inside, warm and sunny—she vacuumed Paul's car and wiped down the interior with wet wipes, cut the grass with his little push mower, and made both sweet and dill pickles from the cucumbers she picked from his garden. The next day, she cleaned his house top to bottom: dusted the woodwork with Pledge, mopped all the floors, scrubbed every surface and nook and cranny clear of gunk—even the grates of his oven and the glass shelves of his fridge—with sponges and Brillo pads. By dinnertime she was slick and itchy with sweat, her T-shirt soaked completely through. That night, like the night before, she went to bed early and slept like a stone.

On the morning of the third day, however, within minutes of waking up, she felt the momentum she'd created go totally slack: she sat up on the pullout couch, looked at her brother's now immaculate kitchen, the low hum of the refrigerator the only sound, and felt hopeless. Almost a month now she'd been with him, and what was there to show for it? Back in May, when she'd decided to leave St. Louis for a few months to be with him through all this, she'd had such high hopes—absurd, considering the situation, but so be it. Don had died suddenly—a massive heart attack in his den; by the time she'd gotten there, he was slumped forward on his desk, gone. With Paul, she would have the chance to *do something*. Give him comfort as he deteriorated. Be there at the very end. But also, she'd wanted to come because she hoped the experience would make her feel like a good, loving person again and help her avoid doing what she'd done last summer, which was to spend most of every day diligently getting drunk.

So far, on that front, she'd been doing neither horrible nor great. She'd been heeding the rule she tried to keep during the school year: no more than a bottle a night on school nights. Then a big glass of water before bed, and coffee and two ibuprofens the next morning, to recover. Most people, she knew, would still consider this having a problem. And it probably was. But considering the stress she was under, what with Paul and Maura's troubles always on her mind, on top of everything else, the escape felt necessary. Deserved, even. Though of course it was exactly this attitude that got her in trouble.

The previous two days had been the only ones since she'd arrived in Wisconsin in which she hadn't gotten the slightest bit drunk, but that was only because there was no wine in the house when they'd returned and she hadn't gone to the store to get any yet. If she simply didn't get more wine, then, she thought, as she got up to make coffee, there wouldn't be a problem. No temptation, no sin. But it was already too late: thinking about not driving to the store to buy wine was no different really from thinking about actually driving to the store to buy wine, and with both shame and relief, as she dumped the coffee grounds into its frilly white filter, she realized that was exactly what she was going to do.

She didn't want Paul to wake to an empty house, so she called Jean over from the church office, to sit in the living room until he woke up. At the store, she bought a case of Pinot Grigio and three cartons of orange juice: when she drank early in the day, it felt less wrong to drink mimosas, with wine instead of champagne. By noon, she'd had three glasses and felt much better. Half a bottle: that was probably her sweet spot. The invisible little weights fastened to her shoulders fell away, her forehead smoothed, and the world narrowed to a simple, attainable goal: to keep on drinking. Buzzed, as Shade called it, she could retreat to the center of herself, a tiny warm spot cushioned from pain, and when she moved from one room to the next, or even sat at a table scrolling through Facebook, she felt fluid, like a surfer probably felt riding an easy wave. The problem was it was impossible to stay a little drunk.

The afternoon passed as so many had passed last summer: as she drank she did whatever she felt like the moment she felt like it, like a child following her whims. An hour with a John le Carré novel from Paul's library, then some Facebook, then some judge show on TV, a full bag of chips and veggie dip, four or five cigarette breaks outside—and then, seeing she needed one, a nap. When Paul finally emerged from his room around five thirty for something to eat, she felt self-conscious of how drunk she was; this sometimes happened when the FedEx guy showed up at her front door back home, often with boxes full of things she didn't remember buying, deep in her cups, a few nights before. She said hi to Paul and Paul said hi back, but she was safe: he was so in his own head he didn't notice anything different about her. As he stood at the microwave, heating his soup, she wanted to cry: he looked like a person who'd been unplugged. Eyes without light in them; cheeks rough with white stubble. He still wore the sweatshirt he'd put on three days ago and stunk strongly of old sweat. *Maybe,* she thought for a moment, *if he just threw caution to the wind and drank some wine too—we could get drunk together!* But the idea was beyond idiotic, she realized: the man had liver cancer. What could possibly be worse?

"How are you feeling?" she asked, once he was eating his soup. It occurred to her that in all their time together, he hadn't said grace before eating once. Usually he took a few moments of silence, head bowed—the silence a form of deference to her. She wondered if he'd stopped praying in private too.

"The same," he said, and lifted his spoon to his mouth.

After grimly rinsing out his bowl and setting it to dry on a towel by the sink, Paul winced a smile at her, then walked stiffly back to his room. For a moment, the evening and its many mindless hours to fill loomed large, and she felt unsure what to do. To help her figure it out, she began what was now her third bottle, the pop of the cork the lively announcement of the start of another round. The feeling now was less like surfing and more like jogging down an endless hill. For a while, she sat on the front stoop and pretended she was back at the beach in Sister Bay, seagulls squawking, her eyes closed against the blazing evening sun. For dinner, she ate most of an eggplant casserole one of the altar society women had put in the freezer for them, then she got the idea to look through Paul's photo albums, all lined up on the lowest shelf of the living room bookcase.

The first album she looked at was the one she was most familiar with: the leather-bound memento made by their mother for Paul to take with him to seminary, the year he was thirteen. All the pictures but for the last three pages' worth were black and whites faded to sepia brown. Bald little Paul in his baptismal gown. Toddler Paul, uncomfortable in a tiny winter hat with earflaps, slouched on a sled, frowning. Proud Paul at his First Communion, wearing his first pair of many horn-rimmed glasses, standing stiffly in a tight dark suit in front of their mother and father, their father holding the baby that was her. Glued to some of the pages was a spelling test (the only mistake was "hlep," his misspelling of "help"), a whale he'd made out of cardboard, holy cards he'd won for good behavior. Jesus with his exposed pink heart, arms out. The Virgin Mary with her starry halo, cradling Baby Jesus in her arms. Saint

Francis with hands pressed together in the woods, surrounded by birds, squirrels, and a deer, like Snow White. Paul looked so serious in the pictures, which was a shame. In her memories, he was more expressive—laughing at something in a book or throwing their old, falling-apart baseball to Shep, their dog, or him feeding her shelled peanuts out of his hand, like she was a chicken, mischief in his eyes. What the album was, Britta knew, was a carefully curated exhibit, created by their mother. A document befitting her chosen one, the future priest.

There were eight other albums, in rough chronological order, and though she was sure she'd gone through them before, she wanted to do it again. There was the album that began with his seminary years and ended with pictures from his ordination—Paul bookended proudly by their parents, a few pictures of her and him together too: her, at nineteen, with her wavy, shoulder-length hair, a sensible green dress—only two summers away from going full hippie. His Rome album she lingered over carefully, looking for the places they'd just seen, looking for signs of Luca (there were none). The two albums that covered his years preaching with Tim at St. Matthew's and the first decade or so at St. Iggy's she flipped through quickly— most of the pictures were of Paul standing with strangers, his hair progressively graying, his sideburns shrinking. The Holy Land album, the India album, an album mostly devoted to the harvest fest fund-raisers at St. Iggy's over the years. And then, finally, the album he'd devoted to her and her family—the one Shade and Maura always pored over when they visited as kids.

When she and Ray, the kids' father, were still together there had been pictures of her and Ray holding the kids as babies, pictures from their first apartment; but sometime after Ray left them after years of cheating, the year Maura was four, Paul had removed all evidence of him, as if trying to write him out of her story completely. The album began with photos of her holding baby Maura, with her little swirl of chestnut hair, and then, two year later, her holding Shade, Maura peeking over her arm, her hair at chin length, to see her baby brother. In the pictures of thirtysomething Paul holding them as babies, his upper body and arms were very stiff; he was so worried he would drop them. The picture Maura and Shade had loved to find and giggle at was the one of them both sitting naked and furious in the plastic pool she set in the backyard of her apartment in Madison, Maura maybe five, Shade, three. When she found it, she laughed again too. But the picture they'd liked the best was the first one with Don in it—the photograph that signaled the start of the life they knew: in it, Maura sat in his lap, ripping apart a big red package, and Shade sat in his lap as well, frowning at the big red bow stuck to his fingers. Don's face was turned to Britta, about to say something, but she was looking right at the camera and beaming. *Look,* Maura had once said, pointing. *Mommy's smiling because she found Daddy.*

By the time she reached the end of the album—marked by the kids' high school graduations—the sun had set, and she was very drunk, and she missed her kids very much. She knew that Maura hadn't been in touch, but she didn't care: she pulled out her phone. But after ringing four times, an automated voice said the mailbox was full. When she called Shade, he picked up, but he was in the middle of some gaming thing and said he'd call her back tomorrow.

Minutes later somehow, she was swaying in the backyard so much it was hard to light her cigarette. The wave she'd been riding had crashed. Rarely did she throw up; her head and stomach had learned to absorb the punishment she inflicted on it and carry on. But she knew that tonight she wouldn't be able to avoid it. Slowly, careful not to fall, she walked inside and sat on the sofa, crouched forward, her head in her hands. If Don were here, she would have called for him by now and told him she was going to puke. He would have appeared with the teal-green bucket from under their sink and told her to wedge it between her knees, the way he had when she got food poisoning on their tenth anniversary trip to San Padre Island. He would be sitting beside her, not a memory but a real man, rubbing her back, alternating between smooth circles and up and down. His big right thigh would press against hers. He would smell faintly of his cologne—cedar and mint. *Just let it out, Britty,* he'd say. *As soon as it's out of you, you'll feel better.*

When it was no longer possible to hold it off, Britta remembered that she didn't have a real bucket in her lap and rushed too late to the toilet. She threw up on the bathroom floor and a little bit in the sink, which seemed slightly better. A big one, a smaller one, and a horrible, eye-watering one that was mostly liquid. When she raised her head to the mirror she was beyond pathetic: pale, the hair on her temples dark with sweat, eyes red and teary, a glob of yellow spit hanging from her bottom lip. She poured water into her cupped hand and washed out her mouth. In the kitchen she sought a roll of paper towels, with the intention of cleaning up. But at the door to the bathroom, when she surveyed the mess she'd made, the idea of cleaning it up made her very tired, and plus she didn't know where she'd put the towels when she was done, so she just set the roll on the floor under the sink, for later, and sank down into the hallway carpet. She would sleep here tonight, she decided—this was comfortable enough. And she did for a while, until there was a tug on her arm. It was Paul above her, saying her name, telling her to get up. His eyes were worried, but he also seemed to have a plan for her she trusted. With him holding her arm, she rose to her knees, then to her legs. The bathroom, she saw with a glance, had already been cleaned. Also, it smelled like lemon. She wondered, as she staggered with him to the living room, what time it was exactly, so she asked him, and all he said was that it was late. Once she was on the sofa, with the sheet over her and the Tupperware that that night's casserole had come in placed below her head on the floor, he said, "Use this if you need to. And get some sleep."

When she woke, light poured through the front window, and she had a headache so intense it made it difficult for her to see. The sheets were a tangle around her legs; there was a faint taste of bile in her mouth. She remembered what Paul had done and wanted to thank him and apologize immediately, to purge her gratitude too. But he was probably still sleeping, recovering from his late night with her. So she walked to the sink and sipped water until the foul taste in her mouth was mostly gone, took four ibuprofen, and fell back asleep.

The blind on the window was drawn when she woke back up, which meant Paul was awake now too. She pushed herself up to sitting, her headache dimmer now, and there he was: sitting at the kitchen table, still in the same gray sweat suit, sipping from a Gatorade, watching her.

"She lives," he said.

"What time is it?" she managed.

"Almost noon."

"Jesus. Really?"

"Yes."

He had something to say to her, she could tell by the way his lips were slightly parted. He was deciding whether to say it. His eyes were liquid, but not lost.

"I'm sorry about last night," she said first. "I guess I overdid it."

"I would say so."

"I appreciate you cleaning everything up."

"Sure."

"That never happens to me," she said. "Never."

"Well," Paul said, "maybe it should happen more often. Maybe you'd stop drinking so much."

There was a clarity in his eyes she recognized: the old Paul.

"I know I should cut down," she said.

He nodded. "Do you think there's a part of you that's trying to kill yourself? I'm asking in all sincerity."

She frowned, then recoiled at the thought. "Of course not!" she said. "I'm surprised you'd even ask me that."

"Well," he said, "that's what it seems like, whether you're trying to or not." He remained perfectly still. "And if you don't get help, I worry you'll end up like Don."

It was a harsh thing to say, but fair: at the time of his death, Don had been more than 325 pounds. Diabetes. High blood pressure. Cholesterol through the roof. She'd had problems in those areas too, even before he died. And now? Worse, probably. But she didn't know for sure because she hadn't gone for a checkup the past three years, afraid to find out. Afraid of more bad news.

"It's been really hard," she said.

"I know it has."

"I know I should be getting over it. But I can't."

"I know."

Her whole face winced, and when she began to cry, Paul set down his Gatorade and walked over to the couch, sat, and put his arm around her. And as she shook, his arm didn't move.

For the rest of the morning and early afternoon, Paul stayed close by. Available, it felt, if she needed him. When she put on one of her stupid judge shows, he sat with her, and when she told him she was going to take another nap, he checked email quietly at the kitchen table, and when she woke again some romaine lettuce and tomatoes from his garden were draining in a strainer in the sink. She didn't want to jinx things by making too big a deal out of this small reversal, or ruining it with conversation, so they agreed without saying so to keep a warm distance. Around three, Paul excused himself to the basement to look through some boxes as she settled into what had become her armchair to read, calmly pushing away the hope that kept surging inside her, to spare herself disappointment. Around five, she started to feel hungry and decided to make dinner from scratch, as a thank-you to him, for helping her, for listening. Spaghetti carbonara—what he always made her family when they visited him. She would make him that.

When she walked down the stairs to the basement to let him know she needed to go get a few groceries, Paul was sitting on a metal folding chair, a thick black binder open on his knees. He turned and smiled faintly, as he might have done if interrupted in his office, at the church.

"Fine by me," he said. "I don't expect I'll be going anywhere."

The air-conditioning at the grocery store was so incredibly cold—so much better than the window units at Paul's place— she took her time moving through the aisles. She got the bell peppers and bacon the recipe required, then a small tiramisu, two cannoli from the bakery, and a bottle of Chianti, to complete the theme. How nice it was, she thought, to be out in the world like this, to have a delicious dinner to look forward to. But as she set her bags down on the passenger seat of Paul's car, she had an awful thought: What if he'd been waiting for her to leave, all this time, and now was going to kill himself? This would be an ideal time; he was down in the basement, alone. She'd once read that, after they had decided to go through with suicide, some depressed people would experience a surge of relief unmistakable from joy: maybe that's what she'd seen. It was a crazy thought, she knew, but as she drove the eight miles back, her heart pounded in her neck. As she put the key into the lock of his front door, she prayed for the first time in years: *Don't let him be dead*. But when the door gave way, Paul was sitting in the middle of the sofa, watching *Wheel of Fortune*. He was in exactly the same pose he'd been in when she left him, except he'd changed out of his sweat suit and into a light blue polo and khakis and black socks. He'd combed his hair and looked freshly washed. And the white stubble was gone from his cheeks.

"You shaved!"

He smiled faintly. "I thought it was time I cleaned myself up a little."

She set down the grocery bags where she was at the door and walked over and sat beside him. She wanted to hug him until he burst, but he was delicate. So instead she just held his hand.

That night, after dinner, Paul told her he might finally be up for having visitors, and by the next morning, Jean had sent an email to the whole parish letting them know. For the next few weeks, people appeared at the door nearly every day: single people, couples, families, most of them bearing gifts—rosaries blessed in Medjugorje, peanut M&Ms (his favorite), flowers to brighten things up. Britta made sure to always have snacks on hand and coffee brewing, though rarely did anyone accept anything but coffee. At first, she wasn't sure whether to give Paul and his visitors privacy, to excuse herself to his bedroom or outside for a smoke. But Paul insisted she join him on the couch and meet everybody who came in. He wanted her to understand this part of his life too.

Those who shared stories about him and tried to make him smile Britta liked the most; those who were awkward and pitying she liked least. But she was thankful to each and every person who showed up. The couple whose son had committed suicide, whom Paul had counseled for years after. The single mom who had a daughter who was a server at Mass. The fortysomething guy who brought over a little cooler full of walleye fillets from his recent fishing trip up north. The McNamaras, again, who gave her the biggest hug when they left. Whenever someone made a reference to something she wouldn't understand, Paul paused to explain it to her, his usual manners resurrected. And in return she typed notes on her phone about the sweet things his visitors said, so she could repeat them to him later, if his mood took another turn for the worse.

Over the course of these few weeks, he became visibly weaker, his liver doubling down on its mission to kill him. He started eating less, and what he did eat, he often threw up. His skin turned the pale yellow of old candlewax; the whites of his eyes were tinged orange. The tumor on his right side bulged like a perverse pregnant belly, blotchy purple and brown and yellow, and Dr. Shaw prescribed water pills to redirect the fluid in Paul's abdomen to his kidneys. But the pills made his hands and feet cramp up so badly he'd cry out in the middle of the night, as though he were being stabbed. To ease the pain, Britta sat beside his bed and rubbed his hands with lotion and pushed her thumbs deep into the joints of his hands and feet. One night he told Britta that his back was really hurting (he gasped whenever he got up or lowered himself into a chair), and she took him in the following day. An X-ray confirmed their suspicions: the cancer had spread to his bones.

But even so, when he was lucid and well medicated, sitting on the sofa, propped up with pillows and facing his guests, the unbroken Paul she'd always known him to be flickered to life, for fifteen minutes or a half hour at a time. His eyes were pained but they smiled when he smiled. His face calmed, and he closed his eyes when he was hugged. He seemed in these moments to be accepting the love being showered on him from all these strangers who were, she knew, his other family. They were blessing him, though they didn't know it.

More than once, she felt so moved she had to excuse herself to the bathroom to sob into one of his big soft towels. It wasn't a total victory, but it was victory enough.

By the middle of August, Paul needed a wheelchair, and in the early evenings, at his request, they went for walks—Britta pushing him first into the church parking lot, then down the long entranceway and onto the paved county road that ran past the church. Sometimes he dozed as the wheels crackled along the shoulder of the road; sometimes he looked around him, gazing out at the world like a tired child. Often, the drivers of the cars that passed by, recognizing Paul, would tap lightly on their horn, saying hello.

Their first time out, she made it maybe half a mile before her body said, *Fuck this*. Her hips were on fire, her lower back throbbed, and her mouth filled with so much saliva she felt like throwing up. Back at the house, she felt so sore and light-headed she took three ibuprofens and lay on the couch with a cool hand towel on her forehead. That night, feeling nauseated, she barely touched her dinner and skipped her wine and went early to bed. The next morning, as she knew it would be, her back was so tight it took great effort to stand up. On the other hand, she felt very rested; she'd slept deeply and straight through the night. So when Paul asked her to take him out again that night after dinner, and the night after, she said okay. She wanted to be useful, and this was the only thing he had directly asked her to do, and by the end of their third walk, she knew that they would go out every day like this after dinner until he asked her to stop, that they were creating a ritual, and that every time she would try to go a little farther than the time before.

It was possible Paul had asked her for this favor because he knew the exercise would be as good for her as the sunshine and fresh air would be for him. But she didn't ask him, and honestly, she didn't want to know: if this was his plan to help her, she wanted no part of it. However, if walking a little farther every time happened to require smoking fewer cigarettes, and eating less of the rich casseroles the altar society women kept dropping off and more of the vegetables from Paul's garden, and recorking her wine bottle after a few glasses at night, then fine. She would try, at least, to do it.

And then one day in early September, as she was climbing up the basement stairs, a boxful of Paul's college textbooks in her arms, Britta heard, first, a *thump* and then an awful moan, like the lowing of a cow. Quickly, she set the box on the step and rushed up the stairs. In the hall, she found him sprawled in his underwear, dark blood worming out of his nose, his eyes open and scared. He'd been trying to walk to the bathroom without his walker, lost his balance, and landed hard on his face, unable to throw out his arms in time: that was her first guess. But when she pulled him up to a sitting position and got a good look at his face, the left side of his mouth hung slack, his left eyelid drooped. When he said her name, it sounded like *Bitta*, without the *r*. He'd had a stroke.

Awkwardly, she propped him against the wall, like a giant doll. On her knees, she dabbed the blood from his nose as she talked to the woman who picked up when she dialed 911; an ambulance was on its way. She didn't want him to show up at the hospital half naked, so she dressed him, moving his heavy legs and arms for him as needed. His eyes, one bigger than the other, were alarmed, so she told him it would be okay; whatever that could possibly mean she didn't know.

Two days later they returned from the hospital, and the day after that, two hospice nurses—a petite Filipino woman with a long black ponytail named Mai and a large, flushed guy with rimless glasses named Tony—arrived in a white van. When they asked Paul if he wanted the hospital bed they'd wheeled in to stay in the living room, where there was more space, he said no, his bedroom was fine. So Tony and Mai moved the sofa and the end tables to clear a path to roll the bed through and then rolled in the IV and a box, in which Britta saw a silver bedpan, not unlike the kind their mother would slide under their beds as young kids, before they got the indoor bathroom. They were sweet, these two, but their sweetness seemed practiced, institutional, a Walmart greeter's shtick. Their hustle reminded

her of ants blindly performing a ritual, assured of their purpose, and for a few minutes she hated them and their heartless
competence. But once the room was set up and she wheeled
Paul over, and they demonstrated how to raise and lower and
adjust the bed and explained how Britta might help Paul lower
himself onto the bedpan if needed, and after they sat altogether
on the sofas making small talk about Mai's eight brothers and
sisters (she was Catholic too) and the two Rottweilers Tony
raised with his partner, Dane, her hatred disappeared. Her
pride had been bruised, she realized: she'd enjoyed being his
one and only savior, and now she had to share him. That's all
it was.

The funeral suddenly loomed, and Britta knew if Paul
wanted to help plan it they should start now. She asked him
what readings and hymns he might like read and sung, and
by that evening he'd jotted his selections down on the legal
pad that hadn't left the side of his bed since his stroke. When
Tim suggested they hand out CDs burned with some of Paul's
favorite music on it at the service, Paul agreed, and for a day
and a half he made his list.

Up at the cottage, he'd told her about the fleeting hallucinations
the morphine sometimes gave him: a feeling he was in the
stands at County Stadium, watching the Milwaukee Braves,
when he opened the fridge; the overwhelming sensation that
he was back on the farm, watching a storm from the safety of
the barn, when he was standing outside on the porch watching
the rain. He'd not talked about these episodes since Sister Bay,
but she knew he still had them, because she saw him in their
thrall. They arrived most reliably when she wheeled him into
the backyard to look at the birdfeeder and the cornfields behind his house. Three times she'd come upon him, eyes glassy,
frowning, mumbling to someone who wasn't there. *Who are
you talking to, Paul?* she'd asked. *Harlon,* he said the first time:
their old hired man, a hardworking but unreliable drunk. The

next time it was Luca (*Don't go too far out,* she heard him say). And the last time it was their mother, who, apparently, was holding Hammy, the runt of a pig that had been, during the year after her last miscarriage, her beloved pet. *Can't you see her?* he said. *She's right there.*

One morning, after he woke from a long nap and she was feeding him a few teaspoons of Ensure, his eyes cleared and he said, "How Maur' doing?" His words were clipped and slurred like this now, but rarely did she not understand him.

"I don't really know," she said. She wondered if he'd forgotten they were out of touch. "I still haven't heard from her."

She could be living in Maine with this David or wandering the Appalachian Trail, searching for the meaning of life, for all she knew, she said.

Paul nodded. "I 'ope she's 'kay," he said.

"Yeah," she said, "me too."

Later that day, Britta found Paul writing something on his legal pad, more carefully than he did to jot down notes for her, when he wasn't in the mood to talk. He asked that she bring him an envelope and some Scotch tape from his bottom desk drawer, and once she had, he folded the piece of legal pad paper twice, slipped it inside, and taped the flap down. He wrote *For Maura* at the bottom in small, precise block letters.

"Can I ask you what that is?" she asked.

"You can," he said, blinking heavily, "but I'm nah go' tell you."

Come mid-September Paul was so fragile, he asked that when she pushed him around outside she stick to the parking lot: even the slight rumbling of his chair's wheels moving over gravel was painful. For a while she did that, but going in circles in the parking lot felt silly, he said, so they stopped their walks together. And though she knew this was her opportunity to stop walking, she didn't want to stop; the walking was one of the things that grounded her these days, so every day at the same time, she walked alone along the road, and without Paul and his chair to push forward, she felt as light as she'd felt as a girl. The first night she walked without him, she checked her weight on his digital bathroom scale. It read 223, and the number didn't change when she checked again. Back in St. Louis she'd weighed 245: she'd lost more than twenty pounds.

She was still fat, of course. Nobody—not even Jean—had noticed the change in her yet.

But that was fine. She preferred it being her secret.

When Tony arrived to give Paul a bath, every other day, Britta helped him remove the white T-shirt and black sweatpants Paul wore most days and laid out a plastic sheet over the cloth one. She would watch through the crack in the door as Tony washed Paul with a damp, slightly soapy sponge, careful not to press down too hard, always checking to see if everything was okay. The scene reminded her of the pietà: Tony as Mary; Paul, an old dying Christ.

He'd come to the end of privacy, the end of shame. He belonged to them now the way he'd once belonged to their mother. There was no avoiding his (big) damp uncircumcised penis, his unruly thatch of pubic hair, the saggy wattle of his scrotum. Here was Paul at seventy, as God made him. In other circumstances, he might have cracked some wry joke about this strange intimacy, though she couldn't imagine what. But now, as Tony washed his broken body, Paul lay very still, eyes closed, chest rising and falling, concentrating, she was sure, on Tony's touch. The warm slippery suds. The tiniest differences in pressure. For a few minutes every other day, his existence reduced, wonderfully, to this.

One unusually hot night Paul asked Britta to sing to him, and when she asked what he'd like, he said it didn't matter, whatever she liked. So she sang what she could remember of the songs their mother would sing to them before bed, growing up. "The Yellow Rose of Texas." "Red River Valley." "How Great Thou Art." Her voice wavered, but she remembered all the words. On hearing them, his mouth didn't so much smile as smooth, contract. Another night, when he was lucid, Britta, sitting beside his bed, asked him if he felt ready. She didn't have to say the words *to die*.

"I thin' so," he said.

Then his voice broke. Tears welled in his beautiful eyes, the irises as blue as ever.

"Thank you," he said. "For be' here with me."

"Well," she said, "you're the one doing the hard part."

He closed his eyes. Tears raced down his cheeks, two faint paths, slightly darker than his skin. "You make me feel so loved."

She bit her lip to stem the swelling in her chest. Then she lifted his hand and kissed his knuckles. "You are, Paul. By so many people. You always have been."

He looked at her and nodded. He believed her.

"It's been my honor to be here," she said, and it was true.

When Tony pulled her aside one night to say it might be time to call family if anyone wanted to fly in to say goodbye, Britta got out her phone and did so. Shade first, because he was easiest, then her aunt Ginny who certainly wouldn't be able to make it, frail as she was. Then cousins in Illinois, and then Maura. If anything was going to end the standoff with her daughter, it had to be this. And she was right: within an hour of leaving a voice mail, there was Maura's name in all caps on her phone, for the first time in months.

"Hi, Mom," she said, her voice breaking.

"Maura. Sweetheart. It's so nice to hear your voice."

"Yeah," Maura said. "You too." And then: the muffled sound of a sob, Maura probably holding the phone away from her face. "How's he doing?" she asked.

"Well," Britta said, "it's a matter of days now. But I think we're managing his pain pretty well."

"That's good."

"It's all you can really do at this point."

"I'm sorry I've been out of touch," Maura said, after a brisk wet sniff. "It's been a really messed-up summer."

"I don't even know where to start."

"Well," Maura said, "in case you're wondering, we're still together. But I asked for a divorce. And then I took it back. And now we've decided we're going to try to work it out."

Britta felt a door unstick inside her: "I'm glad to hear that. I think that's wise."

"Yeah," Maura said. "I guess so. I still don't really know what's going to happen, though. We just started seeing a counselor a few weeks ago. We've only been twice. But that's the plan. To just keep going and see if we can fix it."

"Good. The more you go the easier it'll get." She didn't know if that was true, but it sounded true enough. "Do the kids know what's going on?"

"Not really. They know we've been fighting. But they don't know about David. And we're trying to keep it that way."

Britta nodded. "Good."

Maura sniffed again. "I can tell you more about it when I'm there, if that's okay."

"So you can come?"

"Yeah. But Thursday morning is the earliest I can leave. And it'll just be me."

"That's just fine," Britta said. "I'll take whatever I can get."

The second they hung up, Britta cried quietly on the couch, then poured herself a glass of wine and walked outside. She finished the wine quickly, then smoked three cigarettes one after the other, breathing deeply until she felt relief.

That night, after checking on Paul, she fell quickly asleep and had a succession of vivid, fleeting dreams: in one, she and Paul were running with their old dog Shep through the woods behind their house; in another, Ray showed up at the door of Paul's house dressed in black, holding a gigantic bouquet of pink flowers; in another, they were at the lake they sometimes went to in the summers, and Paul was floating on his back near the dock, as old as he was now, but lively, spitting plumes of water high up in the air, like a whale, happy as could be.

Early in the morning, something jolted her awake—she wasn't sure what. And though she hadn't heard a sound, she walked the ten steps to Paul's room without hesitation and pushed open the door. His eyes were closed but he was awake. "Get Jean and Tim," he said, and nothing more, and she saw the time had come. It was four thirty in the morning, so it took three calls to get Jean to pick up the phone. But within forty-five minutes they were both beside his bed, solemn, their hair uncombed, tears already in their eyes. There wasn't much space to stand around his bed, but they made it work. Jean massaged his hands with lotion and told him that soon he'd be with God; Tim cleared his throat to keep from crying and gave him last rites as he sat beside him holding his right hand.

For a few minutes Paul struggled to breathe, gasping horribly, his mouth opening and closing like a banked fish. Sunlight glowed in the belly of the window curtain. The room was quiet. The world outside was quiet too. The little bottle of hand lotion stood at attention like a loyal, broad-shouldered soldier. And then, as she said, "It's okay, sweetie, it's okay, we love you, we love you," Paul's eyes closed and stayed closed; his mouth opened and didn't shut.

Both Maura and Shade canceled their Thursday flights, there being no rush anymore, and instead arrived at St. Iggy's a few days later, the Saturday before the funeral—Shade by himself and Maura with her family, their arrivals an hour apart. Shade would stay with Britta at Paul's; Maura's family would stay, for free, at Father Tim's insistence, in the two spare rooms at the rectory at St. Boniface in town. This was the plan.

When their rented SUV pulled up, Britta threw on her coat and walked urgently to the car. Maura broke into tears at the sight of her, mouth pinched, nostrils flaring. She looked healthy, despite everything she'd been through. Thin as always, arms strong. Britta hugged her longer than normal, pressing herself into Maura as hard as she could. Then she hugged the kids and Harden too.

"I'm so glad you came," she said into his right ear, like he was a boxer and she, his coach. He pulled away from this quickly. She saw in his face a reserve that wasn't normally there.

"It's good to see you," he said. But something was off: usually he called her Mom.

They ordered in pizza, and Shade drove to the gas station near the highway for beer. As they ate, Maura asked about the service and Britta told her what she knew: overflow seating in the back and basement, and even then it might be standing room only; a big meal in the fellowship hall after. For dessert, they shared a frozen key lime pie one of the altar society ladies had brought over, and Shade thankfully did most of the talking—just as Don would have done if he were here, to relieve the burden for everyone else. He told stories about the idiots he worked with and got everyone to laugh, even Harden, who looked so uncomfortable. Evan showed off what he could do with his ten-sided Rubik's Cube, and Shade made paper airplanes out of white paper from Paul's printer and flew them in the front yard with Ella. When Maura started a pot of decaf, Shade slyly produced a bottle of Chivas Regal he'd picked up for himself along with the beer—and everyone decided, yes, they'd have some. Just a little.

At quarter past eight, Harden looked at his watch and said it was time they went to Father Tim's place. But Maura said she'd like to stay a little longer. Britta's heart leapt.

"Does that mean I'm supposed to come back to get you?" Harden asked.

"No, it's okay," Shade jumped in. "I'll drop her off later. Don't worry about that."

"Okay, well," Harden said, "I guess we'll see you tomorrow then."

He glanced at Maura, then Britta, making sure this wasn't some sort of conspiracy against him. Britta felt bad for him, but her sympathy for him only went so far: her love for her children trumped all.

"I think I'll have another jab of that booze," Shade said, a little while later, when it was just the three of them at the kitchen table. "Any takers?"

"Yeah, I'll have some more," Maura said, offering her empty mug. Shade poured a little and raised his eyebrows at Britta.

"I'll pass, but thanks," Britta said. If she had more right now, she would want even more later, and the last thing she needed in the morning was a headache.

"So," Shade said, swirling his booze and looking at his sister, "Mom said you and Harden are having some issues or something? What's going on?"

Maura looked at her. "Is that all you told him?"

"I wasn't sure how much to tell."

"How much to tell me what?" Shade looked at them back and forth.

Maura inhaled deeply and looked at him abstractly. "I got involved with someone for a while. And Harden found out. And now we're trying to work it all out."

Shade bugged out his eyes. "You mean like an affair?"

"More an emotional affair than a real affair. But yeah, I guess it was an affair."

Shade stopped swirling his drink. "Who was the guy? It was a guy, right?"

Maura shot him a look. "Yes, it was a guy. I met him at that art retreat I went to last fall." She hesitated, unsure of how much more to say. "His name was David. *Is* David."

"So emotional affair means no fucking, right?"

"Shade, for Chrissake," said Britta.

"What?" he said.

He could be such a child, so guileless and direct. But actually, Britta was curious to know. She hadn't dared ask, though she wondered, presumed the answer was yes.

Maura hesitated, then said, "Right. No sex."

But she was lying: Britta knew from the set of her mouth and the way she'd flared her nostrils. This was her tell forever. Britta took a big, exhausted breath. *Oh, Maura,* she thought.

"Does he have a ponytail?" Shade asked.

"What?" Maura replied.

"That's what I picture an art retreat guy looking like. Ponytail. Black turtleneck. Vest. Maybe some skinny jeans."

"Please stop," Britta said.

"Sorry," Shade said. He nervously drummed his fingers against the tabletop and took another swig. "So what did Harden say when he found out?"

"What do you think?"

"I don't know. That's why I'm asking. Should I not even be asking questions?"

"He was upset. Let's just say that."

Shade nodded, biting his tongue.

"And now I'm fucked," Maura added.

"Oh, stop," Britta said. "You are not *fucked*." She looked at Shade. "They're in counseling now." Then back to Maura. "That's not confidential, right?"

"I mean, I guess not, since you just shared it."

Blood rose to Britta's face. "How am I supposed to know what I can say or not, Maura? You haven't talked to me for four months."

Maura looked at her, more sad than irritated. "I'm sorry. You're right. I don't know why I'm being so bitchy. I just—I don't know how to talk about it yet, I guess. It's all so new."

"Fine," Britta said. "I get that. Just don't take it out on me."

"Okay. I'm sorry."

If Don were here right now, Britta thought, he would already be pushing them past this awkwardness with some practical advice. Sympathetic but firm. *You're paying the piper now, Maur, but that's good. That's a start. It's going to feel shitty at first. But you have to keep at it. Just keep plugging.* She could hear his voice so clearly, even now. His confidence.

"Anyway," said Shade, "I'm sorry to hear about all this stuff. I hope it works out. Harden's a good guy."

Maura looked at him and smiled weakly.

"Thanks," she said. "I'll keep you posted."

Soon after, they were all watching Anderson Cooper. Shade sat in the BarcaLounger and Maura sat beside Britta, an afghan wrapped around her legs. Some togetherness, but only thin comfort: the tension from earlier still hung in the air. Finally, Maura yawned and said she should probably get going.

"Why don't you just stay here tonight?" Britta asked. "You'd be waking people up at this point anyway."

"Yeah?" Maura said.

"Of course."

"Where would I sleep?"

"With me, if you want. In Paul's room. There's room for two."

"Oh. Okay."

"Don't worry. He was in a hospital bed for weeks," Britta said. "Everything's clean. Promise."

"I don't know," Maura said. "I don't want to make Harden upset."

"Oh, I'm sure he can spare you for one night," Britta said. "And if he makes a big fuss, just tell him I wouldn't take no for an answer."

Maura brushed her teeth in the bathroom, then paused in the hallway to announce she was hitting the sack. And after a few minutes of watching baseball highlights with Shade, Britta decided to do the same.

Britta's makeshift pajamas—gray sweatpants and a huge Cardinals T-shirt—were sloppily folded inside the suitcase she'd set, open like a clamshell, in the closet, and her first instinct was to gather them and change in the bathroom. But that was silly. With her back to Maura, facing the closet, she changed out of her blouse and slacks, but kept on her bra until she had her pajamas on. Twenty pounds lighter or not, she still felt slightly embarrassed to be half dressed around her daughter—Maura, who was so thin.

The bed creaked dramatically when she sat with care on the edge of the bed and rolled over on her right side, and Britta had a vision of the slats underneath the mattress busting in half, like a gag in a movie. But of course that didn't happen. Beside her, Maura lay on her back, holding a pillow tight, like it was a life preserver, just above the edge of a thin gray blanket.

"Let me know if you want the blanket off," Britta said. "I'm always cold."

"No," Maura said. "I'm good."

Britta watched her daughter close her eyes, and for a while they said nothing, though it felt to Britta as though they should. Was she actually trying to sleep? Or was this just her way of avoiding awkward mother-daughter conversation? Britta considered what she might say to Maura if her eyes opened—a place from which to begin. There was so much she didn't know: about David, the past few months, where things stood now. They needed a real talk soon. When Maura was ready. But maybe she wasn't yet. Maybe that was what the closed eyes meant: *I know we should talk, but if you love me, let me be.*

"I never called him," Maura said now, eyes still closed. "I never even said goodbye."

At first, Britta thought she meant David. "You've been going through a hard time. I think he understood that."

Maura opened her eyes and looked at the ceiling. "That's no excuse. I mean, I didn't even send him an email. Even Shade probably did that."

It was hard to excuse it, that was true. Paul hadn't said directly that he was disappointed not to hear from Maura, but she could tell it hurt him. If he in his terrible state could write her a note, Maura certainly could have at least picked up the phone. Emailed. Like Shade had done, yes. Many times, in fact. But she hadn't. It was testament, Britta supposed, to how carried away her daughter had been.

"There was part of me that wondered if you didn't call him just because I'd asked you to."

"What do you mean? Like out of spite?"

"Not spite. Anger. I thought you were still mad at me. For not being more supportive."

"Come on, Mom. You think I'd really do that?"

"No, I guess not."

"I didn't call because I was afraid that if I *did* talk to you or Paul you guys would talk me out of it. And I didn't want that to happen."

Britta felt like putting a hand on Maura's shoulder.

"It's a really stupid excuse," Maura said. "I realize that."

"Well," Britta said, "no point in beating yourself up over it. He knew you loved him, and he loved you back. That's all that really matters."

"I'm not sure about that," Maura said, "but thanks for saying so."

They grew quiet again, but the silence wasn't tense this time. It was like a long, necessary exhalation, in which Britta knew Maura was beating herself up. Always, she'd been tough on herself, a perfectionist. So rarely pleased with the art she made, so sensitive to the slightest criticism. So eager, at the end of high school, to shed her dissatisfaction with suburban St. Louis and fly away from home, to some bigger, better life. Harden had curbed some of Maura's severest tendencies. With him by her side, steady person that he was, Britta had felt she could stop worrying about her. Maura was safe. Then motherhood, which grounded her even more. But, Britta thought now, thinking about Maura and this David, there was more to life than being safe, wasn't there? There had been something missing from her daughter's life all along.

Now, almost coquettishly, Maura tilted her head to meet Britta's eyes. "I have to say, Mom...you seem better. As weird as that sounds with, you know, what's happening."

"Well," she said, "I suppose I am. I've been a little healthier lately. Actually, since Rome I've lost twenty pounds."

"What? Mom! That's so great! I thought maybe you had."

"Yeah, well, we'll see how it goes. It's not even been three months."

"Sure," Maura said. "But it feels like a good first step."

Her daughter's gaze narrowed and grew softer. The intimacy was almost too much to take.

"We've been worried about you, you know."

"I've been worried about me too."

"Yeah?" Maura said. "I guess I couldn't tell."

"When you're a control freak like me it's hard to admit you're not doing great," Britta said. "Bad for my reputation."

"Well, I hope you keep at it," Maura said. "I want you around for a long time."

"Thank you," Britta said, "for not wanting me to die."

There were tears in Maura's eyes as she turned to Britta, chuckling, and Britta couldn't help laughing too, tears in her eyes. When Britta reached out her hand, Maura took it, first squeezing all her fingers together, then slipping her fingers between her mother's, interlaced; it reminded Britta of the way she and Don had sometimes held hands after sex or just watching TV on the couch. She hadn't cared enough about herself—that much was true. She hadn't wanted to die, exactly. But her life had stopped mattering to her. She'd kept teaching, she'd remained a functioning human being. But in all the important ways, she'd given up.

Right now, though—whether it was just the passing of more time, or being with someone who really was dying, or the care she'd taken with herself lately—that bitterness and apathy had left her. Reading through the obituaries the other day, she'd noted the ages under all the headshots and thought, *I'm only sixty-four, I may have twenty years left.* And for the first time in ages, the thought hadn't filled her with dread.

Maura slowly moved their clasped hands to a spot just below her breastbone, as though claiming their bond for herself. "I'm sorry I was such a shit."

"You were, but I've already forgiven you."

Maura sniffed and smiled. "Thanks."

"I will at some point be interested to know more about what's going on, of course," Britta said. "I have a lot of questions."

"Yeah, I'm sure you do."

"But for right now," Britta said, pressing their hands into Maura's chest, "I'm just happy to have you back."

VI. Goodbyes

Maura and Evan are hiking in the Berkshires, except instead of pines and dusty rock, hovering over them are gigantic prehistoric plants, leaves the size of cars. The light breaking through the cover puddles on the forest floor in soft underwater shapes. There's a sense that they're lost, and if so, Maura understands that she's to blame, because the hike was her idea and apparently they have no map.

She walks beside Evan, trying to hide that she's afraid. She takes bold steps, points to a path ahead, pretending confidence. And then, just as she's beginning to feel like maybe this confidence will pay off, they turn a corner and there's David, standing in a clearing, staring at them. Stopped in his tracks like a deer, gripping the straps of his backpack tightly.

Her first instinct is to veer away for Evan's sake, but David calls her name and is suddenly right there in front of them, as if launched by a gust of wind. He looks a little off, as people often do in dreams. His careful stubble is a pointy Van Dyke. He has a bit more hair.

Do you know this guy? Evan asks.

Yes, she replies. *He's a friend from work.*

At this, David bugs his eyes. *A friend?* he roars. *A friend? Do friends do this?* And from his backpack he unfurls a poster. On it is one of the cell phone pictures she sent him: herself, topless, wearing her pajama pants, pretending to read a book.

She's speechless.

Is that you? Evan asks.

There are her breasts and stomach. Her laptop with the St. Louis Cardinals sticker on it. Her unmistakable face. The look Evan gives her—mournful, shocked—makes her almost pass out.

Angry at being ambushed, she runs toward David, hoping to rip the poster away. But he sidesteps her like a bullfighter, and when she looks back over her shoulder, David and Evan are both staring at her, disgusted. Like she's barely human. A *thing*.

It's the worst feeling there is, this judgment. It's too much to take. So Maura does the only thing she can think of. She runs deeper into the woods, like her hair's on fire, all lungs and limbs. Like she used to do as a girl. And when the forest floor gives way to a cliff, she jumps, heart beating in her neck.

The granular darkness of the room around her takes a few moments to form into shapes. Up on her elbows, chest heaving, her mother snoring softly beside her, Maura remembers where she is and why she's here. The nightmare slinks back into its hole. But even as she understands the dream wasn't real, the guilt remains. A thickness behind her eyes. A sickly swooning in her stomach that makes her short of breath. For weeks now, a constant companion, despite her choice.

During the almost ten months she and David were in love, back when she was texting every day, sneaking time to talk, exchanging photos, she didn't feel guilty: that was what had felt so strange. She lied in order to make time for him, yes, which was wrong. But it served a higher purpose. He made her so happy. How could that be wrong?

It's only since she called things off—three weeks ago now—that she's felt retroactively guilty. Revisited the naughtiest bits, imagining the hidden camera footage a stranger would have seen. A thirty-eight-year-old woman with her hand down her pants, her breathing fogging up the windshield. On the sofa in the basement, holding her phone with a stiff, outstretched arm so he could see every inch of her the afternoon when Harden and the kids went apple picking and she stayed in, pretending to be sick. What they'd done on the hotel bed that day in Boston. All of it in the service of love, though the stranger wouldn't understand that.

When Harden promised to keep her secret for her, at their first session with their couples' therapist, she felt closer to him than she had in years. It felt like a step forward, a bread crumb dropped on the path that would lead them back. Since that first session, her job, as she's come to see it, has been to seek out more bread crumbs. Maybe drop some herself. For the first time in years, her purpose has become crystal clear: to turn away from David and back toward her old life, such as it is. When the guilt threatens to overwhelm her, or when she's tempted to take out her phone and text *I miss you* to David, she thinks of the goal and holds tight.

Now, still up on her elbows, she wishes she wasn't fully awake, but she is. There's no hope of falling back asleep. No point in even trying.

Paul's house is quiet. Carefully, Maura slips out of bed without waking her mother and moves into the living room. On the pullout couch, Shade lies sideways in a T-shirt and plaid boxers, one arm extended, one at his side, like he's Superman, flying nowhere. In the window above the sink, a bold band of light leaches into the darkness above the gray field of cornstalks. It reminds her of a Rothko painting: dark field below, pale gray field above, rose-gray field on top.

The world is her oyster right now.

No kids, no Harden. Nowhere she has to be.

Which means, for the next maybe hour or so, she's free to do whatever she wants.

Seven weeks ago, she was still really going to leave. It was only a matter of when.

The night they returned from vacation, back in July, instead of telling the kids, she stalled again. Told Harden that she'd let him know when she felt ready. To which he'd bitterly said, *I won't hold my breath.*

After two weeks of this, David began to get worried. *Are you having second thoughts?* he texted one afternoon.

It feels impossible, that's all, she replied.

Remember that I'll be helping you. It's not all on you.

I know, she replied. But really, she thought, it *was* mostly on her. What he would have to give up—a single man with a dog—was basically nothing. You couldn't even compare. Not being with her kids every day would be the worst part—that she already knew. But also: some friends would drop her. Harden's parents would never forgive her. And she'd really miss her house.

She barely functioned, hardly ate. She fell behind at work, unable to concentrate for more than ten minutes at a time. At night, she needed three Tylenol PMs to sleep. Mornings, after she made the kids' lunches and got them on the bus and before she drove in to work, she took a shower and sobbed. Sometimes, through the steam, she would watch her curdled face in the mirror like an anthropologist observing a specimen of grief. In a single day, she might change her mind about Harden and David three times, each decision feeling ironclad—until it wasn't. It was like being seasick. Like vertigo. All she wanted was to sleep until she woke up so rested and clearheaded a direction would be obvious. But no amount of sleep was ever enough.

Then she received a call from Evan's principal, on the fourth day of school. During earth science, one of Evan's classmates had called him a spaz, and Evan had lost it and stabbed the boy in the hand with a pencil. The graphite tip went all the way in. The school nurse had had to use tweezers to pull it out. Evan's aide was with him right now, the principal said. Understandably, the parents of the boy were very upset. If she or her husband could come as soon as possible to pick him up, that would be very much appreciated.

Three times in five minutes she'd called Harden, but he didn't pick up. Not picking up was his new thing. It reminded her he had power too. So she'd driven straight there by herself.

When she walked into the front office, Evan was slumped forward on a bench, head in his hands, his aide Janelle sitting meekly beside him. When Maura said his name, he looked up sadly, then stood like a little soldier, his giant yellow backpack high on his back. Only when he was sitting in the passenger seat beside her in the parking lot did he start to cry.

On the ride home, Evan sniffed and wiped his nose with his sleeve, and all the things Maura could have said—about *using your words*, about *using your calming rituals*—didn't need to be said. He knew what he should have done; he just hadn't been able to do it. So instead of talking she held his hand with her free hand, moving her thumb over his knuckles like a tiny windshield wiper, all the way home.

In their kitchen, she served him a bowl of rocky road ice cream and sat beside him watching as he ate it, taking gulps of air between each bite, still recovering. Once he was done, he set the spoon respectfully in the bowl, looked straight at her, and asked if she and his dad were getting a divorce.

Why would you think that? she asked, trying desperately to buy time.

I heard Dad talking about it.

To who?

Just to himself. He was mumbling in the bathroom.

She snorted instinctively, but the serious look on Evan's face erased the little curl of her lips. She'd imagined the awful moment of truth so many times. Now here it was. He was waiting for her to say no, terrified she would say yes. It was all there in his brown eyes and his shut mouth, a watery smudge of brown ice cream on his upper lip.

No, sweetie, she said. *We're not.*

That night, she called David from the backyard to tell him she couldn't do it. He was quiet for maybe fifteen seconds, then said, *You said you didn't love him anymore. You said the marriage was dead.*

I know, she said, and tried explaining, but she did a bad job of it, and a few minutes later David said he was hanging up and did. A first.

Driving to work the next morning, in the soundproof vacuum of her car, she screamed and sobbed and swore, and fuck all the people craning their necks in the cars nearby. That night, she found Harden on the basement sofa watching ESPN. She told him she and David had broken up. Tomorrow, she was going to call a therapist for them and try to fix this.

For a while, he watched her stand there, breathing heavily, unsure what to do. Eventually, he turned off the TV, stood up, and walked over, like an actor tentatively following stage directions. He hugged her, stiffly, like it was job. Which, in a way, it still was.

I'm glad to hear you say that, he said. Then he pulled away and looked at her. *But I'll believe it when I see it.*

It just feels wrong, David wrote her three days later, finally breaking down. *We make each other so happy.*

Though she'd desperately wanted to reply, she didn't. Nor did she reply to the other two texts he sent a few days later, equally heartbreaking. Only when he called and left a voice mail, clearly very drunk, did she take pity on him.

I got all your messages and I love you, she texted. *But I need to stop this now or I never will. It hurts me too.*

I was afraid it might end like this, he texted a minute later. *So be it. I'm not going to beg. Hope you figure out your life someday. Xo D.*

His last words to her three weeks ago. She hates them, and wishes they never existed, and knows them by heart.

Moving across the church parking lot to the road that winds through the countryside, Maura's mind is empty—the gift of still being barely awake. The sun peeks over the horizon, warming the sky and lightening the trees so they're no longer silhouettes but brushy three-dimensional things, the lightening a reminder that change is natural, change is the story of life, and as she moves along the gravel collar of the road, she feels her tense body loosening up, the kinks from sleep ironed out by the swinging of her arms, the grasping of her legs.

She sees but doesn't think: for a change, she feels truly present to the moment, the way her former yoga teacher always challenged her class to be. Naked to the world like a child. To her right is an abandoned barn, splintery and gray, the morning light casting a thicket of shadows inside. An old pickup moves slowly on the opposite side of the road, the driver wearing sunglasses perched on his head. Above and all around her, a big sky clear but for a few long cotton candy clouds.

What she *could* be thinking about, she knows, if she let herself, is David: lately, when she isn't completely locked in on something—a work project, cooking dinner for the kids—her mind goes there almost automatically, and she tries to resist. Thinking about how she isn't thinking about David, of course, usually turns into actively thinking about him—in fact, she can feel the shift happening now—but she also senses a resolve in herself that isn't usually present. It has to do with this being the day of Paul's funeral. If she should be thinking about anyone right now, it should be him. Especially considering how negligent she's been.

Uncle Paul, Uncle Father Paul, ol' UFP—what enters her first now is a feeling: solidity, support, warmth, though behind the warmth there's coolness too. He was a fixture in her life from day one. Benevolent and constant as this rising sun. A card every birthday her whole life; a short, sometimes awkward chat every time he called to talk to their mom when they were kids. More recently, likes on her Facebook posts, birthday cards for her own kids. She loved him and he loved her, no doubt about that. But he'd never been someone she opened up to the way she did with her mom or Don or good friends. He'd always seemed so self-contained. To need so little. To be content being the one who gives. Maybe this was why she'd taken him for granted for so long.

As a girl, she'd been fascinated by him: the first time she watched him say Mass, apparently she told her mom he was like a wizard, in his colorful robes, casting spells the crowd obediently repeated. But then she'd grown up and became fed up with the Church the same way her mom had. She stopped thinking of him and priests as special and instead as company men: fussy managers of an antiquated business that sold comfort and community, custodians of a cyclical world that didn't evolve on purpose.

Rarely, Maura realizes as she reaches an intersection and turns right, did she wonder about his life. He was her priest uncle who did good, vaguely boring priest things—surely not one of the sick ones you read about in the news. A person who supported her, from whom she'd grown apart in the end. But of course, he was more than the sum of her half-hearted imaginings. Being here in Northfield, where he'd spent his days, she can feel the weight of her ignorance.

It hits her again, the guilt. Different cause, same feeling. There's nothing to be done about it anymore, of course, but she wants to make it up to him anyway. Right her little wrong.

According to Kate, her life drawing instructor at Boston College, the key to seeing things as they really were was to unsee them first. To illustrate her point, Kate had them bring in photos of family members, tape them upside down to their easels, and draw them that way. Doing this blinded you to the image of your mom or dad or brother you held in your mind's eye and forced you to reckon with their faces and bodies simply as shapes in relation to other shapes. To see them fresh.

The images that arrive first are the usual ones: Paul slightly hunched forward, saying the prayer at their wedding in a blue polo; the Polaroid of her and him holding up drawings of monarch butterflies they'd made one Easter; the Sears photo studio portrait of him a few years ago that graced his Facebook page—white hair, kind eyes. They evoke tenderness but offer nothing new. So she searches her memory more, her mind wildly casting nets. Here's Paul smoking on their back porch after Thanksgiving dinner, looking wistfully up at the moon. Paul cleaning his glasses with his handkerchief, looking at her blindly as she spoke. Paul squatting uncomfortably to talk to Evan when he was a toddler, about who knows what.

It's a comfort to know she can recover more if she cares to. That the past still lives inside her. But the connection she craves, she realizes, will require her to do more than remember. She needs to see what she never actually saw. So now she imagines him in bed, heavy eyes looking up at the ceiling. In a shower, water barraging his closed eyes. Walking along this very road, like she is now, in comfortable old-man shoes. In the past few months, though, he couldn't have walked this path—he was too sick. So she sits him on a chair, looking out at water. Stands him in front of Michelangelo's *David*, beside her mom, before she remembers the statue is in Florence, not Rome. Imagines him thinner, with fuzzy chemo hair, though no—he didn't do chemo. She forces herself to see him crying, calm face curdling, as he did at her grandma's funeral. He's crying because he's just told her mom about his diagnosis, he's crying because he knows he's dying. To comfort him, she imagines him receiving love. She makes her mom hold his hand, rubbing her thumb over his knuckles, the way Britta did to her when she was a girl, the way she herself now does with Evan and Ella. She imagines him getting hugs. She hears Paul's phone ringing—the portable one that still sits charging in its little port on his kitchen counter—and when her mother answers, asking who it is, she says, *It's me, Maura. Can I talk to Paul?*

A tiny cannonball seems to sit on her heart. She can barely see through her tears.

She keeps on walking. An intersection is up ahead. When she reaches it, she'll stop, turn around, and head back.

I'm so sorry, she thinks. Then she says it out loud too, as if, wherever he is, Paul might hear her.

An hour later, after an egg and toast breakfast with her mom and brother, Shade drives her to the rectory at St. Boniface in town, where her family is staying. It's one of those cathedral-style numbers built at the turn of the century, mortar and gray stone. Maura knocks on the back door, and half a minute later Harden opens it.

"Hey," he says, and immediately he leads her toward their two bedrooms down the hall. "The kids need to get dressed. And I could use a break."

The viewing starts at nine thirty, the service at eleven thirty, and it's a quarter to nine right now. After quickly putting on her dress and pulling up her hair, Maura dives into helping the kids. Curls Ella's hair, as she's asked her to. Irons Evan's pants and shirt, which he'd balled up into a duffel bag. Meanwhile, Evan watches a YouTube video on how to tie a Windsor knot, but when he tries it for himself, he fails three times. "This stupid tie's too thick!" he shrieks. "I can't fit it all in the fricking loop!" He throws the offending thing across the room, where it lands, like a sad, flattened little snake.

"Evan," Harden says firmly, "just calm down. Let me help you."

"I wanna do it myself!" he yells.

"I know. But this is hard for even grown-ups to do. So just take a breath and let me show you."

Evan hates attention when he's hyper and vulnerable, so Maura watches only in glances as she toasts bagels in the kitchen. Evan takes the first stab, then Harden makes adjustments. First, he tightens the bulb. Then he tells Evan to press his thumb on it to help it keep its shape as he pulls the long tail through, and that works.

Disaster averted, Harden palms Evan's shoulder. He's always been nothing but competent, she thinks. Another possible crumb.

"Now just leave it," he says. "'Cause I'm not doing that again."

Three hours later, they're all outside, the sky is a faded blue, and there's an Ansel Adams clarity to the clouds. The coffin has been positioned on a golden rail above the hole in the ground, which itself is tactfully shielded by what looks like bright green Astroturf.

When they pulled up to Paul's house, the parking lot and the grass along its edges were entirely filled with cars and trucks. Men in dark suits blocked the entrances and waved to cars to move along, park on the side of the road, their demeanor firm but warm. On the short walk to the church, Britta asked her and Shade to hand out programs, and they did. She watched strangers file up the aisle, as if for Communion, and pause before the coffin, before crossing themselves and moving on. When Mass began, the choir sang enthusiastically if not exactly in tune. Kneelers clattered and people stood to sing. Father Tim welcomed everyone, then Jean and another friend of Paul's read from Scripture, careful with every word...but the meaning of what they were reading escaped her; it was like trying to concentrate at a poetry reading: impossible.

In his eulogy, Father Tim talked about Paul's great work ethic, his brilliant mind, his generous heart. He told the mourners that Paul couldn't bear to sing the "wretch like me" part of

"Amazing Grace," because he thought no child of God could possibly be a wretch, and Maura had to fight back a sob. Her mom's speech was great—warm stories about Paul as a boy and a nerdy teenager—then swiftly, the Mass wound down: more hymns, Communion, and finally the processional. Six men rolled the casket reverently down the aisle and out the front door to the grave.

Over the course of the next few minutes, the mourners pool around the casket, like slow-moving lava. When they stop, Tim says a few more blessings, the heel of his hand on a corner of his page to keep the wind from fluttering it. There's a bit about entering the kingdom of heaven, then one of the funeral home guys hustles over with a gold baton filled with holy water. Tim shakes it twice, then hands the baton to her mother, who shakes it and hands it to Shade, who shakes it and hands it to Maura to do the same. Less and less water flies out of the little holes until the baton is empty. Then Tim gestures to someone behind them, and when Maura turns, four teenagers she hadn't noticed before come forward, carrying balloons, each the shiny pink white of pearls, twenty-some in each hand, bopping in the breeze. They begin to hand out the balloons, though there won't be quite enough. "Please do share," Tim says, "and wait for my instructions."

When the time comes, everyone lets go and cranes their heads to watch the balloons rise. Maybe there's two hundred. The sun is so bright Maura has to shield her eyes with the flat of her hand, even with her sunglasses on. Some go perfectly straight up. Some wriggle, resisting, before accepting their fate.

At first Maura watches them as a group, but soon she focuses on one balloon in particular, on the fringes; she's pretty sure it's hers. She watches its ascent even as she senses other people losing interest, turning to each other, murmuring things. The balloons are supposed to be symbolic of something, but it's not clear to her *what*—Paul's soul going up to heaven, maybe. The ongoing beauty of life in the face of death. Their collective purge of grief. All of these would make sense, but as her personal balloon gets very, very small and darkens against the sun, all she can think of is David.

Who has been let go. By her.

Who has left her life. At her insistence.

Who has all but disappeared.

Suddenly, she's sobbing: it's too much, too soon. Some people turn and kindly stare. Thinking this show of grief is about a woman and her beloved uncle, Harden moves closer and puts his hand lightly on her shoulder, doing what a husband should do.

There's a big meal in the fellowship hall—ham, mashed potatoes, baked beans, milk—and Maura fills her plate to be polite to the old women hovering near the Crock-Pots, but she barely touches her food.

Back at Paul's house, her mother immediately changes out of her dress into stretch pants and a big striped T-shirt, and Maura wishes she'd thought to bring a change of clothes for herself and the kids too. Jean and her husband have walked over, as has Tim, so Shade starts a pot of coffee. As the kids watch *Homeward Bound* on the portable DVD player they brought, the adults talk about the service and Paul. Jean's husband guesses the attendance was between a thousand and twelve hundred. The balloon idea—Jean's—is praised as a beautiful touch. A decency is on display here that feels like a challenge she's not up to meeting, but Maura decides it's okay to just sit and listen.

By six, everyone but their family has left. They order pizza for dinner, and as Maura's great-aunt Priscilla dutifully does the dishes after, her mom asks her and Shade if they and the kids would like to come downstairs and look through Paul's things. The estate sale is on Thursday, but she wants them to get first pick.

The ceiling is low: if she jumped even half as high as she can, she'd hit her head. Britta leads Evan to the coin collection she's already set aside for him, and Maura and Ella look through the books and records, Ella leaning into her, head on her shoulder. The girl's in no mood to search for treasure now, understandably, and that's fine. To be honest, neither is Maura. But they're here and there will be no better time.

From the book pile, she takes an old copy of *Roots*; from the record pile, some Shostakovich and Dave Brubeck, just in case they ever get a record player. Under a folding table she finds some photo albums, and with Ella half draped over her back, she pages through them.

In the first album are pictures from his India trip; in the second album, pictures of him at St. Iggy's harvest fests over the years—sitting drenched on the edge of a dunk tank, manning a hamburger grill, posing and smiling with various families, his glasses tinted in the sun. The third album she picks up has Rome written on the spine in marker, and here all the pictures are black and white. There's twentysomething Paul standing by the pietà, hands clasped behind him. Paul at the Trevi Fountain, a hand over his eyes to keep out the sun. Paul all over the city, taking all the required landmark pictures. Exactly what one might expect.

Except, that is, for the last picture, which is centered all by itself on the last page. It's a close-up of Paul without his glasses on, propped up on his elbow, on what looks to be a bed. A soft wedge of light falls on his squinting morning face, his mussed hair. His face is in sharp focus, but the background is blurrier: the work of a quality camera with depth of field. He seems on the verge of a smile. Weirdly, it reminds Maura of a magazine ad for cologne: mysterious squinting man in bed, almost sexy. Except the sexy man here is Uncle Father Paul.

Maura stands up and walks the opened album over to her mom. "Have you seen this picture?" she says.

When they look at it together, her mom's face smooths. "I have. It was loose in a box and I thought I'd put it in there. It's beautiful, isn't it?"

"Yeah. Who do you think took it?"

Her mother blinks quickly and looks Maura calmly in the eyes. "He had a friend over there who was a photographer," she says. "It must have been him."

When Evan has concluded that all the most interesting things have been unearthed, considered, and claimed, they climb the stairs, a few mementos in their hands, Britta pulling up the rear so she can click off the light. But as Maura's about to walk back into the living room, her mom says her name.

"Come with me for a second. There's something I need to give you."

"What is it?"

"Just come."

She follows her mom into Paul's bedroom. Britta moves to the little antique desk near the window and pulls an envelope out of the top drawer. "Paul wanted me to give this to you."

"What is it?"

"A note for you. That's all I really know."

The flap is sealed with thick clear tape. *For Maura* is written small in the bottom right corner, like a signature on a painting.

"He told me not to read it, and for once in my life, I listened."

In the living room, everyone is watching *America's Funniest Home Videos* on Paul's old TV. The perfect stupid thing to break the day's awkward spell: Shade's idea, no doubt. On screen, a toddler totters around with an ice-cream bucket on his head, walks into a wall, and falls on his giant diapered butt. Evan and Ella laugh, Shade puffs air out of his nose, but Harden isn't watching: he's reading things on his phone. She should probably read the note later, when she's alone. But she can't wait.

She hurries to Paul's bathroom, closes the door behind her, and rips the envelope at the top with her house key, ignoring the tape, and pulls out the single piece of yellow legal paper inside. To read it, she sits on top of the closed lid of the little toilet. His hand is a little shaky, the cursive words keening left, like passengers bracing for impact. But it's easy enough to make out. *Dear Maura,* it begins:

Your mom has told me what's going on and I've wanted to write for a while. Please know I love and support you and have been praying for you often.

I'm not sure what you'll have decided to do about your situation by the time you read this. Whether you and Harden are working to save your marriage or not. I know how much your children mean to you and how much you love them. And I know Harden is a good man. Over the years, I've advocated for working things out as a rule, and often this can be done and the relationship can recover.

But I want to say this too: there are worse sins than following the call of true love, as long as the love is honest and equal. In fact, to call it a sin at all I don't think is fair. I want there to be someone who says this to you too.

What are we supposed to do when what we want isn't possible unless we hurt others?

Scripture tells us: "You, my brothers and sisters, were called to be free. But do not use your freedom to indulge the flesh; rather, serve one another humbly in love." But then it also tells us: "No one lights a lamp and puts it in a cellar or under a basket. Instead, he sets it on a lampstand, so those who enter can see the light." I find this inconsistent and confusing.

All this is to say that I have felt conflicted myself on matters similar to yours over the years, Maura, and I may know a little of what you're going through. How difficult it must be. Your mother can tell you more if she wishes; by the time you read this I won't be here to have a reaction to it. Lucky me.

Anyway, I love you, dear niece. Please give Evan and Ella a hug for me. Sorry if any of this doesn't make sense, I'm a bit out of it with these meds. Know that I will always "have your back."

Love,

UFP

On reaching the end, Maura folds the bottom part back in on itself, like she's disabling a trap. She looks blankly at the segmented plastic shower curtain in front of her, faint brown speckles of mildew along the bottom. Canned laughter swells and retreats a room away.

Her face and neck are suddenly very warm, her arms and fingers suddenly cold.

I may know a little of what you're going through. But how could he?

She'd known he was gay for years—that's what her mom had told her, at least, when she'd asked her in high school. But his sexuality had always seemed...inconsequential. Gay or straight, he'd chosen to live a life where those inclinations weren't acted upon. To her mind he was as sexless and tame as Mister Rogers. As Jesus himself.

And yet: this note folded in her hands, seeming to offer permission.

When she emerges from the bathroom a few minutes later, Maura walks right over to her mother, who's making a new pot of decaf.

"Can I talk to you for a second?" she asks. "Outside?"

"Is everything okay?" Britta says. "You look like you saw a ghost."

"I just want to ask you something."

Maura doesn't want to stand in the front yard—Harden could spy on them from there and ask her a question about their discussion later, and she doesn't want that. So she curls around to the other side of the house and her mother follows.

They stop at the edge of Paul's vegetable garden. And this is where Maura tells her mother about the note and where Maura finds out everything her mother only recently found out.

"Did he tell you why he didn't leave?" she asks, after the shock has faded a little.

"I think he was afraid," her mother says. "Afraid of what people would think. Or that it wouldn't work out, and he'd have nowhere to go. I'm not totally sure. I think the older he got the harder it seemed."

Maura has such sympathy for all this it makes her want to cry. But it appears she's all cried out. At least for now.

"I think part of it," her mother continues, "was that he was a very loyal person. Always had been. Which can be both good and bad, depending, I suppose."

"It makes me sad to think he felt he couldn't do it," Maura says.

"I know," Britta says. "I felt that too. But I've also thought—maybe he was making more of it than it was because he was so depressed at the end. I think his judgment was a little clouded."

"I guess."

"I mean, he always seemed pretty happy to me. When I think back to our lives together, I think of him laughing. At least as much as I think of him sad."

"He always seemed pretty happy to me too."

"And maybe he was. Maybe this is all overblown."

Maura nods. She hopes so, but doubts it's true.

Everyone is still glued to the TV when they return. There's a free spot on the couch but Maura doesn't take it; she's content to stand behind everybody, hands clasped behind her back, a little apart. On the screen now, a boy and a girl are sitting on a blanket in the grass, party hats cocked on their heads. The girl leans in, kisses the boy on the lips; the boy looks around with a huge smile, giggles, and rocks back and forth with joy so hard he tips over. Meanwhile, Harden, she senses in her peripheral vision, is keeping an eye on her again; she looks, and he is. How she wishes he'd stop.

"Everything okay?" he asks.

"I'm fine," she says. "Emotional day. That's all."

Once the show is over, Harden slaps his knees as he does when he feels that it's time for everyone to go, and she thinks, *Yeah, probably a good idea.* They gather their things, say their goodbyes. They'll head back to the rectory tonight, and tomorrow morning they'll drive straight to the airport, so this is it. She and her mom cry one last time as they hug, they can't help it, and hold on to each other longer than they usually would. "Call me when you get home," her mom whispers loudly into her ear. And Maura says, "I will."

As they drive along the long country road that will take them to the highway that feeds into Green Bay, her family, for a change, is quiet. Chastened, almost. Harden looks dead ahead, face calm and opaque. In the back seat, Evan is reviewing his new coin collection again, plucking coins from their sleeves and turning them around inches from his face. Meanwhile, Maura looks to the west at the setting sun, a pink smear over the horizon, as is Ella, her little face visible in the side mirror.

Maura's glad for the silence because it's helping her conjure David more vividly. If they were still together, he would have sent a note this morning: *Thinking of you today, Maur. Hang in there.* Later tonight, she would have slipped outside to call him, to recap the day. Her mom's eulogy. The out-of-tune, but lovable, choir. How the cheesy balloon release had gotten her more emotional than she'd expected. Though of course, if they were still together, she would have felt something else. Because he's a curious man who understands that it helps most people to talk about their dead, David would ask her to tell him more about Paul, and she would. She'd talk about how kind he always was to her, what an art lover he was, the awe she'd felt watching him serve Mass as a girl, everyone answering him in unison. Maybe she'd share what her mother just revealed... though she's not sure she'd feel ready yet—it needs more time to sink in. For a while they'd share memories about their own dads' funerals, only a year apart. David would have things to say about grief, personal truths he'd worked through, things she couldn't have expected. Remembering his dad, he might get emotional, as he sometimes did. And after all this catching up, when the subject of grief had started to sag, either she or he would steer them somewhere playful. Try to make the other laugh. And then, before they parted, *I love you. I love you too.*

"How many people do you think would go to your funeral, Mommy?" Ella asks her now, breaking the silence. Maura looks at her reflection in the side mirror. Their eyes meet.

"Not as many as Paul got today, that's for sure. I'm not that popular."

"Would there be a hundred people?"

"I might get a hundred, yeah. But not much more than that."

She's never really thought about it, but now's as good a time as any. The crowd size would depend, of course, on how old she was when she died, how many of her loved ones were still alive. The service wouldn't be held at a church, but ideally somewhere beautiful and dignified. A small sea of white folding chairs facing forward; a lectern and, behind it, maybe a screen on which photographs or videos of her could be projected. Like Paul's service, there would be music and eulogies. Shade would give one; the kids, grown up, surely would too. She imagines Ella as a woman, her baby fat gone, small breasts and wide hips like hers. A husband beside her, maybe a few kids. She imagines Evan as a man too, at first alone, but then, no, she gives him a partner too. A woman. Though, of course, for both of them, who knows? She pictures Harden in his seventies or eighties, hair gone white, with a big neck wattle and stretched ears, like his dad. And lastly, there's her, the star of the show, laid in a casket. She'd have a stylish white bob, the old-lady look she admires the most. Except, no, she wants to be cremated. She almost forgot.

Standing before the little crowd that showed up, her loved ones would attempt to bring her briefly back to life. Shade would lean on funny stories, uncomfortable as he is with anything serious. The kids would be earnest, emotional. But Harden's speech...for some reason she can't imagine it. Who would she be to him by then? What would he have to say? Would he mention something about *bumps in the road*, how *it wasn't always easy*? Or would all their trouble be paved over by then?

She tries to hear him saying her name, gnarly old hands gripping the edges of a podium, but something in her balks at even trying. And then—without much drama, the truth pouring into her as pure as water—she realizes why: he's not the man she wants talking about her up there...he who barely knows her at all.

It shakes her, the bluntness of this wish, and she glances at Ella in the side mirror, as if to check if she's noticed the betrayal, then at Harden too.

"How many do you think you'd have at your funeral, Daddy?" Evan asks now. He's holding up a half-dollar to examine it the way a wine snob might raise his glass to the light.

"Oh, I don't know," Harden says. "A hundred and one, at least."

He looks at her sideways, wanting a reaction to his joke.

But she's sorry—she just can't.

When they push open the back door of the rectory house, Father Tim is sitting at the kitchen table, sipping brandy and listening to classical music playing on a little black boom box on top of his fridge. Paul's CD, she presumes. The one from the service.

Tim looks up and says hello, a sad, inward look on his face.

"Sorry for just barging in," she says.

"Oh, it's fine," he says. "It's not barging in if you have a key."

The kids stream past him and down the hall to their room, eager to be reunited with their stuff, to take off their uncomfortable clothes. But she and Harden linger.

"Is that the CD from the service?" Maura asks.

"It is," Tim says. "I'll leave it on for you if you want. I was actually just about to hit the sack."

"Oh, great," Maura says.

He rises from his chair, slightly hunched, holding his glass. Maura feels bad that they're here tonight, crowding him as he grieves. If she were him, she'd wish she could be alone.

"You're welcome to the rest of this too," he says, lifting his glass. "There's still a half bottle up on the fridge."

"We just might," Harden says. "Thank you."

"Better you help me finish it than I drink it all myself."

They smile, not sure how much to make of this.

"We'll do our best to keep it down," Maura says. "With the kids, I mean."

Tim swats her concern away. "Oh, don't worry. I sleep like a log."

Speaking of sleep, all Maura wants right now is to lie face-down on a bed, totally still, as the dread she feels shivers its way completely through her. She feels unwell. Her mouth is dry; her skin is hot, almost feverish; her arms and legs feel hollow, as if they're barely under her control. She could beg off child care tonight—it's her uncle who died, not his. But it's nearly eight thirty, the kids' bedtime, and she wants this to be a regular night. For her sake, she senses, more even than theirs.

When she tells Harden she'll handle bedtime, he says, "Cool," and a minute later he's in the kitchen with his laptop, earbuds in, an almost full glass of brandy on ice sweating beside his wireless mouse. In the kids' room, Maura finds a fresh T-shirt for Ella in the suitcase, picks up the wadded pajama pants from the floor, shakes them out, and helps her daughter step into each leg. Evan has already undressed himself and is in his underwear playing with his Rubik's Cube. When she asks him to put on his gym shorts and Pokémon shirt, he says not now, like he always does. Which is her cue to give him a beleaguered, insistent look until he says, "Okay. Fine."

She does all of these things the way she always does, but it's as if she's split in two. There's the mother saying words to her children, and then there's this other person hovering just a few inches to the side, watching. Crammed together in the room's one twin bed, the three of them barely fit. She feels her daughter's warm head pressing down on her right shoulder. A few inches away, Evan with his skinny knees up at eye level, fiddling with his Rubik's Cube, half listening, half not, as she reads. Her job is to read, so she does. But she's not keeping track of the story at all, merely reciting words, lilting her voice occasionally to sound convincing.

"'The cows held an emergency meeting. All the animals gathered around the barn to snoop, but none of them could understand Moo.'"

Instead, she's tipping over into a different place. Lying beside David in a different bed. She's reading out loud, but it's something interesting from a magazine, something interesting that she thinks he'll like too. His reading glasses are wedged above the narrow bulb of his nose; a book is facedown in his lap: he's just set it there in order to listen. His attention to her is a heat she can feel on her neck and ears like sunlight. The thing she's been missing, the thing she enjoys so much. The thing Harden will never give her, not the way she wants it.

"'In a faraway place in a long-ago time there lived a man and his wife. They were very poor. All they had was a tumble-down house and tiny turnip garden.'"

When story time is done, she shuts the book and lays it on her lap. *All right! Fun's over. Time to hit the sack:* that's what she usually says. But tonight she can't muster anything close. Their bedtime ritual, she's told her therapist, is one of the things she doesn't think she could give up. And she does love this, she really does: her two kids snuggled up beside her, that warm animal thing. But is it so precious that she wouldn't trade having it every night for anything else? Is *this* more important than *that*?

"Today was a weird day, wasn't it?" she says, her chin brushing the hair on Ella's head. "You guys doing okay with everything that happened?"

"What do you mean?" Evan asks.

"I just mean it was sad, that's all."

Ella shrugs. "I'm not that sad," she says brightly.

"Me either," says Evan. "I didn't even really know him."

It pains her to hear this, but it shouldn't surprise her. They're right. How honest they are, her beautiful children.

"Oh, you guys," she says. "Come here." She pulls them closer and holds them tight, as if trying to stamp this moment into her body for later, so it forever holds its shape. Only when Evan says, "Mom, you're squeezing too hard," does the ache rushing through her relent. Only then does she let go.

Ella is asleep by the time she leaves the room, and Evan is well on his way, holding his Rubik's Cube with both hands like a groggy Golem. He prefers to fall asleep alone anyway. And the melatonin will kick in soon. Maura looks down the hallway into the kitchen where Harden is behind his laptop, sipping brandy. She could use some right now—she can already feel the rush of warmth to her brain—but to get it would mean walking over there and having a conversation. And she doesn't want that.

Instead she walks into the room across the hall and closes the door behind her. Standing beside their unmade bed, she

takes off her skirt, black blouse, red flats, then squats and rum-
mages through the suitcase on the floor, on the far side of the
bed, for fresh socks and her pajamas. Dressed, she realizes that
what she wants to do is read Paul's letter again, so she plucks
it from her purse, unfolds it, and sits on the edge of the bed.

This time, Paul's voice wanders in, replaces the usual voice
in her head. It's hard to remember voices: faces for her are easier.
But it comes back. A gentle baritone, Wisconsin vowels. Reading
his letter to her, like she's a child sitting on his lap. Finished, she
exhales, chest trembling. She looks at the door, to make sure
it's shut, then scans the room, as if the walls and floor have just
shot up around her.

It's a drab little space, despite Tim's best attempt to make it
homey: a jelly jar full of water with cut gerberas slumped inside
it on the chair positioned beside the bed, a makeshift end table.
The faint tang of Febreze. Ugly dark brown wood paneling,
broken into sections like pieces of Hershey's chocolate on the
bottom half of the walls. Above that, pale gold wallpaper with
a repeating fleur-di-lis pattern, stained from ancient cigarette
smoke. Near the window, a half-opened closet, three peeling
particleboard shelves. It's a place that screams loneliness. Veiled
neglect. The sort of charmless hotel room she could imagine
a person sitting on a bed inside of, desperate, but calming by
the minute, knowing they're here to end their life. A grim, nowhere sort of place.

And yet, as she absorbs the sadness of this space around her,
she doesn't feel sad. Instead, an improbable, swelling fondness.
It will always be special to her, this room: it's where she'll have
decided to change her life.

A minute later, she's outside, walking, shoes back on, her phone
in her hand like a weapon, and Harden left behind in the
kitchen.

Four times it rings before she hears David's outgoing message. Just after it beeps, she hangs up.

She imagines him out in his studio, measuring something with a tape ruler, making a tiny line in a plaster block with a pencil, a cold beer on a worktable not far away. Though it's just as likely that he's on the couch, Ralphie at his feet, watching the Travel Channel. As is his wont.

It's been twenty-three days. Enough time for him to have begun to hate her, to have left her forever. He might have already started moving on. And if he has, she'll have no one to blame but herself. But then her phone rings and it's him. As she brings the phone to her ear, she closes her eyes.

"Hi," she says.

"I almost didn't answer," he says. "But I figured, what the hell. Let's hear what she has to say."

She's right that he's angry with her. And hurt. The ache in his voice as he tells her how much is so raw she can't stand it.

"I thought we had something really good going," he says. "But now I realize, for you, it was just a game. Once it got a little scary, you chickened out."

"I know," she says. "I did chicken out. I won't pretend that I didn't. But that was a mistake. That's what I'm trying to tell you."

David says nothing, waiting for more.

"I was scared," she says. "But I don't feel that anymore. I understand if you don't trust me when I say that. But I swear it's true."

"You're right," he says. "I don't think I can trust you. Not after all of this."

At this, Maura's face curdles, fighting back tears.

"So what is it that's changed?" he asks. His voice isn't quite as angry: she can already detect a change.

"I thought I could fix things. Or that I should fix things. But I realize now, there's nothing left to fix. And even if there were, I'd still want to be with you."

"You figured that out in three weeks?"

She likes that he's been counting too. "Yeah. Though I think part of me already knew."

"Could have fooled me."

"I'm so sorry, David," she says—she can't really say it enough. Already she knows she'll say it many more times. As many as it takes. "After everything I've put you through, I'd understand if you hated me a little. I really would."

"No comment," he says. But he's joking a little, she's pretty sure.

She's been staring at her feet this whole conversation, but now she feels the need to look up and out. Coming toward her, walking with big stomping steps, is a gay couple with two gigantic wolfhounds. Across the street, a sweet, fat little boy sits on his stoop, looking at his phone.

"Are you at home right now?" he asks.

"I'm in Wisconsin. At my uncle's funeral."

"Oh, I'm sorry. I remember you talking about him."

"Yeah, thanks. It's been a long day. Lots of emotional ups and downs. But I swear I'm not calling you because I'm just a mess from the funeral. This is how I really feel. As soon as I'm back home, I'm going to call an attorney. And tell the kids."

Three sharp sounds hit her ear: it's Ralphie barking in the background.

"Just so you know," he replies, "I don't think I could handle you backing out again. If that happened, I'd have to move on. Just for my mental health."

"I promise," she says, and this time she means it.

"Okay," he says.

"Okay."

"How about you call me after you do all that, and we'll go from there?"

"Okay. I will."

"Okay."

"I'm just going to say 'okay' one more time for fun," she says.

And finally, he laughs—two little puffs of air from his nose. "Okay."

"Maybe, at some point, I could come up to Maine for a while," she says. "For a weekend. Or longer. Whatever would work for you."

"Okay," he says.

"Are you saying 'okay' as a joke or did you really mean that?"

"I really meant it."

"So...that's just 'okay'?"

"I mean," he says, "I'd like that. I really would. I'd like that a lot."

"You don't sound completely sure."

He exhales into the receiver. "Well, Maura, I guess maybe I'm still getting used to the idea a little. Ten minutes ago, I thought I might never talk to you again."

"I did kind of spring this on you, didn't I?"

"You could say that, yes."

"That's fair. I'm sorry."

"Okay."

"Can I call you tomorrow then? Or at least send you a text?"

"Yeah," he says. "That would be nice. I've missed hearing your voice."

"Okay then," she says. "I will. I'll give you a call tomorrow."

For a while, she looks at the traffic passing by her on her left: a minivan, a Prius, a red truck advertising plumbing services.

"I realize this conversation was a little awkward," she says. "But I think we'll do better tomorrow. Don't you think? I mean, there's nowhere to go but up."

She thinks she can hear David smile.

"Let's hope."

"Okay."

"I'll prepare my throat with tea and honey."

"Good plan."

"Okay," he says.

"That 'okay' didn't really make sense," she says, and he laughs: "I know."

"I love you, you know," she says. "That never changed. And it never will."

"Thanks for saying that, Maura," he replies. "I love you too."

All the kitchen lights are off when she returns, and Harden isn't there. The only place he could be is their room, but when she opens the door it's still odd to find him there. He's lying flat on the bed in a T-shirt and boxers, a heavy forearm resting on his forehead like a bandage. When he turns his head to her, his arm moves with it.

"You can turn the light on if you want," he says.

"That's okay. I can see fine." Maura sits on the side of the bed, her back to him. Takes off her shoes: one, two.

"You went out to call him, didn't you?"

She didn't even consider whether he might figure that out, but what else could he have thought? He who is suddenly so watchful.

"I did, yeah." She realizes there's no longer anything to hide.

"I figured."

She turns to look at him over her shoulder. He doesn't deserve any of this. But there's no other way it can go now.

"Harden," she says, "I can't do this anymore." She said something similar to him at the cottage that night, but in retrospect that was a test run. After nearly twenty years, maybe she needed one.

He nods. "Yeah."

She softens her face. "I'm sorry. I really am."

He takes this in, staring at her blankly, before looking back up at the ceiling.

"I don't want to waste your time anymore," she says. "You deserve someone who will love you better. I mean that."

"Wow," he says bitterly. "How big of you. How nice." The way he says it, she can tell he's a little drunk.

"I mean it. It's true."

He shakes his head. "You've got it all figured out, don't you? You go off and have your big love affair, and I'm the one who sticks around and does all the hard shit. Good old Harden. *Yeah, I'm sure he'll be fine.*"

"We'll share the hard shit," she says. "We'll co-parent, like a lot of people do."

"Oh, is that how it's going to go?"

"What do you mean?"

"I *mean* I'm going to fight you for custody. That's what I mean. If you want to be with your boyfriend, fine. But I don't want my kids shuttled back and forth like it's no big thing. They need stability, Maura. Evan especially. And if you can't give that to them, which it's pretty clear you can't, then I will. Somebody fucking has to."

"You can't be serious."

"Actually," he says, "I totally fucking am."

Maybe it's the brandy talking, but it seems like more. In an instant, he's become her enemy, more than she ever thought he could. There's menace in the air. She reminds herself that Tim is only a few doors down. Not that Harden would ever do something for which Tim would be required. But it's where her mind goes, even so.

"Know what's funny?" he says. "About a half hour ago, before you went outside, I was actually going to ask if you wanted to have sex. Just to try that again. But I guess those days are over, aren't they?"

She doesn't know how to respond, but he's right, they are. She sizes up the full length of his body, lying on top of the sheets: his gray boxer briefs with the black waistline and little flap; his strong legs; his still muscular, slightly hairy arms; the line of his jaw. She remembers lusting over his body long ago, back when his was the only body she cared about. She finds herself wanting to remember the first time she saw him naked, but before her mind has time to entertain the project, something extinguishes it—just like that.

"I know you're angry at me and I know you're hurt," Maura says. "But you can't do this to me, Harden. It's not right and you know it. I deserve better."

He doesn't bother to look at her. "Yeah, well, I guess that's what the lawyers are for, isn't it?"

"You're serious."

"Yeah. You better believe it."

She opens her mouth but nothing comes out. Slowly, as if savoring the power he's exerted, Harden pushes himself up to sitting. Then, even more slowly, he stands and faces her and crosses his arms. He's decided to skip the defeated part and go right for revenge. Or justice. Maybe that's how it feels to him. Though surely half of this is about pride.

"I'm going to go sleep in the other room," he says.

"We can talk about this," Maura says. "Okay? We can find a way to work it all out." She feels like an old, feeble person, begging for her life. She wishes she seemed stronger.

He ignores her. Her words have already evaporated. "I'll just say this," he says. "I hope it works out between you and this guy, because no way in hell am I taking you back. And this time I mean it."

Which means he didn't mean it before. She looks at him, this strange man she's known for so long.

"Set your alarm for seven," he says. "We need to leave here by eight."

"I will," she says.

Once he's left the room and she's alone, Maura positions herself L-shaped on the bed—butt and back pressed against the headboard, hands clasped in her lap, legs flat—and looks out the window. The air's gray now. The sun's long gone. Framed there is the edge of the grade school beside the church, a playground with a twisty slide, monkey bars, a four square court. Dark trees behind.

The position she's sitting in, the way she's looking out the window, a little stunned, makes her think about college, first semester freshman year—the fall she got her first taste of independence. Her roommate, Wendy, usually stayed the night at her boyfriend's apartment, the dorm room just a front for her parents' peace of mind, so Maura basically had a single all to herself. Nights, after watching TV in the lounge, or studying, or masturbating under her comforter, she'd sit just like this, looking out at the quad through the big window to the left of the poster of the Cure she'd taped up on moving day—and the magnitude of the freedom now hers would wash over her in waves. It was like the air in the room literally pulsed.

After what had felt like an endless childhood, she'd come to understand very quickly that she could become whoever she wanted to be. Her parents were a thousand miles away. Nobody was keeping track anymore, except maybe the student adviser she was supposed to check in with a few times a semester. It was miraculous. Almost too good to be true. But it also terrified her. Because now, if she screwed things up, there was no one to blame but herself. And who, exactly, was she? The terrible, wonderful power she possessed, and the fear that she wasn't up to using it well, would paralyze her sometimes, to the point where she felt unable to leave the bed.

Here now, she feels a similar paralysis, but it's because she's in shock. That must be it. She didn't expect this from Harden. She knows it doesn't bode well. He's been angry for a long time. It's been building, like steam in a pipe, waiting to escape. And he's a man who sticks to his guns, capable of holding a grudge.

If she has to fight him for joint custody, she will. With everything she has. She'll cash out her retirement to pay for the lawyers. Ask her mom for help. She's pretty sure her mom will agree. When push comes to shove, she'll say yes.

But even then, it's possible he'll get his way. She is, after all, the one who cheated, the one who would be punished.

For a few moments, she feels foolish and afraid. This could turn out to be the worst decision of her life. But no, she thinks. The time for agonizing is over. She needs to have faith. Her heart aches for everything she'll lose, but it's an aching heart that's fuller than it's ever been. A heart that's finally been opened up. *This is my one short life,* she thinks, and imagines being in David's arms, and what settles over her is what she sometimes feels after sex: a sweetly debilitating exhaustion, a reduction to her purest self. Invisible rings radiate out from her warm, spent body, as from a dropped stone in a pond. Until, slowly, beautifully, the water heals.

Her body is what usually lets her know whether she's recovered from a shock or not, and after a time it tells her to scoot off the bed and stand up. Her hands are no longer cold; her head and neck still feel hot. She's extremely thirsty, she realizes. Parched.

She moves lightly but with purpose. She feels nimble and bold. The hall is dark but for the tiny wedge of light coming from under Tim's door. When her socked feet hit the linoleum in the kitchen, Maura resists the urge to turn on the light. The darkness in the room feels better. It makes her feel like she's dreaming.

In a cupboard, she feels around for a glass, fills it at the sink, and drinks it down. Still thirsty, she drinks another. She feels better, but her face and ears are still very hot. Leaning forward, so her head hangs over the sink, she fills her cupped palm with faucet water until it spills over, then slaps and rubs it on one hot ear and then the other. She does this three times, until her skin tingles with the bracing cold. Then she fills up her hand again and pours water on the top of her head, feeling it trickle quickly down her hair and stream off her ears and onto her shoulders. She stands there very still, receiving every path.

Only when the last of the droplets have fallen off her earlobes, the water's movement on her body complete, does she open her eyes. She finds a dish towel in a drawer and pats it along her neck and shoulders, rubs it around in her hair. When she's done, she wets it with cold water and presses her face into it, before setting it on the counter. Then, thinking ahead to the evening, she fills her glass again and carries it out of the room and down the hall.

Beside her kids' room, Maura pauses. She puts her hand on the knob for a moment, wondering if she should dare, then twists it and opens the door.

On the little bed, the children have switched positions: now Evan is on his side and Ella's the one on her back. Through the slats of the blinds, a dusting of light falls on them, just enough to make out their forms. Their lips are slightly parted, as if about to blow bubbles.

Standing here unnoticed in this strange room, Maura feels like a thief. An intruder with dangerous intentions. How silly, she thinks, until she realizes it's true.

There will be nights when they lie in bed, maybe in these same positions, crying over what she's done. They won't understand her choice so they'll blame themselves, especially Evan. They'll see how cruel life can be, before they're ready.

And so her devotion to them will have to be as strong as her devotion to David. And not just until they all settle into a new arrangement, but for the rest of her life. Even when she's not physically there, she'll keep watch, as she's doing now. Even if they can't completely forgive her, they'll always have her support and love. Looking at their sleeping faces, Maura promises them this.

Now, from below, a voice whispers, "What is it?"

It's Harden, of course, lying flat on the floor on a comforter, head propped up by a pillow bent in half.

Quietly she clears her throat. "What's that?" she says. Not that she didn't hear him. She's just buying time to think of an answer.

"What do you want?" he asks.

She doesn't know how to respond. There's too much to say. In the dark, she can barely make out his eyes.

"Nothing," she finally replies, "I was just leaving." And with one last glance at her children, Maura carefully closes the door.

Acknowledgments

There are so many people to thank.

Thanks to my friends near and far for your encouragement and love over the years—in particular, my Cornell, Chicago, and Ragdale writer-pals. It meant a lot.

To the cheap suburban hotels I wrote big chunks of this book in, especially the Extended Stay Holiday Inn in Skokie, thank you if not for the peace, at least the quiet.

Many thanks to Rob Roensch, Jerry Gabriel, and Shawn Currie for reading parts of this book and having such smart things to say about it; to my most excellent agent, Arielle Datz, who believed in this book way back when; to Chris Heiser and Olivia Smith at Unnamed Press for your faith and editorial guidance; to Dr. Helen Te and Jack Melloh for help in filling in important knowledge gaps; and to the Californian priest who candidly shared his experience as a gay man with me years ago.

Extra special thanks to the Vandermeer clan, especially Kitty Vandermeer for helping keep our household running when I was doing a residency at Ragdale; to my brother, Andy, for keeping me laughing and for the unflagging moral support; to my dad, for his enthusiasm for this project and indispensable insights about farm life, seminary life, and Rome in the sixties; and to my mom, a certified genius at loving people, for always being there, no matter what.

Lastly, thank you to my wonderful sons, Arlo and Emmett, who really wanted to be mentioned in the acknowledgments ('sup, guys), and to my wife, Maggie Vandermeer, who for more than a decade always gave me the space and time I needed to write this book and the most astute, helpful feedback. MV, you're the best.

Mark Rader was born and raised in Green Bay, Wisconsin, educated at Tulane University and Cornell University, and now lives with his family outside of Chicago. His fiction has been published in *Glimmer Train, Epoch, The Southern Review* and shortlisted for an O. Henry Award, the Best American Non-Required Reading anthology, and a Pushcart Prize. He has taught creative writing at Cornell, Northeastern University, Grub Street, and the University of Chicago's Graham School. *The Wanting Life* is his first novel.